ISΛN

INTERNATIONAL SENSORY ASSASSIN NETWORK

Other books by Mary Ting

The Crossroads Saga
Crossroads
Between
Beyond
Eternity
Halo City

Descendant Prophecies Series
From Gods
From Deities
From Origins
From Titans

Secret Knights Series
The Angel Knights
The Chosen Knights
The Blessed Knights
The Sacred Knights

ISAN

INTERNATIONAL SENSORY ASSASSIN NETWORK

MARY TING

ISAN

ISBN: 978-1-944109-56-1

VESUVIAN BOOKS

Published by Vesuvian Books
www.vesuvianbooks.com

Printed in the United States of America

10 9 8 7 6 5 4 3 2 1

"Dystopian fans, prepare to be blown away!"
~Ednah Walters, *USA Today* Bestselling Author

TABLE OF CONTENTS

CHAPTER ONE
MENTAL MISSION

I ran to live.

Bullets whizzed by my ears. Adrenaline pumped through my body like a high-speed train. I peeked around the corner to confirm no enemy remained, then charged down the hall faster than humanly possible. Justine and Brooke hot on my heels. I halted when I realized Justine had slowed.

"Crap. It nicked me." Justine's long blonde hair screened her face.

"How bad is it?" Metallic scent spiked my senses. I cringed and reached for her arm, but she jolted back and flashed daggered eyes at me.

"I'll be fine. It's not bad." Justine pressed a hand over the wound and snarled.

Blood soaked her shirt and seeped between her fingers. Crimson beads dotted the floor. Hopefully, her shirt would catch most of it.

My jaw tightened. "The hell it isn't. Make sure you don't leave a trail."

Steady the anger, Ava. No time to argue. Since she didn't want my help, I checked my digital watch. Ten minutes left to reach the other side of the building before time ran out with my team. *If we didn't end up killing each other first.*

Justine liked to test my leadership. I would not let her intimidate me. I knew when to bite back, and harder if I needed to. A charming trait I'd learned from being in juvenile detention.

"Shhh ..." Brooke placed her finger to her lips. "They've stopped shooting at us."

"That's because they can't see us. They went the other way, idiot." Justine smirked, then wiped her bloodstained hand on her pants.

Brooke placed her fists on her hips and glared at Justine. "I was only making an observation. My hearing is awesome right now. Better than usual."

"You're not the only—"

"Shut the hell up. Stop arguing." I sighed heavily. Both of them drove me nuts when they bickered—the possible reason we might fail our mental mission.

As I smeared sweat off my forehead, I listened for the clicking of guns and squeaks on the laminated floor. Then, at footsteps vibrating like thunder, I poised to run.

"We need to get moving." Justine stiffened, her eyes darting every which way. "Where's the freakin' door, Ava?"

"This way. Follow me." I swept the long hallway to my left, then to the right. When I didn't spot the computerized soldiers, I took off toward the left, then halted when the hallway split again.

"Do you know where you're going?" Brooke panted. "We've never been here before."

"I do. Trust me," I said, catching my breath.

Brooke knew I stored a blueprint of the structure in my mind. My mind projected a map in front of me like a hologram, visible to only me when HelixB77 serum had been injected in my system.

As the soldiers' footsteps got louder, their precise location became harder to detect. The sound bounced from wall to wall, echoing.

"They're coming from behind us, too." Justine tapped her foot, rooting her eyes on my watch. "How much time do we have?"

"About four minutes."

So little time. My heart pounded. I needed to go faster. I took deep breaths to keep from freaking out. The image faded as fear took over.

No, no, no. Not now. Focus. Focus. Focus.

Justine pointed at the air vent. "How about up there?"

"Are you nuts?" Brooke gave Justine the evil eye. "I'm not going up there. What are we going to do, crawl our way to the exit door? And what if they start shooting the ceiling? We'll be trapped. We'll be dead. Ava, hurry up. Which way?"

I closed my eyes and tuned out their squabbling voices. *Breathe. Stay calm.* I inhaled deep breaths, letting serenity wash over me. Then a few heartbeats later, I opened my eyes. There. The image came back.

"The exit is this way." I dashed down another long hallway and stopped at a door bearing a sign for the stairs.

Brooke's eyes beamed hopeful, but her muscles remained rigid. "It's the exit, right, Ava?"

"Yes." My hand trembling, I turned the knob.

It wouldn't budge. What the hell? Yanking didn't help, so I kicked the door in frustration. Pain shot through my leg like an electric shock. I lost precious seconds.

What next?

"Move out of my way." Justine knocked the door open with one swift kick, the door now becoming one with the wall.

I bolted down the steps, the ping of dampened gunfire behind me. *Faster. Go faster.* Power and exhilaration surged in my muscles. As I descended, the footsteps pursuing me disappeared.

Twenty feet from the exit ... eighteen ... fifteen ... so close ... almost there. I could almost taste sweet victory, my heart leaping for joy. Then ...

My watch beeped.

Damnit to hell.

The ground rumbled violently. I slammed against the wall. Justine barked a curse behind me as I braced for another impact.

The blast roared and tossed me in the air. Flames engulfed me, followed by another loud boom. The building groaned and shrieked as it collapsed. I died.

Again.

CHAPTER TWO
RECAP

My body jolted. I gasped like a drowning woman breaking the water's surface. My heart calmed when the room came into focus, and then everything cleared. Coming back always felt that way. Disheartened I had failed my team, I slammed back against the black leather chair and gnawed the inside of my mouth.

My damp shirt clung to me and my hands slipped on the armrests. As I wiped the sweat trickling down my forehead, wire tangled around my arm. The red wire monitored my heartbeat, the blue measured my brainwaves, the green checked the level of HelixB77 serum in my body, and the purple monitored my fear.

Justine's loud, hoarse voice reconfirmed I'd kept my team from succeeding the mission again.

"Shit." Justine rubbed the arm where she'd been shot.

Since the mission had only been projected into her mind, she didn't bleed but still felt the pain. Justine tore off the lead tapes. Still swearing under her breath, she stormed toward the door, her blonde hair bouncing with the rhythm of her steps.

"Watch your mouth," Russ said in an even tone. He stood by the large, flat screen that filled half the back wall.

As our training director, Russ observed and evaluated us through these 'mental mission'—or MM—sessions.

"Screw you. Screw the test. Screw the network." Justine quickened her pace.

She seemed taller and leaner in the black, skintight uniform they made us wear.

5

Here we go again. I released an exasperated breath, imagining sealing Justine's mouth with tape, or perhaps with a stapler.

"I suggest you watch what you say if you want to continue with ISAN. And by the way, you've just lost a point for your team." He shifted his gaze back to the screen.

Justine stopped when she reached the door and gave Russ the middle finger. "I really don't care."

Russ, still looking at the screen, didn't see her lovely gesture. "That's another one for your positive attitude."

"Geez … is that all?" She stiffened when the automatic door didn't slide open for her.

Dropping to a sprinter's crouch, I thought she'd try to break it down, but she'd only hurt herself. However, I would have loved to see her try it. The small dose of Helix serum she had been given before the training session would have worked its way out of her system already, leaving her without the power to push through.

For one long moment, Justine glared at the door, jaw so tightly clenched her muscles pulsed. Then she closed her eyes, wriggled her shoulders, and straightened her stance.

"Calm yourself and sit down." Russ never raised his voice, though his jaw was set in a tight line.

Beside me, Brooke sat quietly, seemingly in deep thought until Russ replayed our mission on the screen.

"We were almost out." Brooke peered at the ceiling.

She didn't seem to care we'd failed for the third time.

"When can we do it again?" Brooke asked, as if MM was merely a fun game.

Russ didn't answer. He continued inputting the measure of our heartbeats, our brainwaves, and level of our fear into the TAB—technological advance board. He did this for every mental mission to keep track of our progress, individually and as a team.

Justine couldn't peel her eyes off the screen, still scowling.

"We needed one more second. We would've made it out. You could've at least given us a weapon."

Russ pushed back his shoulders. "I don't have to tell you anything, Justine, but I gauge how you work with your team in all situations. Sometimes you might not have weapons accessible."

"Relax, Justy." Brooke waved her hand like it was no big deal. "It's not even real. It's all in your mind."

Justine strode over to Brooke, her blue eyes flaring with anger. "Don't call me Justy. Sounds like a guy's name. You may not care, since you and Ava have been out before, but I want my chance. It's my ticket to the mission in the real world." Then she sauntered back to her seat and crossed her arms like a spoiled child.

Brooke studied her fingernails and picked at them. Then she slowly peeled off the lead tags one-by-one, speaking with cool composure. "If I recall correctly, we never failed an MM before you joined the team, so the problem must be you."

Justine held a murderous glare. She jumped out of her seat with fists rounded into balls. I yanked off my tags and lunged forward. Justine scoffed and surrendered. My glower warned her to back off.

I had known Brooke longer and I would defend her with my life, not that Brooke couldn't defend herself. As their leader, I needed to control the situation before it got out of hand. Although I wished it wasn't my responsibility.

"Well, that was productive." Russ lifted his eyebrows. "Justine, you ready for evaluation?"

Justine's shoulders tensed. "Not really." Then her eyes roamed down Russ's tall, lean, but toned body.

I didn't blame her. Besides his drool worthy body, he had an attractive, kind face and a smile that made you feel like you'd been friends for a long time. But Russ and I really *were* friends, and he seemed to favor me above his other students.

Though I had small talks with him here and there, I wouldn't flaunt our friendship in front of his students, not even to my team. I'd never seen Russ out of control, a quality I admired. He always seemed collected, even when Justine got in her moods. And she wasn't the only one with an attitude.

All the girls had come from juvenile detention or from foster homes. Some had lived rougher lives than others. I could always tell which ones had had it bad.

After Justine's and Brooke's evaluations, Russ instructed them to leave the room. As he replayed the last few minutes of the mission once more, I waited in my seat for him to tell me how I'd failed miserably. Even after months of MMs, I still thought it was cool how the screen could play back the mission like a movie, even though it had happened in my mind.

Russ glanced my way. "Sorry. It'll be a minute. I want to show you something." Grinning, he spun back to the screen and glided his fingers across it.

A few seconds later, he stepped in front of me. Heat rushed to my face. For a moment, he wasn't my instructor but a guy with a nice ass. After months spent around mostly females, my heart turned funny flips around a decent looking guy. I brushed off the sensation, especially since we were friends, and blamed it on being deprived of man-candy.

Russ pointed to the screen. "That's where you lost your one second."

I squeezed the armrest, my stomach constricting. "I don't understand."

I shifted away from the screen, embarrassed. But I did understand. I recalled how I'd let fear encroach on my map image. But hearing those words from him felt like a punch to my gut.

That's where you lost your one second. I'd failed the team. I wondered if Brooke and Justine knew. I hated being a leader. I'd never wanted to be one in the first place. The guilt of failing my team came strong.

Russ closed the gap between us, pushing his face in front of mine. Those twinkling emerald eyes stared back at me. "You hesitated. Why?"

I couldn't breathe with his lips hovering so close to mine, especially when his breath brushed my face. Pleasant shivers rippled up my back, and his musky scent spiraled through my senses.

My instructor. My friend. I reminded myself. Then my mind registered what he'd said. *You hesitated.*

"I … didn't …" I didn't know what else to say when his eyes trailed down to my lips, and then up to my eyes.

Russ backed away, his fingers pushing through his hair. "Ava, are you aware the average human has five senses?"

Duh? Really? He did not just ask me that. Hold your smartass tongue, Ava.

I rolled my eyes. "Yes. You've told us many times." I tried not to sound sarcastic. Once the lecture started, all my inappropriate feelings withered.

"Then show me you understand. Most humans have the potential for more, but all of you here—and you, especially—are more gifted than average people. From what I've seen from the test results so far, the serum brings out the most in you. Everyone gets heightened sight, hearing, and smell, but your location sense is rare. ISAN could use more compasses like you."

He chuckled lightly, but I didn't see what was funny.

Russ continued. "Embrace your inner strength and the powers within you given by Helix serum. Don't second guess, don't let fear make you hesitate, and you won't fail next time."

I hated that word—*fail.* My face stung. He might as well have slapped me. "So, it was my fault we didn't make it."

Russ shoved his hands into his white lab coat pockets, his

expression calm as the steady sea. "Those are your words, not mine."

"Are we finished? May I be excused?" I accentuated each word with a little attitude, and then chastised myself for taking it out on him.

"Yes." Russ pressed his fists on the table with his shoulders slumped.

He didn't need to say a word. His body language confirmed my blame. Needing to release my frustration, I cursed under my breath and punched the black leather chair. Why should I care what he thought of my performance? What gave him the right to make me feel like a failure? I dropped my timer into my chair, then swung my legs over and sprinted out.

I passed a web of gray hallways housing the classrooms where I learned everything from world history to social etiquette. My finishing class instructor, Diana, would have been appalled at Justine's cursing. Justine still had a lot to learn in that department. And so did I.

Peeking into the gym, I cringed as I caught a whiff of stale sweat from the fitness and weapons training sessions. I ignored the grunts and groans from the girls inside the gym sparring and meandered on.

My footsteps squeaked in the empty, cold hallway. Two security guards stood like statues at either end of every passage. Even the juvenile detention center had been better than being locked up with a bunch of weirdos and mad-scientist types.

Though I had been locked away from the outside world before, with all ISAN's rules, I might as well have been back in prison. Not one window existed in the whole complex. Not a single one. *Creepy.*

What did I expect, though? ISAN was located underground, after all.

ISAN

I'd had a wonderful life before ISAN with my mom, but unfortunately, she'd passed away four years ago. Foster care became my only option.

I missed my mom. I missed my mom's tender voice, her loving touch. I missed her gardenia-scented perfume, and especially her home-cooked meals. Gone were the days I'd binge movies with her and chat about the love of digital books. The warm hugs and late-night talks had been replaced by curfews and resentful foster-siblings. I'd have given anything to hear her nag about keeping my room clean or see her eyes narrow at me right before a scolding.

The ache in my heart stretched too deep, and I closed myself off. Drowning into an empty heart was better than living with gut-wrenching pain. So, I buried the viselike ache clawing deeper and deeper as every year passed, until I couldn't recall the pang. It helped me move forward and be strong willed. Helped me survive.

But sometimes in my dreams, she planted her favorite flowers on our high-rise apartment balcony. She stopped tending to the roses to smile at me, to remind me I wasn't alone. That she would always be in my heart, my memory, and she would watch after me. And that no matter how deep I buried her, she would surface when I needed her.

Later, I'd run away from my abusive foster family with only a few dollars in my backpack. I'd rather live by myself than have strangers pretend to care about me. Life on the streets had made me grow up fast, and I'd become independent and resourceful.

When you've got nothing, you learn to steal.

I hadn't watched my back one winter night and got caught. Juvie had kept me warm during the harsh cold season, but nothing compared to freedom. Nobody, including my foster parents, had claimed me. Thank God they hadn't.

Russ had come for me when I turned seventeen; I'd thought a savior had come to my rescue.

CHAPTER THREE
THE PAST

One year ago ...

One of the juvenile detention guards escorted me back to the meeting room after some guy administered a blood test. When I entered, the same blood-test guy sat by a square table for two.

"Ava, do you remember me?" He scooted his chair out a bit and reached inside a black bag.

I recognized his tender voice and his pretty green eyes. "Yes. Your name's Russ."

His neatly pressed suit and grown-up tie contrasted with his youthful face. My eyes kept flashing to the glass of water so close to the edge of the table, but I didn't say a word.

"That's right. Please, have a seat." He waited until I sat. "The results showed you have a special DNA marker we're searching for. That means, if you want, I can take you out of here."

Take me out of here? You better not be lying to me.

I raised my eyebrows to hide my eagerness, especially since I had no idea if he could deliver. But my heart hammered from the excitement of the possibility.

Russ came around the table and held out a syringe without a needle. "This is another test. It won't hurt. May I?"

What the hell?

I jerked, chair scraping the tile floor. I almost tipped it back in the process. Rubbing my arm, I'd anticipated the pain.

"I promise it won't hurt."

His tone calmed my racing heart.

"Okay." I'd trusted him before, so I figured it would be fine.

"I'm going to show you what I mean when I say you're special. Give me your arm, please."

"Is it a shot?" I hesitantly extended my arm and rolled up my sleeve.

"No. Don't worry. You won't feel any pain, just some pressure. It's a volatile compressed gas that passes through the permeable layers of your skin."

The what? Passes where? I didn't want to look stupid so I just nodded.

After Russ finished, he went back to his seat while I unrolled my sleeves. He placed the item back in his bag and gave me his attention.

"I'm offering you a place at a secret institute called ISAN, better known as International Sensory Assassin Network. Don't be afraid of the word *assassin*. We're highly classified, and only people in the highest levels of government know about us. If you decide to join us, you'll be trained to kill criminals. I won't paint a pretty picture. You'll work hard; however, you'll be compensated. Your needs will be fulfilled."

You're freakin' kidding me.

I laughed, thinking he was crazy. "Look at me." I tapped my chest for emphasis. "I doubt I could kill anyone. I'm tiny. They don't feed us well here."

He frowned and nodded as if to tell me he agreed. "Believe me, Ava, you'll be well taken care of. You'll eat three full meals a day. You'll get your own room and sleep on a comfortable bed with fresh, clean sheets and blankets. You'll have your own clothes. You'll even get your education. You can make a difference in the world. You can be somebody. It'll be better than being here, wasting your life. Let me show you something."

Tingling heat coursed through me as Russ reached inside his bag again. My heartbeat escalated in a way it hadn't before, and my breathing sped up. The blue stripes on his tie appeared more vibrant. Musky scent from his cologne permeated the air heavier and thicker. My hands on my lap hotter at the touch. Voices I hadn't heard earlier murmured in my ear.

What's wrong with me?

My senses sharpened in a superhuman way.

Impossible.

I rubbed my temples, trying to calm the rush of adrenaline racing.

When Russ swung around with a paper and pen, his left elbow knocked the glass. I caught it before it could fall, my hand moving on its own accord. Not even a drop spilled. Bending low, I stared open-mouthed at the glass and how it seemed to have happened in impossibly slow motion. My gaze shifted to Russ, his green eyes somehow brighter, like the sunlight reflecting on emerald stone.

"How?" I sat back down and placed the glass on the table with trembling hands. My mind whirled with questions.

"HB77 or just simply Helix." He beamed a smile. "I injected you with a serum called HelixB77 to show you what you can do. With the proper training and practice, you can be so much more. Ava, you can be a superhero. There are other girls like you where I'm from."

"I don't understand."

"With Helix, your senses become heightened. You'll experience an increase in ability—especially the five senses. Images will be sharper, colors brighter, and you'll see farther. You'll be stronger. Your reflexes will be faster, and you'll be able to hear from longer distances. However, your senses will tame a speaking voice not to boom in your ear. The reason why it doesn't sound like I'm yelling at you."

"Incredible." The word barely left my mouth.

"Some lucky ones have more. We call that extrasensory perception. Based on the blood test, I think you might be one of the lucky ones."

Something flashed. I caught it with my right hand, then another projectile with my left. Again, my reflexes had taken over and when I looked down, I'd caught two golf balls. I gawked, trembling. The hair on my arms rose.

"Like I said, fast reflexes." His lips spread in satisfaction.

I clenched my jaw and stiffened. "You could've hurt me."

"No, Ava. Helix doesn't wear off quickly. I'd never hurt you. I bet you feel pretty powerful right now. Pretty special. What if you can do something good with that? What do you say?"

"Are there side effects?"

I rolled the golf balls over my fingertips. I imagined the balls colliding with my face. The thrill of what I had done—there was no denying it made me feel amazing.

Russ slowly curled his lips to a grin. "I like the way you think. It's been thoroughly tested and we've seen no side effects in all the years of the program. We give you just enough to do a job, and then it's out of your system."

I nodded.

"So … Will you be joining ISAN today?"

I shivered, not just from the cool draft from the vent, but the thought of being an assassin, even if my victims were criminals. Could I really do it? Trained or no.

My mother's last words echoed in my mind. *When life shoves you down, you get right back up. Be strong. Be brave, Ava. Be someone important.*

Oh, Mom, what do I do? I feel so alone and I'm so scared.

My chest caved in. I wanted to burst into a sob, but I slammed it back down. As tears pooled, thoughts of my mother twisted the dagger in my heart. My heart leaked, bleeding from the mountainous pain of missing her, needing her guidance.

I wouldn't be in juvie, desperate to get out and resort to being an assassin if she were alive. Having no choice, I succumbed to the reality of my life and the cards I had been dealt. I pushed back my shoulders and held up my chin. Boring my eyes into his, I gave him an answer that would change my life forever.

I will be brave, Mother. I will become someone important.

* * *

Thinking I'd be taken care of, have warm food to eat and a roof over my head, not to mention a get-out-of-jail-free card, I didn't have to think twice. My mom hadn't believed lives were given to be thrown away and neither did I. I wanted to be somebody important, to make something of myself. I still had my whole life ahead of me. ISAN seemed like my only chance.

But ISAN proved no better than jail. I couldn't go out into the real world except on special assignment, which I'd done twice. Russ told me the next one would be even more difficult and dangerous. If it was like any of my mental tests, I might as well go ahead and die.

I had net access, but with restrictions. Rule number one: No contacting family and friends. A useless rule for me since I didn't have any. Rule number two: Net access is limited to fifteen minutes daily, and if I went beyond the time allowed, the TAB shut down. Rule number three: No social connections. No contacting or communicating with strangers.

I curved the corner of the drab gray wall to get to my room and passed another security guard. Standing in front of my door, I placed my palm on a square metal plate. The cold steel warmed to the touch as it took the imprint of my hand, red laser zigzagging back and forth.

The laser passed over the web between my thumb and forefinger, where the tiny silicon-based chip used to be. Every citizen got one when they turned sixteen. But ISAN had taken mine out and given me another one in the middle of my inner forearm—less likely to be damaged in physical combat. Not only was ISAN's chip used to track me, a cyanide capsule was attached it. Triggering the capsule would induce a massive attack and I would die.

With a whoosh, the metal door slid open.

My room—a perfect cube—barely fit a bed and a small desk. When I'd first come to ISAN, I'd had no possessions but what I wore. Not even a photo. Once in a while, the inspectors checked my room unannounced. I had no idea what they thought they'd find. My room stayed clean and pretty much empty. No evidence of the past; no evidence of the Ava before ISAN.

I changed into something comfortable and waved my hand over my metal desk to initiate the voice-activator. The voice-activator could do pretty much anything in my room, like release my bed out from the wall, open my closet, or turn off the light. Or I could simply do it manually. Sometimes I turned the activator off when I didn't feel like talking to a fake person. It gave me the creeps.

"Turn TAB on," I said.

"Good evening, Ava," the female with no name said. "Initiating."

"Thanks."

The TAB projected in mid-air. Searching the net had become my comfort, where the walls around me didn't exist. I stripped away Ava the assassin and became Ava the normal teenager.

It was my time, my freedom, and my world.

CHAPTER FOUR
DINNER

Reading about fashion, movies, TV shows, and actors' gossip entertained me. As I searched for news about my celebrity crushes, a word appeared on the bottom right of the projected screen.

Hello

At first, I thought Russ or one of my teammates from ISAN had messaged me, but their faces would've popped up. Puzzled, I debated whether to click on it. One of the ISAN leaders might have sent me a message to see if I'd break their rules. I didn't want to find out or get in trouble, so I ignored it.

The screen shut down automatically. Had it been fifteen minutes already? I cursed and commanded the voice-activator to open the door. When it slid open, I jerked back, startled by Brooke peering at me from under her long eyelashes.

Brooke and I had hit it off pretty well from the start. Maybe Brooke being the same height as me, same gray eyes, and having brunette hair just past the shoulder blade like mine, bonded us. From behind, I could pass for her twin.

Being new together at ISAN also made a difference. She would stick up for me, fight for me, and even get in trouble for me. She wasn't like that with everyone, but working as a team built trust between us. Brooke still kept her guard up, though—like everyone else, she pretty much kept to herself. I understood. I'd been burned

18

before.

"Hey, Ava." Her gray eyes beamed and she flashed her white teeth.

"Hey. Did you need something?"

"Nope, just waiting for you."

"You hungry?"

"Starving."

"You want to move out of my way so we can go to dinner together?"

She blinked, stepped aside, then cruised down the hall with me. I veered right, then took another right, and came into view of the cafeteria door.

"I wonder what we're having tonight," Brooke murmured.

The aroma of pot roast and mashed potatoes spiraled through my senses when I stepped in, replacing the sterile scent of the hallway. My stomach churned, reminding me of my mother's cooking, reminding me of my home before. For a second, I let myself feel the pain, and then quickly shut out my thoughts. I inhaled again, moaning, my mouth watering.

"Don't have an orgasm over food, Ava." She chuckled. "Better yet, go ahead. It's the only one we're getting."

True. So damn true. I snorted as I picked up a tray and got in line. For Brooke's ears only, I moaned longer.

I giggled when she moaned loud enough for everyone to hear. Brooke, on the other hand, not only made her audience bellow a laugh, she caught the guards' attention.

Two guards stood at the front entrance with their hands behind them. Tasers hung from holsters on their belts. Shaped like a gun, the Taser was silver to distinguish it from a regular firearm. It had one purpose: to incapacitate an opponent for roughly thirty minutes.

The Taser had a laser attachment to allow precision accuracy when shooting from a distance and fired an electrically charged pellet that stunned on impact. Since the Remnant Councils had a no killing policy, guns had been outlawed. Only the most elite possessed them.

One of the guards looked away when no problem arose, but the other one surveyed mine and Brooke's bodies from the corner of his eye. He tried not to make it obvious, but his eyes did not lie.

I wanted to say, "Do you like what you see, or are your eyes burning from staring at our asses?" but I held my tongue in check. Asking guards questions or even talking to them was prohibited. And I didn't want to find out what my punishment would be. Rumor said it had something to do with our fears, and that alone hit the brakes for me.

Brooke tapped my tray with her spoon to get my attention. She smiled giddily while piling mashed potatoes on her plate and mine. Then Brooke groaned when the girl in front of us took too long scooping pot roast.

I snorted. "The food isn't going anywhere."

"I know, but it'll be on that girl's face if she doesn't hurry."

I knew she meant it, so I tried to reason with her. "She's probably deciding how much to take. What're you going to do, start a food fight?"

Brooke's eyes twinkled, and she flashed a wicked smirk. "Not a bad idea."

I chuckled, catching the girl's attention in front of Brooke. She glanced over her shoulder and scowled. Brooke gave the girl the finger after she turned and held it up longer than needed, so I crushed it down. Sometimes Brooke's temper flared from something small—unpredictable.

The girl whirled, fury in her eyes. "I saw that, bitch. I'll break your finger next time you flip me the bird."

The clanking of the utensils stopped and the room went silent.

Brooke parted her lips to say something, but I stepped between them when the guards focused their attention on us again, their hands on their Tasers.

"Stop. Enough." I said it more for Brooke's sake. I didn't want her to be sent to isolation over something trivial.

They both cursed and then went back to minding their own business. I looked at the ceiling and released a long breath.

Finally, I passed through the line and searched for empty seats. The tables were full—not that there were many of us. There must've been fifty girls from different cultures. I knew only a few by name. Selected groups trained on different schedules; not to mention girls were regularly shipped in and out unannounced. I hoped Brooke stayed in the same group as me for the sake of my sanity.

Brooke picked a seat across from Justine. I sat between Brooke and a newbie.

"Hello," the girl said. "My name is Tamara Lee. I mean Tamara. Just Tamara. I was told I don't have a last name anymore." She twisted her inky hair with her finger, and her brown eyes beamed when she smiled. "I'm new here ... well, since last week, but I'll be easy to recognize since it looks like I'm one of the few Asians here."

"My name is Ava. And you're in good company. I'm actually half Asian myself, on my mom's side." I pointed to my teammates. "Brooke and Justine."

"Hi," Brooke said, her mouth stuffed with food.

Justine jerked her chin, a way of greeting.

Tamara forked a portion of roast beef, and her eyes glistened with excitement. "I may be new here, but I know who you three are. Russ used your MM training video as examples to follow."

"Oh?" My interest piqued, I soaked in her enthusiasm.

Mr. Novak, the head of ISAN, had introduced the five

newbies the week before. For the first five to seven days, the newbies were confined in one area for further testing.

I remembered my first day—more blood tests and mental mission training to determine my level of tolerance and my capabilities. The grueling testing exhausted me. After tests, I had been sent back to my room.

Mr. Novak had prohibited me from mingling with other girls and I'd realized then ISAN wasn't a place of comfort and home. My destiny had been set. They owned me. They would use me. I had no choice. I had no money, no friends, and no family.

Russ preached I would be somebody important one day and make a difference in this world. I held onto that thought and reminded myself why I had committed to ISAN in the first place.

I took a gulp of my vitamin-laced water and almost gagged.

Justine grimaced. "I don't know how long I can drink this awful protein shake."

Brooke tapped Justine's cup and almost knocked it over. "You drank it all."

"Well, I don't have a choice, do I?" Justine gripped her tray until her knuckles turned white.

"You do." Brooke stared, eyes unblinking, challenging. "You could've opted not to sign your contract. You knew what you were signing up for, so stop complaining. We're all going through the same shit."

I scrubbed my face and sighed, preparing for anything to happen. Justine jumped out of her seat, her fingers flexing, and her eyes cold as stone.

What the hell? Not again.

"Stop." I held out my hand. "You'll be deported." I shook my head. Then I snickered at the image of pot roast and mashed potatoes on Justine's face and hair. Oh, how I would love to dump food on her head one day.

Justine sat as if nothing had happened. Brooke gossiped about what she'd found on the net, telling us all about fashion dos and don'ts. Tamara smiled. As for me, I exhaled in relief; my team hadn't disturbed the peace. I took my last bite of broccoli as I thought of the weird message I'd received on my TAB.

After dinner, I went to the meeting room as announced during meal time. When I arrived, Russ and Lydia stood side-by-side on a raised podium situated in the center of the room.

"Good evening." Lydia spoke through a tiny microphone clipped on her red, long-sleeved shirt.

Lucky Lydia. As a superior, she wore any color shirt she wanted. Even without makeup, she was beautiful. Her smooth skin appeared soft, and she looked as sweet as her voice, with a friendly smile and dimples.

Lydia waited until the shuffling stopped. "Tomorrow, some of you will be in session with Russ and some of you will be with me. Then we'll switch, depending on your last score from this point. The two teams with the most points will be on the next special assignment."

Cheers filled the room.

Russ raised his hand and the noise faded. "We have a big assignment next week. I'm not authorized to say more, but know I'll be picking the best of the best. Also, I'll be adding one more person to each team. You'll be notified tomorrow. Don't forget to do your homework. Good luck. You're dismissed."

"I hope I get to be on yours. I heard your team was the best," Tamara said.

"You bet it is." Justine raised her chin, slinking past me.

"Is she always this cocky?" Tamara kept her steps even with mine.

You have no idea. I raised a corner of my lips. "Always."

Brooke took a step to the other side of Tamara. "Who told

you we were the best? We were short by one second. Surely some other team made it. But, then again, we never know the other teams' scores."

"All the newbies know. Russ, the cute instructor, said so." Tamara twisted to find Russ.

I did the same in curiosity. I was sure he'd be gone, but when his eyes locked on mine, my face warmed. I pivoted away. Surely, he wasn't just focusing on me, rather making sure everyone headed to their rooms.

"Wow. That's awesome." Brooke almost ran into the wall when the hall split east and west.

"I'm going to the left." Tamara waved her hand. "See you guys tomorrow."

"Goodnight, Tamara." I smiled.

"See you tomorrow, newbie." Brooke rounded the corner with me.

I really liked Tamara. Rarely did I meet an amiable newbie, especially in this environment. ISAN encouraged competition—something you didn't do with friends. For this reason, I understood the hostility among peers. I just hoped Tamara would remain the same after the hell she would have to go through. She had no idea what was in store for her.

She'd be fine, right? She'd come out of juvie or from foster care, like all the rest of us had, and she still acted bubbly. But deep in my gut, doubt grew—she wouldn't be fine.

I had been in her shoes once—compliant, hopeful, and gullible—but now I questioned everything. After all, I had become a weapon—an assassin. No matter the reasons for my killing, I would be playing God and taking people's lives. In the end, I would become a darker version of myself.

"Who do you think will be on our team?" Brooke asked.

"No idea. Do you know something I don't know?"

"No. Your senses are better than mine. I thought you could read their minds or something by now. I would love to have that kind of power. I'd especially want to know Russ's thoughts." She waggled her brows.

I snorted. It felt good to let out some stress. Sometimes Brooke knew just what to say. Brooke seemed to be the go-getter type, but she never judged or competed with me.

I shrugged. "Sorry. I have no idea. Wouldn't it be great if I *could* read minds? Maybe I could eventually with Helix."

Brooke's eyes sparkled. "Maybe you should try it. It might work if you use a higher dosage."

The sound of the footsteps dissipated around us.

"Why just me? We can both try it."

"You and I both know you're special. It's why you're the team lead." Brooke stopped at my door. "You think faster, move faster, and hell, you have a map in your mind. You can see it in 3D, can't you?"

"I can." I dipped my head, shuffling my feet.

Brooke had never raved about me before. I didn't like to brag, and I didn't want to admit aloud to being different or special, but secretly I agreed.

"That's so freakin' awesome." Her eyes scanned my name on the door. "Well, here we are."

"Yup." I lowered my voice. Any louder and my voice would have reverberated to the guards. "The halls are so dead quiet and freaky like Mr. Novak."

"He definitely creeps me out. I don't like the way he scrutinizes us, like we're his pets."

I gasped at her boldness, even though I felt the same way. He reminded me of my foster father, especially around the eyes. His bottomless pit coal eyes impaled me like spears.

I wished I could've defended myself from my foster father

25

when he'd come at me with a belt, since my foster mother hadn't done anything to stop him. But he would've beaten her, too. Helix would've been good to have then.

"Pets? Don't think like that." I frowned. "He's probably shaking because if given a chance, we could beat the crap out of him with Helix."

"I guess." Brooke lifted her shoulders. Her scowl replaced her somber expression. "He reminds me of one of the people who killed my parents. I never told anyone how my parents died. They were murdered in our house right in front of me when I was a little girl. Men in dark clothes came during the night when we were asleep."

"I'm sorry." I thought about what my mom had done to give me comfort, so I wrapped my arms around her. It was the first time I'd shown her affection. Then I immediately regretted my action and stepped back. "Sorry, I didn't mean to do that."

I tensed. First, I didn't know how she'd react since she hadn't returned the hug. Second, I didn't know if anyone was watching us besides the guards. Not that showing affection was a crime. Cameras hung from the ceiling, but I didn't know where, exactly.

Brooke squinted her eyes, then eased back a step. "Anyway, I'd better go. I need to finish my homework."

"See you tomorrow morning." I placed my hand on the scanner.

"See ya." Brooke headed toward her room as I entered mine.

I gathered my supplies to wash up at the community restroom. After I did my business, I went back to my room and finished my homework. Once in a while, I'd run my fingers along the length of the three faint scars on my body, wondering how I'd gotten them.

One spanned my lower back and another my left rib. The third scar was a burst of distorted streaks that might have once resembled a sunrise on my right side. I might have gotten these scars when my foster father whipped me, or when I'd been wounded in fights at juvie. No matter how hard I tried to recall, it remained futile. Dismissing the thought, I got into bed.

As I stared at the ceiling, I replayed the day in my mind. Today had been better than the day before. Brooke and I were getting closer to developing a real friendship; albeit it had taken us six months.

It had been so long since I'd had a friend. Ever since I'd gone into foster care, I'd hidden my life from everyone else. I made sure I stayed invisible, especially when it came to making friends.

Many people stayed away from me, anyway. Everyone in our small town knew about my alcoholic foster father, and they wouldn't allow their children to come over to my place. Couldn't blame them. So, when I ran away, I hadn't missed anyone and no one missed me.

I'd also met a potential new friend. I hoped Tamara stayed as sweet as she'd seemed. With real friends, I might actually like it here after all. Though I complained about ISAN, it beat sleeping out in the streets, stealing food, and being utterly alone.

The stranger on my TAB came to mind. All sorts of nonsense invaded my thoughts. *What if one of the girls had pranked me? What if Mr. Novak had tested me?* Violating a rule would likely result in harsh consequences, but I had no idea what. Surely ISAN wouldn't just send me back to juvie knowing what I knew.

Too tired to think, I drifted away to my fairy dream world— a place where my mom was alive. A place where I had a family, friends, and even a sister and a brother … and I was happy.

CHAPTER FIVE
TEAMWORK

The suspense drove me crazy.

I stood on a yellow line in a giant circle while Russ and Lydia stood in the center. They wore their training outfits—dark gray pants with matching red shirts. Lydia had her hair tied back as usual, but for some reason, she and Russ seemed different—more tense.

In the center of the circle was the ISAN logo—a compass with the initials ISAN in the middle—the same symbol imprinted on the front of the guards' vests and all outfits.

With my hands behind my back, spine stiff, eyes forward—ISAN attention stance—I waited for my training to begin.

"Good morning." Russ produced a barely noticeable smile. "Hope everyone had a restful sleep. In a few minutes, the screen will display the schedule for your team, indicating when to report to the fitness workout with me, or self-defense with Lydia."

Lydia stepped forward. "As I've mentioned before, the top two teams will go on a special assignment. As an extra incentive, the winning team will be allowed to go out on a Friday night for three hours to a place of their choosing."

Cheers erupted but faded. Mr. Novak appeared and raised his hand to silence the crowd. His eyes—cold as a gravestone—fell on me, rooting me to the spot, singling me out. I bristled, heart racing. Despite the perfect temperature in ISAN, I shivered.

Look away. I couldn't. His gaze held power over me, making me weak and stiff.

In addition to the fact he walked like he had a stick up his butt, he never smiled. His chiseled jaw clenched, his shoulders pushed back proudly, and his onyx eyes warned me not to mess with him. Sporting a black suit, his tie perfectly straight, he always dressed like he was going to a funeral. Too bad it wasn't his.

Lydia squared her shoulders and cleared her throat. "We'll give you some time to look over your schedules. Russ and I will be in our offices if you have any questions."

With a nod, they ambled out together.

The room went silent. The hunger to contact the world outside the building fed my desire to win. I presumed everyone felt the same. Only two teams would go on a special assignment and one team for Friday night for three hours.

Did my team have a chance?

"Come on. Let's go find out who goes first," someone said.

As if the words were some kind of cue, girls jostled each other in the race to check the list. Brooke pulled my T-shirt, ensuring we would stay together, but someone rammed my shoulder in passing. If Brooke hadn't grabbed me, I would've fallen flat on my face.

"What the heck?" Rage surged through my veins. I searched for the rude girl who didn't apologize as I straightened my shirt.

Brooke narrowed her eyes. She had no shame in pointing her finger at the culprit. "The girl with the black T-shirt. The big mean one. Her team calls her Roxy."

Roxy towered over me and bulged with muscles. I soon learned running into me wasn't an accident when she glared at me. Her scowl promised there would be more trouble ahead. Guess she didn't like Russ telling newbies we were the best. My assumption only, but I couldn't think of any other explanation. I had never interacted with her before.

I ground my teeth, my fists hard as rocks. I wanted to rush over there and hammer her face into the ground.

Steady the anger, Ava. You're a leader. You're better than that. Think of your team. So I simply offered my fake charming smile and gave her the bird.

She schooled her face so tightly, her cheek muscles twitched. When she lunged forward, her team held her back. Roxy swatted at her friends to release the hold on her and then scampered away.

Good. You best scurry away. I lit a victorious smile for the win.

The crowd stopped and I rooted my eyes on the screen that ran the length of the wall.

"Do you see our names?" I asked Justine.

"Nope. Nothing so far ... can't see the bottom. There're too many people. But there goes Tamara."

Tamara's petite frame slinked through the throng. She found us a few minutes later with a bright smile. "Justine, Brooke, Ava and me—we're Team Ten. Oh yeah, oh yeah, oh yeah." She twirled her hips and her neck simultaneously.

I giggled at the hilarious display—her version of the happy dance—she had no rhythm, but I had to give her credit for moving to her own beat.

Justine leaned on her hip and crossed her arms, staring at Tamara, appalled. "Great. We get a clown."

"You're such a bitch." Brooke shook her head, like a mother reprimanding a child. "You're jealous because you can't dance like her."

I smiled, secretly thanking Brooke for sticking up for Tamara. Tamara didn't say anything, although her lips parted and her eyes darkened. One day soon, she would be brave enough to fight back, once her newbie status changed.

Justine pushed her chest to Brooke's and I prepared to step in the middle.

"Look." Justine stabbed her finger in the air for emphasis. "I want to see the outside of this place. If any one of you messes up,

I'm asking for a transfer, understand?"

Go ahead. That would make my day.

Brooke's lips spread broadly. "No one is stopping you."

Justine gazed up at the ceiling and scoffed. "I'll meet you guys in fifteen minutes." She pointed down. "Right here on this spot. You see those idiots, huddled together?"

I considered the group Justine pointed to.

"They're Team Nine," Justine continued. "We're up against them. I suggest you get some rest and think of ways to beat those girls, or they'll kick our asses. They look like they've been drinking steroids." She stomped away.

Tamara gasped. Her eyes widened. "Maybe Justine is right. Maybe we should rest before—"

"Don't worry. Justine is all talk. She's just scared." Brooke waved her hand as if she could dismiss Tamara's anxiety.

Everybody headed to their rooms, except for me. Reviewing the list once more, I noticed all teams had five names. Tamara had failed to mention the fifth line read *M*. Just the letter *M*. Strange. Did I know someone whose name started with M? And why was she in all the teams?

Having some time left, I sprinted to my room, planning to check for another strange message on my TAB. I rushed through the door, powered my TAB, and checked the clock. Plenty of time.

Anticipation heated my blood. I waited, but no message appeared. Despite being suspicious of the unknown message sender, I was disappointed. Then after five minutes, three words popped up at the right corner like the last time.

Are you there?

I had a strong urge to peek over my shoulder when fear pricked my skin. I should ignore the message, but I couldn't help myself.

My heart drummed faster. I felt nervous and excited at the same time. Oh, what the hell? I hadn't done anything wrong. I hadn't reached out first. I typed back.

I hesitated. Had I just failed a test? I debated whether to shut down my TAB. If it was a test, I was already screwed.

I wrote back.

I thought about questions that wouldn't cause suspicion, and I could only think of one.

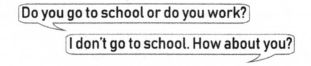

My fingers paused as I debated what to type. The urge to respond before time to leave outweighed the consequences of being caught, so I continued.

I don't go to school either.

A lie.

> **I want to meet you.**

What? Had he just asked me out on a date? Was he some kind of psycho killer? He didn't even know me. Wouldn't a name like *Adam* put the brakes on? Maybe the stranger was female. Or maybe he was gay. I snorted and noted the time.

Crap. I had a minute left before I had to report to my station, so I typed as fast as I could.

> **I gotta go. I can't.**

I shut down my TAB and ran as fast as my legs would allow. I booked it down the hall, the echoes of my stomping tennis shoes reverberating loudly.

Why were there so many damn halls?

Justine glared at me, pointing at the digital clock on the wall.

"Sorry," I mouthed.

Standing next to Tamara, I examined Team Nine. They were muscular, bigger, and their eyes held no mercy. In the dead center stood Roxy. Roxy's face paled sickly against her black hair. Her nostrils flared like a bull ready to charge, and her lips twitched when she spotted me.

Roxy lifted a fist and smacked it against her palm, as her dark steel eyes, hard and cold, gazed straight at me with purpose.

I swallowed, but reminded myself this was like sparring. Something I had done many times, and the size of the girls shouldn't daunt me. So I squared my shoulders and I glowered back. Challenge accepted.

Lydia stood in the middle of the yellow ring, looking young

enough to pass for one of us. I wondered if she had ever been an assassin who had switched to a different department when her time expired. Curious, one day I would ask her.

In one hand, Lydia held a digital stopwatch. In the other, she held two black vests. While Lydia paced, she scanned the workout room, then each of us, and then stopped in front of me.

"Glad your team didn't have to have one less. Keep the time, Ava."

She turned her back to me before I could explain.

Explain what? Someone had contacted me and I secretly wished the stranger was a hot guy? I had to stop thinking about the message and get my head in the game or my lack of concentration would hurt my team.

"We're doing something different today," she continued. "I'm not going to teach you any tactics or self-defense. I'm going to dose you with a small amount of Helix. Keep in mind, unlike when you get a full dosage, you will feel pain. And your team will lose a point for face contact. So be careful and remember the rules. One person will wear the vest from each team, and the rest of you will need to protect it. The team that steals the other team's red X from the back of their vest is the winner. Your timing is crucial. I rank by time. Good luck. Do you have any questions?"

I stepped forward without making eye contact.

"Ava?"

"On the screen, a letter *M* was added to our team. Will she be joining us?"

"No, not on this round." She examined me, her eyes lingering longer than usual.

Was something up?

Oh God. Was she the stranger contacting me on my TAB? My face burned at the possibility. Then I realized she had been busy with the girls while I had been talking to the stranger. My suspicion died.

"Is that all?" she asked.

"Yes."

"Return to your position."

I acquiesced and took a step back into the line.

My team voted Tamara to wear the vest. I would stay behind and protect Tamara while Justine and Brooke went for the other team's X.

Helix spread through my blood after Lydia gave me my dose. The red X on the vest grew vibrant. My mind clicked in full alert, strategizing, and my eyes darted back and forth.

Everyone's unique pheromones whiffed through my nose. Tamara, closest to me, smelled like jasmine. Justine and Brooke gave off wild flower scents. But, oh God, the odor from the other team, something between sweat mixed with bad breath, made me want to vomit.

I winced and tried not to inhale deeply, and failed.

Tamara grimaced. "What's that smell?"

Clearly their tactic had worked, but I needed her to focus.

"Tamara, it's their plan. They're distracting us with their stench. Don't let it get to you."

"Okay." Tamara's voice sounded off, like she had a bad case of stuffy nose.

Clever, Roxy. Let's see if you're smart enough to beat my team.

As if Roxy knew I was thinking of her, she pointed at me with narrowed eyes, and mouthed, "You're dead."

I scoffed. The nerve of her. Instead of feeding my wrath, I did something she never expected, something that might flip her switch. I winked and blew her a kiss. Then I gave her my back as if she wasn't worth a second of my time and swaggered away.

When I turned back, Roxy's face blazed with enough rage to start a fire.

Team Nine charged when Lydia gave the green light. My heart pounded against my rib cage. Justine ducked a swing and rammed her fist into the gut of a fighter named Carol.

Carol's head thrashed forward while her body curved around her stomach. She recovered and swung higher, smacking Justine on the left cheek. I winced. Justine swore. Team Nine had lost a point for making face contact.

The wicked side of me snickered. Justine deserved that. How many times had I wanted to punch Justine in the face? Justine would have a bruise, but Dr. Machine could make her look good as new in a matter of minutes.

I shifted my eyes to Brooke.

Come on, Brooke. Do better than Justine.

A redhead charged like a jaguar toward Brooke. Brooke effortlessly leaped upward and landed behind the redhead. She swung her leg around like a baseball bat and knocked the redhead to the floor, face down.

Atta girl.

When the girl lifted her head, blood trickled from her nose. The smell of iron came strong, thanks to Helix. Then, Brooke charged for the girl in the vest, Faya. I itched to help when I observed Justine struggling with Roxy. But the X couldn't be taken. I had to protect Tamara.

I extended my arms in front of Tamara as the other team advanced. The redhead wiped her bloody nose with her shirt and came for me. When I threw a punch, she got a hold of my arm and twisted it behind me. I groaned.

With my other hand, I reached behind me and wrenched a fistful of her hair. I landed on my back with a thud when she flipped me over, but I popped back up. Rage rushed through me, and I swung my leg as Brooke had and knocked the redhead over. Not realizing she had a grip on my shirt, I fell on top of her.

I bit my lip when my head hit hers and I tasted warm metallic liquid. After tumbling several times, my body came to a halt with redhead on top. When her hand wrapped around my throat, I lost my concentration.

What's wrong with me? I'm stronger than this. Get the hell up. Your team needs you.

Tamara yanked the redhead off me and tossed her to the side. Coughing relentlessly, I got up to protect Tamara again. The room spun and I stumbled forward a bit. I scrubbed my face and shook my head, hoping to clear my vision.

"Are you okay?" she asked.

I had no time to respond.

I pushed Tamara aside and dove for the redhead. I managed to get a grip on her T-shirt and shoved her across the polished floor. I'd predicted Roxy to be the troublemaker, but I'd thought wrong. The redhead charged, her eyes pinned on me with promise of death. Some people would do anything for a night on the town.

You can go with the black eye I'm going to give you, Red.

The redhead threw herself at me. Instead of blocking, I jumped over her. She stumbled, gripping only air, and fell. Growling at me, she got up and threw a sloppy punch. I moved faster, and she missed.

"We did it," Brooke exclaimed.

Cheering and screaming erupted. Justine and Brooke gave each other high fives.

I glanced over my shoulder to the redhead as a cautious measurement, wondering if she would attack me. Though she didn't, her gaze screamed bloody murder and held me on edge. I've learned through experience; some girls didn't care about rules.

Roxy cursed under her breath, pacing the length of the mat.

I punched the air and gave Tamara a pat on her back. Justine and Brooke ran toward us. For the first time, I felt we were a unit.

There was no yelling or bickering among my team. A sense of trust and sisterhood I'd never felt before wrapped around me; which I assumed was the reason for this specific training.

One step closer to getting some free time in the real world. I especially wanted it for Justine and Tamara. They deserved some happiness, too.

"Congratulations, Team Ten. Let's see what happens to the other groups." Lydia tapped the small TAB device she held. "Team Nine, you need to stay for round two. Team Ten, go get some rest and report to Russ in half an hour."

Team Nine kept their heads down. The redhead's bloody nose became worse and Lydia offered her a towel. I felt bad for them, but one of us had to lose. Better them than us.

I shuffled out and past the guards, then separated from my team to head to my room. I rubbed my still-throbbing throat and sucked on my small split lip. No biggie. The intensity of the pain would have been a lot worse had I not received the serum. Besides, months and months of physical training had made me tolerant to pain. Pain or not, I felt the strong need to punch the redhead.

As soon as I entered my room, I went straight to my TAB. I had about five minutes left. I waved my hand to wake it up. My eyes zoomed down to the corner, and sure enough, a message awaited me.

Why?

Sorry. My parents are very strict.

Stupid answer, but a believable explanation. Why was I apologizing?

Come meet me for a drink.

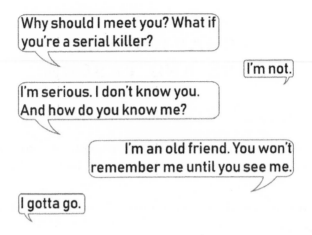

Why should I meet you? What if you're a serial killer?

I'm not.

I'm serious. I don't know you. And how do you know me?

I'm an old friend. You won't remember me until you see me.

I gotta go.

I shut down.

I didn't know what frightened me more, getting caught or exchanging messages with Sniper. *Sniper* sounded more like a guy's name, so I pretended he was. My sensible half didn't want to talk to the stranger anymore, but curiosity about the mystery person ate me alive.

How had he tapped into my TAB when ISAN had a highly classified system deemed untraceable? I didn't want the blame to fall on me if the person broke through the main system and crashed everything.

Sniper said he was an old friend, but I didn't have any friends. No explanation how the stranger had found me was fathomable.

Why had it happened to me? I'd always believed nothing happened by chance. I thought about asking Brooke, or maybe Tamara, but definitely not Justine. As those thoughts circulated in my mind, I noted the time. I sighed through my nose.

"Open. Door," I said.

When the door whooshed, I stepped out.

CHAPTER SIX
GUNS AND TASERS

I sat on a black training chair and patiently waited for Russ. The large screen above reminded me of the last failed mental mission.

"Do you want the room brighter?" I raised my hand to wave at the sensor.

"No. It's fine." Justine leaned back in her seat. She placed her arms behind her neck for support and crossed her ankles.

I shivered. Unlike the just right temperature in my room, the sterile room seemed as cold as it felt. Bored out of my mind, I eyed the high dome-shaped ceiling and marveled at the sophisticated equipment that monitored me during mental missions. Then I examined the machine with countless switches and buttons. I yawned since there wasn't much to see. A complex room, yet so simple and lackluster.

"So, what brought you here?" Brooke asked no one in particular.

"None of your business." Justine twirled her chair and gazed up at the lights.

Justine was a tough nut to crack. One minute, she'd act like your best friend, and the next, she hated you. Everyone had a difficult past. Perhaps being insufferable was her defense mechanism.

"I didn't ask you, Justine," Brooke said. "You assumed I did and opened your fat mouth."

Justine growled like a wild animal.

Brooke hiked her eyebrows. "What's wrong, Justy? Don't have anything intelligent to say?"

The mocking hostility in Brooke's tone made Justine flinch.

"Easy." I reached over and pressed a hand on Brooke.

Yep, I had a fantastic group. What happened to the bond we'd found half an hour ago?

"I killed someone when I turned sixteen," Tamara said in a monotone. Her eyes were focused on the gray wall.

No way.

The room grew silent. Not even the machine hummed. Not only did Tamara appear fragile, she had a baby innocent face, and with one pout, she would more than likely get her way. Perhaps not in ISAN, though.

"My lawyer tried to win the case by presenting what I did as self-defense, but actually it was premeditated." Tamara broke the awkward quiet. "I shot my boyfriend. He beat the crap out of me day after day. He deserved it."

"He *did* deserve it, Tamara." Justine sounded sympathetic— unusual for her. Whether it was the topic or she genuinely cared, surprisingly Justine opened up. "I know you're from juvie, but how about your parents?"

"I don't know who my dad is. My mom left me with my grandmother and took off somewhere. My grandmother passed away when I was in juvie. I never got to say goodbye to her."

I sucked at comfort talk, so I kept quiet.

"How about you, Brooke?" Tamara swirled her chair to face Brooke.

Brooke idly ran her fingers on the lead tags, and then cocked an eyebrow. "I didn't kill anyone, if that's what you're asking. I went through a line of foster parents. None of them could handle me. I sucked at school and got into fights. I beat the crap out of anyone who stared at me wrong. Hot Russ entered my life about

41

six months ago. He did blood tests on a few of us at juvie. I had the lucky genes, and here I am." She stretched her arms sideways with bravado.

"And you, Ava?" Tamara locked her eyes with mine.

I stretched my neck and cracked my knuckles. "I never knew my father. My mom told me he passed away when I was a baby, and my mom passed away when I turned thirteen. I didn't even know she was sick. My foster father drank heavily and beat the crap out of me. I didn't want to get smacked around anymore, so I ran away from home. I slept on the streets and stole whatever I needed to get by. I had become an expert at stealing, but I got careless. My foster parents never came for me, so they locked me up in juvenile detention. Then Russ came along."

None of us had ever opened up about the past. Talking about it helped the hole in my heart heal a bit, but I didn't let it go. My past had made me Ava the assassin. I hoped one day I would find closure. Through life lessons, I wished to become a new me.

"Wow ... our lives totally suck." Tamara tucked her fist under her chin. "I guess we're the lucky ones. At least we have decent food to eat and live under a warm roof."

"Yeah ... but the kids—" I stopped when footsteps squeaked. *The kids still in juvie are not assassins*, I finished in my mind.

Russ entered, taking long strides across the room. "Sorry, ladies. I was in a meeting."

"Wow, boss." Justine jumped out of her seat. "You look like a hot angel with your white lab coat on."

Indeed, he does. My heart skipped a beat, and I burst the bubbling feeling slowly rising from my stomach.

Color coated Russ's face. "Very funny, Justine. Based on your cheerful mood, I'll assume your team won the first round."

Justine gave a sidelong glance and sat back down. "I'm always cheerful, boss, and we kicked their ass." She paused. "I mean ...

Yes, we won."

Polite and ladylike wasn't usually her style. I almost gagged at her change of words. *Kiss ass.*

"Congratulations. I knew you would. Today's round will be more difficult than the last. You won't be timed. You just need to make it out alive." Russ knitted his eyebrows together, and then narrowed his eyes at me.

Brooke gulped and let out a nervous laugh. "It's only a mental test, right?"

Russ picked up his hand-held TAB and a small black case from the table next to the screen. "It's different."

"What do you mean, different?" Tamara's tone rose.

"I'll explain after I introduce you to the fifth member of your team."

"You mean M?" I asked.

Hopefully she would be easy going like Tamara and Brooke. God help me if she was anything like Justine.

"Yes, M. Come on out, M." Russ whistled.

I gasped when a man appeared through the door—tall and built like Russ and sporting an ISAN black training uniform. The man's light brown hair was brushed back, revealing thick eyebrows and tantalizing blue eyes. I bent forward to get a better view of my team, and sure enough, they practically drooled.

"Ladies, this is Mitch. If your team gets chosen to go on special assignments, he'll be your director, also known as field operative. Today, he's going to assist you with Tasers and guns."

"Hello, ladies." Mitch grinned. He eyed each of us.

Justine leaned a hip against her chair, biting her bottom lip. "Hi there." She greeted him in the most seductive way with those two simple words.

Russ coughed to interrupt her daze. "Make sure you pay attention to his instruction and not his face. When he feels you're ready, your team will move ahead to the next stage of training. Though we mostly use Tasers, sometimes you might need to use a gun."

"Or body," Justine murmured.

Brooke removed her hand from the tags and sat taller. "Sounds exciting. I'm up for the challenge. When do we start?"

"Right now. Ladies, follow me." Russ's black shoes clicked along the polished floor.

"Gladly." Tamara made an *I'm hot for him* smile.

Yeah, she had it bad for Russ.

Russ took us through the double steel doors, across the hallway, and several floors down into another dim room. The room was divided into five shooting ranges. A dummy stood at the back of each. A gun and a Taser lay on top of a table in front of each station.

"I won't be staying." Russ glanced about the room. When his eyes settled on me, he parted his lips like he wanted to say something, but then thought otherwise and gazed at my team. "You're in good hands." Then he locked eyes with Mitch. As if Russ could read Mitch's mind, he nodded and walked away.

"Have any of you ever held a gun before?" Mitch asked.

One by one, my team answered they had.

"I have, but I mostly practiced with Tasers." I lightly poked Brooke to get her attention. "Brooke and I used Tasers on two small assignments. Justine and Tamara have never been on one."

Mitch nodded. "Tasers are easy to use. The laser marks your target. Since you've handled Tasers before, a gun should be easy to adjust to. You only need to work on your aim. But with Helix, you should have no problem."

"Lucky them." Justine's tone became sarcastic. "I never got to use a Taser on a real person before, just on the dummies. I'm going to need more assistance from you."

"You're the lucky one." I tried to keep my annoyance at bay but failed. "It doesn't feel good to hurt people, even if they're criminals. You saw the videos in class. Their bodies shake like they've been electrocuted, and then they fall on the ground lifeless."

Mitch made his way to the center. "Ava's right. It's awful, but you're helping our society. It will get easier every time knowing you're keeping everyone safe. No one knows you exist. No one knows your name. You joined ISAN, not for the fame, but because you're special. You want to be somebody. You want to make a difference. You got out of detention for a reason. Destiny chose you."

Sometimes destiny sucks. I thought of my mom. The only person in the world who had loved me had died too young. *Sometimes destiny is wrong.* I thought about my abusive foster father and wondered how the hell the social worker could have sent me to someone like him. *Sometimes destiny presents a new journey ... maybe.* The message on my TAB came to mind.

Before he had a chance to finish the rest of the sentence, Justine interrupted. "So, how long have you worked here? I've never seen you before. I would've noticed you."

"I've been here longer than you." Mitch paced between the station tables, assessing the weapons. "In fact, I know all your records. Your height, your weight, and every bit of personal information you don't want me to know. I get into your business, but you don't get into mine, got it?" His sharp tone shut Justine up quick. Especially when he ended his sentence standing in front of her.

Justine dared to meet his gaze with an obsequious grin, and then cowered. Nobody asked questions after that. I went straight to my assigned station and waited for his instructions.

Mitch pointed his gun at the ceiling. "Let me refresh your

memory. This is a 9-millimeter Luger, which you have seen before. This is deadly. I repeat, *deadly*. Don't point it at anyone unless you plan to kill the person. Keep it pointing down at all times, especially when you're running. In order to shoot, you must first release the safety lock on the side. Right here." Mitch pointed to it and released the handle.

"You see these? Eight bullets in the clip, and one in the chamber ready to go. You get nine shots before you have to reload. These bullets are not made from solid lead. They are compressed air bullets. When the silver pointy part of the bullet hits the target, it will explode inside their body. After you release the clip, you get your new one and push it up like this. Don't worry about putting on earphones because you won't need them. These guns are not just deadly, they're quiet, too. Now, pick up your guns."

The gun felt cool to the touch, slightly heavy, but easy to hold with two hands.

Mitch directed us. "Hold your gun with one hand and cup it for support with your other. Arms firm, but not tight. Relax, or else the recoil will hurt your arm."

Mitch helped Justine, Brooke, and then Tamara hold the guns properly. Then it was my turn.

"Relax, Ava." His soft voice helped me unwind and the musky scent of his cologne had me temporarily distracted. "There," he cooed, his arms still wrapped over mine. "I feel you relaxing. Now look through the two sights at the top of the gun. Pretend to draw a line from the gun to your target ... just like that." He moved us slightly to the right. "You see that dummy, don't you?"

"Yes."

"Good. Let out your breath as you squeeze the trigger. Now you're ready. Aim ... I'm right behind you. Actually, I'm pretty much on you so don't be afraid. Shoot when you're ready."

Unsettled by his closeness, I pulled the trigger when he gave me the green light. I jerked back and let myself adjust to the recoil. The bullet flew, and, to my surprise, penetrated the dummy's head between the eyes.

"Now do it by yourself."

Though his words sounded encouraging, they also sounded like a demand. It took me several more tries before I successfully did it on my own.

"Not bad." He gave me a thumbs up, then headed back to my team.

I exhaled a long, deep breath. After a few more rounds of practice, I had a handle on holding the gun and shooting the targets.

"Great job, ladies." His words were sincere and proud. "Now, round two. You'll be using your Tasers. In front of you, you'll see a screen. There will be innocent civilians, but some of the civilians may be holding a gun. Only stun the ones holding the guns. Your scores will be automatically entered through the TAB data. Good luck."

The screen glowed with real life images. To the right—a shopping plaza, a bakery, pizza store, and a coffee shop. On the left—a tall office building. When I tilted the Taser to the right, the screen shifted in the same direction. When I leaned forward, it moved me ahead. It reminded me of my foster siblings' video games.

I shot a man holding a gun without hesitation. More figures popped out. There was no pattern I could detect, just random civilians and attackers.

Three women came at me, but only the one on the left held a gun. I shot her just as she fired. Then I shot a young girl to my right stationed at the shoe store. *Shit.* Not a weapon. She'd held a flashlight. No time for regret. Move onward.

My aim and differentiating whether it was a weapon became

sharper. But still, occasionally, I mistook innocent items like umbrellas for guns. Even knowing the figures I'd stunned were animation, it churned my stomach, especially when I'd shot innocent bystanders.

I maneuvered swiftly street to street, and even through alleys. Focused, I became lost in the digital world. When the test ended, the screen scrolled back up. I turned to my team. They were still in the simulation. I gasped and jerked back when Mitch appeared in front of me.

"Not bad."

"Not bad? That was horrible. I shot innocent people." I gnawed the inside of my cheek.

"Not shot, stunned."

"Same thing, sort of."

"Not true, but you shot all your enemies, and your team is still searching for them. You did this without Helix."

I shrugged. Since the others couldn't hear us, I risked a personal question, even though he'd told us not to. "So, do you live here?"

"Sometimes." He raked his hair back and rubbed the back of his neck.

"I've never seen you before."

"Maybe I didn't want to be seen." His tone was light and playful.

There was something about Mitch I couldn't wrap my head around. My gut told me not to trust him. Perhaps it was the way his blue eyes constantly studied me, and the way his answers were clipped. Or maybe I was being paranoid. But he had said, 'I've been here longer than you.' So why hadn't I seen him around? It didn't add up. My mind reeled with ways to find out.

Mitch grabbed a beige hand towel from his shoulder and wiped my gun and Taser. "Never leave your fingerprints."

"So, you design these tests?"

"Do you start all your sentences with 'so'?" He chuckled.

I frowned and whirled.

"Ava. I'm teasing. I'm sorry." His tone dipped softer.

Surprised by his friendliness, I blinked.

"Well, aren't you cozy? You two know each other or something?"

I hadn't noticed his hands on my shoulders until he dropped them when Justine spoke.

Mitch backed away. "You're supposed to stay at your post until I come." The words came through gritted teeth.

"Why? So I can't see what you're doing? Just in case you care, I need help." Justine scowled and stomped back to her post.

Bitch.

Though Justine had never shared her story of her past, I was sure she drove everyone she knew insane.

"Is she always like this?" Mitch shifted the gun and Taser on the table and tossed the towel over his shoulder.

"Only when she's in a good mood. You should see her at her worst. Russ told us Helix had no side effects, but I think he's wrong. I think it made her emotional and unstable."

He chuckled and headed to Justine.

CHAPTER SEVEN
SECOND TEST

After the practice session, Mitch took us to one of the restricted areas on the eighth floor. Silence fell as the elevator whizzed upward—the longest five seconds of my life. The elevator door opened, revealing Russ with his hands behind his back and legs apart—the way I was trained to stand, no doubt out of habit for him, too. He had once been a field operative, someone like Mitch.

"Welcome back." Russ showed no emotion, leading us down the hallway and into another room.

Something like a massive jungle gym materialized when Mitch waved a hand over the light scanner. The maze-like contraption soared to the ceiling and stretched from wall to wall. It resembled a nightmare for an adult if they were being hunted. But to a kid, it would appear to be an awesome playground.

Wooden bridges of varying sizes connected to one another, going in different directions throughout levels. Some bridges were linked to platforms that led to barrel tunnels—about ten feet tall and thirty feet long. Some seemed longer. I gasped when I saw ropes dangling from rings bolted to the walls.

Being afraid of heights, I swallowed the thought down. No use worrying in advance.

"Ladies," Russ began, "your task is to get to the other side. You'll start here, at this entrance. Easy enough, right?"

"Piece of cake." Justine squared her shoulders.

"Umm … do we work as a team or are we racing against each

other?" Tamara crossed her arms and rubbed them, as if to steady her nerves.

Russ didn't answer. Instead, he placed a hand on a metal square on the wall. A red line scanned his handprint, and a large tray slid out of the wall with four black guns and four black vests, like the ones I had to wear at team combat.

"Cool." Justine's eyes gleamed at first, and then her excitement disappeared. "Wait. We don't have to shoot each other, do we?"

"No, not each other. You'll have to outrun Mitch."

"What?" Justine's eyes rounded in alert. "But he's the expert. That's not fair."

I brushed up against Justine. "Afraid of a little competition? Let's show him what we've got." I grabbed a black vest, slipped it on, and picked up the gun. "This feels fake."

Russ handed the firearms to my teammates. "It's not real. It shoots low-powered lasers instead, but it sounds and feels like the real thing. Your vest won't protect you against a real gun. It's laser activated and will flash when you get shot. If that happens, you're out. However, if you get hit, you'll feel the impact."

Tamara gulped and blanched. With shoulders hunched, she puffed out air, like she was already defeated. Justine crossed her arms and bit her lip, and Brooke inhaled deep breaths like she was having an anxiety attack. We didn't have much time to strategize as a group.

Think of a plan, quick, Ava. You're their leader.

As I thought about ways I could help my team get across, Russ took out four Helix filled special syringes from the sliding wall and administered one to me. Like all HelixB77 serums, it was needleless and given to me through volatile compressed gas that passes through the permeable layers of my skin.

Brooke pulled up her zipper and pushed her hair back from

her face. "Doesn't Mitch need a vest?"

"I don't need one. I never get hit. You ready?"

Mitch's tone, so confident and relaxed, made Brooke pale like she had seen a ghost. He smirked and winked. Then he cocked his gun, just like he'd shown us.

His question sent shivers down my back.

"It's time," Russ said.

Crap. I had no plan. Run, for now. Stupid plan. Some leader I am.

"I'm counting to ten, and then I'm coming after all of you." Mitch's tone rang deadly. His flat eyes touched all of ours, one at a time, as he counted. "One … two … three …"

"Run!" My steps pounded on the platform, adrenaline soaring through my blood. When I crossed the first small bridge, I stirred right, and Tamara trailed behind. Justine and Brooke followed suit; however, a wall jetted up from the ground to the ceiling, separating us.

Shit. Shit. Shit.

"Brooke. Justine." I smacked the wall, but to no avail. I realized at that moment, they couldn't hear me.

The wall—thick and solid—even Justine couldn't break it down.

"This is bad." Tamara bent forward and planted her hands on her thighs, like she was going to vomit.

"It's okay. It's better this way." I placed my hand on her shoulder to give her reassurance. Although I didn't believe my own words, I had to say something to keep Tamara from having a meltdown. "This way."

Crossing another bridge and a short barrel tunnel, I ducked instinctively when a shot whined in my ear. Tamara grabbed me from behind, startling me even more. My heart about burst out of my chest and fear locked my muscles.

"He's coming," she sniveled.

I embraced her to still her trembling. "You have to calm down. You can do this." It seemed like the right thing to say, as I tried to convince us both. Gripping Tamara's hand tightly, I sidled, hand in hand, with my back flat against the wall.

Dozens of shots resonated, and then a loud screech of rage halted us. So soon? Only one person could make such a sound.

"Shit. I'm dead. Run, Brooke." Justine's voice boomed throughout the room.

"It's okay," I said. "We have a chance. He's on to Brooke. Let's go."

I trudged my way through more barrel tunnels with charged energy, my steps echoing. If Mitch hadn't known where I was, he did now. Then I hopped onto a longer and wobbly bridge connected by wooden beams. Once again, my steps loud as I raced across from plank to plank, more shots raining behind me.

"Wait." Tamara halted, out of breath. "Are you going the right way?"

"Yes."

"How do you know? You've never been on this thing before. I feel lost, like a mouse in a maze. We keep going on bridge after bridge and tunnel after tunnel. We're going in circles."

"I don't know how to explain it, but I just know the way when Helix is inside me. You're not supposed to be this scared."

Tamara's actions worried me, but I didn't have time to analyze it. The serum had a different effect on each one of us. Perhaps it didn't help her as much, or she needed more rounds of mental missions to help her calm her fears.

"You've got to trust me. Are you coming?" I tapped my foot rapidly, trying to calm my anxiety flooding like a broken dam.

She nodded, terror filling her eyes. "Yes. Russ told the newbies your mind worked like a compass. I remember now. I trust you."

"Good. Think of something happy. And hurry."

I'd forgotten how to explain my special gift to new people. Though I'd never been on the obstacle course before, my mental blueprint appeared.

I climbed on the protruding man-made rock to assist my hike up a twenty-foot wall. The coarse, jagged rocks abraded my skin, making the scaling difficult. As I proceeded higher and higher off the ground, I tried not to gaze down. My muscles went rigid and my stomach recoiled from the height I'd traversed.

"Ava," Tamara yelped. Her foot had not been secured and she crashed onto the rocks, sliding downward, but managed to stay on them.

"Tamara." My pulse quickened, worried for her. "You're doing fine. Just breathe and continue." *But hurry the hell up.*

When Tamara caught up to me, I flung over the top and used the rope to slide down to the platform. My palms burned like they were on fire. I winced and rubbed them together. Too fast. I had descended too fast.

"Something feels hot, Ava." Tamara rubbed at her hands and knees. She must have bumped hard on the rocks.

I'd thought Tamara was whining when she repeated her words, and I almost gave her a sarcastic remark. Sure enough, when we rounded the bend and entered a tunnel, fire blasted. Scorching heat brushed up against me so close, I thought the flame had engulfed me. I cursed from the burning pain and rubbed my face to confirm I wasn't on fire. My eyes stung and the smell of gas assaulted my nose.

The digitally enhanced blaze died, as if it had never happened when I backed away. I rubbed my eyes to clear the lingering smoke. Searching through my mental map, I found another way.

I clutched Tamara, my fingers around her wrist like handcuffs, and hauled her forward. "Follow me."

I took us to another route, more vigilant than before. My map showed me the road to the exit, but it couldn't detect unexpected surprises like the one we'd encountered.

"Watch out!" My heart lurched to my throat.

I shoved Tamara back when I took a cautious step on a cement platform. Countless sharp metal spikes poked out all at once, blocking my way. Again, digitally enhanced, but so life-like.

"Oh, God. Oh, God." Tamara folded her arms in front of her stomach. "What now? What now?"

I stilled, and rifled through every possibility on my mental map. *Hurry, Ava. Where the hell is it?* There. Cleverly hidden in the dark. Grabbing Tamara's hand, I took her to the last option.

"Trust me, and please don't scream."

"It's so dark." She stared at the pitch-dark entrance and whimpered.

I slid down a dark slide spiraling like a coil with Tamara beside me. She didn't scream, but instead, she released a strange strangled noise when she landed on her butt.

"I'm alive." Tamara hinted at a smile behind a mask of horror.

"Come on. We've gotta keep moving. We're almost there."

Tamara placed her hands on my shoulders, forcing me to halt. "Did you hear that?" She dabbed the sweat beading on her forehead. "I think Brooke is out. He must have caught up to her. I'm pretty sure I heard a faint scream."

Crap. Breathe.

"Let's go then." I turned the corner and stopped at a gap with no bridge.

Tamara gawked. "What do we do?"

"That." I pointed. A rope was tied to a ring bolted to the wall. "We're supposed to swing over."

"What? I'm not doing it."

"You want to stay here and get shot?" Anger coursed through

my blood.

Calm down, Ava. She's new to this. Yelling won't do any good.
She shook her head.

My jaw clenching, I pointed over the cliff. "There's a safety net down there. If you fall, you'll be fine. If you stay, you'll get caught. You don't have another option right now. Remember, you can do things you normally can't do. Take charge of your fear or it will conquer you. I'll go first."

Tugging on the rope to ensure it would hold my weight, I stepped backward to give me momentum, ran and pushed upward when the timing felt right. I swung, landed on the other side, and then heaved the rope back to Tamara.

Tamara caught the rope and copied me. Instead of landing, she held on to the rope, swinging back to the other side. Tangling her arms and legs around the rope so she wouldn't fall, she swung back and forth like a pendulum clock.

Crap. Tamara will be the death of me.
"Ava, go without me. You can win for us."

Cursing under my breath, I shoved my gun inside my pants. "Did you do this on purpose?" I huffed, heat rising to my face, my heart palpitating faster.

Mitch had eliminated Justine and Brooke and no doubt he was hot on my tail.

Her eyebrows gathered to the center. "No, why would you say that?"

I narrowed my eyes. "Don't be ridiculous. I'm not leaving you behind."

I didn't understand. Helix should have kicked in. Her coordination should be sharper. I couldn't leave her there. If I went through without her, I'd feel guilty beyond words.

I smeared the sweat on my forehead with one swipe, but I couldn't do anything to the sweat clinging to the back of my tight training outfit. Rubbing my sweaty palms on my pants, I judged the distance.

I sprinted, my leg muscles throbbing, and leaped to grip the rope. Luckily, I made it. I swung out and back to where I had stood a few seconds before. When I let go of the rope, Tamara fell, knocking the wind out of me.

"Thanks." I grumbled.

"Sorry." Tamara got up and offered a hand. "Thanks for not leaving me behind."

"You can thank me all you want later, but we gotta get out of here."

I led the way again until the last rickety, swaying rope bridge came into view. On a hunch, I peered below. Sure enough, Mitch hid under us. He knew the course. He'd probably won that way hundreds of times.

"Come out, ladies, and surrender." Mitch's tone rang confidently.

"No way. We still have a chance." I swept the perimeter. Given the options and the limited space, I could only do one thing—cross the bridge.

Mitch let out a victory laugh. "I've never lost. And today won't be my first time."

Perhaps today you shall. You don't know me, Mitch.

Anger fueled my determination. "Never underestimate the power of teamwork." I grabbed Tamara's arm and bore my eyes into hers. "You can do this, but you have to do as I say. Don't look back, okay? Bend low and run when I say run, got it?"

After Tamara confirmed with a nod, I positioned myself. I held the gun in a tight grip as my heart pounded in my ear. "Ready? Remember to run with me and stay low, out of his sight, if possible. Now … Run."

Hoping Mitch hadn't heard me, I aimed straight for him. I

fired continuously as I sidestepped on the bridge, trying to get to the other side while protecting Tamara at the same time. Mitch fired back. When I tried to dodge the laser, Tamara and I collided and fell. My legs tangled with hers in the middle of the bridge.

I snarled from irritation. "Come on. Get up. We're almost there."

I dropped to my hands and knees and crawled. The ropes crisscrossed, keeping the bridge together and blocking Mitch's laser from directly hitting me. I could have kissed the person who designed the bridge.

I'd thought crossing the bridge would make us the winners, but I assumed wrong. We also had to cross a small plank. We would be open targets and we couldn't get across without Mitch spotting us.

Since I didn't tell Tamara to stop at the end of the bridge, she kept on going, never looking back, just as I had instructed. Once she reached the plank, I shot one after the other, continuously at Mitch. *So close. Go Tamara.* My heart thumped faster and faster the closer Tamara neared the end.

To ensure Tamara got to the finish line, I distracted Mitch by leaving Tamara's side and going the opposite direction. By the time he realized what I had done, it was too late.

Tamara crossed over just as the red laser shot the center of my chest. Pain ripped through me. The impact pushed me off the bridge and I plummeted three stories to the ground, chest up on a cushioned mat.

A barely audible groan shuddered out of my mouth.

One sacrifice equaled victory for the team.

Worth it.

CHAPTER EIGHT
SECRETS

"We did it," Tamara squealed. "Ava. Where are you?"

I moaned. "I'm fine." I lay on my back with my arms and legs spread out, unable to move through the throbbing pain.

As my chest heaved, sweat trickled down the sides of my temples. I'd been thrown around during training before, and I'd been taught to relax my muscles on impact. With Helix in my blood, the hit should have been tolerable. Either the serum had worked out of my system or Russ hadn't given me enough. I doubted he would make that mistake.

Tamara made her way down and hovered above me.

Mitch offered his hand. *Prick.* I had no right to be mad at him, but anger flared in my bones. To show my sportsmanship, I took his hand anyway. My head spun and muscles continued to ache as Mitch pulled me upright. Russ, Justine, and Brooke rushed over.

"You're awesome." Brooke gave me a high five, but I recoiled from the pain. "I saw the whole thing. I cheered for you on the other side."

Tamara drew her eyebrows together. "You tricked me. In a good way, I mean. You sacrificed yourself so I—we—could win." Her eyes dampened with tears. "Thank you. I've never won before at anything."

I smiled, not knowing what to say. My heart softened a bit, knowing I had done something good, something selfless.

Mitch patted my back. "I have to admit, Ava, this is the first time any team has beaten me. And you managed to find the hidden slide. Well done."

I didn't know Mitch well, and I didn't know how he would react to getting his ego smashed, but I was pleasantly surprised.

"Does that mean we won?" Brooke batted her eyelashes.

Russ input something on his TAB. "I have to add up the scores, but since you're the only team to beat Mitch so far, I would say yes. But try to pretend to be surprised when I announce the winners. Shall we go?" He extended his arm.

Justine strode happily, matching Russ's stride. "If we're the winners, then we get to go out this Friday night, right?"

"Yes, but you'll be escorted."

My team sauntered out of the room behind Russ, but I lagged behind. A sharp pang in my right shoulder stopped me. Wincing, I placed my hand on it to rub the area.

"The hero who sacrificed herself. Some things never change. Are you okay?" Mitch stepped beside me.

Instead of an answer, I gave him a faint smile. *Some things never change?* I didn't remember sacrificing myself for my team before.

"Let me take a look." He extended my arm and then slowly rotated it back.

I held my breath when he stood too close for comfort. He gently massaged the muscles, moving his hand upward to my collarbone. My shoulders eased and his touch soothed me. I didn't want him to stop.

"Let me know if it hurts." Mitch continued to knead it. "Where would you like to go, Ava?"

My heart raced. "What do you mean, where would I like to go?" At first, I'd thought he'd asked me on a date. Such a silly thought.

Mitch gingerly guided my arm downward. "Does this hurt?"

I shook my head, but pressed my lips together anticipating a rush of pain.

"I meant Friday night. I'm making the reservation for you ladies. Assuming you are the winners."

"Somewhere nice and fun, I guess. I don't know too many places. How about Shooting Stars? I read on the net that it's a fun place."

Mitch guided my arm toward my back. "Perfect. I'll arrange it after I check it out. You were brave back there. You could've been the person on the other end. Why did you let her cross?"

The answer sat on the tip of my tongue, but I couldn't get the words out. "I knew ... I mean, I—"

"Let me answer for you. You knew she couldn't do what you did. You sacrificed yourself for the team to win. It was ..." He moved closer. "Well thought out. But when you're on assignments, don't sacrifice yourself unless it's the last resort. I don't want to see you dead."

I closed my eyes, trying to stay focused. My arms were still behind me, locked in his hold. When he let go abruptly, I opened my eyes to see Russ glowering by the door. My face burned, even though I had no reason to feel guilty. I wondered how long he'd been watching us.

"I'm checking her shoulder. We'll be right there." Mitch's tone oozed authority and Russ left without another word. "You should ice that shoulder and let me know how you feel in the morning. Or you can go to the medics and get that taken care of right away."

"I'll be fine. It feels better already." I meandered away.

Mental note to self: Ask Russ why Tamara acted so scared while on Helix and why the hell had I felt real pain?

* * *

Later that afternoon when I had free time, I excused myself to my room to power on my TAB. I had a couple of minutes left for the day. I tried to keep Sniper out of my mind, but I couldn't. This person bugged the life out of me. I needed some answers.

I tried to keep my mind occupied as I scrolled through the net with no purpose. When that didn't help, I started reading a novel about zombies, but my eyes kept moving to the right corner of the TAB's screen. *Ugh.*

Just as my finger neared the power button to shut down, a message popped up.

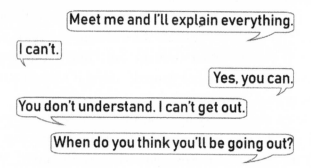

He was either persistent or … did he know where I was? He couldn't know.

Sniper wasn't getting the point. I pushed my hair back, set my elbows on my desk, and propped my chin on my fists. My mind raced on what to do, and then my fingers danced on the letters.

Shooting Stars.

I immediately regretted what I had done. *Stupid. Stupid.*

ISAN

Stupid.

> When?

The TAB automatically shut down. *Freakin' hell.* Time had run out. Or someone had enough evidence to report me. My back prickled with alertness. I prepared for the possibility of several guards rushing through my door and taking me to Mr. Novak for breaking rule number three.

I waited in silence, still as the cool air around me. Holding my breath, I begged for release. When the door remained closed after a long stretch of silence, I let it all out. No one had come for me ... at least not yet.

* * *

After dinner, I went to Russ's office as instructed. Before I had the chance to knock, the door slid open, revealing Russ sitting behind his desk. Two brown leather sofas sat facing each other in the center of the room, separated by an ottoman. Behind him, nothing but blank, white wall. No paintings hung, and no photos lined his desk; no evidence of his life before ISAN.

Had he even had a life before ISAN?

Of course he had. Don't be ridiculous.

Russ wouldn't flaunt his personal life in his office. He was a professional in every sense of the word.

"Come in and have a seat." His words were sharper than usual.

Warm air bathed me like the sun's rays when I stepped in, and the scent of lavender permeated the room. In my chemical class, I learned lavender relieved stress, anxiety, insomnia, and agitation. Good choice of scent, especially in his position.

"You wanted to see me?" My steps were quiet as I moved

63

across the impeccable white marble floor.

A black leather chair rose up from an opening in the floor; then the opening sealed shut as if the chair had always been there. Taking a seat, I placed my hands on my lap.

"Yes." He sighed.

I'd known Russ long enough to know it wasn't going to be a friendly conversation from his tone.

He exhaled again and rubbed at his temples. "Your team was chosen to go on assignment."

It took me a second to register. "Great ... I think? Does my team know?"

His face held no smile, and his green eyes lacked their spark. "Not yet. I wanted to tell you first." Russ pressed his chest to the desk, leaning forward. "This isn't going to be easy. Your team will have to assassinate a political figure."

Not bring someone in but to assassinate. To kill. I leaned back as blood boiled through me, not from anger, but from fear. *Holy cow.*

"I've never—"

"That's right. This will be the first time for your team, too. You have to understand you're assassinating a criminal. You don't need to know the details. Just do your job. Get in and get out as fast as you can."

I crossed my arms and legs, swiveling my chair from side to side, as I tried to grasp the purpose of it, the unfairness of what I had been asked. My life was on the line in many different ways and so was my team's.

Building courage, I asked, "What if I said no?"

I didn't have the right to question the authority of my superiors, but he was a friend, too. And I was going to take advantage of it to get some answers.

As usual, he showed no emotion. "Ava, between you and me, okay?"

"Okay."

He knew I was good at keeping secrets, not that he told me many. It felt good he trusted me with highly classified information.

"I don't like sending you on a dangerous assignment. This political figure will have bodyguards surrounding him twenty-four hours a day. It will be nearly impossible to kill him. But I know you can do this. It won't be just your team. I'll be sending the guards and Roxy's team, too. You've all been training for this."

"Roxy's team?" I jumped out of my seat, my teeth grinding. "No." With my fists on his desk, I leaned forward, challenging him.

"Ava, sit down. You don't have a choice." Russ arched his eyebrows, obviously displeased. But his tone remained calm.

"Sorry." I sheepishly plopped back.

He scowled. "I don't care if you don't like Roxy's team. Besides, they won second place, and with their help, you'll be safer. Their job is to protect your team and nothing else." He pointed at me. "Your job is to get into his house, eliminate him, and get out. You'll have Helix in your system, so mapping out his house won't be an issue."

I narrowed my eyes. I wanted to tell him Roxy's team had cheated, though I had no proof. "Why don't you send Roxy's team instead?"

"You know why." His words drew out harshly.

"So, you're just using me for my ability to project a blueprint of his house and intended to send my team along—test or no test."

He scoffed. "Yes, I'm using you. If you weren't so damn good at it, you would be picking up trash and scrubbing the toilets instead."

"The toilet cleans itself. It does a better job than I could." I smirked.

Russ shook his head and twitched his lips. "You know what I

mean."

"Do I?" I released a defeated sigh. "But what if I freak out, like I did on the mental training? I missed it by one second."

He stiffened and shifted his eyes from mine. "That's different."

He was hiding something. I wasn't sure, but I thought I'd take a chance. After all, what would he do to me?

"You took a second away from me, didn't you?"

"I have no idea what you're talking about." He folded his hands in front of him.

The second he wouldn't meet my gaze, I knew I was right.

"You did." I gasped and hid the hurt of betrayal, masking my face to neutrality. "Why? To humiliate me?"

Russ's head snapped up. "Humiliate you? Of course not. I had to prepare you, make things more realistic for you. I knew your team would be picked for this assignment."

I peered down at my legs and rocked my chair to calm my fury. "Did you give us less Helix when we were up against Mitch? Is that why Tamara was so scared and I felt more pain than I should have when I fell?"

"Tamara hasn't had as much mental mission training as your group. I figured with your guidance, she could overcome it. I suspect she has a special ability, but I haven't found out what it is yet. I know you don't agree with some of the things I do, but I needed to push you and test your limits. You know damn well you won't do it on your own. The answer is yes. I took away the second, and I gave you less Helix, but look what your team has accomplished anyway."

I didn't mention it to Russ, but even with the smaller dosage of Helix, my mind had mapped out the blueprint. Some secrets were mine to hold.

"You care about me?" I gave him a sweet smile to apologize

for crossing the line. He was my superior, and I was surprised he hadn't reprimanded me thus far.

Russ set his hard eyes on me, as if to decide what to say or do. After a brief moment, we exchanged a warm smile until he broke his gaze.

Sliding his fingers through his brown hair with a sigh, he leaned forward. "Let me show you something."

Russ placed his hand on his desk and then raised his hand up. A large screen appeared in mid-air. When he waved a hand across the screen, a picture of a man in his late sixties, with clean-cut white hair, materialized. The wrinkles across his forehead marked his age.

"This is Thomax Thorpe, a representative from the East territory. Its urban population sustained heavy death tolls in the meteor and tsunami aftermath, and its agricultural regions have been hit hard with drought. Thorpe has been in office since the Remnant Councils of the Former United States were formed, but you won't have heard of him. Each territory's national representative has been kept anonymous to protect them and their families. Only the councils and a few trusted members know their identities."

I stopped rocking. "Why do they need to be kept secret? I don't understand."

Russ waved his hand again to change the picture. "It's political. You can't kill someone you don't know. Why does one try to take another down?"

"For power," I mumbled under my breath.

Russ's gaze moved back to the screen. "These representatives not only guide the councils, they are spies and trained to protect."

"I still don't understand."

"Influence, bribery, blackmail … you name it. It all happens and has happened in the past. It's to keep everyone safe. It keeps our world in order and running smoothly. The councils want to reassure the people they're doing their jobs. That's why you don't see homeless people sleeping in the streets anymore. Everyone has a roof over their head. People have enough to eat. Crime rates are low."

"What'd he do, or what's the reason to terminate him?" My words came out so uncaring—like he was an object, not a person.

"You're not authorized to know that kind of information."

I drummed my fingers on the arm of the chair. "You've already told me this much. Who am I going to tell? Mr. Novak?" I was pushing it, but curiosity hammered my mind. "I'm going to be assigned to kill him—at least give me a reason so I can feel somewhat good about it."

Russ shook his head and pressed his lips together. I batted my eyelashes and pouted to convince him. A heartbeat later, he reconsidered.

"Okay. But don't say a word. We think he's talking to the other reps, organizing a group to take over the councils."

Holy shit. "Why not just bring him in instead of taking his life?"

"Like I said, there are other reasons. Other reasons even I'm not privy to. Sometimes matters have to be given special attention. I would like to close this conversation."

"Okay." I'd heard enough. It didn't matter anyway; Thomax Thorpe's life would end soon, either from my team or someone else's. "You know, I lived on the streets. So, the system can't be perfect."

"That was different and you know it. You chose to run away instead of finding shelter. They would've taken you in."

I shrugged and twisted my lips. "Maybe."

"It's different now."

I didn't believe it, but I didn't want to talk about it anymore. Sometimes talking about my past gutted me.

"When do I get to meet Thomax Thorpe?"

"Tomorrow night." Russ poured two glasses of water and slid one to me. "Want a drink?"

"Is this going to be another test? Or that better be alcohol."

Russ almost choked taking a sip. He wiped the drops trickling out of his mouth. "You can drink in two weeks when you turn eighteen."

"How wonderful for me," I said sarcastically, waving a hand. "I'll be able to drink whenever I want, except I'm not allowed to drink here. And, oh yeah, I can finally have a place of my own, but I'm stuck here, not allowed to leave … ever. What else?" I drummed my fingers on his desk, as if thinking. "I'll be eighteen and have never been kissed, and since I can't date, I'll never get married or have kids. And the best part … I'll never have sex."

I took a sip of water to cool my rising anger. Russ flushed the brightest red I'd ever seen. He blinked rapidly. The clink of ice when I placed my cup down sounded too loud at that quiet moment. As always, he would listen but be terse with his advice.

"Be grateful, Ava. You're alive," he said gravely.

His words slammed into my chest. Goosebumps rose on my skin. A feeling of déjà vu spiraled through me. But I blinked it away.

"Am I?" I lowered my head down in shame and peered at him under my eyelashes. Russ was the one who had taken me out of juvie; albeit I had special DNA ISAN sought, but I should be grateful he had come to my rescue. "Sorry. I didn't mean it."

"It's okay. I understand." His lips softened their hard line, and the sparkle came back into his eyes.

Russ had a kind heart. I couldn't remember how we'd become close, but I recalled we'd just hit it off. It wasn't an overnight kind of friendship, but more like a progression. But I did question why he had opened up to me.

Russ waved a hand to close the images. "Do me a favor. When you're on this assignment, just get in and out as fast as you can.

Remember your training. Don't look at their faces. Don't make eye contact."

I ran a finger across the rim of the glass, soaking in Russ's words. The reality of the danger hit me again, but I had another question nagging at me. "Can I ask you something?"

"Sure. I'll do my best to answer it."

"Do you or anyone else send out private messages on our TAB anonymously?"

I didn't know how to ask the question without getting myself in trouble. I didn't know where the line crossed from Russ being my superior and friend. And I was sure I had reached my limit.

"What do you mean? Did someone try to contact you?" Russ sat taller and his shoulders tightened.

"No." My pulse raced as the lie left my lips. Sinking into my seat, I wanted to take back my question.

Russ's jaw relaxed, and he pulled back his shoulders. "If that ever happens, don't reply. ISAN will find out and you'll be sent back. I don't want that to happen to you, got it?"

"Sure," I murmured.

The reality of Russ's words hit me, and my worries about ISAN finding out what I had already done knotted my stomach so thoroughly I couldn't untie it. But if it wasn't ISAN, well, that bothered me, too.

"Your team will be directed to Kendrick before you begin your assignment tomorrow. He's new to ISAN. He's built some interesting gadgets. You'll be amused." Russ stood and gestured for me to do the same. Placing his hand behind my back, he led me to the door and stopped. "Be safe, Ava. Follow your instincts, and don't be afraid. It will only cause you to shut down. Pretend you're on the mental mission. Block everything out."

"I failed, remember?" I cocked my brow.

Russ gave me the biggest smirk; his lips practically reached his

70

eyes. "Yeah, you did."

He caught my hand easily when I swung at him. It would've been a light punch to his arm. I would never hit him hard, even though he deserved it.

"I'm still mad at you for taking away my second." My nostrils flared. "You owe me a second. You …"

My tongue stopped working when Russ tenderly rubbed the back of my hand. He had never shown this amount of affection before. Tingles ran up my arm and in places they shouldn't. With his other hand, he pushed my hair away from my face, his fingers feather lightly caressing my cheek in the process. My breath caught in my throat and I closed my eyes to fight the heated sensation leaching onto me.

What the hell is he doing? My fault for acting like a lovesick fool. My instructor. My friend. Friend. Friend. Friend. I repeated to chase away false hope.

"Good luck tomorrow, Ava." His voice sounded more like a whisper when his lips brushed my face.

The scent of musk and lavender spiraled up my nostrils, coaxing me. Heat infused my body, sending quivers through me. *Oh, God. Had he just kissed me?* Slowly, I fluttered my eyes open. When his eyes caught mine, his lips inched closer, and I thought he was going to kiss me, but he pulled away.

He couldn't kiss me even if he wanted to. ISAN frowned upon any romantic relationship, especially between a superior and student. I wondered if he had a wife or a family, but that thought was ridiculous and impossible since he lived there. Then I recalled how Russ used to be out in the field, too. From that alone, I was certain he had no family to call his own.

"Thanks," I managed to say finally, then left, dazed and a bit flustered.

CHAPTER NINE
GADGETS

"Good afternoon, ladies." Kendrick stood from his chair behind his desk when I entered his office.

I'd imagined someone older, but he appeared young and amicable.

"It's nice to meet you." Tamara's eyes rounded.

Justine lifted an eyebrow and surveyed him silently while Brooke offered a quick smile.

"Hi, Kendrick." My nose crinkled from the scent of burnt metal and something else I couldn't detect. No doubt he had a lot going on.

I'd marveled at the various inventions filling the room. The open cabinet on the back wall shelved steel, iron, bronze, wires, and tools. Bright light from the ceiling concentrated on the tables, strewn with half built or dismantled objects, varied in size.

Kendrick took his hand out of his white lab coat pocket and adjusted his glasses higher on the bridge of his nose. "Come. Let me show you my designs."

I followed behind Kendrick and weaved around some chairs and standing gadgets with wires and metal dangling.

"Here they are." Kendrick's tone matched the excitement in his eyes, but Justine squashed it.

"What the hell are these? It's a lipstick, a compact mirror, necklace, hair clips, and earrings. What am I going to do? Kill them with a makeover?"

Justine had a way with words, and most of the time it was the way of pain. She needed to be taught manners, or maybe she needed extra classes with Diana. I probably should have said something, but I didn't want to make a scene, and I didn't want to cause a rift between us with a mission around the corner. Besides, Kendrick seemed like he could put her in place.

Kendrick's smile froze. He ruffled his dark curly hair and pressed his lips together tight. With his level of intelligence, probably no one spoke to him that way.

"You didn't let me explain." He held up the lipstick. "After you apply it, blow out air. The carbon dioxide and the chemicals from the lipstick will bond together. It will put the person facing you to sleep."

Justine's eyes grew wider. She clamped her mouth shut and gave him her full attention. As did the rest of us. Russ had mentioned gadgets, but I had no idea they were one of a kind.

Kendrick picked up a fake—I assumed—solitaire diamond necklace from the table and continued. "If you press the center, it will disperse a toxic chemical reaction into the air. They will feel intense pain and will wish for a quick death." He pointed to the compact mirror and the brush. "Use the brush to grab the powder. When you dust it off, you'll be able to see any hidden laser beams."

"Is that all we get?" Brooke asked. "What are we supposed to protect ourselves with?"

Her concern was warranted.

Kendrick pointed to the shelf behind him. "You'll each get a Taser. Remember, these Tasers incapacitate the person for thirty minutes or so. You'll either have to tase them again or make sure you're out of there." Kendrick shifted his attention solely to me. "You get the gun, too." He took it out of his drawer. "It's small, and it will fit inside your pocket or wherever you'd like to keep it safe. Keep in mind, this will do the job. I was told to show it to you, but Mitch will give it to you on your mission. Nothing like assassinating someone the good old-fashioned way with one bullet to the head."

"You make it sound so simple," Brooke chimed in. "Have you ever—?"

"No, I haven't. I would suck at it. At least you've got HelixB77. It doesn't work on me."

It doesn't work on me. His statement, as if it was conclusive, piqued my interest. "Why?" My gut instinct told me there was more to tell.

"You should know that answer. I don't have special genes like you." He busied his hands by adjusting a pen inside his front pocket, as if to distract me.

I sighed in disappointment. I should have known if there was information to hide, he would keep it to himself.

"What if I'm locked with my hands behind me and I can't get to the lipstick, or the necklace, or any other gadgets?" Tamara asked. "Do you have something for that?"

"Good question," I said.

"What would you do, Ava?" Kendrick's eyes met mine.

I wasn't expecting that. Glancing at the items on the table, I thought of the possibilities. "Well, according to my morning training class, I guess I could throw my head back and hit his chest or his nose. It would be better if it were the nose. He'll let go, and then I can swipe my leg to knock him down, or punch him where it would hurt him the most." I raised my chin with the confidence of my answer.

Tamara gawked. "It sounds like you've done it before."

I went around Tamara to Brooke. "Brooke and I were on a couple of assignments before, but we never assassinated anyone. Unfortunately, I didn't have these gadgets with me. Our assignment was to bring our subject in, not to kill." I picked up several pairs of the clip-on earrings and handed them to my team.

"Be careful with those." Kendrick flickered his hand as if to stop me, nearly hitting me in the process. "Do you know what they're used for?"

I gave Kendrick an evil stare and almost shoved him into the wall. *Steady, Ava.* I did not appreciate his condescending tone. And I was sure he read my expression well when he cleared his throat and twisted away from me.

After Justine put them on, she picked up the small hand mirror from the table, admiring her reflection. "I don't know, but these fake diamonds are gorgeous on me."

Tamara placed a finger in her mouth, pretending to gag. I spat out a laugh and blocked Tamara from Justine's view so she wouldn't get caught.

"Anyway …" Kendrick coughed lightly. "You can communicate with each other using these earrings, even if you're in the next room. They also double as small bombs, so don't drop one in front of you. You won't be able to blow up a house, but you can knock out a door."

I bared my teeth, blood draining to my toes. "You should have warned us first."

Kendrick shrugged, schooling his face into a portrait of innocence, and turned his back to me. Brooke took them off her ears immediately and placed them gingerly on the table with shaky hands.

"That's pretty clever and dangerous, Ken." Justine carefully handed hers to Kendrick and headed to the next table. Not an ounce of fear in her blood. "What are those?"

Kendrick bolted to Justine, bumping into her in the process. "My name is Kendrick and don't touch anything." He grabbed hold of Justine's arm, and some kind of metal wire came out from his watch and coiled around her wrist.

Justine arched her eyebrows, and leaned into her hip. "Trying to get kinky with me, Ken? You don't need to tie me up. Just tell me it's none of my business."

Oh, please. Her sultry tone made me nauseous.

"Awesome," Brooke exclaimed. "I want one."

"Me too," Tamara added.

Kendrick pushed a button on his watch. The wires flew back inside. "You'll each get one when I'm done making them. Now, take the things you think you'll need. You'll be seeing Lydia next."

"Why?" I asked. "Russ didn't tell me about Lydia."

Kendrick moved his glasses back up into place and touched his mini TAB screen on his desk. "Those were my instructions. I guess Russ forgot to tell you."

"Why Lydia?"

Brooke must have had the same reservations I did.

"To get dolled up, ladies. You're not going to catch anyone's attention looking like that." Kendrick lowered his glasses again, gawking at each of us. "But she"—he glanced at Justine—"might need more makeup."

Yup, I knew it. Kendrick could hold his own, and he'd made sure to insult Justine when offered the opportunity.

Justine's eyes darkened. She curled her fingers, no doubt ready to punch him.

I grabbed Justine's arm. "Don't. You'll get suspended and won't be able to join us for Friday night."

Kendrick pressed a button on his desk before Justine could lunge at him. A sliding door opened in front of us. For a second, I considered letting her punch Kendrick, just so she could experience what it would be like to be reprimanded. Maybe it would do her some good. And also, because I wanted to do it myself. But I needed her for the mission. Replacing her in such a short time would be out of the question.

"Lydia will see you now." Kendrick flashed a grin fake. His

narrowed eyes said, *get the hell out.*

* * *

"Ladies." Lydia smiled warmly, her dimples deepening.

She wore a silky lavender blouse and tight black pencil skirt. Her hair surrounded her face with soft curls. Earthy makeup complemented her brown eyes. If I hadn't known I was going to her office, I wouldn't have recognized her.

"Hello, Lydia," we all greeted in unison.

"Come in and have a seat."

Lydia's office was three times larger than my bedroom. Two brown leather sofas faced each other, separated by a small steel table. A clear vase set to the left of her desk held peonies of varying colors, filling her room with a sweet scent. As I sat and waited for her instructions, I admired the beautiful flowers and wished my room smelled and looked like hers.

I also admired her back wall. It projected a garden with various types of colorful flowers with a fountain in the middle. Then it switched to a white sandy beach and a rowboat softly rocked near the shore. Quite different from Russ's office.

Locked up in the compound, I didn't have the opportunity to be surrounded by Mother Nature or breathe in the fresh air, though perhaps not so fresh ever since meteors had struck the world. Ironically, the meteors had enhanced technology and medicine, helping humanity advance centuries ahead of schedule.

"You're probably wondering why you're here." A wall slid open at the touch of Lydia's hand, revealing a rack of clothes. "We're sending you on an assignment full of men. We can't have you dressed like that."

I gazed down to the comfortable workout clothes I wore every day, which were branded with the ISAN symbol. The four of us wore the same outfit—black jersey pants and white T-shirts. Yeah, not attractive—at least not compared to what Lydia wore.

"I get to dress like you?" Tamara's eyes sparkled with excitement.

She sounded more excited than I felt.

Lydia bent down and pulled out some boxes. "Almost." She paused to take out black boots. "You can't fight in the heels I'm wearing, but you can in these."

"Wedge heels." I stared in disbelief.

They were about two inches and squared. I supposed a real heel wouldn't be practical.

"A wedge heel isn't a real heel." Justine clucked her tongue, as if she was the fashion icon. "ISAN takes the fun out of everything."

Lydia handed a pair to me, and then to Brooke. "These are different. You'll see. Put them on. I have your measurements, but let me know if they don't fit right."

I took off my comfortable flat shoe, slipped my toes through the boots, and then zipped up the sides.

"I love it." Brooke admired her boots, staring at her reflection.

The wall with the beach scene had switched into a mirror. I wished my wall could project like hers.

"Here." Lydia passed out a pair to Tamara and Justine.

After my team put them on, Lydia instructed us to spread out an arm distance apart. "Stomp on your heels and see what happens."

"Whoa." Brooke sat back down, examining the small, plastic knife that had slid out just enough so she could grab the handle.

Tamara mimicked Brooke's action and held it out. "This is way too cool."

"Mine's not working." Justine frowned.

"Try again," Lydia said.

I touched the short blade. "Pretty ingenious. Plastic knives can't be detected. How do you—?"

Lydia answered before I could finish my question. "The same way you got it open. Slide it back inside."

"Why're we dressing like this?" Tamara clicked her shoes to put the plastic knife back in.

"To answer your question, Tamara, Mr. Thomax Thorpe is single and likes to be entertained by beautiful women."

"I don't have to ... um ... um ..." Brooke tugged on the hem of her shirt.

"No, of course not. I'd never ask for more than flirting, but you won't even get that far. As soon as you get inside, you start attacking the guards. You have to take them down before you can reach Mr. Thorpe."

"What if he's not home?" I asked.

"Wow." Justine's reaction was delayed. Her boots finally worked.

"We've been monitoring him. One of the guards inside is our source. He's been keeping me informed of all Mr. Thorpe's activities. He's always home on Wednesday nights. Seems like Wednesday is his fun night. I've canceled his appointment with the service. There won't be any confusion."

Lydia rose and opened another level of the sliding drawer from her wall. "This is where the fun begins. Let's pick out some sexy outfits. Though your outfits will be Taser and bullet proof, unfortunately because of the design, you'll have some exposed area. Now ... I'm going to make you irresistible." She tossed wigs at us. "I don't want anyone to identify you."

"Why are we all blondes?" I ran my fingers through my wig, engrossed with the silky-smooth texture.

"I'm already blonde." Justine flipped her hair from side to

side in exaggeration.

"Yes, you are, Justine." Lydia laughed, but her humor quickly faded. "Your hair is about shoulder length, but it needs to go to your waist." Lydia held up the extra wig, inspecting it as if she was seeing it for the first time. "I was informed Mr. Thorpe likes blondes. Then blondes you shall be."

CHAPTER TEN
FIRST MISSION

An assassin. That would forever be my life. But how huge was ISAN? I only knew they were a secret organization. I had no way out. Maybe they would let me go when I was no longer of any use. I hadn't seen anyone much older than me; maybe they found other uses for older girls. Or I would be dead before then.

I woke my TAB with a wave of my hand to tune out what was to come in a couple of hours. No message appeared from Sniper—another mystery. Russ would've told me if they were running some kind of test. If Sniper had asked another question, I would've told him off, even if it meant getting caught.

Nothing on the net held my interest, so I paced about the small cramped space in my room. I paused when I caught my reflection in the long mirror attached to my closet.

I traced the curve of my hip. Dressed up and wearing makeup, the girl in the mirror seemed like a stranger. Blonde hair did nothing for me, but the black leather pants and tight corset top made me thin and sultry.

After I shoved the special lipsticks and earrings into the side pockets of my pants, I tossed my long wig over one shoulder, wondering how in the world I was supposed to fight with it on. Then I wondered what Mom would have thought if she had seen her only daughter wearing such an outfit to assassinate a political figure.

Thoughts of her seized my heart as the pain of losing her consumed me, and I felt as though she had just died.

Be brave, Ava. Be someone important. Mother's words rang in my head. If being an assassin was the only way I could be someone important, then I would do it.

The hospital hadn't let me see her when they'd told me she died from an illness they couldn't explain. Being only thirteen, I had no rights. If I had been bolder then, maybe …

I stopped thinking of her when something caught my eye. My heart leaped to the ceiling when Russ's face materialized on my TAB.

"Russ." My hand flew to my chest. "Give me a warning next time, will ya? What if I was changing?"

He rubbed his jaw and forced a hand down his face. "Sorry. I do this all the time. You must be doing something you weren't supposed to do." He flashed a grin.

I rolled my eyes. "I was looking at myself."

He smashed his lips together, angling his eyebrows. "Don't girls look at themselves all the time?"

"Ha, ha … very funny."

"You look very nice." His tone softened.

Heat flushed through my face, and I craned my neck sideways. "Yeah … well … Lydia made me like this."

I dropped my finger when I realized I had wound a strand of my fake blonde hair around it. For heaven's sake, I couldn't believe I acted like this.

"Lydia can't make a person beautiful when she already is." Russ's words were laced with sincerity.

My cheeks burned, as I took in his unexpected flattery.

To change the subject, I asked in a respectful tone, "Why did you call me? Did you need something?"

Russ's expression changed from earnest to stern. "It's time."

* * *

The cool draft made me shiver. I didn't make eye contact when I whisked along the dim hallway where Lydia, Russ, and Mitch waited. Being literally dressed to kill left me uneasy. My team seemed to be fine with it, or they hid their fears well.

A wolf whistle from Mitch made me blush, but he wasn't going to get a smile from me like he did from my team. Justine fidgeted with her wig. Brooke kept touching her clip-on earrings. Tamara played with her bustier zipper, most likely trying to decide how high or low it should stay.

"Nice suit," I said to Mitch.

Mitch pressed his lips into a tight smile as color stained his cheeks.

No way. Mitch blushing. Now that's a first.

Mitch sported a classy dark suit and blue tie. The suit conformed to his broad shoulders and every inch of his muscular frame. Then I remembered he would play the role of the handler.

Not a bad looking handler.

"Nice leather pants. They're perfect with those killer boots." Mitch spread his lips wide, keeping his eyes on me longer than necessary. "Nice choice of top, too."

The black leather tops Lydia made us wear were smooth to the touch and beautiful, but showed a bit more skin than I was used to.

"How's that shoulder?" Mitch asked.

I was surprised he'd remembered. "It's good as new." The pain had vanished shortly after and I had forgotten it had even bothered me in the first place.

"Ladies, you are beautiful. You have been well trained, but keep in mind this isn't a training mission. It is for this reason Mitch is going with you." Lydia's dimples became apparent when her lips spread. "Ava, you're our map. I'll have no contact with you, so make sure you stick to the plan. Roxy's team and the bodyguards are already inside the ISAN sub-glider. Good luck. See you all back here soon." Lydia shifted her attention to me. "You're their leader. Everyone was told to listen to your directions. Mitch will help guide your team."

"Everyone," I murmured to no one in particular. *No pressure there.*

"What if something goes wrong?" Tamara gnawed on her bottom lip, her tone panicky. "I mean, what if one of us gets shot or injured and we can't move?"

"Didn't you read the handbook, newbie? We leave you behind." Justine unzipped her top a little lower and clicked her tongue.

I wished I could have taken her zipper and zipped her mouth for good. The nerve of her. I glared at Justine for that asinine remark as I waited for my team to pass me. I could've said something, but I dismissed it. We didn't have time for a discourse, one likely that would turn into a bitter argument. But I swear, one of these days I was going to lose my patience with her.

Tamara knew what to do. Diana had discussed the topic in class that morning. She had only asked because she was freaking out. I would remind her when I had the chance.

A chill seeped over my exposed skin when the sliding door opened. I shivered from the sharp breeze and anticipation. Just before I stepped in, someone yanked me back. I whirled. Russ had gripped my arm.

Russ leaned closer, his eyes filled with concern. "Be careful. I want you to come back in one piece, you hear? Don't do anything foolish. If you don't think it's going well, get the hell out of there with your team. Stay close to Mitch. Understood?"

I nodded and left when Russ released me. He wouldn't have said that unless he thought I might not come back. I'd been uneasy before, but Russ's words shot a bigger dose of fear through me. I had no time to think, just do. Marching forward, I kept my ears open.

"Keep them safe," Russ said to Mitch.

"Don't worry, you know I will. Especially the one in front of me."

In the sub-glider, Roxy and I locked eyes. She scowled until she saw Mitch coming in behind me, and then the other three from her team gave me half smiles. Carol sat next to Roxy, and Faya next to Carol. I had forgotten the fourth girl's name. I didn't bother to ask, so I just kept calling her *redhead*.

Roxy's team wore all black, with black masks covering their faces like a second skin. They could pass for men with their hair tied up and bulky clothing.

Roxy concerned me. Would she watch my back? I didn't know if I could trust her. But I trusted Russ, so I shut down that thought quickly. Too late, anyway.

"Sit down, please." Mitched glanced behind his shoulder at me and turned back to the panel.

When a screen materialized in front of Mitch, he used his voice to command the location. Then the screen slid back down and the engine hummed softly. Still standing by my seat, I ran my hand against the expensive fine metal. Cool to the touch, it felt smooth and refined.

ISAN's private glider was shaped like a saucer—One could mistake it for an alien ship. There were plenty of seats to transport at least two dozen of us if needed. Small backpacks, filled with medical and dry food supplies in case of emergency, hung above each seat.

Brooke gave me a side long glance. "What're you doing? Sit down."

I couldn't help myself. Being inside the sub-glider thrilled me.

"Ava," Mitch said. "I'm getting ready to take off. I need you to sit down now."

When I sat, the straps from the metal wall behind me automatically secured my body. My stomach dropped and my muscles squeezed when we took off, the engine still quiet as if no motor existed. Holding onto the strap, I relaxed into the ride.

The sub-glider had no wheels. High-tech and super-fast, it traveled more than one hundred miles per hour. It emerged from underground and launched to the sky. Outside the tinted glass, the scenery stole my breath. The ocean came into view first, along with the destruction from the tsunami, damaged buildings and debris never cleared away.

The meteors had hit in my grandparents' time. Hundred-foot tsunamis had devastated the Atlantic and Pacific coastlines of the United States. Many other countries suffered equally cataclysmic devastation. Massive atmospheric debris had led to decreased sunlight and profound weather changes caused crop failures, drought, and famine.

The old United States was now four quadrants: North, South, East, and West territories. An elected council, the Remnant Council of the Former United States, governed each sector. The councils chose secret representatives to meet at the national level. I was on my way to kill one of those representatives. My reality would have been unimaginable to people one hundred years before.

After passing the debris, which I assumed would eventually sink into the ocean, tall buildings blurred in my line of view. The bright blue, red, yellow, and green lights from the buildings at night created one long rainbow streak.

Enjoying the scenery and being out of the compound, I had forgotten where I was headed. A peaceful hush wavered through me, coaxing me into sleep. Reality came back when the sub-glider landed quietly and gracefully—not even a thump to shake us from the landing.

"What's going on?" Roxy's eyes shifted with concern when a soft vibration waved around us.

"Don't worry. This baby is now invisible to the world." Mitch stood when the belt around him slinked back in place.

"How will I find my way back?" the redhead asked.

Oh, this was so not good. Roxy's team was asking questions they should already have the answers to. They were freaking out. I should have pushed and demanded Roxy's team not be placed with my team.

Mitch handed Tasers to Roxy's team. My team got nothing, but he gave me the small gun Kendrick had shown me.

"Don't wander off. Stick with me. Let's go."

His serious, assertive tone stunned me.

My steady heart drummed as fast as the sub-glider's speed. I needed to breathe, to focus. Damn, I needed to take a piss—a bad habit when I got nervous.

Mitch administered the Helix serum to us, but he shot me up twice. I wanted to ask why, but we didn't have time to discuss it. As soon as I got my doses, my muscles relaxed and my heart eased to a steadier beat. My fears and my doubts vanished. *Kill* reverberated inside my mind. Nothing could stop me.

When I got off the transporter, the ocean wind enveloped me and the sting of salt assaulted my nose. The crashing of the waves on the shore sounded pleasant to my ears, but louder due to Helix. No stars graced us—only the dark—but ominous clouds bunched up together like black ghosts floating above us. Perhaps they were warning me about what was to come.

"Preston." Mitch nodded a greeting.

The back-up group waited for us below. They came out of the second vehicle, their sub-glider, also invisible.

"We're ready." Preston slid on a solid black mask, matching his suit. "I'll take Roxy's team and we'll head in from the back. The door to the balcony on the second floor is wide open."

"Ava, what do you think?" Mitch dusted something off my hair.

I took a second to register his question, gazing at the guards and Roxy's team blending as one, especially with their masks on—phantoms ready to kill.

"Since they can't come in with us, I think that's a good idea." A stupid answer. I sucked at being a leader. Having super power to map out any premises didn't warrant my ability to be a good guru.

"Perfect." Mitch straightened his tie. "Preston, see you inside. Ladies, come with me."

CHAPTER ELEVEN
THOMAX THORPE

My team and I stood in front of the gate with purpose. While Mitch pressed a button on the box by the gate, I eyed the several men rotating on the rooftop with guns.

"What do you want?" a manly voice asked.

So much for friendly greeting.

Mitch smiled. No doubt the men could see us through a camera attached to the monitor. "We have a meeting with Mr. Thomax Thorpe. Open the door. Mr. Thorpe doesn't like us being late. I'm sure you know what I mean."

The gate slid open. I exhaled; I hadn't realized I'd been holding my breath. As I strode over the cobblestones, I patted all the gadgets on my body, ensuring they were in place.

The exquisite Spanish style villa had arched doorways and a red tile roof, reminding me of the expensive older homes I'd seen on the net. White lights strung on trees and the rose bushes near the front door permeated the air with a heavenly scent. Though they no longer built this kind of house, it was nice to see one. Most citizens lived in sleek skyscrapers, or towering concrete buildings.

The front door seemed to be made from dark oak, a rarity because of the scarcity of trees. In fact, having a wooden door was against the law, but for some reason he'd gotten away with it. I frowned and lost respect for him. Who was I kidding? I didn't want to think of him. I didn't want to know him. He was a target I needed to eliminate, and that was all.

Don't think, Ava. Just get in and out as fast as you can. Russ's words played in my mind. When the door opened, seven hulking men came into view.

"Come in," one of the men with the biggest muscles said.

The first thing I set my eyes on was the scanning device held by each guard. Then I noted they had a Taser inside a holder belted to their waists. Since none of us had Tasers, we would be cleared.

The plan required us to steal one. Then I understood why Russ had us do a mental mission with no weapons. I hadn't thought to steal one during the MM, but then again, we'd been short on time. But what about the gun inside my boot? I panicked, but only for a second. Helix had already circulated through my blood and it helped me suppress the anxiety.

Breathe, Ave. Mitch knows what he's doing. You'll be fine. Your team will be fine.

The crystal chandelier above caught my eyes as I waited for the bodyguards to give us the green light to move on ahead. While they examined Mitch, I did a quick survey: the decorative iron banister, the oil paintings adorning the walls, the beige marble floor, and the ornate furniture. They'd most likely be destroyed after we were done.

The guard pointed at me with an astute grin. I spread out my arms, just like my team, but with a wry smile. *Come and get me.*

The scanner traveled from my head to my toe. Everyone in my team kept cool and gave the bodyguards fake grins. Inhaling and exhaling deeply, I cleared my thoughts. My heart rate shot up again when the muscle man stopped in front of me, tilted his head and squinted as if he could read something in my features.

Don't look at him. Look away. But I couldn't. Helix made me bold, and my cocky expression offered him a challenge.

Mitch took a step to me, calm and collected, coming to my aid. "Something wrong? Why don't you ask Mr. Thorpe to come out and see the girls? Aren't they beautiful? Don't keep him waiting."

The muscle man ignored Mitch and circled us, checking every inch of me, making me extremely uneasy. Hell, he might as well have sniffed me like a dog.

The muscle man stopped to check his scanner and then back to me. His nose twitched and his lips quivered. "This one has something. Hand search them all."

They'd find my gadgets, and if they figured it out, I was done for. It was time to do what I was trained to do.

One of the men placed his hand on my neck and took his time running his other hand down to my hip. I held my breath, wanting to puke from his strong cigarette odor. Sometimes, Helix sucked. Knowing where his hands were headed next … hell, no, he wasn't going to touch me there.

"I can take it off for you. Want to see something that will knock you off your feet?" I asked in a breathy voice. I'd never flirted before, but Helix left me empowered and in control.

His eyes gleamed with lust and he gave me a nasty smirk. Holding his stare, I licked my lips with one seductive stroke to start the chemical reaction, then blew him a kiss. Smoke puffed out, engulfing his face, and he collapsed.

Don't look at their faces. Don't make eye contact.

Then, chaos.

I didn't know if Mitch made the first move or if I had. The next man in front of me dropped, knocked out with two red lights beaming on his body. I had taken the Taser from the first man I'd gassed, then silenced the second man, but Mitch held a Taser, too. He must have taken it from another guard. I spun to see the rest of the guards on the floor, except one pressed a gun to Tamara's head. Her eyes were wide with terror.

Mitch raised his hands. "Wait. Don't shoot. We'll put down our Tasers."

The man pointed the gun at Mitch. "Who sent you?"

I needed to do something. What would I have done? "Tamara, remember what I said when you asked that question about what I should do if someone held us hostage? You can do it. You have *it* in you."

I wasn't allowed to mention the word Helix outside the ISAN compound, so *it* became my code word.

Tamara raised her lips into a knowing smile. Then, *whack!* Her head flew back. She jabbed the man's eyes. Blood spewed down his nose. He howled in pain, no doubt alerting more guards. Tamara ducked and gave me the perfect shot to bring him down with a punch.

"Excellent guidance." Mitch moved stealthily up the stairs.

"This way." I initiated the blueprint. "Watch out!"

My team dispersed. Laser lights flashed down from the second level and across the foyer. I ducked, hiding behind a sofa. *Thud. Thud. Thud.*

The firing came quick, pelting the padding, cleaving through. Not just the sofa, but the marble floor, too. Chips from the debris flew like mini bullets, and dust coated the air which blocked my view. Yet with Helix, nothing stood in my way.

Stupid idiots. They couldn't shoot a cow if one stood right in front of them.

As I crawled swiftly away from the demolished sofa, Taser pellets continued to rain down. I found my footing and shot back. I might have been outnumbered, but I was trained to aim with precision. In less than a minute, I had tased them all with my team's help.

I led them up the stairs, Mitch at the end, watching my back. Footsteps echoed down the hallway. Not only did the blueprint appear, invisible to everyone else, but red dots inhabited the map. Each dot represented a body. I assumed having a double dose of the serum had caused the new effect.

I scanned through my blueprint, my mind searching, calculating the distance. "There are bodies in the room at the end of the hall, but we have to take two more turns, and more men are coming toward us."

Sure enough, Taser lights flashed across my vision. I shot back and retreated to keep from being hit.

"Now what?" Brooke brushed her blonde wig out of her eyes.

"Who wants to give up their earrings?" I asked.

"I will." Justine didn't wait for anyone. She dodged to the side and threw one of her earrings. Justine jumped back just as the small bomb exploded.

The opponents scrambled.

When lights shot at me from behind, I ducked for cover.

"Where are you Preston?" Mitch spoke into the top button on his suit.

"We were under attack. We're on our way."

Preston's voice projected clear and crisp in my ear, thanks to Helix.

The laser lights from behind me stopped, blazing in the other direction. Thank God for Preston and Roxy's team. I launched forward again after stunning the second group of men. Then I veered to the left.

My steps quiet, I backed up against the wall from either side and ambushed another group with my team's help. With the last group down, I was free to move ahead. Mr. Thorpe wouldn't be alone, and he certainly wouldn't be an easy target.

I parked my team around the bend of the hallway, told them to stay there, and only I moved ahead. Slowly, I crept forward down the long hall and tugged off one of my earrings. Then I tossed it in front of the door and shielded myself with my arms from the explosion as I dashed back to my team.

When the smoke cleared, smack in the center stood Mr. Thorpe, leaning back against his wooden desk. His smirk alone taunted me to dash through the door and kill him, but just as I tensed, Mitch placed his hand on my shoulder.

"This is too easy." Mitch clenched his jaw, his eyes shifting in thought. "Who has the powder?"

"I do." Brooke unzipped a side pocket on her pants and took out the compact.

"Throw some by the door when I say to. We'll be right behind you." Mitch guided Brooke to stand in front of him.

With a nod, Brooke rubbed off the powder with the brush from inside the case and cupped the loose granules in her hand.

"Welcome," Mr. Thorpe said. "I may not be able to see you, but I know you're there. Surrender now and no one will get hurt."

Mr. Thorpe greeted us happily, as if we were old friends. I grimaced, not just from his bravado, but from the strong smell of cigar indicating he had recently enjoyed one.

"I'll take my chances." Mitch unloosed his tie, ready to use it as a weapon.

I stood behind him, Tasers aimed and ready.

"Do you know why your organization sent your team to kill me?"

"Shut up." Mitch took a quick peek and turned to us. "Ready?"

A click. Then another click. My heightened senses picked up on multiple guns in Thorpe's office. I swallowed, my heart thundering in my chest. Not Tasers, but guns. *Oh God.*

"They have guns." Tamara shuddered.

"You've got this. Same as a Taser. Move faster. Just don't get hit." Mitch patted her shoulder as if we were playing a simple sport.

Tamara's jaw dropped. His humor did not amuse her.

"You've got this all wrong." Thorpe seemed desperate to be

heard. "I believe in keeping the council number count at four. The person who sent you wants to be the only ruler. That person will have everyone killed."

"Go." Mitch gave the order, ignoring Thorpe.

Thorpe glared at the sight of us dashing down the hall toward him. "I warned you. Too bad you'll all die today."

His tone, confident as he appeared, did nothing to discourage my assertiveness.

Brooke had charged down the hall first. I trailed right behind her, firing away with a Taser to keep the guards back. When she reached the door, she tossed the powder.

Mitch's concern was warranted. Red laser lights appeared before my eyes, crisscrossing in countless directions. My team would've been fried to a crisp. Then the lasers disappeared. The smug *you-can't-touch-me* attitude on Thorpe's face blanched.

Bullets showered one after the other when I entered. I ducked from side to side, moving swiftly like a hummingbird. My pulse soared.

Good lord, how many men did he have?

One tried to grab me and missed. I jabbed him in the gut, knocking him back several feet, then I finished him with my Taser. Another guard advanced toward me. I rotated around him and snapped his neck.

Helix made me strong and brave, but the extra dosage Mitch had given me made me feel like Superwoman.

I delivered a roundhouse kick, connecting with the man who came charging at me, and knocked him out cold. Pivoting to my left, I threw myself back when a bullet whooshed by, inches from my neck.

A guard socked my face. I thumped on the marble floor, blood spewing from my lip. Sucking hot liquid from my mouth, anger flaring inside me, I pounced on him.

I felt no pain. I had no fear. I had become invincible. And though impossible, the guards seemed to move in slow motion as the sounds of fists upon flesh, bones snapping, groans, and curses trickled through my ears.

Mitch proved to be smooth and skillful, too. He had no problem taking down the bigger men. He squeezed his tie around a bodyguard's neck, chocking the life out of him and using him as an anchor, and kicked the men coming at him from both sides, one after the other. Bodies surrounded him in various states of agony.

I tried to fight my way to Mr. Thorpe, but like Russ had said, Thorpe had countless bodyguards surrounding him.

Tamara struggled with two men. I flipped over bullets to get to her and I knocked down the guy nearest to me. When he fell flat on his back, I elbowed him in the chest while Tamara kicked the remaining man in the groin.

"Thanks," Tamara said.

Tamara and I stood back to back, panting, and I advanced in a defensive position the way Lydia had taught me.

From the corner of my eye, I saw Justine escape a bodyguard's hold and punch him hard in the face. Blood jetted out of his nose as he dropped. Justine proved once again she was the strongest when she moved Thorpe's desk and knocked down a group of men as if they were bowling pins.

Brooke had told me she was extra sensitive to vibrations, and she could hear the sound of movement before the contact. Before the bullets touched Brooke, she fired back and hit them in time to counteract the direction, sending it right back to the person that fired it.

We needed to be off his property soon. Mr. Thorpe slid his hand under his desk when I entered, probably signaling for more help.

All the guards were down, except the ones near Thorpe. The few men remaining built a wall around him with their bodies. Thorpe huddled in the corner like a coward with a gun in his hand. He slid up the wall to stand and pointed the gun at me, glaring with anger and determination.

I snarled right back, smearing the blood that trickled down my forehead from a bullet nick. Pointing at him, I mouthed, "You're dead."

When my team surrounded me, I gasped at blood on their arms, torn fabrics, bruised faces, and the countless bodies spread about the room, dead or injured. I didn't dare look at my injuries. Blood dripped from Justine's arm at her side. Like the Mental Mission. But real. This was real.

Eliminate Thorpe. Home free. Such an easy kill.

A triumphant smirk tugged my lips as I pointed my Taser and pulled the trigger.

"Put your Tasers down," a voice said behind me.

I gasped, whirling. My heart ricocheted in my chest, victory fading right before my eyes.

A group of men held Roxy's team hostage with knives at their throats.

Thorpe's trepidation turned into a triumphant grin. He moved closer to the window along with his bodyguards. I didn't know what would happen if I failed an assignment, but I didn't want to find out.

"Put them down," another one said.

Roxy cried out. The man holding her hostage nicked her neck.

When Mitch placed his Taser down, I followed.

"You should have run when you had the chance." Thorpe pushed through his bodyguards protecting him, exposing his body like a fool. "It's too bad. You're much prettier than last Wednesday's girls." He pointed the gun at Mitch, edging closer to him. "I'm going to kill you all."

Arrogant bastard. Not if I kill you first.

A tiny piece of me had wondered if ISAN had made the wrong

decision to terminate Thorpe, but when he ordered us dead, I felt nothing for him. If he was a decent human being, he would have us locked up for trying to assassinate him instead of having us killed. He deserved his punishment.

I hissed and bared my teeth. "I'm going to kill you."

Mr. Thorpe let out a sardonic chuckle, halting momentarily.

I took this moment of opportunity, praying my team would understand my message. "You know why I love my boots and my earrings? Women's accessories are such great inventions. *Now.*"

I snatched off my last earring and flung it in front of the men holding the hostages. The smoke caused disorder. My team had done the same and more smoke filled the room in sections. Bullets whizzed by my ear. With my heightened sensation, I sensed the direction they flew and I dodged them with ease.

Sharp plastic projected out from my right heel with a stomp of my foot. I grabbed the small daggers out of my boots and leaped off the floor to slice across the neck of the bodyguard coming for me. Blood dripped on the floor, pungent metallic scent stung my nostrils. Then I flipped over backward to see Preston's team. It was about time. When more came at me, I became a slicing machine.

I hadn't wanted it to get to that point, to shed blood, but I had no choice. Desperate situations called for desperate actions. I'd intended to kill only Mr. Thorpe, but my plan had changed. My superiors had often told me sometimes I would have to change the course because things could go wrong. I believed them now.

A gun fired and Roxy screamed. My heart stopped, muscles rigid. Roxy's deafening cry became unbearable with my heightened sensation. I whirled to see Faya bleeding on the floor. Then another one of Roxy's girls went down, and then another.

My heart and stomach crashed in the center together, and the urge to vomit came strong. Shocked to see blood on ISAN girls, I took a few seconds to register what had happened. A teammate dying was a possibility. I knew that. Seeing it firsthand was something else.

When the bodyguard with the gun directed the weapon at Roxy, something dangerous ignited in me knowing my team would be next. This foreign existence in my core wanted blood. It wanted death. It wanted destruction. I became a monster. Helix transformed me into a shallow shell to servitude—a perfect model of ISAN assassin.

I pulled my gun from the side of my boot and took aim. The bodyguard who had shot Roxy's team went down first, followed by the others.

Don't look at their faces. Don't make eye contact. But I did look at their faces, and I did make eye contact.

Each guard held my foster father's cruel face, his steel malevolent eyes. I saw the man who ripped the happiness out of my soul, who towered over me into submission, and molded me into a terrified little girl. For a heartbeat I froze, knees buckling, heart palpitating with trepidation and regret. I became that little girl. A rat, he had called me, and beat me until I stopped crying from missing my mother.

No more. No more. I am no longer that petrified girl.

Then, one after the other, as hunger for revenge drove me, as if each of the men was him, I shot them until they were all down.

I spun toward Thorpe, open and exposed with no guards around him, and I fired at him. *Stupid fool.* Surprisingly, he managed to dodge my bullet. Then Thorpe pointed his gun at me when I jumped on the desk, and leaped into the air for him.

Two gunshots whiffed past me. At the same time, the bullet tore through skin, muscle, and bone. As my body slammed into his, shattering glass crashed in my ears as pain wrenched through me. I flew out the window.

I didn't know which one of us had been shot.

CHAPTER TWELVE
A DREAM

I n the darkness, a faint light illuminates. A woman with brown hair appears in the glow. The light blocks my view of her face, even as she stands a touch away from me. She caresses my cheek like a mother would her child's. In that contact she feels familiar, and her scent of gardenias soothes me. I lift my hand to cover hers.

"Mom?" My heart expands with joy, but she slowly fades.

No, no, no. Mom. Come back. *My chest caves as a sob shudders out of me from missing her.*

"Is she okay?" Brooke's panicked voice hummed in my ear.

At first, I had no idea what had happened, or why Brooke spoke with such concern, until I recalled crashing into Mr. Thorpe.

Someone shifted my body. Pain sliced down my leg and traveled to my head. Then I felt nothing. I wanted to open my eyes to see the damage from the fall, but no matter how hard I tried, I couldn't. Blackness took me again.

I am four years old. Skipping down the hallway of a building, I come across a door. Two voices murmur on the other side. I swing it open and peer in to see my mother stroking my face.

100

"You can't do this to her. It will change her," my mother begs.

"I have no choice." The man wears a white lab coat. I squint to identify him, but to no avail.

"Everyone has a choice," she cries. "This is all your fault. I'm her mother. I forbid this."

"It has already been done. This is the only way to ensure her safety. I can't keep her safe if I'm gone."

The man's face whips to the left. He doesn't say a word. He stands there while my mother slaps him again.

"I hate you. Do you hear me?" Tears stream down her cheeks. "You've sold your soul to the devil."

"Maybe I did." He grips his hair in frustration. "It was always inside her, through you. I never told you."

My mother drops to the floor at this news, sobbing. I stare at the man's face as he turns to me. His jaw drops and his gray eyes turn gloomy. He bends down to me. "Ava. How long were you standing there?"

I stiffen from his scolding tone and my body goes cold. "I'm sorry, Daddy."

Daddy? How could I dream about my father when I've never known him? I wanted to know more, to see more, but …

The bright light blinded me and my mind went blank.

"Ava. Open your eyes, damnit." Justine's concerned voice sent warmth to my core.

Wow. She actually cared about me.

I tried to say something, but no sound escaped my lips.

"She's not going to be brain dead, is she?" Tamara's worried tone concerned me.

The words brain dead scared the life out of me. Why couldn't I speak? And where the hell was I? My body shifted and something warm gently pressed my chest and temples.

"Ava is going to be fine," Mitch answered finally, and then something tightened around my leg. "She's going to need stitches."

My body rocked back and forth. The sub-glider hummed, ready for takeoff. My eyes became heavy again, and then everything went dark.

"Ava. Stay close to me." He sounds unfamiliar, but his voice beckons my attention. Then his body presses into mine, so I peer up, but can't see his face.

My dreams sucked. Knowing I was attracted to him, I at least wanted to see what he looked like. Then my dream flashed to another time and place.

"Ava." The same guy sings my name tenderly as if it were a song. Caressing my cheek, he continues. "The only good thing about this place is you." He takes my hand and places it on his chest. "Do you feel that? No one can take away my beating heart for you. You're imprinted right there. You are my forever."

I answer him, but I don't know what I said. Sadness floods me and tears warm my face. I jump into his arms and hold him tightly. My heart overflows with completeness, and takes me to another level of euphoria. I can fly, soar high to the sky, and never fall ... because of him.

Then he is gone.

* * *

My eyes fluttered open. I lay on a thin mattress inside a clear rectangular case. Blue and green laser lights crisscrossed up and down my body. When I craned my neck to the side, Brooke's face came into my view. Clear. Clean. No blood. The guards I had shot, bloody and dead on the floor flashed in my mind. *Oh God. How many had I killed?*

"It's about time you woke up." She scowled playfully. "Don't you know sleeping on the job can get you fired?"

"I think I want to get fired." I grumbled. My muscles ached like I had worked out beyond my limits, but I would rather take the soreness over pain. "What happened?"

I glanced about the dimly lit room. On the wall to the left of me were monitors. Above me, another monitor scanned the length of my body. And on my right leg, two mechanical machine hands had just finished sewing me up.

"What *didn't* happen?" She arched her brows. "Where shall I begin? What do you remember?"

I opened my mouth to speak when the mattress I laid on flipped me over by mechanical hands connected to the case. A soft and flexible material wrapped around my body, like an enormous bandage. After the machine evaluated my body, it set me back in place.

"The last thing I remember ..." I trailed off when Russ, Mitch,

Justine, and Tamara entered.

"Next time you decide to jump out a window, do it on your own time. How are you feeling?" Russ lit a small grin, but his green eyes flashed a look of concern.

"Awesome," I drawled. "What happened to Thorpe?"

Mitch came to the forefront. "Thanks to you, the case is closed." He gave a victorious smirk. "You were all brave. We saw blood this time around, but considering the unforeseen circumstances, you all handled yourselves professionally. After we left, a team of sweepers came in and disposed of the bodies. Our technician also tapped into their system and erased any video evidence."

"What happened to Roxy's team?" I asked hesitantly. From what I could recall, they were in bad condition or worse.

"Roxy's fine," Russ replied, but his eyes told me something else.

I tensed. "How about the others?"

Nobody said a word. The soft whirring of machines answered my question.

I didn't like Roxy, but I felt sorry for her. I knew what it felt like to lose someone. She had lost three of her teammates. No matter how tough Roxy played it, she had to be devastated.

I lowered my eyes, overwhelmed with dread.

"It happens. When it's your time, it's your time. It's the nature of what we do. Don't dwell on it or it will set you back. It won't be the last time." Mitch brushed it off like it was no big deal.

I winced. *When it's your time, it's your time?*

My blood boiled. Maybe it was no big deal to him. He didn't care about the girls who had died. Or perhaps he was trying to ease my mind. But a life was a life.

Russ must have seen my frown. He changed the subject. "You'll be dismissed in five minutes. You'll need to report to Lydia for a debriefing. She'll want to know how you're doing. Then, you'll need to stop by to see Vanessa in counseling. She's going to help you deal with psychological distress. Don't forget about Friday night. You've earned your free night. Mitch and I will be on our way so you ladies can have a private moment to recap."

Then they left.

"Were any of you hurt?" I asked. I recalled the blood on them.

Justine came around to the other side of the case. She had tied her hair back, exposing her fair skin. As always, her lips were pencil straight with no expression. I prepared for her sly remark, but then her face softened.

"No. We're fine. We had some cuts and bruises, Tamara more than us, but nothing that the Dr. Machine couldn't fix." She gently tapped the metal. "Besides, Mitch injected us with pain killing serum, so we're all good."

Tamara extended her arm to me and wiggled her fingers. "Oh, don't forget I fractured my pinky, but Dr. Machine fixed me up."

"How long was I out?" I attempted to get up, but the case held me in place.

Brooke held out a hand. "Stay down. Not yet." She glanced at the time on the machine. "To answer your question, you were out for an hour."

Tamara cleared her throat and wrung a few strands of her hair about her ear. "Mitch had to drug you. You had some glass embedded in you from the impact. Thank God you landed on Thorpe. His fat body saved you." She giggled lightly. "You bounced off him and landed on top of more glass. What were you thinking?"

That explained the weird dreams. Drugs could jumble the mind I assumed. Ignoring her question, I tried to bring the night's action to the forefront of my thoughts, but I only remembered the powerful need to save my friends and kill my enemies.

"All windows are supposed to be made of fiberglass. I should've bounced off the glass and not gone through it." I wondered if I'd even gone through the glass at all.

"You shouldn't have done what you did." Tamara's scolding came as a surprise.

Brooke narrowed her eyes at Tamara. "Hey, newbie. Watch your tone. Ava is right. None of us could've known."

"Sorry." Tamara shrugged sheepishly. "I thought I'd lost you." Her tone became somber, and her eyes glistened. "After the girls from Roxy's team got shot, I ... I froze." She dipped her head as if in shame. "When fear overpowers you, I don't think anything can help, even Helix."

The machine lowered me. As my team moved to the side, my bare feet set on the floor and I stood upright. I shivered. The cold beneath me stung through my bones. I hated the tile floors on my skin. They made me feel like I was in a lab.

"It's all in your head," I reminded her. "Helix is a tricky serum. It helps you but doesn't fully take away fear, which is the reason we do those stupid mental missions."

I had a difficult time taking the first step, like a newborn colt, but my muscles regained their mobility soon after. Thank goodness for inventions like Dr. Machine to speed up the healing process.

Brooke handed me a clean top. "I know what I signed up for, but I don't know if I can do that again. We've never killed people. I mean ... except for Tamara."

"Geez, thanks for pointing that out." Tamara spiked her eyes to the ceiling.

"Sorry. I didn't mean it that way. We spoke to Vanessa while you were healing. She wanted us to express our feelings and get everything out of our system. She said time would help and the first time is the hardest. She also said we should keep in mind it was self-defense, and we had nothing to be ashamed of."

"I'm glad you had a talk with Vanessa. We didn't have a choice." I pulled my shirt down, trying to help Brooke feel better, even though I felt the same way. As their leader, I needed to say something to make her snap out of it. "I don't think we have a choice whether or not we do this again. They own us. We gave our lives to ISAN. Now we have to deal with it. At least we're doing something to help society, instead of picking our noses in jail."

"What if I tell them I don't want to go on the next assignment?" Justine asked.

"Maybe that's what Roxy's team said."

Tamara's words froze me in place.

Brooke whipped around to face Tamara and stopped her in her tracks. "You think that's the reason they were terminated?"

All these questions seemed to have stirred her into a frenzy.

"Brooke, they weren't terminated." I needed to keep her calm. "How could you say that? Thorpe's bodyguard shot them. I saw him do it."

"Were your eyes glued to the bodyguard at all times?" Brooke challenged. "What if Mitch took the shot? And which bodyguard was our source? If Roxy's team got the same amount of Helix as us, why couldn't they escape their hold?"

One of the guards inside is our source. He's been keeping me informed of all of Thorpe's activities. Lydia's voice rang in my head as my imagination ran wild.

"What's causing you to be suspicious?" I asked. Though I wondered about her last question.

This was the first time I had killed. No amount of therapy and reminding myself it was self-defense would ease my heart and mind, and I could assume Brooke felt the same which was the reason for her outburst, ridiculous or not.

She shrugged. "I don't know. Maybe I'm just freaking out."

I glanced at the ceiling, wondering if there were any cameras, or if somehow they could listen to our conversation.

"You're going to be fine. Let's get out of here." I put on my pants and shoes.

Brooke didn't move. "They say there're no side-effects from Helix, but what if it's a lie? What if I develop a tolerance for it? What if I need double the dosage? Then what? Can my body handle that much more?"

"Not here, Brooke. Let's talk later in private," I whispered curtly in her ear and tugged her along.

Brooke gave me a sidelong glance, and then her eyes grew wider in understanding.

The doors slid open as I approached them. "Let's keep this conversation to ourselves. It's better if we find our own answers instead of asking our superiors, just in case."

"Fine," they all said in unison.

I headed in the opposite direction.

"Where're you going?" Brooke asked.

"To Lydia, then to Vanessa. See you at dinner." I tried to sound cheerful. I needed to maintain my composure, to convince my team everything was going to be fine, but I suspected it was just the beginning of something huge.

* * *

After meeting with Lydia and Vanessa, I went back to my room. Though Sniper had stopped messaging me, I still checked. I had to wash the thoughts of Sniper out of my mind. The possibility I would get kicked out of ISAN if I got caught made me dislike that person even more. However, I couldn't fight my curiosity.

Waiting for a message made me question my sanity. I scolded myself for letting an anonymous stranger get to me, though in my fantasies, he was a hot guy. I had better things to do, like complete my homework or train on my own. Just as I scrolled to shut down to go to dinner, a message appeared. My heart pitter-pattered in a pleasant way and blood rushed to my face.

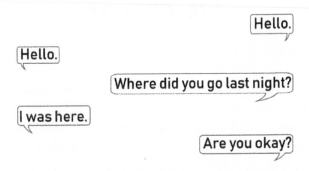

Strange timing for Sniper to ask such a question.

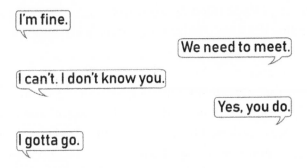

For all I knew, Sniper could be ISAN's enemy or a spy. Suspicion overcame curiosity. I made a decision to never reply again. Knowing Brooke waited for me by the door like she had been doing the past week, I shut down my TAB. When the door slid open, Brooke's smile greeted me.

CHAPTER THIRTEEN
THE FUTURE

After dinner, all the girls gathered in the meeting room, patiently waiting for Mr. Novak to make a few announcements. Curiosity nagged at me when I didn't see Roxy during dinner. If Mr. Novak didn't address Roxy's absence, I'd have to visit Russ. I didn't know why I bothered to care, only that the answer would give me better insight of how ISAN ran.

Lydia, Russ, and Mr. Novak walked out of the top floor shadows. Mr. Novak filled the air with his arrogance, like an actor commanding the stage. He intimidated me with the ability to send me back to juvie.

"Good evening," Mr. Novak announced through a mic pinned on the lapel of his fine, tailored suit. "As you all know, ISAN takes pride in our network. We take pride in sending out our best. We have proven Helix is successful. There will be more incentives coming your way. I know some of you have doubts about our program, but I want you to know we're highly classified and we're working under a secret operative group. Nothing we do is illegal. If you wish to leave this project, you are free to go. However, you'll be sent back to juvenile detention or the same foster care you came from."

Loud ruckus erupted in the room.

Brooke and I exchanged wearily glances.

His words seemed to answer my concern, as if he knew, or maybe just had good timing.

Mr. Novak raised a hand to stop the commotion. "If you have

any questions, please feel free to ask your superiors." Then he was gone.

The tension in the air eased.

Lydia took over the stage, looking prim and proper as usual. "Starting tomorrow, we're going to increase the dosage of Helix. If anyone has any kind of reaction, please let me know."

"Can it kill us?" one girl asked.

"Yes, it can." Russ raised a hand to silence the murmuring crowd. "Which is the reason we need to be notified. Vomiting, fever, rashes, hot flashes, blurred vision, and restless sleep are some of the side effects. Regardless, I need to be aware so I can help you and treat it immediately."

Bastard. I recalled Mitch giving me a higher dosage without my consent when I'd gone to terminate Thorpe. But then again, I guessed, being my superior, he didn't need my permission. He hadn't warned me about side effects, either. I reasoned he knew I'd be fine. If I found out he'd gambled with my life, I planned to give Mitch a piece of my mind.

"You're dismissed. Enjoy the rest of your evening. You are allowed to visit your friends until bedtime." Lydia concluded the meeting.

Everyone dispersed.

Brooke grabbed my arm when I stepped away from her. "Where're you going?"

I leaned into her. "Meet me in my room in thirty minutes."

I weaved around others, keeping my head low as I headed to Russ's office. The door was already ajar, the scent of lavender drifting out.

"Russ?"

"Come in. I was expecting you."

I scampered in to see Russ at his desk, pouring two cups of water.

"You were expecting me?"

"I figured you would have a lot of questions." He slid a glass toward me.

I took a seat and folded my hands on my lap. "You know me so well, boss."

Russ pressed his lips together and cocked an eyebrow. "Don't call me that. I'm not your boss. I'll do my best to answer your questions."

"Justine calls you boss. You don't seem to mind."

"It's different. Justine isn't my friend. I didn't bring her into ISAN."

"Fine." I furrowed my brow. "Be a good *friend* and answer my questions honestly. No holding back, because that's what friends do." I picked up the glass and took a sip. "What happens to the girls who ask to leave?"

"You already know the answer." He released a taut breath. "Mr. Novak answered that question tonight."

So vague. What are you hiding, Russ?

I scooted the chair closer to his desk. "What happened to the girls who died on our mission?"

"They were incinerated. ISAN doesn't do a ceremony. There will be unfortunate incidents. We move forward."

"Where's Roxy? I didn't see her at dinner."

"She's not well. She needs more rest."

From that answer, I had a feeling in my gut I would never see Roxy again. My confidence diminished. Listening to Russ's sharp answers, I knew he wouldn't tell me the truth. Every reply sounded rehearsed.

Russ leaned back in his chair with his arms crossed. "Don't start asking questions about things you know nothing about. This is bigger than you can comprehend. Now, I think it's time for you to go."

I gaped. I didn't like Russ's harsh tone or his words. Sometimes he treated me like a friend, and other times he sounded like he didn't care. I tried to hide my hurt when I rose from my chair and headed for the door.

Russ gripped my elbow, stopping me in my tracks. Then he stepped back, as if he noted he stood too close.

"Ava, have a good rest." His eyes softened and he lowered his eyelids.

Thinking about what Brooke had said, even though my gut told me I would regret it, I opened my big fat mouth. "One of Mr. Thorpe's bodyguards was our spy. He killed Roxy's girls, didn't he? Or Mitch did? They wanted out and they had to be terminated."

He bristled and clenched his jaw. It took a few seconds for Russ to meet my eyes.

"That's not true. I don't like Mitch, but he's not a cold-blooded murderer. And ISAN does not kill our own. Please, Ava, for your sake, I'm begging you, don't ask these questions."

I scrubbed my face and forced my anger to subside. "I don't understand why Roxy's team couldn't fight back."

"There are many possibilities. Maybe they needed more training. Maybe I was wrong to think they were ready. I can't foresee the outcome. I prepared you the best I could, but there are many factors I can't predict. Maybe—"

"Maybe they needed more Helix. Or got too much. Mitch gave me double the dosage. I didn't think anything of it until you mentioned the side effects. Something could've happened to me during the attack." I stopped after my voice rose disrespectfully.

"Ava ..." He closed the space between us and rested his hand on my shoulder.

I rolled my shoulders back, causing his hand to slide off. He was not going to soften my rage with tender touches and soft voices.

"I checked your blood sample's reaction to a high concentration of Helix. It was Mitch's idea. He was worried the dosage I suggested would not have been enough for you. This was your first kill assignment. You were their map. They relied on you to get them in and out."

My face flushed. I flicked phantom lint off my shirt just so I could dip my head down to hide my embarrassed expression without making it obvious.

"I'm sorry. I didn't know you tested the double dose."

Russ's shoulders slacked, seemingly less intense. "No, don't be. I should've told you. But I didn't think of it until this morning. I had to work fast. I had planned to discuss this matter with you, but I didn't have a chance. You're welcome to come see me anytime, but please don't discuss this with Mitch. He's not good at answering questions, especially if you are questioning his actions and motives."

I leaned against the wall. "I won't. You don't have to worry." I was about to leave, but paused. "Have you ever killed anyone before?"

Russ raked his fingers through his hair, and then a few heartbeats later, met my eyes. "Yes. I've been on assignments that didn't go as planned. It was self-defense, just as it was for you. If the question was their lives or yours, I'd rather it be theirs. It gets easier, I promise. Just keep in mind they're the bad guys."

"I had double the dosage of Helix, so I wasn't afraid. There was no hesitation. I didn't even blink or care I was taking their lives. I probably should feel guilty, but in a way, I don't remember what happened."

"Because you were defending yourself and your team. Helix helped you. It's okay. I hope your session with Vanessa helped. If you need to discuss this more, come see me tomorrow. My door is always open. Have fun Friday night with your team. You need to release some stress. Going out to the real world will help."

"Yes, boss." I smirked, knowing how much he disliked me calling him that. Without waiting for his reaction, I left.

* * *

Brooke and Tamara were waiting by my door. Had it been thirty minutes?

"What took you so long?" Brooke scowled, leaning against the wall. Scooting over, she gave me access to place my hand on the scanner. "I brought Tamara with me. She doesn't have any friends."

Tamara glared at her. "Thanks, Brooke. You make me sound so popular."

Brooke raised her hands to surrender and winked. "Just kidding."

"Welcome to my beautiful home," I said when the door slid open.

"Love what you've done with the place. It's just like mine." Tamara giggled.

Brooke pushed a button. The bed slid out from the wall. She glanced around and then plopped down. "Looks just like mine, too. What'd you find out from Russ?"

"You went to see Russ? For what?" Tamara's eyes widened in surprise.

Great. Thanks, Brooke. I wished Brooke hadn't brought it up in front of Tamara.

"I asked him what would happen if I wanted to leave ISAN. He said I already knew the answer."

I sat on my chair and opened my TAB. Not having much to do in my small space, I figured I'd check out the fashion world on the net.

"You want to leave?" Tamara asked timidly.

I put the screen to sleep. Instead of answering, I asked a question. "Let me ask you something. Have you ever thought what your life would be like if you lived somewhere else?"

Tamara twisted her lips and squinted as if in concentration. "Since I have no family, I would be stuck in juvenile detention or in the homeless shelter with a bunch of strangers. At least here I have a roof over my head, food to eat, and I have friends."

"Brooke?" I asked.

She bobbed her shoulders. "I don't know. Never thought about it. I don't know what I would be good at to make a living on my own. I think I'm good at being an assassin. I mean, I know I freaked out, but ... How about you?"

I turned back to the screen and played a section of the Fashion Show. "I think I would've loved to be the designer of that dress. I would love to travel the world and live a glamorous life. One day, I know this sounds strange, but I want to be on top of the highest building and see the city lights. I want to feel the breeze and be a part of society. It would make me smile."

"It all sounds amazing," Brooke said. "Maybe I could travel with you and hook up with hot models. It's too early to think about marriage, but maybe I would get married to a model, and we'd build a family together. I would have at least two children, and he would be a great father and husband. I would be a better parent than my foster parents ever were. I would make sure to help my kids with school so they wouldn't feel stupid. I would give them everything I wish I had."

"I like your plan, Brooke." Tamara's eyes sparkled, as if she pictured her future. Then her face lit up. "I wish for better things for myself, too. I wish I'd had good foster parents who would've helped me when my boyfriend beat me. I was alone and had no friends. I'm so glad both of you are nice to me."

Brooke nudged Tamara's shoulder. "I'm glad you're here with us. I'm glad you're nice, too."

I smiled to agree, but was mostly surprised at how much we were sharing.

Brooke sat up taller, humor gone. "Did it freak you out to kill someone today?"

Tamara leaned to her side, patting her leg on the mattress. "I'm not sure. I feel bad, but at the same time, it was their lives or mine. I assume after so many kills, you become numb to it. I killed my share this time, but Ava did most of the killing. I think you should ask her that question."

I stiffened, my eyes bouncing from Tamara to Brooke.

"Ava, do you remember?" Brooke studied me carefully. "You did fall out the window."

I chewed on my bottom lip, contemplating how to answer. "To tell you the truth, I don't remember much. I wanted to be out of there."

I wanted to tell them Mitch had increased my dosage, but I thought it was best they didn't know. If what they were telling me was the truth about me doing most of the killing, I didn't want them to think I had morphed into some kind of anomaly. Though a part of me felt like I had. I recalled the overwhelming rage and power pumping in my veins. What if I'd lost it and shot my team?

I didn't want to think about it anymore. It was done and over with. I wouldn't be able to bear the gruesome details.

"I think life is about your choices." Brooke clicked her tongue, seemingly a world away. "What if I hadn't signed my contract with ISAN? My destiny would've led me to a different path."

Tamara wrinkled her nose, shifting her eyes back and forth. "What if life made you think you had a choice, but instead, the choice you made was really your destiny? Have you thought of that?"

Brooke lifted her brow. "I'd never thought of that. If you're right, then I was meant to be here. This is where I belong."

I don't belong here, I wanted to say.

Something held me back. Like Tamara and Brooke, and Justine, I should want to be there. Something was missing. Maybe destiny had done wrong by me. The hole my mother's absence had created settled in. I changed the subject to create a more cheerful atmosphere.

Staring at the screen, I pointed at the girl gracefully swaying her hips down the runway like she owned the stage. "It's too bad I don't get to wear clothes like that. I'm sick of wearing black, white, and khaki. Doesn't it bother you?"

Tamara and Brooke exchanged knowing glances, then looked back to me. "No," they answered in unison.

"At least I'm not naked." Tamara giggled.

Her bright side cheered me up and unnerved me at the same time.

"Oh, God. I wouldn't want you to be." Brooke covered her eyes for emphasis.

"Hey." Tamara elbowed Brooke.

Brooke fell off the bed. I laughed out loud, and so did my friends. Belly busting laughter rarely happened at ISAN and it felt good ... so freakin' good. Tamara helped Brooke up, and they planted on my bed again still giggling.

"Have you read any interesting books lately?" Tamara asked. "I started one, but the list they allow us to read sucks."

"I have to agree with you," I said. "I started reading about zombies, though."

"I bet Mr. Novak approved that one. He even looks like one." Brooke grimaced. "I don't read much. You shouldn't ask me."

"Mr. Boring, straight by the book, dead in romance, and no personality." I laughed. "Mr. Novak lacks creativity, humor, and action, the components you need for a good read. I read a lot of those before I went to juvenile detention. They were my escape. I wish libraries still existed with paper books. It's too bad we only have access to digital books."

"When you come across one, let me know. I held a book once. There's nothing better than holding a book in your hands." Tamara hugged herself and inhaled, as if she could actually smell one.

"Well, we would have to visit the museum and I don't think ISAN would just take us to one so we could admire them." I shrugged and snorted. "I wish I had tons of money. Only the rich still have books, so I've been told. It's too bad most of the books were burned or destroyed after the meteors."

I twitched my nose and got back to the fashion show on screen. I stayed alert for any messages. Though the TAB would shut off automatically in five minutes, I prayed Sniper wouldn't message me. I didn't know how I would explain it to my team. I trusted Brooke, but I didn't know Tamara well enough.

My blood pressure rose, so I shut down my TAB. I talked about places I would like to visit one day and the junk food I wanted to try, like chocolate, since ISAN didn't allow us to have it—if and when I ever got out of ISAN.

"I would like to visit the West, except I don't like the earthquakes," Tamara said. "Before my grandmother passed away, she told me it was important to know my roots, because only then can I truly become the person I was meant to be. I think my grandmother wanted me to be a doctor like her. I wonder what she would think of me now."

Just as Brooke opened her mouth, soft instrumental music echoed in the hallway, signaling curfew.

Tamara pushed off the bed. "Time goes by fast when you're having fun."

"Well, until next time." Brooke got up as well.

"Too bad we don't get visiting time more often," I said. "They should make it longer."

"I agree, but this was fun. Thanks for letting me join in." Tamara smiled.

Then both of them scurried out.

I recalled how other girls in juvenile detention had envied me when I had been chosen to join ISAN. They had no idea what happened behind closed doors and thought I had been adopted. If only they'd known they had nothing to envy. They were safe, and I wasn't.

I didn't know what tomorrow would bring. I figured I should expect a short lifespan if I stayed with ISAN, not that I had a choice. I might be stronger, faster, and better at strategic thinking, but I was no Superwoman.

There were no guarantees I would not die on an assignment, as I had seen firsthand. But it was good to know I wasn't alone, and I had friends—real friends for the first time.

CHAPTER FOURTEEN
FRIDAY OUTING

Friday night couldn't come soon enough. It was hard concentrating during classes when all I thought about was going out with my team.

We coordinated outfits, each wearing slim-fitting, dark pants and colorful tops. I wanted to wear red; Justine picked blue; Brooke chose purple, and Tamara went with pink. Borrowing clothes from Lydia's wardrobe and getting ready in her room made the outing a lot more exciting. With light makeup and my hair in soft curls, I slipped on my boots and was set to go.

I took the elevator down to the front entrance where I would make my way to the sub-glider. Exhilaration couldn't even come close to describing how I felt to finally spend time in the real world with my team. It took every ounce of my energy to keep calm, cool, and collected. My team wore happy smiles, and no one talked smack about anyone or anything. Peace and unity filled the air.

"Ladies, you're beautiful." Lydia greeted us with a smile.

"Be careful." Russ gave a pointed look. "Don't do anything foolish."

Justine tossed her hair to the side and leaned into her hip with her arms crossed. "We have three hours, boss. That's just enough time to eat. There's no time for misbehaving."

"Exactly." Mitch came out of the shadows. "Your bodyguards will be escorting you tonight. Pretend they're not there."

"Great." Brooke planted her fists on her hips. "A night with our bodyguards. This should be fun."

Mitch leaned in with a snarl. "Just be glad you get to go out. I'm sure someone else would love to take your place."

Brooke kept her mouth shut.

"Look." Tamara pointed.

I turned. To my surprise, a black limo drove up in front of us. The engine made no sound.

"We get a limo?" Tamara's eyes widened.

Cars were a rare commodity, and even rarer to find a flying limo. It appeared to be in perfect condition, and I couldn't wait to get in. I'd only seen pictures of them, but to physically be in one … there were no words to describe my excitement.

"I had to kill someone to get here, but hey, at least I'm doing it in style."

Justine threw in an unwarranted comment, but I let it go. Nothing was going to stop me from having a great time tonight.

Russ offered a small grin. "Have fun, ladies. You deserve it. No talking to strangers."

"I understand, Dad." Justine sighed.

Russ's lips pinched to the center. Inhaling a deep breath, he shook his head in annoyance.

Sometimes I wished he would reprimand Justine, but he wasn't the scolding type.

Three bodyguards were already seated when I got in, while the one who had opened the door for me went around to the driver's side. I found out his name was Hank when Russ instructed him to drive carefully. The thick arms and necks of the bodyguards—like they had been injected with dangerous doses of Helix—proved without a doubt I was safe.

Like in the sub-glider, the limo jetted from underground. The windows remained dark until the transporter approached the city. From then on, I soaked in the beauty of the scenery.

The twenty-minute ride went fast. I kept myself occupied with conversation. I didn't want to say much in front of the bodyguards, not that I had much to talk about. My topics were limited to classes and training.

When I stepped out of the limo and onto the rooftop landing pad, I shivered in a sudden brisk wind, a contrast to the perfect weather inside the ISAN complex.

The magic began when I entered the eightieth floor. The aroma of delicious food engulfed me, making my hunger pangs even worse. Star-shaped lights sparkled along the entrance archway, blinking to the rhythm of the music's beat. Farther in, planets were painted on the walls.

Perfectly lit, not too bright and not too dim. The atmosphere seemed hospitable and enticing, giving the impression of being in space. A streak of light started from one corner of the room and zoomed across.

"Did you see the shooting star?" I drew a line in the air in the direction it traveled.

Justine looked up at the wall. "Where?"

"I saw it, Ava. That was cool," Tamara said.

Brooke glanced around, taking in the twinkling silvery lights. "It's amazing beyond words."

Customers were dressed in their best. Some wore uniquely colorful, large designer hats, while others wore hats that projected butterflies dancing about in 3D. Another wore a hat arranged with flowers. Some men wore pants and shirts that puffed out like a clown's suit.

"Can I help you, ladies?" a woman asked.

I had never seen hair that shade of red before. Her eyes lit up when she gazed behind us to the bodyguards.

"Yes, I have a reservation under Ava Novak."

I examined her dress. It reminded me of the dresses I'd seen in the fashion show. Her top formed into a heart, emphasizing her figure. The back of her dress, my favorite part, flared out into a train of blue and purple.

"I hate we have to use Mr. Novak's last name." Brooke's breath brushed against my ear.

I met her eyes, darker in the dimly lit restaurant, and frowned to agree.

The lady glanced at her screen, asked me to place my chipped hand on it, and then peered down on the screen again.

"Yes." She flashed her gold teeth. "There you are." Then she asked my team and the bodyguards to do the same as I had. "Two tables for four. Helen will seat you."

Another waitress approached us, dressed in the same outfit, but yellow and red, and her teeth stained completely silver. She led us to our table.

"Here you go."

A hologram popped up in the center of the table.

"You can order your dinner from there." She waited for us to settle into our seats and then left to take our bodyguards to the next table.

The upbeat music—jazz and pop—created a blissful ambiance. In ISAN, music was censored—I was only allowed to listen to music during my free time. My choices consisted mostly of classical.

"What are you going to eat?" Justine peered to where the menu appeared 3D in mid-air.

With my elbow propped on the table, I rested my head under my fist to read the menu. "There are so many choices. I can't decide."

"Pick the expensive one," Brooke said. "Expensive meals always taste better."

Tamara pushed her finger through the 3D image. "I don't know. I think I'll have the Jupiter salad."

"Salad?" Justine's pitch rose. Her voice boomed clearly over the loud music. "Are you crazy? Have soup with it, then. You can order anything you want, and you want salad? Let me decide for you."

Justine scrolled through the menu by swiping across the air. "Let's get the seafood dish. It's called The Galaxy Special. And let's order some appetizers." She touched the screen to order.

"Order what you want," I said.

My mind wandered back to Sniper. When Brooke and Tamara had left my room, I went back to my TAB. I'd had a gut feeling Sniper would message me, and I was right. Though I'd told myself a thousand times not to reply, I had gone against my better judgment.

Was that even a word?

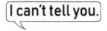

I can't tell you.

Then have fun.

For some inexplicable reason, I felt terrible. I hadn't meant to sound rude. It was a simple question. No harm in that. Except conversing with a stranger outside of ISAN would get me kicked out if I got caught. Would Russ find out? I needed to end it. He was probably already suspicious since I had brought it up. Damn. Why had I opened my big fat mouth?

I had messaged back.

I can't talk to you anymore. I'm not trying to be rude. My parents are very strict. They are taking my TAB away.

I hated lying, but for some stupid reason, I wanted to be nice to the stranger. God, I hoped Sniper didn't turn out to be a crazy person who would ruin my life.

"Ava."

Brooke's voice hummed in my ear. My body swayed, making me snap out of my thoughts.

"Aren't you going to eat?" Brooke lifted her hand off my shoulder when I caught her eyes.

Had I zoned out that long? As I picked up my fork, the sensation of being watched prickled my neck.

"You don't like your food?" Tamara blinked, her brown eyes reflected by the shooting stars soaring from wall to wall behind her.

"No, it's fine. I ..." I considered telling them about Sniper, but I decided against it. Besides, what could I tell them? "I'll be right back."

My team stared at me as if I had grown a third eye. I gave them a pointed look and went to the bar, even though I wasn't old enough.

Sliding on the stool, I cautiously glanced around, trying not to be obvious. When I spotted the bodyguards, I flashed my phony smile and wiggled my fingers, then reached over as if to ask the bartender a question. One of them came closer but didn't make eye contact.

"Psst."

I pivoted behind me to see who the bartender was signaling. When I couldn't see anyone, I faced the bartender, who stared straight back at me.

I pointed to my chest and mouthed, "Me?"

"Would you like something to drink?" The bartender's eyes drifted toward the bodyguards, then back to me.

"Uh … no thanks."

"Yes, you do." He placed a napkin in front of me.

His assertiveness caused me to flinch.

"No, thank you. I … I'm fine." I slid off the stool.

He slipped the napkin closer, and this time I saw something written on it. I looked up before I could read it, sure he had given me the wrong napkin, but he was gone.

> Meet me by the back exit door.
> Don't tell anyone.
> −Sniper

My breath caught in my throat as I read it again, and then once more.

My heart hammered against my chest. Sniper? I hadn't let him know where I was going, had I? Oh hell, who was I kidding? I wanted him to be a hot guy. And I had mentioned Shooting Stars in one of my messages. I had told Mitch to set the dinner there.

Sniper had even asked me if I had plans to go out. I surveyed the area once more and then headed back to my team.

Brooke drew her eyebrows together. "What are you doing? Just because you'll be eighteen soon doesn't mean you can drink. You know ISAN rules."

Justine reached over to my plate with her fork. "Are you going to eat? 'Cause if you're not, I can finish it for you."

Brooke lightly slapped Justine's hand. "Hey. Ava needs to eat, too. Let her at least nibble on it."

I only heard half of what they said, and I might have taken several bites of lobster. "I'm going to use the restroom. I'll be back, okay?"

I couldn't help the curiosity. I needed to find Sniper or I would regret I'd left without meeting him. Curiosity was a bitch.

"Sure. But hurry up or your food will be gone." Justine eyed my plate again and pitched her fork into one of my shrimps.

I scanned the back area to find the exit door. In one corner of the room, people danced as the strobe lights flashed, making them seem robotic. Thank God, the lights localized only to the dance floor. Once I'd located the exit sign, I knew where I had to go, and then went back to my team.

I cleared my throat. "Can you do me a favor and distract the bodyguards? You know, like flirt with them? Or see if you can get them to dance with you?"

"Are you serious?" Brooke raised her voice, matching the volume of the music. "What are you up to?"

"I'll tell you later. Just do me this favor and I'll owe you one."

"I have to flirt with *them*?" Tamara's lips twisted into a frown. "They're not good-looking. You're going to owe me big time."

Justine flung her hair back and puckered her lips. "I think the one on the left is cute."

"Hurry up. Make it fast. Please—"

ISAN

Tamara's voice faded when Justine tugged her out of her seat.

As my team headed to the bodyguards, I wove through tables and crowds. Curiosity overtook my good sense. I knew going alone was a stupid idea, but I couldn't waste any more time, and I certainly wasn't going to let my team in on my secret. Although having Helix in me would have been better.

Then a thought occurred. What if ISAN found out and decided to terminate Sniper? I would have his blood on my hands.

Stop over thinking. Get in and get out. Tell Sniper to stop messaging you.

I took a deep breath and headed down the long dimly lit hallway. The cool breeze caressed me gently, causing more goosebumps to rise. I zeroed in on the door that sat ajar, ignoring the others.

About midway to the open door, someone grabbed me from behind and pulled me aside. My heart dropped. Fear shot through me as an earthy scent and hint of citrus whiffed through my nostrils.

"It's me, Sniper." His hot breath tickled my ear.

A scream died in my mouth and my galloping heart eased. Sniper was no doubt a guy. His whisper was low and deep, but then again, Roxy had that kind of voice, too.

One of his hands wrapped around my waist, locking my arms straight down. The other hand covered my mouth and one of his legs tangled with mine. I should've brought Brooke with me.

It's too late. That's what you get for being reckless. Now, find a way out.

Sniper used a move I'd learned in training. That confused me. How would he know? What if it was a test? What if Mitch or Russ or, even worse, one of the bodyguards who reported to Mr. Novak had captured me?

"Shhh … it's me. Don't say a word. I'm not going to hurt you.

I'm going to let go. Nod if you'll do what I say."

I nodded. At that point, I would agree to anything for him to loosen his grip. It would be the only chance I'd get. If I had been injected with Helix, I would've been able to take him down. My punishment for being too curious.

As soon as he let go, I flung my head back, but he had stopped the momentum with his hand before my head smacked his face. Worse, he had the audacity to laugh at me. Anger flared inside me. What was so funny? Shocked I had been outsmarted, it took me a second to gather my thoughts. As I tensed to bolt out of there, he whisked me around.

"It's me. Don't you recognize me?"

I stumbled away from him as icy chills skidded down my back from his words.

His eyes burst with life, and my heart did as well just at his expression. A heated thrill flushed through my core. A sense of familiarity, like déjà vu, slapped me alert. With all the perfect curves and angles of his face, down his arms, to his lean ripped body, he was a vision I had not expected.

He sported black pants and a black T-shirt, framing his muscular chest. As his warm amber eyes surveyed me, a lock of light brown hair fell across his forehead. His voice—all of him— gave me pleasurable tingles I didn't want. Or did I?

Sniper watched me soak in his hotness. His eyes bored into me so hard, I was sure he could see right through my soul. He waited for me to answer, but I couldn't.

Don't you recognize me?

His question stunned me into silence.

"Are you Sniper? The same person who's been messaging me?" I asked after I got my mouth moving again.

I spotted the same type of ISAN gun in his holder, the type of weapon supposedly non-existent to the world except for elite networks like ISAN.

"Yes." Though his tone dipped softer, a bit somber, his facial muscles hardened. "You're looking well. Are they good to you?"

Something inside me went weak. I felt his torment, though I had no clue why he would feel that way. Did he know me? He couldn't.

"Sure, my parents are good to me." My face flushed as the lie parted from my lips. "Why would you ask me that?"

When he took a couple of steps toward me, arms extended, I scurried backward until I bumped into the wall. I glanced around for a way out or anything to use as a weapon. The room was empty. I tightened my fists, the next best thing to defend myself with.

"How do you know me?" I asked.

"I told you. You and I have a history."

I glared at him and kicked the wall with the back of my heel in frustration. "I don't believe you. I don't have any guy friends. Not that you need to know that."

He grinned, too happily. "Memories can be erased, but you can never forget emotions."

Why did his words sound so familiar? As I dug into my thoughts, I only felt lost and confused.

I shook my head.

"Maybe you'll remember this."

It happened so fast I couldn't have stopped him. He swooped in and pressed his lips to mine, so soft, tender, and so enduring. Sparks burst in my mind and I kissed him back. I didn't know I knew how. It seemed so natural, like I had done it many times, but I was certain I had never kissed a guy before. Maybe I was just an awesome natural born kisser.

A part of me wanted to keep kissing him. Shoot, I wanted to suck face with him hard and make up for not getting to be a normal teenager. When I snapped out of it, I pushed him away and slapped him. His hand went to his cheek.

"Don't ever talk to me again. You don't understand. I'll get in trouble." I pivoted on my heel to leave when two people entered. *Shit.*

"They're coming. We'd better go," a tall, dark-skinned female said. She held out a Taser, ready to use it.

She wore leather pants and a vest, appeared intimidating, not someone to mess with. Her outfit reminded me of what I had worn when I visited Mr. Thorpe. The guy who had entered with her was muscular like Sniper, sharp and fit. Just like the girl, he also held a Taser. They were stone-faced when they saw me. They gave me a once over and that was it.

"Does she remember?" the guy asked Sniper.

Sniper turned his back to me without a word.

"You've lost her," the girl said. "It's over. We're not doing this again. It's too much of a risk and you know it."

The sound of approaching footsteps and a door slamming drew my attention.

"We need to go—now." The guy ruffled his hair and paced to the door to peek out.

Sniper stared at me, then grabbed my arm. "Ava, let's go."

My chest tightened and my blood ran cold. *He knows my name?* "I'm not going anywhere with you. You have the wrong person. I don't know who you are." I yanked my arm, but his firm grip would not relent. *Fine. You had your chance.* I curled my lips impishly. "I'm in here."

The three of them glared daggers at me.

"We *have* to go." The guy forced a part of the crude wall that shouldn't have opened.

The wall thumped on the ground. Treacherous wind slapped my body and pushed me back with a force like a punch. They had cut out a section and entered through there, large enough for two bodies to fit through.

"Let her go. You're not the only one who lost her."

The girl's sympathetic tone had me puzzled, and the ache in Sniper's eyes made me stop resisting. Did I know him? If I did, how could I have forgotten?

"I can make her remember. I have to. I can't … I won't …"

His tormented voice, like he'd lost a loved one, squeezed my heart so tight, I wasn't sure I was breathing. His voice triggered a memory long forgotten, and a hazy vision formed in my head. Like floating endlessly through a fog and unable to find my way out, I couldn't grasp it.

He dropped my arm when a bullet whizzed by us. He must have been hit, or he wouldn't have let me go. More lights shot from both sides, keeping me momentarily stagnant.

I gasped when Sniper's friend jumped through the open wall. I thought he had dropped eighty floors to his death but was relieved when he sprang into a topless glider, a small version of a sub-glider.

Sniper gestured the girl to go next with a jerk of his head and dropped to a knee and returned fire. The girl flipped back to avoid a laser and jumped right off like a graceful gymnast. He could've used his gun, but he used the Taser instead. He wasn't shooting to kill.

One of the bodyguards dropped to the floor.

Sniper's anguished gaze extended across the room to me, calculating. I had managed to move out of reach during the commotion. He heaved a quick sigh of disappointment and shot his Taser in rapid succession.

"I'm not giving up. This isn't over," he said.

"No. They'll kill you." I winced as another bullet whizzed by. Though the guards wouldn't shoot me, accidents could happen.

Sniper ducked and cocked an eyebrow, as if to say, *the hell they won't*. Doing a backward somersault like a professional diver, he dropped through the opening. As he disappeared, he bellowed my name.

Something twisted painfully inside my core at his gut-wrenching cry. Then an old memory flickered. I saw myself running down the ISAN hall, and then I was somewhere else in the ISAN compound with my hands held up while guards surrounded me. But like before, I couldn't hold onto it.

Terror and regret filled me, but I didn't know why. Perhaps it triggered a memory I buried deep within? Impossible. Running, yes, but I'd never had guards point their guns at me before. Perhaps my vision was merely a long-forgotten dream?

Sirens wailed. No doubt the council guards chased after them. If they were ISAN gilders, there would be no warning.

I had to admit the way Sniper moved was pretty impressive. My eyes lowered to where he had stood a second earlier. A few drops of blood gleamed on the floor. I sprinted to the chunk missing in the wall to see where they had gone but pulled up short.

An arm wrapped around my waist and wrenched me back. The strong wind continued to steal my air and envelop me with a forceful grip. As the bodyguard carried me away, the walls spun around me. Even with my eyes closed, I saw Sniper's intense stare. His words would haunt me. My mind opened to more questions, and my world had turned upside down.

What have I done?

I was in a whole lot of trouble with ISAN.

CHAPTER FIFTEEN
INTERROGATION

"What the hell happened?" Russ paced the length of his desk.

Taken aback by his tone and his stone-cold gaze, I turned away. I had never seen him so furious. The veins on his neck throbbed, and his fists rounded to tight balls.

"I ... I ..." What could I tell him?

I had fabricated a story when my team had asked me the same question on the ride home. That was the lie I would stick with, even to Russ, for his own protection.

Russ towered over me. With his hands on the armrest of my chair, he shoved his face into mine. "You need to tell me the truth. I'm the only one who can help you. In a few minutes, Lydia and Mitch will be walking through that door."

I kept my mouth shut. That seemed to aggravate him further.

With a frustrated sigh, he went back to his desk. "Last chance. Do you know what will happen if they catch you in a lie?"

"I won't be lying," I said with a straight face.

"They have been interrogating your team. Your story had better be the same."

My body went rigid as Mitch and Lydia strode in. When they took a seat next to Russ, I met their gazes—hard and steadfast.

"Want to tell us what happened?"

Mitch's glacier gaze alone could intimidate anyone, but not me.

I sat tall, rolled back my shoulders, and tried to keep my cool.

"I wanted to get a glass of water."

"Why didn't you ask the waitress?" Lydia used her handheld TAB to record my words.

"I was thirsty and the waitress took forever."

Lydia shifted in her seat, seemingly uncomfortable with my answer. "What happened next?"

"I went to the bar. The bartender handed me a napkin. There was a note written on it to meet in the back."

Mitch narrowed his eyes. "Why did you go?"

I shrugged and idly tangled a strand of my hair with my finger. "Don't tell me you wouldn't have been curious, too. I thought a good-looking guy wanted to ask me out."

Lydia crossed her long legs, slightly rocking the chair. "One of the bodyguards told me there were three of them, two males and one female. Have you been contacting them? Or have they contacted you?"

I folded my hands in my lap. "I have no friends outside of this compound. I was in juvenile detention as long as I can remember prior to ISAN. I especially don't have any *guy* friends."

Lydia nodded, seemingly satisfied with my answer. But Mitch tilted his head and glared at me.

"Did they say anything to you?" he asked. "Did they tell you their names? Did they want something from you?"

"You're asking me a lot of questions at once, but the answer is no." I fashioned a quick smile.

Mitch fixed the lapel of his jacket and stood next to me. After a long pause, he drummed the back of my chair.

What the hell are you doing, Mitch? Trying to intimidate me? It won't work.

"So, you're saying they asked you to meet at the back, and they had nothing to say to you?" he asked.

Sniper kissed me and I liked it, I wanted to say, but I knew better. My memory took over, and warmth flushed through my body, as I recalled how Sniper held me, wanted me, kissed me. A part of me felt guilty and dirty for enjoying it. I couldn't shake the hurt and joy in his eyes when he saw me. His expression followed me everywhere.

"Want to answer me?" Mitch leaned closer.

Having Mitch inches away made me nervous. I had to keep it together and continue the lie. I had never been in this kind of predicament before, and I never wanted to be in one again.

"They didn't have a chance to tell me or ask me anything. The bodyguards started shooting at them."

Mitch's face pressed even closer, and he pierced his stormy eyes into mine. "You're lying. I'm sure one of your teammates will tell me the truth if I beat it out of them."

He wouldn't dare. Would he?

"My team wouldn't know. I'm telling you the truth. The others grabbed me, wanted me to go with them, but they didn't give me a reason. Maybe they wanted to start an 'I hate Mitch' group. I would join them in a heartbeat." I dug my nails into the cushion of my seat to suppress the urge to punch his face. How dare he threaten me.

From the corner of my eye, I thought I saw Russ's lips twitch, but when I faced him, his mouth was pressed into a thin line and concern filled his eyes.

Mitch's hands pounced on the armrests. I flinched. My heart jumped out of my chest.

"You think you're funny, Ava?" His nostrils flared. "You're lucky your story matches with your team; however, one thing doesn't add up. The bartender that the bodyguard, you, and your team described doesn't exist. I had it checked out. In fact, the owner told me there were no male workers that night."

"I have no clue." I shook my head, pressing my lips together.

"I didn't do anything."

Enough was enough. Tired, confused, and hungry, I had to end this meeting. I let the painful memory of my foster family come to the forefront of my mind. Forcing the tears to roll down my cheeks, I cradled my face in the palms of my hands and sobbed.

"I just wanted to have fun. I didn't ask for trouble." I shuddered a breath.

Tears kept flowing. It felt good to cry, but I also knew it would make them uncomfortable. Most likely, they would end the interrogation quickly.

It worked. Their expressions were all distraught. Russ rose from his chair to pour me a glass of water.

"Enough," he said to Mitch. "You got your answers. Obviously, this wasn't premeditated. How could it be, anyway? None of the girls knew they were going to Shooting Stars until they got there."

"That's not true. Ava suggested the restaurant." Mitch casted a challenging glance at me.

"You didn't have to make a reservation there. I didn't force you."

"She has a point there," Lydia said.

I wiped my tears, my lips quivering. "I've never been to a nice restaurant like that in my entire life. I was happy to be out. Why would I ruin a pleasant evening? I didn't even get to eat."

Mitch's expression softened. I didn't know if my crying or my words convinced him. Hopefully he would stop hounding my team.

"Okay, I believe you." Mitch sighed through his nose. "One got nicked from the gun. I have a sample of the blood. I'll find out who he is soon enough."

I leveled my stare at the wall, keeping my body still, trying to show no emotion as Mitch headed to the door and waited for Lydia to do the same.

Sample blood? Did I need to worry?

Lydia turned on her heels and gave me a small smile. "Mr. Novak will be happy to hear your team was not involved in any way. I'll close this case."

Mr. Novak can kiss my ass.

"Thank you." I looked right at Lydia as I said those two deceitful words. Mixed emotions bottled up inside me, ready to explode, but I remained composed.

I realized my actions affected my team and how ISAN viewed them as well. We were a team in every aspect of the word. Not one, but all got punished. That wasn't fair. And seeking out Sniper on my own had been a bad judgment call on my part. I sucked at being a leader.

"Can I leave now?" I relaxed my shoulders and sank into my seat from exhaustion.

Russ slid me the cup of water. "Drink. You'll feel better."

I drank and wiped the lingering tears. Though Russ was a friend, a fine line existed I couldn't cross. Above all, he was my superior, the reason I would never completely trust him. And no matter how badly I wanted to tell him about what exactly happened, I couldn't.

Russ leaned into his desk. "You may go."

"Thank you." I raised the empty glass to him and placed it down.

The glass always reminded me of the test he had used on me when he'd first administered Helix. It was that moment I had begun to trust and respect him. I headed to the door, but stopped when he called my name. I rested a hand on the wall and pivoted sideways.

"I'll have dinner sent to you. Whether you want to eat is up to you. You're going to have a hard day tomorrow. I suggest you eat and rest well tonight."

I closed my eyes and opened them to smile. His unadulterated care sank into my heart, and warmth flowed through me. I treasured his friendship.

"Thank you, Russ."

His smile let me know he felt the sincerity of my words. Satisfied, I bustled out the door.

* * *

Someone knocked on the soundproof door. When I opened it, Brooke stood there.

She stared and lifted her arms as if to give me a hug, then lowered them. "Are you okay? Did they hurt you? You're not going to be sent out, are you?" She rambled, not giving me a chance to answer.

"Come in." I gave her space to ease through. "I'm fine. And no, unfortunately I'm still here."

"Well, that's a fortunate *unfortunately*." Brooke moved to my desk and saw the empty plate of food I'd just finished. "Wow, you got food in your room? What did you do?" She planted herself on my bed while I sat in my chair.

"I told them the truth. I told them I didn't have a chance to eat." I didn't want to tell her Russ had done a favor for me. "Is everyone okay? Did you get grilled like me?"

"Pretty much." She picked at her nails and pushed her hair back from blocking her eyes. "I mean, I had nothing to tell. I told them how it went. I hope you didn't get in trouble because of us."

"No." I shook my head. "We didn't do anything wrong. Well, maybe I shouldn't have gone to the back and maybe I shouldn't have asked you to flirt with the bodyguards. So technically, it's my fault. I'm sorry for causing trouble."

"Nah." Brooke waved her hand flippantly. "It was fun. I got to stare at Mitch's gorgeous face and have naughty thoughts while he asked me a bunch of questions."

Shocked by her comment, I snorted.

"You can laugh all you want, but it's true. You can't deny he's hot, and I'll bet everyone dreams about him. Seriously, one day I might suck face with him and make it seem like an accident."

I moved onto the bed next to her. "You're too funny."

Brooke leaned into me. "I'll blame it on the serum. Helix made me do it. Or maybe I'll do it when I get dosed. I'll be stronger than him. He can't push me away when I jump on top of him and pin down his arms."

I couldn't help myself, my stomach hurt from laughing. "You're killing me."

Brooke and I laughed so hard, tears rolled down my cheeks. After I wiped them, I lay there in silence. The laughing and talking reminded me how my mom and I spent time together.

Brooke dabbed at the liquid lingering in the corner of her eyes. "I'm glad you're safe. When the bodyguards realized you were out of their sight, they took off like the restaurant caught fire. They pushed people on the dance floor and held out both their Tasers and the guns. However, on a lighter note, I wish you could've seen how receptive they were to our flirting."

I propped an elbow on my pillow and rested my head under my fist. "Sorry. I shouldn't have asked you guys to do something you weren't comfortable doing."

Brooke crossed her legs and teetered like she was on a seesaw. "I wasn't uncomfortable. It was good practice. I have no idea what's attractive to the opposite sex. I wasn't sure what I was doing could be considered flirting." She let out a snort. "But you should've seen Tamara. I don't know where she learned how to sweet talk like that, but she was a natural. You'd think someone shy, quiet, and innocent looking like her wouldn't know what to do, but I could learn a lesson from her. Actually, Justine could use one. Justine is all talk and no action."

I sat up and dangled my feet, my legs lightly hitting the mattress. "I wish I could've seen it."

"I wish I'd had more time. I didn't even get to dance."

I frowned. "That's my fault."

Brooke socked my arm lightly. "Please. It's not your fault. It's not like I had guys lining up to dance with me. The guys I thought were cute had dates. And it wasn't like I could talk to them. So you can fool others, but you can't fool me. I know you're not telling the whole truth. What happened?"

I lowered my chin, guilt swimming in my gut. "I want to tell you, Brooke, but I think it's best I don't. I hope you understand. And don't worry—this will never happen again."

Brooke took a moment, tilting her head to glance at the ceiling. "Fair enough. As long as everything's fine, I'll forget about it."

"Deal." My tone rose excitedly.

Brooke slid off the bed. "Anyway, I'd better get going. I got permission from Lydia to come see you. I wanted you to know I'm not mad at you. I also wanted to make sure you were okay."

"Lydia let you come?"

"Yes, she said only one of us could see you. Justine didn't care. Tamara wanted to come, but she knew you and I had been friends longer, so I won."

I got off the bed and stood next to her, wishing I could give her a hug. But Brooke wasn't the hugging type. "I'm glad. Thank you for checking up on me." A sense of warmth enveloped me for the second time that day. I appreciated her effort to see me and for simply caring. "Russ said we're having a hard day tomorrow. Rest up."

"You know I'm ready for the challenge." Brooke pressed the door open and smiled at me before she left.

Though my getaway had been short-lived, I'd had a chance to go out and have fun. I needed to be out of the ISAN environment, to know I still existed in the real world. It made a difference in my mood and my sanity. Surely my team felt the same.

But Sniper ... mysterious, hot Sniper. What the hell had happened? The incident boggled my mind. I had to investigate on my own.

Who the hell are you, Sniper?

CHAPTER SIXTEEN
HELIXB77

Russ strolled in and picked up his TAB from his desk. "Good morning, ladies. I've asked Lydia to cancel your history class this morning so we can have extra mental mission practice."

I shifted in my seat and waited for his instruction.

"Your mission is different this time. Not only do you have to find the exit in a timely manner, you have to find the blue ball. I've administered Helix at double the dosage. I'm monitoring your heart rates and your blood pressure. If your body rejects it, I'll be taking you out of the MM. It won't mean you're off the team, though."

I released a sigh of relief. Careful not to disturb my tags, I craned my neck to see Brooke lying comfortably on the black leather reclining chair.

She gave me a thumbs up. "See you on the other side."

I leaned back into my chair and closed my eyes.

Zap. I was in.

My face thrashed to the right and I slammed into the wall. Pain sliced through me as my vision went hazy. Someone squeezed my neck. I jabbed the man's chest and kicked him off me, but from the force of the impact, I crashed to the floor. I peered up, dazed to see my team surrounded by large men.

The same guy who had hit me picked me up effortlessly and drove his fist into my stomach. I jerked back, moaning. But I knew what was coming next. His actions seemed to be in slow motion. I caught his second blow like a baseball flying perfectly into a mitt.

Then I slammed my head into his. The force of the impact threw him across the open space.

When the next man came at me, I took a couple of running steps up the wall and flipped over to land on his shoulders with his head between my legs. I pressed my thumbs into his eyeballs and jumped off just before he hit the wall, trying to escape my torturous grip. Another one came at me, and again, I had no trouble taking him out. I'd always felt alive and strong with Helix, but the double dosage had me on fire.

I became unstoppable. It appeared my friends were, too.

"This way," I said over a dozen inert bodies.

"In your face." Brooke kicked one in the stomach, her chest rising and falling rapidly.

Tamara yanked Brooke's arm. "That's enough."

"They're not real." Justine shoved Tamara. "It's all in your head. Better get used to it if you're going to stay on our team."

"Hey." I clasped my hands together to get their attention. "Stop bickering." I was tired of their childish ways, especially during mental missions. "Let's go."

As the blueprint of the building appeared in my mind, I led them down the empty hall with more confidence than before. All the buildings in the mental missions were the same—gray walls, white laminate flooring, and a cool draft that stung to my bones, giving me the creeps.

Justine took long strides beside me. "We're waiting for you, Ava."

I halted and held out my hand. Footsteps pounded, and the red dots on my blueprint showed where they were located. The second time I had seen the red dots, and I'd not told anyone. I wanted to keep it to myself. So far, it had only happened with the higher dosage.

Brooke tucked a strand of hair behind her ear. "Shhh …

they're coming from the left. Can you hear them, Ava?"

"What should we do?" Tamara squeezed her hands together, seemingly trying to stay calm. "How much time do we have left? We need to find the blue ball."

"I say we stay and fight." Justine gave a cunning smile. "Don't you feel it? I feel like I can fly. I'm faster and stronger than before."

"I say we stay and fight, too." Brooke nudged me. "You're our map. What say you?"

I took a moment to consider their wishes and calculate the odds. "Tamara, you open every door and search for the blue ball. We'll stay behind here and fight. Once you find the ball, let us know."

"Can you tell which room I should go into?" Tamara asked.

"Every room has a ball. I can't tell what color they are."

Justine threw up her hands. "That's just great. Isn't there a faster way?"

"We're wasting time arguing about it. Go." Brooke shoved Tamara to force her to move.

Tamara dashed to the nearest door.

Brooke examined her hands. "I have nothing to fight with. Are we supposed to find a weapon in a room?"

I didn't answer. I had no idea.

A noise grabbed my attention, and I craned my neck to the sound. "We don't have time. Take weapons from them. They're here."

Shiny silver objects flew by our heads. I noted they were knives when I'd ducked. Blade after blade flew in my direction. When they stopped, I twirled to assess my team.

Justine had caught one, blade side in her hand. She winced, blood dripping, dotting the ground with crimson. Then she lit a wry smile and flung it back to the group of men coming toward us. It pierced one in the chest, dropping him to the floor. Fake blood pooled around him. A few men had long blades, and I had nothing to fight with except my speed and strength.

I knocked one down and stomped on his hand. When he loosened his grip, I picked up the knife and held it to his neck.

"Stand up," I said.

Justine and Brooke held blades across their hostages' necks, too. The fourth guy held a knife, ready to pounce at one of us.

"Don't you dare. I'll cut him." I nicked the hostage to show the fourth guy I meant it. Blood trickled down and soaked into his shirt.

The guy didn't listen. It was all computer generated by Russ anyway. Why should he care about his teammate? When he lunged at me, I slit the hostage's throat, then pivoted to the right with a swing and speared through the fourth guy's chest. He dropped, fake blood pooling around him. Justine and Brooke had done the same with their hostages.

"We have five minutes." I looked down at my computer-generated wrist watch, my breath steady.

Usually, having so little time left made me panic, but today was different. Keeping my composure steady, I searched for one red dot in my mind. I located Tamara in the last room.

"Let's go." I led the way.

Tamara came out of the room with the blue ball.

"Here." She handed it to me.

"We need to get back in." I pushed her back into the room she had exited.

Tamara furrowed her brow. "Are you sure? I was just in there. I think—"

I went inside before she could finish her sentence, her words lost behind me. "You didn't search for it. You were just looking for the blue ball. You wouldn't have seen it. You don't expect to have the exit door in the same room where the object is."

"Clever." Brooke twisted the doorknob, but nothing happened. "Not again. How much time do we have left?"

"One minute." I scanned to see if anyone was coming for us.

"Step aside. I got this. We win this one." I'd never seen Justine's smile reach her eyes before. She pulled the door off. "Oops." Justine shrugged and flung it across the room.

I wasn't sure what sound echoed first—the door slamming against the floor or the unexpected sound of the bullets being fired from the doorway. Justine, Tamara, and Brooke fell to the ground, but before the enemy soldiers could turn the gun to me, I hurled the blue ball at the first guy. The impact of the ball on his forehead knocked him out. Then I took down the other two with my Taser.

Thirty seconds left. I picked up the blue ball and dragged my friends, one by one, through the exit door in four … three … two …

* * *

I heaved a deep breath as my eyes adjusted to the light.

"Well done." Russ clapped his hands.

The vision of my team getting shot kept replaying in my head. How many times had I done MM? It was silly of me to think they would get hurt.

I relaxed in my seat when Brooke gave me the thumbs up. Tamara smiled victoriously, and Justine lifted her middle finger when Russ faced me, making Tamara giggle.

Russ's green eyes met mine, gleaming with approval. "You brought your friends through the door. Now that's teamwork. That's one reason you were assigned as their leader."

I kept my lips tight. I didn't want to be their leader. I didn't want him to praise me in front of my team. We worked hard as a unit.

"Now. Can you smart ladies tell me why you didn't anticipate anyone behind the door?"

"Umm ... because there wasn't one last time." Tamara shrugged sheepishly.

Russ cocked an eyebrow. "You're joking, right?"

"Sure." She laughed nervously.

Brooke gently peeled the tag off her temple. "If you gave us more time, maybe we would have."

"Not a good enough answer, Brooke." Russ shook his head disapprovingly and shifted his attention to me. "You need to be a step ahead. Anticipate the worst in every turn, every door, above or under. Wrong moves like that and you're gone." He swiped across his small TAB. "Thankfully the dosage of Helix was fine for everyone. Let me know if you have any side effects. Tonight, you'll be practicing combat with Mitch."

Hearing Mitch's name left a foul taste in my mouth. I didn't know why, but there was something about Mitch I disliked.

Russ continued, "He's going to review and drill you on self-defense and offense, things you already know how to do. Your team has been designated for a very important assignment. You'll get more updates tonight. You're excused."

"We're not getting any feedback?" Brooke adjusted her shirt and combed her hair with her fingers.

"I just did. You did everything right, except at the end, when you got shot because you were too busy worrying about getting out on time." Russ's voice increased in volume. "You think you're safe? You're not safe until you're home. Understand?" Russ bored his eyes into hers.

"Got it. Jeez." Brooke craned her neck as if she couldn't stand to be stared down.

"I'm thinking of your safety. You shouldn't be ..." Russ stopped, seemingly distracted by something.

If I could fill in the words for him, I would have said, "You shouldn't be here. You should be out in the real world with a family who loves you. You should be worrying about fashion, gossip, and what other girls your age worry about."

I would never know what his true words might have been. I wasn't sure if I wanted him to say what I'd thought. It would only break my heart, because I would've agreed with him. My destiny was irrevocable. I had to make the best of it. But again, the hole somewhere inside me, as if I lost a piece of my heart, reminded me I belonged elsewhere.

I wondered if I would have found that missing piece if I had run away with Sniper. Crazy thought. I would not let a whacko and his friends ruin my life. But his words, disclosing we had a past, crazy as it sounded, I couldn't stop thinking about him.

I felt his lips on mine, smelled his earthy scent, and pictured his toned body and handsome face. Then I chastised myself for having such thoughts about a stranger who had tried to kidnap me.

I'm not giving up. This isn't over. His words echoed in my mind.

Sniper haunted me while awake and in my dreams. My gut told me something wasn't right. And the *what ifs* nagged at me. I shoved Sniper out of my mind.

"You're dismissed," Russ said. "It's time for lunch."

CHAPTER SEVENTEEN
TRAINING

I didn't say a word to my team as we headed to the cafeteria. On my way, two medical personnel dressed in blue with masks over their noses and mouths pulled a gurney. A white sheet covered it, framing and confirming a body lay beneath it.

Brooke gawked at me, and her bulging eyes asked if I saw what she saw. I picked up the pace to pass the personnel. Justine and Tamara caught up with Brooke and me, and they gave me the same expression.

My thoughts ran wild. Assuming the dead person was a girl, I wondered how she had died. Had she been given more Helix than her body could handle?

"Don't stop." I kept my head low and rushed ahead, "Keep your eyes on the floor. You didn't see anything."

Surprisingly, they listened.

I entered the cafeteria. Groups of girls sat together, leaving few spaces available. I checked out the selection: salmon sandwiches, salad, and chicken soup.

"I'm starving." Justine slid her tray next to mine. "Smells delicious, but I'm not a fan of salmon."

I took a step with the moving line. "Grab it for me. I'll take yours if you don't want it." Beyond starving, I could have eaten two of everything.

After I filled my tray, I scanned the room for seats since our usual spot had been taken by a group of newbies.

Justine growled, marching toward the girls. I stopped her and

151

told her to let it go.

"Here." Tamara found empty seats and planted herself in one.

"Roxy's team used to sit there." Brooke shrugged and sat next to Tamara.

Knowing it was where Roxy's team used to sit made me uneasy, but since my team didn't seem to mind, I let it go. The conversation softened, and the forks clanking the trays and glasses contacting with the tables sounded louder than the voices.

"I can never get away from this protein shake, but I wish I had something other than water to drink." Justine grimaced, taking a sip. "At least give me flavored water once in a while." She picked up the salmon sandwich and set it on my tray.

"Thanks." I agreed with her about the water but didn't voice my opinion.

One of the girls at the table reminded me of Sniper's friend I had seen at Shooting Stars. They both had dark skin, similar closely cropped hairstyle, and both had heart-shaped faces.

While I ate, I tuned in to the conversation at the table where the dark-skinned girl and her friends sat. I couldn't help myself; their English accents were adorable. I loved listening to every word they spoke.

"Did you hear?" the blonde asked her friend. "They say one girl got dosed with too much Helix and her body couldn't handle it. She keeled over and died. With all this advanced technology, they couldn't revive her. What a shame." She took a bite of her sandwich.

"Are you sure?" the girl with short hair asked. She scooped up a spoonful of chicken soup and slurped it.

The blonde glanced around and then leaned in. "She was a member of my team. So is Jackie." She pointed to the girl sitting next to her. "I didn't know her that long. She was new."

"How long have you been here?" the girl with short hair asked.

"A few months," the blonde answered.

The dark-skinned girl took a sip of her drink. "I've been here longer."

"Have you been on an assignment before?" the blonde asked.

The girl with short hair nodded. "I have with my team, but it wasn't a big one. Not like the team behind us."

"Ava?"

"Huh?" My attention snapped back to my friends.

Brooke looked past me to the group of girls and then came back to me. "I called you three times. Were you trying to listen to their conversation?"

Try? I was surprised Brooke hadn't heard any of it. Their voices were clear as day.

"Sorry," I said.

Hearing about another death had made me lose my appetite. It could've been one of my team members. It could've been me. My team had had a higher dosage last time around, but we were safe. Would they triple the amount of serum?

"Anyway ..." Brooke stabbed her salad with a fork. "It wouldn't be so boring if there were hot guys to admire every day. I'm tired of having crushes on Russ, Mitch, and the celebrities on the net. If I ever tell you Mr. Novak is hot, then you know I've gone over the edge. Just shoot me. I've been locked up so long any male looks good to me now."

"Mr. Novak?" Justine schooled her face as if she ate something sour. She stuck her finger into her mouth and pretended to gag. "You're really desperate. I just lost my appetite." She pushed her finished plate away.

"Are you guys done? I think I want to rest before we meet with Mitch." Tamara got up and waited for me.

"I'm done." Brooke dropped her napkin onto her tray. "Let's go."

I went back to my room. The dimly lit hallway seemed as though the walls caved in with loneliness, mistrust, and confusion. Guards lurked everywhere. I thought at one point there could be a sense of home and belonging at ISAN, but I had accepted it was impossible, especially after the encounter with Sniper and his friends. I had been lying to myself.

I gazed around the room where I had tried to make my home for the past six months and the only thing close to making me feel a sense of home was my TAB. Would it have been too much to ask for pictures in my room? I wondered if others did. I knew I shouldn't complain when kids in juvie had it worse, but at least they didn't have to kill to stay alive.

Russ would never admit it, but I was almost positive if I ended my contract with ISAN, I would be terminated. Why would they let me live knowing I had a bunch of classified information stored in my memory? But I would never share my thoughts with my team. They had enough to worry about.

I should have been reviewing my notes for history class, but I turned on my TAB instead. A part of me wished for a message from Sniper, and another part of me wished I'd never met him. His words haunted me. His face and his intense, tortured expression stayed with me. I wanted to forget him, but I couldn't, no matter how hard I tried. Every silent moment, my thoughts were of him. I needed answers but I had no idea what questions to ask, or *how* to ask without giving him away. My need to protect him boggled my mind.

Obviously, he thought he knew me, but he wasn't the only one. His friends, though seemingly indifferent, seemed to know me as well. Either they were crazy or I was, but it didn't make sense. Unless I went searching for answers, I would never know.

I jumped when a message popped at the bottom corner of my screen.

It's me, Russ.

Disappointment flushed through me.

Sending you a warning. Walk away if you are undressing.

A face appearing on my screen made my heart leap out of my chest.

"What the hell, Russ?" My hand flew to my chest protectively as breaths puffed out of my mouth.

Russ rubbed his face with his hand and sighed. "You told me to give you a warning. What do you want me to do, make some noises, too?"

Russ had called me from his room. His room seemed bigger and the color scheme similar—white walls and a metal door. Boring. I searched every corner of the screen, but no pictures could be seen. Maybe pictures were forbidden. I hadn't seen any in Lydia's office either. After all, I wasn't allowed to have family contact anyway, an unnecessary rule since it seemed none of us had family.

I straightened in the chair, folded my hands on my lap, and gave him a polite smile. "I need more than one second to move away if you're asking me if I'm undressing. Unless your intention was to see me without clothes on?"

My cheeks burned, and so did Russ's. Why the hell did I flirt?

I cleared my throat, composed myself, and smiled. "So, how can I help you?"

Russ cocked an eyebrow. "You okay?"

I nodded. "Are you going to answer my question?"

"It's time."

Narrowing my eyes at him, I powered off my TAB. "Your favorite phrase."

* * *

My room was the farthest from the classrooms, and I was always the last one through the door. My team was already seated on a thick black mat with their legs crossed and hands on their laps. Their faces seemed to shine brighter with my presence.

"You're late," Mitch said.

Mitch wore a black training outfit, something similar to the gray one I had on. When he wore that type of outfit, he seemed less threatening.

"I'm right on time." My tone was cold as his.

With a knowing smile to my team, I found my place on the mat.

Mitch glanced at his watch that projected out from his chipped arm. "You're right."

My eyes widened in surprise when he acknowledged his mistake.

Mitch locked his eyes on each of us, pacing back and forth on the length of the massive mat. "As Russ mentioned before, I'm here to reteach what you already know. The mental training helps you contain your fear and think faster on your feet. However, it doesn't necessarily mean you can conquer terror in real life situations, as you have already experienced. I'm going to drill you, knock you down, and continue to knock you down until you knock me down. Now all of you stand and surround me."

"I didn't get Helix." Tamara shrank in her seat.

"You don't need it." Mitch craned his neck, cracked his knuckles, and rolled up his sleeves. "If you train without it, you'll be much faster when you do have it. Who wants to go first?"

Justine stood, lifting her chin with a cocky smile. "Me." Her eyes grew dark and hungry. Bouncing from side to side, she raised her arms in front of her.

Mitch gestured with a curl of his finger, eyeing her flirtatiously. Lust replaced the fire in her eyes, and her gait was too casual. Justine swung and missed. Mitch had crouched and sprung up to grip her neck with his hand. When Justine swung again, he blocked it with his free hand, then he put her in a choke hold from behind.

"That's what you get for lusting after me instead of anticipating my move." Mitch held her firm, his grip unwavering. "How are you going to escape now?"

When Justine's face reddened, Mitch shoved her. As she coughed, she brought up her knee, trying to reach his stomach, but Mitch jammed her with his elbow. He then swiped his leg, slamming her onto the ground. A hard thud echoed in the room. Justine moaned in pain and rolled onto her stomach. Cursing softly, she crawled on her hands and knees away from Mitch.

"Next?" Mitch said nonchalantly.

Brooke stood with one leg behind her, arms bent at the elbows, fists hard as rocks in front of her chest.

Mitch yawned and glanced about the empty room. "Any time now, Brooke. I don't have all day. What're you going to do, bore me to death?"

Brooke's expression turned baleful, then she kicked high. She missed when Mitch shifted his body and caught her leg. He shoved her, causing her to fall flat on her back. At Brooke's heavy grunt, I folded my arms and winced.

"Get up." Mitch's harsh tone resonated in the room. "You fight like a girl. What kind of assassin are you?"

Brooke growled like a wild animal and charged at Mitch. She

jabbed at his face. Mitch blocked each consecutive blow and drove a hit to her chest. Her body curled as she sucked in air hard and collapsed to the floor.

"Better than Justine," he said. Then he gave her his back, as if knowing she would not rise.

Tamara stood and did her best. She stood longer than the other two, but she was no match for Mitch.

"Might as well admit defeat, Ava." Mitch smirked. "Let's make this easier for the both us. Get down on your knees and beg."

My body boiled, and not from the humid heat of the training room. He was full of shit, and his chuckle made me want to give him pain. Flexing my fingers, I strategized. He'd never said I had to fight fair.

I swaggered, swaying my hips. Keeping my distance, yet staying close enough to jump at him, I did something he would never expect me to do. I crossed my arms and tugged my shirt off in one smooth pull. He blinked in disbelief and lost a precious second.

I leaped. He assumed I would go for his face when my arms went up, and didn't block my leg that went for his groin. Unfortunately, I missed his jewels, but I got him good on his thigh—good enough to bring him down. When I turned away in victory, he grabbed my leg and slammed me to the mat. I should've seen that coming. I'd given him my back when I shouldn't have.

Mitch crawled up my leg, using his weight to keep me down. He flipped me over and pinned my arms above me. "Not bad, but not good enough." His hot breath puffed on my face. "How're you going to get out of this one?"

As his brash words came out of his mouth, he moved his body to a straddling position. I kicked upward to get momentum and swung forward with him over me. I rolled, and ended up on top of him.

"Just like this," I said smugly.

Applause got my attention. I peered up to see Russ and Lydia. I got off Mitch, caught the shirt Brooke tossed me, slipped it over my head, and sat next to her.

"Maybe you should be training Mitch," Russ threw in casually, striding across the mat.

Mitch flashed a dangerous, heated look at Russ as he straightened his shirt. "Why are you both here? I thought you were going to meet with them afterward?"

Lydia's lips curled with a hint of a smile. "To watch you get distracted by a half-naked girl. Ava, good job, by the way. Also, to discuss tomorrow's assignment. Might as well do it now since you're all together. Russ also wants to do another round of mental missions with the girls." Lydia moseyed halfway down the mat to focus on us. "Ladies, always remember to center your attention on the hands and feet."

Russ flipped open his handheld TAB and brought out the screen in midair. "This is your assignment."

A picture of a man with white hair appeared. His wrinkled forehead defined his age, his eyes drooped, and his nose seemed large for his face.

"His name is Jonathan San. He's your target. Don't terminate him. You need to bring him in. You'll be allowed to use your Tasers; however, if you feel necessary, use the boot daggers. We won't know the circumstances of the situation until we're inside. Whatever you need to do to stay safe, do it. Even if it means you need to kill the guards. You'll be going to one of the biggest charity functions held in the Leviathan Hotel in the East. Ava and Mitch will go in as a couple. Lydia will give you identification cards. You'll be attending as Mr. and Mrs. McCann. Tamara, you'll be attending as my assistant. Brooke and Justine, you'll be housekeepers."

"Wow. That's just awesome." Justine leaned back with her arms extended behind her. "Ava and Tamara get to dress up, and I get to dress like a maid. That's not fun."

Russ pressed his lips together and his blade-sharp gaze pinned Justine like a butterfly to a board—the longest, deadliest stare I'd ever seen from him.

"You think this is fun?" His words were slow but lethal. "This is not a dress up tea party."

A long, awkward silence followed.

After a moment, Russ continued in a level tone. "One very important thing you can't forget: if you don't meet us at the assigned meeting time, you'll be left behind. That goes for all of you." Then he shifted his attention to me. "Do you know what will happen if you don't come back? Mitch will activate your tiny capsule filled with cyanide that's attached to your chip with a trigger. Not only will you die from a heart attack, you'll be dead before their security guards have a chance to question you."

I'd already learned about the cyanide capsule, so Russ's speech didn't frighten me. But being it was my first time, trepidation crept in.

"Glad I mean so much to ISAN. Like I have a choice?" Brooke scowled, flicking something off her shirt.

"Why the cyanide?" I asked.

"It's not only used to keep your team focused and on track, but also to keep ISAN's identity hidden. ISAN can't afford to be found if one of you gets captured," Russ answered.

"Lucky us." I dipped my head, saddened at the possibility of one of us not returning.

Words from Russ during a training session entered my mind. *Don't have such negative thoughts. Being a good leader means having a positive attitude.*

Bullshit.

I stretched my arms and legs. "Why does it have to be a heart attack? It seems so brutal. Why not something like a poison?" I wanted to laugh at our conversation.

"Either way, it does the same thing; however, you can detect poison in an autopsy."

"What about Helix?" I asked.

"You won't be dosed at the beginning. You won't need it until it's time. The security will be on high alert. You'll be scanned, and they'll take a breath test to detect any drug in your system if they suspect anything. And yes, Helix will come up as an unknown drug. You'll not only be escorted out but possibly be labeled as a terrorist. It's the reason why you're training with Mitch right now. However, if you stick to Lydia's plan, you won't need to worry. This should be an easy in and out."

"How will this be easy?" Tamara tucked her knees under her chin and wrapped her arms around her leg, as if she needed something to hold onto. "Is Ava going to just walk up to the person and stun him?"

"That's the reason why you're not planning this mission, Tamara." Mitch shook his head.

Russ frowned at Mitch then faced us. "Mr. and Mrs. McCann's room has already been set up by Kendrick. Their room will be next to Mr. San's room. Don't worry about the details. You'll get them from Lydia."

Lydia shuffled black cards in her hands, about the size of a playing card, and handed one to each of us. "All the information you need is in here. Place your thumb in the middle to unlock it. Your thumbprint is the key."

Russ closed his TAB and moved around Lydia to get closer to us. "Your attire has been sent to your rooms. Do you have any questions?"

Justine raised her hand.

Russ dragged a long, agitated breath. "Yes, Justine. This better be important."

"Do I have to do this?" she asked sheepishly. "I'm concerned I might freeze up without Helix."

"You'll be roaming down the hall with Brooke. All that's required from the two of you is to get the housekeeper's cart and make sure our weapons are in place. Our contact will have it ready for you. Read the instructions and you'll be fine. Once Mr. San is on his way to his room, you'll be instructed to leave the premises and meet us at the specific location where the sub-glider will be hidden. However, if I need your assistance, you'll be informed. In that case, you'll get your Helix."

"What about the cyanide?" Justine folded her arms, feet tapping the mat.

A nervous habit of hers, I realized.

"You'll be fine as long as you stick with me," Mitch scrubbed a hand down his face, as if he didn't want to be bothered with questions.

Justine's shoulders relaxed, but she gnawed on her bottom lip.

Mitch stretched his arms behind him and cracked a few knuckles. "If that's all, I'd like to get back to the training."

"After you're done, send them to my office." Russ flashed a quick grin or a scowl—I couldn't tell which—then left with Lydia.

CHAPTER EIGHTEEN
LEVIATHAN HOTEL

The east side of the city was mostly covered with water, where the tsunami had hit the hardest. Citizens lived in skyscrapers and traveled predominately by underwater transportation and gliders.

The Leviathan Hotel was as grand as its name. Standing tall, the structure towered over the rest. Glimmering lights adorned the bridge, leading to the enchanting and magical entrance. I felt like I was inside a fairytale, going to a ball. With my hand over Mitch's arm and the other around my clutch purse, I gracefully followed the line heading to security.

The blazing sun had dropped lower from the magnificent sky painted in periwinkle, illuminating the undulating water around us like sparkling gemstones. So beautiful. I had seen such sunsets before with my mom, but I was young and hadn't appreciated such simple beauty. I had taken it for granted.

I pushed away the thought of my mom, the regrets, the harsh words I had spoken to her before I'd ran out of the house over something so trivial we'd fought about. Then when I came home, the ambulance was there, and that was when …

"You okay?" Mitch asked. "You seem a little edgy, besides the obvious reason why we're here."

I loosened my tight grip on him and took deep breaths, inhaling the salty air. The cool breeze seeped through the thin fabric of my dress, making me shiver. I couldn't wait to be inside.

Mitch leaned in to whisper. "If you're afraid of heights, this isn't the bridge you want to be on. We're almost there. By the way, you look stunning. You should wear red more often."

My face flushed so I dipped my head. I didn't want him to think his compliment got to me. "Like I have a choice. And keep your eyes in front and not on my dress."

Mitch scoffed, then lightly chuckled. "Just keeping your mind occupied. We're almost there. You should be going over your schedule. You remember what to do?"

"Don't worry about me. Just don't do anything to distract me."

Mitch squeezed my arm a bit too tightly, then loosened it. It was his way of telling me to keep my mouth shut, and letting me know everything would be just fine.

Mitch wore a black tuxedo with a red bowtie to match my dress. I loved how his tuxedo jacket flowed downward like a train but stopped short of touching the ground. The men in line wore similar outfits in different designs and colors. The women's dresses were more creative. Some of them reminded me of the ones I'd seen during the fashion show on the net. According to their attire, I assumed everyone invited was of high-class status.

As I approached the entrance, the rippling water became less visible. Soft instrumental music floated through the night air just as the moon rose, casting a silvery glow and dancing across the water. Ice sculptures in abstract shapes dotted the front. After I passed the cascading water fountain, a security guard greeted me. He wore a navy uniform with three silver buttons and a matching box-like hat.

"Welcome to Mr. San's third annual charity gala. May I see your passes?"

Mitch withdrew two cards and handed them to him. The security guard placed them into a machine. A few seconds later, my face appeared, and then Mitch's.

"Mr. and Mrs. McCann, please place your hand on the scanner. Mrs. McCann needs to set her purse on the holder."

The door buzzed and I entered. I placed my small purse on the holder as instructed. The red lights zigzagged across my body and my purse at the same time, and then I took a breath test. The door opening signaled I was cleared. Mitch handed me my purse, helped me take a step up, and I advanced through a curtain.

I sucked in a breath.

The biggest crystal chandelier I'd ever seen caught my eye. Shaped like tear drops, the crystals shined like diamonds, reflecting the surrounding lights. In the center, large rectangular tables decorated with flowers contained gold plates that were filled with drinks and appetizers of various sorts. I had never seen so much food in my life. When Mitch pointed, I peered up to see the long stairway, leading up to a banquet room where I assumed dinner would be served.

At first, I wasn't sure what to do, overwhelmed by the opulence around me. But when I recalled the lessons I'd learned in my finishing class, I raised my head and smiled at those who made eye contact with me. As I reminded myself they had no idea of status, I became elegant and graceful, and I allowed Mitch to lead the way up the stairs. When I relaxed my muscles and observed with ease, I noted both sides of the walls were mirrored.

The first person I saw reflected in the mirror was me, wearing a silky-looking red dress. It showed a little bit of my cleavage, but chiffon material crossed over my shoulders and in front of my chest, giving it elegant but sexy appeal.

Exquisite diamonds sparkled in my ears and at the throat. Wrapped around my arm was a small, black night purse, studded with crystal beads. My hair was pulled up with soft curls flowing down, making me look like a princess. As I ascended the stairs, my gold wedged heels glistened in the light reflected by the mirrors.

"Like I said, beautiful." Mitch's lips moved on the reflection of the mirror as I watched us climb higher and higher.

Not knowing how to respond, I focused on the table we approached. The layout matched the same as downstairs. At the drink tables, Mitch and I grabbed glasses filled with yellow liquid. I assumed it was wine or champagne, so I took a sip.

A deep grumble escaped from Mitch's mouth.

"Why are you growling at me, Mr. McCann?" Luckily the music drowned my sarcastic tone.

"You shouldn't be drinking."

I gave him a wry smile. "They didn't have water."

Mitch took a step. "You're not eighteen. You shouldn't start, especially today of all days. You need to focus. You've never drank before. You don't know how your body will react to the alcohol. Not to mention it's written in our handbook."

Rules. Rules. Rules. Too busy rolling my eyes, I almost tripped over my own feet. If Mitch hadn't had a strong grip on me, I would've stumbled. At least he was good for something. I was clumsy with heels, but I had to be mindful. Kendrick had made them especially for me.

"Seriously, you're going to lecture me about drinking when I'm about to …" I stopped, knowing there were cameras around.

I'd wanted to ask Russ about Jonathan San, but he had been unavailable after my second session. I was pretty sure he purposely avoided me. He'd hardly said a word to me when they were seeing us off on this assignment.

"You're right. What was I thinking?" Mitch released his hold of me, took my glass, and chugged it down. "There. You have no temptation now."

Before I could blink, Mitch had downed both glasses. *Insufferable man.* I scowled, clenching my jaw, but then I thought I saw Sniper and my mind went blank.

ISAN

My heart thundered out of control. My cheeks burned as I recalled his tender lips on mine. I blamed my shallow breaths on the worry that he might try to kidnap me again. If there were a next time, I would have no choice but to tell ISAN the truth. I shook the thoughts away, thinking my mind played tricks on me.

When I entered the dining area, the sweet scent filled my nose. Enormous floral arrangements all around the room had me in awe. From the dome ceiling, to the centerpieces on the table, the archway where I'd entered, and even on the floor, roses of varying colors were the theme for the party. The room became a fairytale garden filled with white linen-covered tables and chairs slip-covered with black velvet. Every inch of the place seemed like a dream.

The host escorted us to a round table. I introduced myself and then Mitch to everyone seated. Two couples were young, while the other two were much older. The scale of luxury reminded me of haves and have-nots, and I wondered what my life would've been like if my parents had been wealthy, or if my mother was still alive. I hadn't known what I was missing until I'd seen it, and I'd seen plenty that day.

"How long have you been married?" The old lady tapped Mitch's arm to get his attention.

The diamond on her ring practically blinded me.

"Oh, we're not …" I said, but stopped when I felt a tug from Mitch under the table.

Mitch placed his arm around my shoulder and pulled me tightly to him. "Two wonderful years."

Mitch twitched when I pinched his thigh.

"Such a lovely couple." The wrinkles on her forehead creased deeper when she smiled.

"Thank you." I tipped my head slightly.

Fortunately, a waitress distracted her by leaning over to pour wine into her glass. I glanced toward the stage and spotted Tamara and Russ taking their seats. Russ wore a dark gray tuxedo with a violet tie. It was nice to see him out of his usual work attire. Tamara looked gorgeous in a violet gown adorned with butterflies at the bottom. She fit right in with the garden theme.

A man appeared at the front of the stage. A hologram image of him popped up in the center of our table.

"Good evening, my friends. My name is Jonathan San and I am your host tonight."

Clapping and cheers erupted.

I almost choked on the water I had just sipped. Jonathan's appearance signaled the start of the mission and my nerves tangled in my stomach. Swallowing, I listened carefully.

Mr. San continued when the noise died down. "We're here to celebrate our third year of success, and with your help, we'll be able to continue to maintain the low cost of water."

Mitch caught my eyes and jerked his head slightly to the side, a silent command to get ready to leave the party.

Mr. San took a moment to pause, then resumed, "Let's face it, everyone. Our unpredictable weather is not likely to change soon. Our unseasonable snowfall and cycles of drought and flood are a blessing compared to the continuing drought elsewhere. However, I foresee it getting worse in the future. We need to find a solution for our children and for generations to come. Water is scarce. In fact, many things are scarce, but we will not survive without water.

"Today, I'm going to show you a home filter called Hydro Home System. It can be managed at your home, from the rain and snow that falls directly on your property. Hydro can filter on the spot. You can drink from the second it falls into your system. You won't need to rely only on one source.

"For those who live in the east part of the world, you're in luck. We have the most rain and snow. With this home system, you'll have clean water that's cost effective. These are your donations hard at work. With more donations, we'll improve this system. Every family in all territories will have plenty of drinking water. I thank you all for making this possible. Enjoy your dinner. I'll be back on shortly."

Soft instrumental music started up again after the clapping died. Jonathan left the stage as indicated on the itinerary.

"Excuse me," I said to the people at our table. "I'll be back. Ladies room."

Mitch stood up. "Let me escort you."

"Thank you, dear." I flashed a fake smile at Mitch and took his arm.

CHAPTER NINETEEN
MR. SAN

Weaving around tables, I glided across the floor. Just as I exited the grand ballroom, Russ and Tamara left their seats.

"This way to the elevator." I clutched my purse sandwiched between my arm and the side of my chest.

"I know. There's an elevator sign." He pointed to the sign, as if I should've seen it.

I smirked. "I'm glad you can read."

Mitch parted his lips to offer a comeback when the elevator door opened. A young couple with wide eyes paused for a moment. Their casual attire informed me they weren't from the party. Returning a smile, I inserted a special cardkey to allow us access to the top floors.

My stomach lurched as we shot upward, and I gasped when the elevator walls opened up to reveal a glass window. The colorful lights twinkled against the dark below. I recalled telling Brooke and Tamara how I wanted to see the city lights. Mesmerized with the view, I hadn't realized I'd reached the designated floor until Mitch gently tugged me.

"Focus."

I sneered at his sharp tone and snapped back to the task at hand.

The young couple stepped out with me, making me more uncomfortable. Then they followed us. Their soft steps on the beige carpet intensified my anxiety and threw my imagination into overdrive. I imagined them being Mr. San's spies or maybe they worked for a competing secret organization. Who knew how many secret organizations existed?

When the hallway split, the couple veered left and I steered right. I released a breath and focused again when Justine and Brooke appeared at the end of the hallway.

I didn't recognize my team at first. They wore wigs and housekeeping uniforms—black pants, black vests, and white long-sleeved, button-down shirts. After I rubbed the back of my ear, I connected the transmitter, so flat against my skin I had no idea if it worked.

Kendrick had created a way to communicate without being detected. Since any form of metal device would have been picked up by the scanner, he'd designed a polymer one to blend with the skin. Brilliant.

I slowed my pace to match Mitch.

He spoke to them through the transmitter, dipping his chin low to shroud his lips from the cameras mounted on the ceiling. "We'll enter our room first. Then you knock, announcing housekeeping service. Were you able to detect how many bodyguards he had?"

"About twenty," Brooke said.

"Sorry ladies, but we're going to need your assistance. He has more bodyguards than I had anticipated."

"Understood," Brooke replied.

"Did you prep the room?" Mitch asked.

"As instructed. Justine and I did an awesome job for our first time. Everything we'll need is in the cart."

"Perfect."

Mitch took out the keycard and inserted it to be scanned. The door clicked open and I went in. A few seconds later, the door chimed.

"Who is it?" I asked.

"Housekeeping. Did you request some towels?" Justine asked.

I pushed a button, allowing the door to swing open on its own. As soon as the door closed behind them, Brooke reached inside the cart full of towels. She pulled out Tasers and guns and placed them on the dining table. The cart was big enough to hide Mr. San's body.

"I assume you had no problems with security?" Mitch took off his coat and placed the Taser in the back waistband of his pants.

"It was the only cart in the basement." Brooke adjusted the weapons around her. "Just like the itinerary said, it was waiting for us. I didn't see anyone around. I'm assuming his identity is confidential?"

"Yup." Mitch adjusted his shirt and took off his bow tie.

Justine pointed her Taser at the tall vase. "I'm ready."

"I'm almost ready." I took off my fake jewelry and slipped off my dress to unveil black leggings and a curve-hugging corset.

Lydia had provided the outfit—the only thing thin enough to fit under my tight fabric. I certainly couldn't be a proper assassin in that dress.

Mitch hitched a brow. His eyes lingered on my body a bit too long for my comfort. "Lydia told you to wear that?"

I picked up a Taser and a gun from the table. "Yes. Don't stare at me. Whatever it takes, right?"

Everything paused. The room spun, and I felt sick to my stomach. *Whatever it takes. Whatever it takes. Whatever it takes.* The words flooded me with déjà vu. *What the hell?* I snuck a glance at Mitch and was glad he hadn't seen my expression. He busied himself by setting aside the towels that had been dumped.

"Hey, Ava. Are you okay?" Brooke's hand on my shoulder took me out of my daze, but I wasn't sure what she had said exactly.

I rubbed at my temples, hoping to focus better. I blamed it on nerves, but I couldn't shake it. "Yeah. Let's do this. Is the room ready, Brooke?"

"Yes," she said with conviction.

I froze when Tamara's voice projected through the transmitter.

"Mr. San and roughly twenty bodyguards are about to enter his hotel suite to change his outfit as stated in our itinerary. His speech is over. Russ and I have changed in our room and we are set to go. Let me know when you're in. When the doorbell rings, you'll know it's us."

While Tamara spoke, the pitter-patter of my heart turned into a roar. I felt the danger, tasted fear, and saw death. Inhaling deep breaths, I counted down from ten to ease my pulverizing heart to control my trembling body. A dose of Helix would have been welcome. I'd have one less thing to fight—fear.

As if reading my mind, Mitch withdrew Helix from his pocket and administered some to all of us.

"You have thirty minutes for Helix and one hour before I jump start your capsule." Mitch rubbed the transmitter. "Russ, Tamara, the eagles are in flight."

"Let's do this." Justine's tone laced with confidence.

"Let's go." Brooke took off.

Passing the sofas, 3D screen, the kitchen, and then another bedroom, I reached the empty walk-in closet. Justine pushed a section of the wall she had cut through, the empty space just enough for a body to enter. She then took out the second wall, opening a door to the closet in Mr. San's suite where a musky scent enveloped me. The sound of many footsteps indicated Mr. San was inside.

Tiptoeing, I passed his bedroom and got into my position as far out as I could without being seen. Right on cue, the door chimed. Then the sound of Tasers and bullets rang out.

Crouching low, I stunned the first guard through the door, shifted my aim, and shot again. Then I bolted across the marble floor to dodge bullets, and shot one guard in front of me. Brooke, watching my back, kicked a guard who was pointing a gun at me and tased him.

With a Taser in each hand, Mitch took out two guards at once. Sidestepping to the right, he shoved one Taser behind his waist and punched the guard coming for him on the chest. Justine finished him off with a swipe across his neck with the plastic dagger she had pulled from her boot. The guard reached for his neck, blood spilling down his shirt.

Tamara jumped on the sofa to evade the bullets aiming for her. Just as she leaped off, the fabric tore and white padding shot out like dust around her. Bullets sprayed across the wall, destroying the television screen, punching holes through the plasters, and shattering the mirrors. Tamara throttled a guard's neck from behind him. As he struggled from her grip, she held him as a shield. The man took the hit instead of her and fell to the ground.

More came at me. I slammed a man against the wall when he yanked a fistful of my hair. His whole face smashed into the plaster, making an imprint before he collapsed. Whirling, I stunned the one to my right. As I held on to him, I threw my legs in the air and kicked another guard on his chest. He flew on top of the glass coffee table, shattering it into pieces. I flinched away from the flying shards. My chest heaving, I assessed the damage.

I didn't know what made me freak out the most: seeing all the bloody bodies on the floor, or Mr. San scared out of his mind and urinating. Mr. San stood in the corner with two bodyguards pointing guns at us. He had told his guards not to shoot.

Why?

"What do you want?" San's beseeching eyes bounced to all of us. "I have money. I can give you lots of it."

Russ held a Taser on them as I cautiously closed the gap.

"Stay where you are or I'll shoot," one brave guard said.

"Not if I shoot first." Russ took out both guards with his Taser in rapid succession, his aim impeccable, leaving Mr. San standing there with his hands in the air, surrendering.

"I'll give you whatever you want … Please."

Mr. San's plea softened my heart only for a tiny fraction when Lydia's voice entered my mine. *Don't listen to the sound of their voices. It will only confuse you. Don't look at their faces. Don't make eye contact. You are there to do your job. You are an assassin.*

A gunshot exploded through the quiet. My heart leaped to my throat as my eyes darted from each member of my team. I even patted my chest. But it was Mr. San who dropped to the floor. One bullet to his head.

Russ gripped the front of Mitch's dress shirt, his eyes fuming with rage. "Why did you do that? We were supposed to bring him in."

Mitch shoved Russ off like he was a nuisance and straightened his collar. "I've been out in the field a lot longer than you. You don't question me."

I stiffened and watched my two superiors as though I had never seen them before. *What if they start punching each other?* Though I would have loved to see Russ kick Mitch's ass.

Mitch pointed to San. "He's not Jonathan San. He's still down there. This one is an imposter. We've been found out. We need to get the hell out of here."

"You better not be playing me." Russ shook San's body and examined him. Mitch did too.

I gasped when Mitch tugged off the imposter's hair and the fake glasses.

Mitch placed the glasses inside his pocket and stood. "We need to go, *now*."

"How did you know?" Russ inspected the wig Mitch had handed him.

"I didn't until I saw his face up close. Then it was obvious. Mr. San's nose is bigger."

"We could've brought him in and questioned him."

"No, he wouldn't have made it. I just saved him from blowing up or having a heart attack. They would use a failsafe like the cyanide capsule on him. These people we're dealing with, they're professionals, too."

Satisfied with his answer, Russ tossed the wig onto the imposter's body. "Good observation. I'll call the sweeper team. They're already in the building."

Blood rushed down to my toes, and acid rose in my throat. Not only was Helix out of my system, I was on the run.

Mitch stretched his neck and rolled his shoulders. "Ladies, don't go out front. Go back through the closet we came from and dress back to your gown. Don't get caught. Stay close to me. I'll lead you to our sub-glider."

CHAPTER TWENTY
KIDNAP

Justine and Brooke left the room with the cart as if nothing had happened. Tamara and Russ went back to their room through the adjoining door, and Mitch joined them to do a quick update to ISAN. With my hands shaking, I held onto my dress and ran to the bathroom.

I fixed my hair to be presentable and slipped on my dress and tried to zip it back up. Unable to finish the rest, I decided to call Tamara when I heard a soft tap on the floor.

"Would you like my assistance? Or you can just stand there so I can stare at you a bit longer."

Startled, I whirled toward the sound of a familiar, seductive voice. Sniper stood by the walk-in closet in a cool, relaxed manner with his hand braced on the door. His hair was slicked back, looking polished and debonair. My heart pummeled, but not in fear.

Was I crazy to be attracted to him? Mesmerized by the black tuxedo forming to his perfect body, I stared at him and wondered if I'd dreamed him up. His presence confirmed I hadn't imagined him above the stairs earlier. Then I wondered if he'd come alone.

"How'd you know I was here?"

Unnerved, I gritted my teeth. He hadn't heeded my warning to stay away. I should scream or plan an escape out of the bathroom, but I couldn't move or think. His presence stirred my curiosity and I wanted answers, especially when the lunatic thought he knew me.

177

"It doesn't concern you," he said.

His nonchalant tone caused me to raise my voice. "The hell it doesn't."

"I'll explain later."

I scoffed. "Are you here to try to kidnap me again?"

I might not have Helix, but I had my heels and months of training backing me up. If there was one thing I was good at, it was bringing a person to their knees. Courage grew inside me and I dropped my dress.

Sniper snapped out of his stupor and his amber eyes grew darker. "Where are my manners? I admire the dress, but I like what you're wearing now so much more." He waggled his eyebrows. "You look absolutely beautiful tonight."

No. Don't say that.

I became breathless when he closed the gap between us. Why was I letting him? When Sniper raised his hand, I flinched. My heart galloped faster when he cupped my face and ran his thumb ever so tenderly along my cheek.

"I wish I could've been your date tonight. We could've danced together. Dancing with me always made you happy."

I closed my eyes for several seconds, hypnotized by his voice, by his touch. I pictured us slow dancing, not because it had happened, but because I desperately wanted the happiness he described.

Then I came to my senses. Leaning into his caress, I pretended to enjoy it, which wasn't hard. Moving slowly, I raised my knee …

He stopped me from kneeing him between his legs. "Good try, but I know you too well."

Sniper whipped me around before I even knew what had happened. Blood rushed to the spots his warm hands touched, and the scent of him spiraled around me. I peered up to see our paired reflection in the mirror. When my eyes met his, I became lost in time and space as I studied him. A second seemed like minutes.

Who are you? What do you want with me?

"Do you want to walk out of here with me willingly or do you want me to carry you out? Either way, you're coming with me." His flirtatious tone had vanished, replaced by something sharper.

"If you think you're going to take me, you're wrong. My team is in the other room. Leave before they come get me. If they find you holding me hostage, they'll kill you. You better hurry. You're running out of time."

"I doubt that'll happen. Besides, I'm not alone." He twitched his lips. "We—"

"We?"

"My team. Look behind you."

The two friends with him last time stepped out of the shadows. The girl wore a shimmering coral gown, and the guy sported a black tuxedo.

"Whoa." The guy raised his hands, blocking his view of me. "When you said you wanted to strip her down, I didn't think you meant literally."

"Shut up, Ozzie. Just do it."

Ozzie approached me. He raised his slightly trembling hands, but backed off. "Reyna, you do it. I can't touch her."

Grumbling, Reyna ran her hands down my body. "She's clean."

"Are you done? Had enough? So, have I."

I kicked my heel upward and caught it with my left hand, then tapped it on the beige granite counter. After I whipped around, I grabbed Sniper and locked my arms around his neck, the plastic blade from my heel sticking close to his throat.

"Well done, Ava. Too bad you won't be awake to celebrate your victory." Sniper didn't struggle or try to break my hold.

Did he plan to kill me?

"What do you mean?" I tightened my grip.

"You were dosed with a sleeping agent when I caressed your face. In the count of five, you'll be in my arms."

"You're lying." My heart leapt to the ceiling. My eyes darted wildly as I tightened my hold around his neck to the point of cutting off his air. "You don't understand. I need to get back. I'm going to have a heart attack. I'm going to die. They're going to trigger my chip. Are you not hearing me?"

"Three ... two ... one."

When nothing happened, their stunned faces almost made me laugh, and I loosened my grip. In my desperation, I had rambled things that shouldn't make sense to them, and I felt as if I had told them ISAN's secrets. My team's faces flashed in my mind—Brooke, Tamara, and Justine.

I'm a coward and an idiot. Think. Think. Do something. Now is your chance to escape.

But I couldn't move. A part of me wanted to be taken, to see where they would take me, perhaps a place better than ISAN.

"It didn't work." Sniper cursed under his breath.

It was my chance to yell for help, but my tongue twisted in knots. I also found myself amused by their blunder.

"You're supposed to start from sixty. It takes sixty seconds once it's applied. But you're not supposed to count out loud." Ozzie rolled his eyes. "It's not my fault you didn't listen and made a fool out of yourself."

"Sixty? What the freakin' hell, Ozzie?" He roared and then shifted his attention to me. "So, Ava." Sniper cleared his throat, rubbing the back of his head. "It seems like I miscalculated the time. You should be seeing the room spin by now. Don't worry. I'll catch you. I always do."

I had made a terrible mistake by keeping quiet. Now, I was good as dead. Before I could part my lips, the room spun. My muscles slacked, my body swayed, and three blurry Snipers wavered. Then I felt a sting on my forearm, where my chip was lodged.

"I know the drill. That will deactivate the chip and the capsule. Though I highly doubt they would risk it with you. You're too valuable to them."

Ozzie's words dragged out, and it sounded like a long, jumbled sound. An arm supported my back, and I knew I wouldn't drop to the floor. Sniper's arms? I fought so hard to stay awake, but darkness came swiftly and Sniper's words chanted in my head.

Don't worry. I'll catch you. I always do.

"I got you. Whatever it takes," was the last thing I heard before sleep beckoned.

* * *

I blinked my eyes open to a white ceiling. As I relaxed my muscles, a sense of serenity filled me. That only lasted for a second before I realized I should be looking at an energy-saving light panel turned on by my command. My memories of the night before crept in.

Oh God, how long had it been? I should have been dead from the cyanide. Why was I not dead? *What do I do now?* My training hadn't covered getting captured.

Breathe. Don't move. Stay calm. I wiggled my toes, ensuring I had use of my muscles, when something clicked. Shoes squeaked on the floor. I closed my eyes again and kept my breathing even.

"How long does it last?" Sniper asked.

"It should be out of her system by now, unless you did something I told you not to do, like apply double the amount." Ozzie sounded aggravated.

I heard clicks with a rhythm like typing, but TABs didn't make any sound when fingers touched the screen in mid-air.

I heard more clicks, but on the floor. Someone paced across. "Why don't you get something to eat?" Reyna's voice.

The sound of the chair rolling made me twitch. "I'll sit," Sniper said, his voice a lot closer than before. "Ozzie, go with Reyna and get something to eat. I'll wait here."

"You sure? Ava's different. She's stronger."

"She's knocked out. She can't hurt me. I'll be fine."

"Okay. I'll bring you something to eat, then."

The tilt of the mattress indicated Sniper had sat. I gasped inwardly when I felt the heat from his closeness while he caressed strands of hair away from my face. Releasing soft moans, I pretended to have a nightmare as an excuse to kick off the light blanket covering me.

"Ava." Sniper shook me lightly.

When I stopped moving, he did the same. Then I slowly opened my eyes. His features expressed sadness and happiness at the same time. Something about him made me pity him. He must be out of his mind to think he knew me. As a moment of silence stretched between us when I locked my eyes with his, I wondered, *why me.*

The sound of footsteps drove me into panic mode. I had to do it or I might never have the chance again. Sniper's pensive stare— as if he was reaching into my soul or drawing up memories—gave me an advantage. Poor guy. It was going to suck for him when he finally realized he had made a huge mistake. He'd made another huge error by telling his friends he would be fine.

I jerked my butt up and pushed against the mattress with one foot to throw him off balance. Then I swung one leg over, and locked him between my knees. At the same time, I used my hands to trap his arms straight up from behind him, as his butt found the ground. His friends came back just in time to see it happen.

"Don't take another step or I'll snap his neck."

Ozzie held out one hand, placing the tray on the counter with the other. The savory aroma drove me insane, and I wondered what they were serving. Missing dinner last night, possibly breakfast and lunch too, my stomach growled.

"Ava, you don't want to do that." Ozzie's forehead creased with pained expression. "We're not the bad guys here, okay? We could've tied you up, but we didn't. See this plate? I brought back something for you to eat. I know you're hungry. See?" He lowered the tray. "Ground beef, mashed potatoes, and corn. It's canned corn. Actually, most of the stuff is canned, but you get the point."

"You can relax," Sniper said coolly, no worry in his voice.

If he was talking to his friends, he was crazy. I had him locked good and tight.

"Ava isn't going to kill me. She thinks I'm hot."

Prick.

He grunted when I squeezed my thighs tighter.

"What is it with guys and their egos? Rhett, you can be so arrogant. You deserve whatever is coming to you." Reyna placed her tray down and picked up corn with her fingers, eating one kernel at a time.

"Rhett?" I squealed. "Your name is Rhett, not Sniper? You lied to me?" I squeezed tighter until his face reddened.

"No, I didn't." His voice came out as a horse whisper. "I can explain. Let me go or I'll have to hurt you."

Ozzie stuck out his hands, as if to stop whatever he thought would happen. "Wait, wait, wait. You like each other, remember? No violence. What the hell's going on?"

"Sit down and eat, Ozzie." Reyna giggled. "This is entertaining. We get dinner and a comedy show."

I scowled. *Bitch. You're next.*

"Last warning," Sniper or Rhett, whoever he was, said, even though there was no escape for him. "You might have forgotten, but you don't have Helix in your system anymore."

How did he know about Helix? Oh God, had I rambled and disclosed information while I had been sedated?

"I dare you to try," I said.

In a blink, I landed flat on my butt on the floor in front of Rhett. Pain shot up to my head. That freakin' hurt! I let the sting run its course. Rhett had somehow placed his hands behind my neck when he lunged back to me, and then flipped me over. Luckily, he was nice enough to break my fall, or it would've been a lot worse.

Wait—*nice enough*? Pompous ass.

When he gave me his hand, I refused to take it. I crawled up to the mattress and laid back down. He wore an apologetic frown, but I didn't care. He *should* feel bad for a lot of things he'd done to me.

"Let me go." I rubbed at my legs still throbbing. "They'll be searching for me, and when they find me—and they will—you'll all be dead."

"We know." Reyna shoved ground beef into her mouth. "I mean the part about them trying to find you. But the thing is, they can't. Our hideout is not on any radar. They don't even know this place exists. It was a secret military base the president of the United States and his staff used during the natural disasters, and no one who knew about it is still alive."

I didn't know what to say. I didn't know if anything she said was remotely true.

Rhett's jaw clenched, and his nose flared. "Ozzie, stay here with Ava. Maybe she'll eat when I'm gone. Reyna, come with me."

Reyna got up, picked up her tray, and followed Rhett. When the door closed behind him, my muscles relaxed, and hunger pangs took over my stubbornness.

CHAPTER TWENTY-ONE
ESCAPE

"I'm not like Rhett. Come here and eat with me." Ozzie tapped the table, his tone softer than Rhett's stomping out the door.

Ozzie reminded me of Russ, the sweet, caring type, especially his friendly and welcoming smile. A big, teddy-bear-with-a-good-heart kind of guy. His gentle voice pegged him as someone I could maybe take advantage of.

Ozzie's deep blue eyes put me at ease. That was the first thing I'd noticed when I'd first seen him, and they appeared even bluer up close.

"Sorry. We don't have utensils. We make do with whatever we have and whatever we can get our hands on."

"Thanks."

I tried to smile, but only curled my lips a little. Though my stomach had raged minutes before, the hunger pangs had vanished, so I took my time eating. Thanks to Diana's finishing class, I didn't want to look or act like a savage.

"How long have you been here?" I asked. I scooped mashed potatoes with two fingers and dropped them in my mouth.

"Roughly six months," Ozzie said, then his eyes grew wide like he'd slipped up.

"Do you think I'm your friend, too? I mean, Rhett thinks we're friends."

Ozzie sipped water from a topless can. When I stared at it, he said, "We don't have cups. We use this instead. But to answer your question, we can't really be friends if you can't remember. How can we talk about anything if we don't even know what to talk about? You can't tell me anything, because what you believe to be true is not, and even if I tried to convince you, you wouldn't believe me."

"You're wrong." I chewed some corn and cringed. "You can't erase memories."

Ozzie shifted his body from the chair and glared at me incredulously. "Think about how much technology has advanced in the last fifty years, thanks to the meteors. We have gliders to take us where we want to go by our voice command or simply by punching in the address. Bank access, our address, medical records, every detail of us are stored in our chip. The doors to our homes open by our handprints. Kids all over the world are taught by specialized grade level teachers on their TABS at home. If we can do all this, what makes you think our technology isn't advanced enough to do anything else?"

I took a sip and twitched, then wiped my lips with my hand. "I guess you have a point there." My hand came away with blood on it.

Ozzie wiped his finger on his pants, reached out to me, but then changed his mind. His sweet gesture softened my anger.

"Are you okay? You're bleeding. Sorry. I should've warned you about the cans. Some can be sharp around the edges."

I sucked the blood from my lips and welcomed the sting. "I'm fine. This is nothing compared to the stunt Rhett pulled on me."

Ozzie gave me a warm smile and leaned back in his chair. "He's not so bad. He wasn't always like this."

"Oh, so he wasn't cocky before? I doubt that."

"No, he's still arrogant, but he kind of lost his way when ..." Ozzie pressed his lips into a thin line and craned his neck sideways. "Anyway, he can tell you himself. I don't think he would like for me to say anything more."

"What time is it?" I rose from my chair.

Ozzie sat taller, eyes wide, and ready to bolt, already half out of his seat.

"Thanks for dinner. I'm used to better, but it wasn't too bad."

"Wait." Ozzie shot up. "Where're you going?"

"Obviously I can't go out, so I'm snooping. I also need to use the restroom." I headed to the glass cabinet and stopped when I saw my reflection. "Who dressed me?"

I hadn't noticed the puffy black pants and long-sleeved, blue flannel shirt earlier. Rhett always left me so confused whenever he was around. He made me forget to notice I wasn't in my own clothes.

"Reyna did. It's more like she put another layer on you. It can get chilly around here."

I shifted my legs, the leggings underneath rubbing against my skin with the movement.

"What are these?" I opened the cabinet and saw a multitude of small bottles filled with clear liquid.

"Medicine."

"Medicine? Why would you need …?" I realized the answer before I finished.

I moved to the steel table in the center. On top sat a bunch of equipment. I recognized a burner and test tubes but didn't know what the rest were.

"Don't touch that, please." Ozzie shoved my hand away.

I spotted a wooden desk in the corner and sauntered there. I had never seen an old desk like that before, except on the net. Mr. Thorpe had had one, but his seemed brand new. Too bad he couldn't enjoy it anymore. I ran my hand over the fine texture.

"How many of you are there?" I pulled the drawer, but it wouldn't budge. "Do you have the key?"

"Why?" Ozzie backed away.

Was he scared of me? Surely, he could take me on. His muscles were just as defined as Rhett's, and without Helix, a regular guy could still overpower me.

I advanced toward him, forcing him back until he hit the wall. "So, I can open it and see what's inside. If it's locked, then something important must be inside."

"It's not my desk." He raised his hands as if to defend himself.

"Whose is it?"

His shoulders tensed. "Rhett's. He'll get upset if I let you see what's inside it."

I planted my hands on either side of him against the wall and peered up through narrowed eyes. "Are you scared of me, Ozzie?"

He shook his head feverishly. "Nope. I don't want to hurt you."

I snickered. "Why would you hurt me?"

He didn't answer my question and lightly tapped my shoulders gently. "Ava, please sit down. They'll be here very soon."

I glanced around the room to find anything I could use as a weapon.

"You can't escape from this room," he said, as if he could read my mind. "We have monitors all over this place. Not because we don't trust each other, but because we need to keep an eye out for attackers."

"I thought it couldn't be found?"

When I wrung a strand of my hair back, Ozzie flinched and flattened against the wall.

"We're cautious. We have to be."

I paced aimlessly, checking out any other exit beside the front. "How big is your hideout?"

"You can find out later. I'm not answering any more questions. You're not supposed to even be standing."

I hiked up my eyebrows. "Says who? Rhett? He can go to hell.

I'm getting out of here and you're going to help me."

"I can't help you get out, but if you did, you'd get captured again."

I sighed and rested my hands on a metal table. "Fine. I'll escape on my own."

Ozzie's cheeks puffed out into a ball. Apparently annoyed, he raised his tone. "Have you heard anything I said?"

"I did, Ozzie."

I unbuttoned my shirt. It had worked on Mitch. Come to think of it, it would work on most men.

Ozzie waved a hand at me. "Whoa ... what're you doing? I know you can't remember, but you love Rhett and he loves you, so don't do anything foolish. He'll come in here and get mad at me. Stay back."

He pushed me away, that time using more strength.

I could've resisted being shoved, but I froze at his words. I loved Rhett? He loved me? *Liar.* I'd never loved anyone in my life except for my mom. Brushing off the attempt to distract me, I continued. My shirt slipped off my shoulders and I tossed it on the floor.

"Sorry, I was a bit hot, but now I'm cold. Can you pick that up for me?" I fluttered my eyelashes and gave him my most impressive angelic smile.

Ozzie didn't move a muscle. His jaw dropped, and he darted his eyes everywhere but at me.

"You don't want Rhett to come in and see me like this, do ya? I'll tell him you tried to take off my clothes."

Good one, Ava, but what a bitch.

I wished I could've framed his shocked expression. Epic. I couldn't wait to tell Brooke as soon as I got out of there.

"You're not the same sweet Ava. What happened to you?"

His askance expression caused me to pause, and I found myself asking the same question. No. Ozzie didn't know me. How dare he fib and try to confuse me. I had planned to go easy on him, but now he was going to pay for his trickery.

With one eye on the shirt and one eye on me, he bent down.

"Sorry, Ozzie. I don't recall being sweet. You've kidnapped the wrong Ava." I delivered a roundhouse kick to his face and punched him between the legs.

Poor Ozzie couldn't say a word. With his lips pressed tight, he grabbed himself and dropped to the ground. His face turned red and his mouth opened but only a wheezing sound came out.

I picked up the shirt and slipped it on, not bothering with the buttons. Recalling the two types of shots I had seen inside the cabinet, I took out the one with the syringe and held it like a weapon with the needle pointing down.

Bending low, I gave him a rub on the shoulder. "Sorry, Oz. Thanks for all your help. This was your own fault. Next time, grow some balls and don't let a girl sweet talk you into anything."

I rushed to the door, not knowing how many people would be on the other side. Hopefully everyone else had gathered at the dining hall and were eating. I pushed the button to open the door and waited anxiously as my heart thumped out of control.

I had no plan, but a faint map of the place materialized in my mind. How could that happen without Helix? If I did escape, how would I get back home? Something else was missing. I wiggled my toes and realized I only had socks on.

None of my planning mattered. When the door slid open, Rhett stood as if he knew I would be there. His eyes roamed intensely over my body, causing me to blush, and then landed on my hand with the syringe.

Crap.

Wearing an irresistibly sexy smirk, he planted his hands on either side of the doorway, muscles flexing, blocking me.

"Going somewhere?"

CHAPTER TWENTY-TWO
EXPLORING

I wanted to wipe Rhett's expression off his face with a spiky sponge because I found myself utterly attracted to my kidnapper. It was twisted and sick. I needed therapy, and tons of it. With a heavy sigh, I backed away.

"Not anymore," I murmured under my breath.

When the door closed, Rhett double tapped the button, punched a few keys, and bent down to Ozzie.

"She got you good, bro." He got up and went to the cabinet. "Don't even try it again, Ava. I've set the door so it can only be unlocked with a code. Now, please put the syringe back."

I grumbled and placed the syringe inside the cabinet.

Rhett shot Ozzie's thigh with medication. Within seconds, Ozzie stopped moaning, straightened his legs, and released a long sigh of relief.

"You let her give you a roundhouse kick and a nutcracker?" Rhett chuckled and got down on his knees.

For a split second, his attention and care softened my heart.

"Take my hand." He helped Ozzie up to the mattress.

"How did you know that's what I did to him?" I tucked a pillow under Ozzie's head.

Though Ozzie didn't say a word, his glare said plenty. He had every right to be pissed off, and I hung my head. I wanted to do what I could to apologize without actually saying it. Then I rethought it. I was the one who had every right to be angry. They had kidnapped me.

"Because." Rhett turned to me. "One side of his cheek is red, and I taught you that move."

I scoffed. *Liar.*

Rhett went to the other side of the bed and opened a drawer. "Here." He tossed me a pair of old blue tennis shoes. "Put those on and button up your shirt."

"Why?"

"If you're desperate enough to hurt my friend just to see outside this room, I'll show you around now."

"Fine." I gave him the same harsh tone back. I closed the last button, unhooked the corset and tossed it on the bed, and I wiggled my feet inside the shoes. "Who do these belong to? They fit perfectly."

"You wouldn't believe me if I told you." Rhett tapped the keys on the panel and the door slid open. "After you." He gestured like a gentleman.

I looked over my shoulder at Ozzie before I took a step out, shame swarming in my gut for hurting him. Ozzie had been nice to me. I was an assassin, but that didn't mean I didn't have a heart. On the other hand, had I hurt Rhett, I wouldn't have felt guilty whatsoever.

Being alone with Rhett didn't seem like a good idea, but from his and his friends' actions, they didn't want to hurt me. They could've tied me up or locked me in a prison, but they hadn't.

I met Rhett's stride. "I'm surprised you have manners."

"You haven't seen anything yet." After taking several steps, he halted. "By the way, I taught you a lot of your techniques. If you want me to prove it, I can. I'll block every move you make against me."

"I'll pass."

I continued into a large, circular, empty space, dimly lit. No sun. I sighed with disappointment. The layers of floors reached so high, I had to tilt back my head.

"I know what you're thinking." He pointed to the ceiling. "That's not the exit, so don't think about it. You'll end up hurting yourself. Would you like to continue?"

Rhett snapped me out of my observations. "Okay."

I followed him and frowned. The dark gray smooth tiles reminded me of the gray walls in ISAN. Moments later, we entered a large cafeteria.

"Is this where you eat?"

Rows of tables filled the space.

"Yes. We also hold meetings here."

"Where do you get your food?"

"Let me show you."

Rhett took me to another door in the same room. It opened up to a massive pantry, more like a storage room. Canned foods—beans, corn, chili, various cocktail fruits, condensed soup, and dry powder boxes—lined the shelves. Off to the right, a refrigerator hummed steadily.

"Where did you get all this?" I made a complete turnaround.

"Once a month, we go hunting."

I strode down the shelves, reading the labels. When I sensed Rhett watching me, I stared right back at him, just as intense. Rhett cleared his throat and slid his hand down the back of his head. I had made him uncomfortable, too.

"Let's move on. Time to close up." He shut the door.

I followed behind him. "Hunting? You mean you steal."

"It's called surviving, not stealing, but you're going to judge me anyway. Your word, not mine. We also have our own organic garden for fresh fruits and vegetables."

"Really?"

"I'll show you in daylight. It's too dark now. You won't be able to see a thing. I'll take you to one more room, and then show you the rest tomorrow."

I followed, admiring the structure of the building. It felt more like home than ISAN. Perhaps the dimly lit halls and gray walls at ISAN created more of a mental institute environment. But the secret lair—at least this part of the structure—seemed as though it had been built around Mother Nature. The rocky mountain-like walls jutted over the uneven floor and the scent of soil created a sense of freedom.

I skidded down a corridor and followed the narrow tunnel. "Where are we going?" My shoulders tensed and my pulse sped up. I imagined all sorts of ways he could take advantage of me and then kill me.

I collided into Rhett's chest, not knowing he had stopped. I'd been watching my steps on the uneven rocky ground so I wouldn't make a fool out of myself and fall. When I realized my hands were pressed to his chest, I stilled. His eyes glistened heatedly under the hanging lights above. His hot breath tickled my forehead and then moved over my lips as he bent to reach for something. I worried what to do if he tried to kiss me, because his eyes never left mine.

Dammit. I couldn't believe I had that thought.

"We're here." He cleared his throat.

The creaking door freed me from his spell. For a few heartbeats, I was Ava, a girl walking with a guy she had a crush on, and not Ava the kidnapped. Why was my life so messed up?

When Rhett switched on the lights, I couldn't believe my eyes. I stood still, taking in my view from one end to the other, wondering if it was a mirage. Shelf after shelf, books were lined neatly to the ceiling. Every part of me tingled with happiness. I wanted to explore inside and live there. It took every ounce of control to keep from hugging Rhett. I became greedy with the need to hold as many books as I could all at once. I wanted to touch the covers, rub my face on the pages, and take a long whiff of their papery smell.

Rhett's smile reached his ears as he observed me. "When we found this room, it was a bit dusty. We cleaned it up and made it presentable, accessible for everyone. I never would've imagined a room filled with books, especially at a place like this. Anyway, I knew you would love it here. You used to talk about how you would love to hold a real book. Now I can make one of your dreams come true."

Tears pooled in my eyes. Not wanting Rhett to see, I turned away, knowing he would watch every move I made. Books were my escape from reality. They took me to places beyond my imagination, and some of the characters became family. Books gave me peace, sanity, and hope. To be able to actually hold a story in my hand, my heart burst with euphoria.

"You can take one back to your room. We have someone in charge of this place, but I'll let him know I let you borrow one. I'll tell him to put it under my name."

With a nod and the hint of a smile, I ran my finger along the bindings. He'd made one of my dreams come true, but it didn't mean I trusted him. It didn't mean he had won me over. Telling me he knew how much I loved books was dumb luck. I would guess one out of every three people felt the same way, if not more.

I pulled one out and slowly opened it as if it was a treasure. The pages were crinkled, and some parts were damaged by water. As I ran my hand across the words, I took in the scent without making it obvious. I didn't want to show Rhett how much I enjoyed the moment. I thought about thanking him, but my thought didn't carry to action.

"I'll take this one." I closed the book and showed it to him.

"*Gone with the Wind.* I've heard about this book."

I wrapped my arms around the book and held it securely. "I've never read it, but I know it will be good."

Rhett twisted the ends of his lips. "I heard the protagonist falls in love with a man named Rhett, and I'm not making this up."

I gave him a pointed look. "Too bad that's not going to happen in real life."

Rhett gave me a defeated soft chuckle. "Would you like to take another one?"

Sudden exhaustion made my muscles weak. I shook my head and hugged the book tighter.

"Maybe tomorrow."

"Sure," Rhett said. "I'll take us back."

"I need to wash up and use the restroom."

Rhett leaned into me. I jerked back.

He raised both hands. "I'm not going to hurt you. Trust me."

I frowned. "You want me to trust you?" I scoffed. "You kidnapped me."

"Hold still." A command.

He leaned into me and brushed his face against my hair. Was he sniffing me? I stiffened and held my breath. Why was I letting him? But his words—*hold still*—sounded all too familiar.

Silence held us in place until he pulled back.

"Washing for sure. You're limited to a two-minute warm shower. Don't try to turn to hot. It doesn't work, and as for the restroom, prepare yourself. It's not the kind you're used to."

I frowned. How bad could it be?

* * *

"How was the shower?" Rhett asked.

"Fine."

I meandered behind the counter, staying far away from him as possible.

His lips twitched and his eyes beamed in humor. "How was

the restroom?"

I crossed my arms and blew out a breath. "I had to squat and plug my nose, but hey, it's better than doing my business by the bushes."

Not by much—I'd pissed into an underground hole. Did they not have a sewage system? If they had built the place for the past president, I figured it would be somewhat comfortable. Maybe he had a real toilet in his corridor.

"This is where you'll sleep for now." Rhett opened a top cabinet to pull out a beige blanket and an oversized shirt.

"Where's Ozzie?" I glanced around, trying not to watch Rhett's every move.

"He went to his room." He placed the things on the bed and headed back to the cabinet.

"Then whose room is this?"

"Mine." He twisted at his waist, regarding me. "Don't worry, I won't be staying."

Rhett crossed his arms in front and tugged off his shirt. He opened the middle cabinet and took out a new one. I should have turned away, but I couldn't. Not only was I gawking at his ripped chest, but I also stared at a scar under his rib cage and another one on his arm that looked fresh. Must have been when the bodyguard had shot him when he'd first tried to kidnap me. Then I spotted a tattoo above the rise of his hipbone. Four jagged points, softened by a lace work design. Though I couldn't identify the design, there was no denying its beauty.

"Like what you see?" He pulled down his shirt. "You've seen them many times."

I flashed my eyes away, heat burning my face. "I … I didn't see anything."

"I meant the scars." He smirked, brushing his hair back with his fingers. "Everyone has scars, Ava, physically and mentally. I know where yours are unless you got more in the past six months."

I gasped when he stood in front of me. "How could you? You're lying." I blanched, afraid to meet his eyes, and also afraid he would prove me wrong.

"I'll prove it."

My heart skipped a beat when Rhett wrapped his arms around me. Starting at my neck, his finger gingerly traveled down my spine ever so slowly. I should push him away, but like many times before, I couldn't. His touch, hypnotic and soothing, sent pleasurable shivers everywhere. When he tugged the back of my shirt, I hitched a breath.

"You have one right there." His finger traced my skin at the lower end of my back, slightly angling down.

"Lucky guess." I sucked in a breath.

"You got that scar when I got this one." He lifted his shirt and guided my finger down the scar under his rib cage.

My traitorous trembling hand lingered and I dropped it when Rhett noticed.

With a smug grin, he grabbed my hips. Spreading his strong fingers, he moved up under my shirt. Heat blazed through me. *Oh God. Please stop.* I closed my eyes for a second to stop my heart from hammering out of control. He'd better not touch me there. I was going to slap him hard.

Or maybe I would let him.

Snap out of it, you lust struck idiot. He's manipulating you.

"This one is small, but just slightly above … here."

His thumb caressed a spot under my left rib, then his other thumb glided on my right side over my faint scar, the one that reminded me of a burst of distorted streaks that may have once resembled a sunrise, as if he knew exactly where it was.

My chest rose and fell in shallow breaths as his hands skimmed my body. His unforgettable eyes, so full of desire and sadness, held me unmoving. He made me want him and I hardly knew him.

I'd never doubted he was the enemy, but what if he'd told me the truth? I didn't want to believe it. It would confirm my life was more messed up than I realized. I didn't know if I could handle any more.

"How the hell did you know?"

He settled his hands back on my hips, keeping me locked in place. "I know everything about you, Ava." His voice confident and bold, I almost believed him.

Maybe he told the truth? He'd touched me like he had touched me many times before, so comfortable, so knowing, and so familiar. If I were a stranger to him, I would assume there would be a little hint of discomfort, but he'd showed none.

"I know your likes and dislikes. We spent a lot of time sneaking around in ISAN."

I drilled my eyes to his with a challenge. "I don't believe you. They wouldn't allow us free time like that."

He shrugged. "Yeah, they had strict rules, but we found a way. If there's a will, there's a way. People are bound to fall in love. It's inevitable."

"Stop it. You're lying." I yanked away, anger swelling. "Don't tell me I liked you."

"I won't." Rhett tugged my elbow, closing the gap between us, his nonchalant tone gone. "I won't tell you how much you liked me, and I won't tell you how much I liked you. 'Cause I'll tell you this, no one in this world loves you as much as I do."

"You … you can't. You don't know me." I shoved him when I could no longer control the rage and something softened inside me. "How dare you manipulate me?" The walls spun and acid coated my throat. Overwhelmed by his words, butterflies slammed inside my gut. "How can you make me feel this way?" I whispered wearily, clutching my stomach.

Rhett stepped away and raked his hair back. "I'm sorry, Ava. Emotions are the one thing you can't forget."

He dragged his feet to the door with his head down.

Before he left, I wanted him to think he didn't get to me. I wanted him to know whatever had happened a few minutes before meant nothing to me.

"They're going to find me." I gritted my teeth. "They're probably on their way now. Maybe you and your friends should consider packing and moving somewhere safe."

Rhett laughed softly, almost sadly. "Like I said before, they won't be able to find this place. Get some rest."

He dimmed the lights and left.

CHAPTER TWENTY-THREE
BREAKFAST

"**I** know a place where we can go," Rhett says, sitting next to me on my bed.

I'm in my room in ISAN. I'm dreaming. "Are you sure? If you're wrong, then it will be the end for all of us."

"It doesn't matter, anyway." *Ozzie plants his hands on my chair.* "If we stay, we're dead. Leaving is our only choice. I'd rather try than go down without a fight."

What's he talking about?

Then they disappear. My mind goes blank. And then I'm sprinting with a gun. Ozzie runs ahead of me.

"Stay close to me," *Rhett bellows.*

Stay close to me. Stay close to me. Stay close to me.

My eyes shot open to the white ceiling, my breath heavy and emotions flustered from the dream.

What time is it? How long had I been sleeping?

I sat up. Fresh clothes and toiletry items lay at the foot of the bed. Someone must have come in early that morning. I picked up the brush and combed my hair, and then changed into dark pants and a light blue sweatshirt. As I wondered when Rhett would come, the door slid open.

"Hi, Ozzie." I smiled.

I needed to get on his good side again, just in case I needed information from him. He growled. Or maybe not? He didn't greet me back.

"I'm here to pick up a few things."

When I approached, he backed away. "Ozzie, I'm not going to hurt you. I'm really sorry about yesterday. This isn't who I am."

Ozzie headed to the medicine cabinet. "I know."

"It's just … I'm so confused. I'm not sure how I'm supposed to act or be around people who think they know me."

"Just be yourself." He took out two small bottles and closed his fingers around them. "You'll figure it out."

"Is Ozzie your real name?"

He cocked an eyebrow, his blue eyes brighter under the light. "Yes. Why would you ask me that?"

"I thought Rhett's name was Sniper."

He closed the cabinet and rotated the silver latch to lock. "It kind of is. Sniper is his nickname. I know you don't remember, but you gave it to him."

"Why?"

"You'll find out soon enough. He'll gladly show you. You actually gave me one, too." He shrugged sheepishly.

"Really? What did I call you?" I inched closer.

Ozzie smiled in a way I hadn't seen before, a warm smile that said *I want to show you.*

"Let me explain." He sat in a chair, and his fingers danced over letters. "I'm very good with technology." He pointed to the screen. "You see that?"

"What is that?"

"It's a server. It connects all the circuits. I can control it from one unit." He swiped his fingers over the screen. "We've managed to post micro cameras around the perimeter, thanks to Rhett's aim, and also ..." He paused, swiftly moving his left hand, then right, in a circular and diagonal motion, like some kind of hand dance. "This is the Leviathan Hotel. And this"—he moved them again—"is the ballroom. Like I said, we have micro cameras. I should go to jail for this."

"You're a genius." I wanted to knock myself on my forehead for praising him. What the hell was I saying?

"No, I'm Einstein."

Had I heard him correctly? My heart thumped in recognition. The word meant something to me. My eyes widened.

He bobbed his head. "That's my nickname. That's what you used to call me. You know, 'cause I'm so brilliant."

Taking a step back, I placed my hand over my chest. "I'm so sorry. I hope I wasn't ... I mean ... did I mistreat you or was I rude to you?"

Ugh! I wanted to take it back. Asking questions meant I believed their stories about me. But, I reminded myself, I needed to be on his good side.

"No. You were cool." He shut down the TAB and shoved his hands in his pockets.

I blinked, surprised by his comment. "How did you know I would be at the hotel?"

Ozzie drummed his fingers on the table. "I can't tell you."

I pressed my lips together, not accepting his answer. I had to probe for more. Then a thought came to mind.

"You're good with technology." I restated what he had said earlier. "You hacked into ISAN's network. You helped Rhett." I emphasized a bit louder, putting pieces together from Ozzie's words. "I know it was you."

Ozzie covered his ears and squeezed his eyes together at the same time, as if my words hurt him, and then a heartbeat later he sat taller with a broad grin. "I'm glad I did. I would do it all again just so we could find you."

It was not the answer I had expected. Something warm, yet painful tugged my heart, so I kept my lips sealed.

The door whooshing broke the comfortable silence. Rhett swaggered in with a hint of a smile, avoiding me. Wearing jeans and a gray sweater, bags under his tired eyes, stubble lining his jaw and hair disheveled, he managed to look messily attractive.

"What's taking you so long?" Rhett asked Ozzie. "You were supposed to bring the bottles and take Ava to breakfast."

Ozzie scratched the back of his head. "Just showing Ava some cool stuff I did."

Rhett took the bottles from Ozzie and shoved them inside his back pocket. "Don't tell her too much." Rhett's impassive eyes turned stone cold. "Breakfast is almost over and everyone will be moving out to do their jobs. Let's go."

"So, bossy."

"Yeah, he can be." Ozzie pushed in his chair.

"Are you two friends now? Ganging up on me?" Rhett's tone became slightly playful. "Someone has to be *bossy*. Nothing will get done around here."

Rhett led the way, and Ozzie and I followed.

"Bossy should've been *his* nickname. Is he always grumpy like this?"

"Only when you're around." Ozzie gave me a huge smile, seemingly more comfortable around me.

I thought I heard a soft chuckle from Rhett.

"Wow, that's so romantic." I mentally slapped myself for warming up to strangers I shouldn't trust. But they made it so easy.

ISAN

* * *

ISAN housed only females, but Rhett's secret bunker seemed to be mostly males. Brooke would have loved it here. She always complained there wasn't enough eye candy in ISAN.

Everyone ogled me as I followed Rhett to a table. Avoiding eye contact in the newly quiet room, I lowered into my seat. A tray sat in front of me—an apple and something oatmeal-like. But trying to elude attention didn't last long. Rhett remained standing.

"Everyone, this is Ava, which you already know," Rhett announced. "You know the history. Be nice and don't bombard her with questions. Enjoy your breakfast."

"Hi, Ava," voices chorused, and normal chatter rose around me.

I didn't say a word. Instead, I hunched lower in my seat, wishing I was invisible.

Rhett slid down next to me, picked the apple off his tray, and took a bite. A smudge of oatmeal lingered on his plate.

"What history?" I asked.

"Nothing that concerns you."

"You always say that." I grumbled and chomped down hard on my apple.

He took another bite and then lifted his eyelashes when Reyna sat on the other side of us.

"How did she sleep?" Reyna asked Rhett.

When Reyna took a sip of her drink, white liquid foamed around her lips. As she wiped her mouth, I wondered what she drank.

"Fine, I guess. I didn't get any complaints."

"Does she remember anything?"

Rhett tilted his head to Ozzie. "Einstein told her a few things.

I think they're friends now. Getting hit in the balls can make you do stupid things."

Ozzie let out a soft growl. "You never told me not to tell her things."

While they talked like I wasn't there, I chewed my apple loudly in annoyance.

Reyna leaned in closer. "We can't trust her, at least not yet. It's too early."

That did it! I banged my hand on the table harder than I meant and winced.

"Hello, I'm right here. *Her* and *she* are listening. Not to be trusted? I'm the one who got kidnapped. I didn't ask to come here. Keep that in mind." I tossed the apple core on the tray. It bounced off my tray and landed inside Rhett's empty cup.

"Nice shot. Are you done eating?" Rhett asked.

Without answering, I got up halfway, but he pushed me down. "Eat." He didn't raise his voice, but it wasn't a request. "You're going to need the energy. We're going hunting today."

"How am I supposed to eat this mush? You didn't give me any utensils to eat it with." I sounded like a spoiled brat, but he made me angry.

Rhett poured the mush into my empty can. "We're very low on supplies. Utensils are not of utmost importance to us. I'm sure Einstein already told you that." He slid the cup. "We learn ways to eat with or without using our fingers. So drink up."

If hunting—*stealing*— meant my ticket out of there and a way for me to find an escape, I was all for it. I grabbed the can and chugged it down, dulling my hunger.

"Here." Rhett set another can in front of me.

"What's this?" White liquid filled the can.

Rhett gave me a sideways glance. His lips perked into a sexy smirk, and then twitched his brow in a playful way. "Got milk?"

"Milk?" I wrapped my fingers around the can, as if I held something valuable. "How did you get milk? It's been so long. I can't remember when I last had milk."

"It's actually baby's milk," Ozzie said, as if he simply read the ingredient off the box.

Milk squirted out of my mouth like a fountain the second Ozzie spoke. They'd given me breast milk? My relentless coughing wouldn't stop.

Rhett patting my back gave me no pleasure. I wanted to twist his arm and flip him over on the table, but nothing good would come of it except the satisfaction of hurting him. That sounded appealing, but I decided not to do it since I was surrounded by his people. Wiping my mouth with the back of my hand, I wished for something to clean up my mess.

Rhett gave Ozzie an evil eye. "It's not *baby's* milk. It's powdered milk."

"It's basically the same thing. I'll bet it has the same formula. I won't drink it."

"It isn't." Reyna set down her can after taking another sip, but she grimaced.

"I'm the one with a brain around here, remember?" Ozzie smirked. "I know science, chemistry, and formulas. All you know how to do is—"

"Everything else." Rhett rose to his feet. "Let's go, Einstein. We have work to do before we go hunting."

"Where are we going?" I picked up my tray and placed the plate and can in a large plastic bin how Rhett had done.

Ozzie gulped his last bit of mush and wiped his mouth with the back of his hand. "We have a little community here. It will blow your mind."

Reyna swung around to plant her feet on the ground and held out her tray. "At least I don't have to drink that awful protein drink and I don't have to be shot up with Helix and forced to take lives." She dumped the plate and wiped her hands on her pants. "Think about it." Reyna strode out.

I followed behind Rhett. How did she know? How the freakin' hell did she know? The truth was, I had been thinking about it.

A lot.

CHAPTER TWENTY-FOUR
THE COMPOUND

Itook one step outside the dining area and would've fallen if Rhett hadn't steadied me. The guys had swept the floor with an old-fashioned worn mop. It was rare to see a mop, let alone four of them in one place.

"Conserve water guys, please," Rhett said.

The boys gave him a thumbs up and went about their business.

"You have mops? How did you get them?"

I kept my steps even with Rhett's, Ozzie and Reyna lagged behind.

"They were already here. You'll see many things that are no longer manufactured and items from the past."

Reyna pushed a button on the side of the rocky structure. "I'm in charge of agriculture. You're visiting my domain."

I entered an old elevator. Thick wires dangled through the cracks above. I gasped when the elevator rattled and jerked before ascending. Rhett focused his eyes straight ahead at the metal door with his fists tight.

"You'll get used to it," Ozzie said. "It only broke down twice this week. Just don't get trapped inside with Rhett." He snickered softly, his eyes twinkling with amusement.

Rhett twisted his neck, pushed back his shoulders, and let out a small grunt. His sound of annoyance made me want to know more. When the door opened, Rhett released a sigh and the tension in his shoulders eased. Then earthy and citrus scents spiraled through me.

"I see. Claustrophobic," I murmured.

"Welcome to my favorite place." Reyna burst out with her arms held up high and her head tilted back. Soaking in the dim sunlight filtering through the fiberglass ceiling, she sauntered on ahead with Ozzie.

Surrounding the outer layer of the ceiling were solar panels, except for where the crops grew under man-made lights that hung every few feet. Stepping out into a field of green, I marveled at the trees and various fruits I hadn't had the pleasure to eat. The other half of the field held a planted vegetable garden—carrots, potatoes, tomatoes, and cabbages.

"This is amazing." I observed their teamwork. "I'm very impressed."

Though I should be fuming with rage for being taken against my will, I allowed myself to step back and submerge in the curiosity of my new environment.

Don't get attached. I belong to ISAN.

"Don't be too impressed." Rhett peered up to pick an orange from the tree.

Just then the sunlight kissed his hair, highlighting the tips to a shade lighter, and his amber irises glowed, reminding me of a sunrise bursting to a new day. He peeled the orange and handed me half.

"Thanks," I said.

"My favorite." He pinched his lips and drew his eyebrows to the center, as if in concentration.

If I hadn't known better, I assumed he waited for me to say something. Did he hope I would remember oranges were his favorite fruit? When I didn't say anything, his face relaxed.

Rhett bit into a piece. "We didn't build this place. We're only utilizing what was already here. It's amazing how they planned the details of what they needed to survive."

"They were brilliant." I chewed and swallowed, savoring the orange. I hadn't had one in so long. The sweet juice going down my throat felt like heaven. "Water is so expensive. How do you get water?"

"There's a filter pump down in the basement. All the water goes through a pipe that leads to a special pumping system to purify the water."

I parted my lips to put another piece in my mouth, when I stopped to think about the restroom. "Any chance of getting a toilet? Not that I plan to stay here, but squatting down to pee is not my cup of tea."

"I'll make a note of that." Rhett pursed his lips together. His eyes glistened in the light again when he caught mine.

I glanced away when I realized I'd stared too long. Needing to focus on something else, I crossed my arms and shuffled my shoe in the dirt. Juice squirted onto my face and I squeezed my eyes shut. Before I could block Rhett, he reached out to me.

"Sorry." His finger traced my cheek, wiping the juice off my nose and then my lips.

The intimate gesture unsettled me. I kept my eyes closed and enjoyed the warmth of the sun as chills waved through me in the wake of Rhett's touch.

"Are we interrupting?"

I opened my eyes. Three men stood before us.

"No," Rhett said.

The dip in his tone told me otherwise.

"We don't know each other well, but I want to thank you." The first guy extended a hand to me.

"I don't know what I did, but you're welcome." Not knowing what he meant, yet wanting to be polite, I shook his hand with a smile.

"My name is Quinn." He pointed to his friends. "This is Kai and Drew. We work here every day. Will you be training with us?"

"Training?"

"In case we have to go to war with I—"

"Everyone should know how to defend themselves," Rhett said.

Was Quinn going to say ISAN? I would have to ask him when I got the chance.

"Anyway … we watch old movies after dinner. Would you like to come?"

Before I answered, I glanced at Rhett, seeking permission because he was my jailer. His lips pressed into a thin line, and his eyes narrowed. Was he jealous?

"That's nice of you, but Ava will be busy."

"Sure. You can hang out with us some other time when you're free." Quinn backed away with his friends. "You too, Rhett. We gotta go back to our station. Bye."

"He's cute." I watched them run across the field.

Rhett hiked an eyebrow. "Who's cute?"

He stood with his feet apart and arms crossed, reminding me of Mitch.

"Who I think is cute is none of your business." I pierced my eyes into his.

He didn't reply. Instead, he rested his hand on my back. "Let me show you something."

Rhett and I took the elevator down and stopped at floor level X. The sound of soft moving water caught my attention. When I got off the elevator, cool mist drizzled and tickled my face.

Trekking down the pebbled path, I trailed my hand over the rocky surface to keep steady. Even the walls felt cool and dewy to the touch. The trail ended, and a stream prevented us from going farther.

"This is where we do our laundry."

The water seemed to be about three feet deep. Rhett's friends washed clothes and laid them on a boulder to dry. The boys hung some on the bridge netted with rope, connecting one side to the other.

"The old-fashioned way? Unbelievable." I shook my head because I couldn't believe my eyes. I almost laughed.

"The old-fashioned way."

"Hi, Rhett. Hi, Ava."

A few of the boys waved from across the bridge.

I waved back to be nice, but they said my name as if we were friends. It only added to the strangeness of everything I felt, happening over and over again. I clenched my teeth from the frustration of being unable to remember. Rhett certainly couldn't have convinced everyone to pretend to know me. But even still, I didn't want to believe he told me the truth.

Rhett shuffled small rocks out of the path. "I'm giving Ava a tour."

"She can help us with the laundry if she wants," one said, holding up a wet shirt.

"We can teach her," the second guy with dark hair chimed in. "Then we can go for a swim."

"Trying to get out of doing your job?" Rhett hopped onto a boulder.

"We're always trying to get out of our duty, Rhett." The third guy wrung the shirt he pulled out of the water. "We're lazy. Don't be surprised if we can't get the stain out of your favorite shirt next time. We're thinking if we do a crappy job, you might reassign us."

Rhett let out a boisterous laugh. "Okay, guys. Let me see what I can do."

"Thanks, Rhett," they said in unison and continued what they were doing.

Rhett jumped off and rubbed the back of his neck. "Where was I? Oh, yeah. Once they get dried, it all goes to one room. We all share. There's no mine or yours. It all gets recycled. However, they do keep in mind my favorite shirts. And some people fight for things that fit better. They'll even trade for something in return, like taking a shift in vegetation or cooking."

"That explains why the clothes feel so rough." I thought about the softness of the clothes from ISAN. "What do you wash the clothes with? I didn't see soap scum."

"We don't believe soap is a top priority."

"You mean you can't find any to steal."

Rhett's lips parted in a light chuckle. "I'll never admit that."

"It's okay, I understand." I shrugged, and took a few steps to hike back up, passing him. "You've gotta do what you gotta do. Whatever it takes, right?"

I halted and planted a hand on the rock jetting out from the wall. Why did those words haunt me as if they were a physical being, someone I should remember?

When Rhett didn't respond and I heard no footsteps, I gazed over my shoulder. His eyes darted in my direction, but he didn't acknowledge me.

"Did I say something to offend you?" I broke his daze. Not that I cared.

"No," he said softly. "You just said, 'whatever it takes.'" Rhett passed me, shaking his head. "We need to get going."

CHAPTER TWENTY-FIVE
HUNTING

"How did you get a glider?" Through the dark tinted window, I saw nothing but the ocean. "Wait. I'll answer for you. It's none of my concern."

"If I could get paid for the number of questions you've asked, I'd be rich." Reyna batted her eyelashes, half mocking and half teasing.

I caught her reflection through the tinted window and scowled. *Bitch.* I wanted to bite back, but I didn't want to twist around in my seat. Sitting in the front was a disadvantage when it came to giving the evil eye.

"That's enough, Reyna."

Surprisingly, Rhett took my side.

"You don't treat your best friend like shit no matter how angry you are at her."

"Best friend?" Baffled, I frowned at the thought.

She didn't show any sign of caring at all. And if this was all a setup, she sucked at acting. I had no memories of us sharing laughter, or stories, or even a sisterly bond. Rhett said we could lose memories, but not our emotions. Brooke was the only friend that felt like a sister to me. I missed her.

Why was ISAN taking so freakin' long to find me?

"Leave Ava alone," Ozzie said.

I hid my smile. My attempt to manipulate Ozzie to be on my side seemed successful so far.

Reyna mumbled something under her breath.

Tense silence filled the space inside the glider. I stole a few glances at Rhett. His hands moved about the control panel, checking the pressure, checking the distance. The steering looked simple enough, but the knobs and flashing colored lights confused me.

I thought about knocking everyone out and flying the glider back to ISAN myself; however, I'd never flown one before, and I had no idea where ISAN was located, so I scratched my escape idea.

At times Rhett glanced my way, and occasionally, my eyes would meet his. Then he pretended to check the screen. In every glider I'd seen, once you input your destination, you could take a nap. So why the fidgeting?

Rhett parked the glider inside an abandoned building. I'd heard about abandoned cities, never knowing if they were real. I wondered if this was one. My stomach fluttered excitedly at the possibility.

"Where are we?" I climbed out of the glider.

The cool, dank building had me shivering.

A large chunk of the building had been torn off, and the asphalt streets had been lifted and tossed about in twisted sections. Weeds as tall as me grew throughout where once trees and bushes rooted. Debris—plaster, street lamps, street signs, glass, metal, tires, and car parts—scattered everywhere and seemed impossible to pass. No animal life inhabited it as far as I could tell. Even the air smelled stale and dead.

Rhett hesitantly handed me a Taser and then a jacket. "Just in case. Make sure not to point it at us." He emphasized the word *us*. "We're in the restricted area and might run into drifters or the council's security. You should put the jacket on. It gets cold."

"What are drifters?" I shoved the Taser in the back of my pants and put the jacket on, silently thanking him for it. In ISAN, I never had to wear one in the perfect temperature setting.

When Rhett swung a backpack over his shoulder, I locked my eyes on the hole in the side of his backpack. A bullet hole? I didn't bother to ask.

"Drifters choose to be here." Rhett adjusted his backpack strap and tapped about his waist for his weapons, ensuring they were secure. "They don't want to have anything to do with the society. They prefer to live alongside Mother Nature."

"What happens when you run into them?" I stepped over upturned cement and almost lost my balance when my foot caught in a crack.

"They'll try to steal your things," Ozzie said.

Reyna hadn't spoken a word since Rhett had called her my best friend. She took long strides to Rhett. Their voices sounded muffled, but I had a hunch they were talking about me.

My focus went back to Ozzie. "They do?"

"Don't worry. We have Tasers. The first time we were here, they were all over us until we stunned one of them. They don't bother us anymore. They're mostly men, but a few are women."

"What do they look like?"

"Like zombies." Ozzie snorted.

"Really?"

"Yes, really. They have dark circles under their eyes and sallow, ashen skin, like they're malnourished. Or dead. They smell like they haven't washed in months. Does that describe a zombie?"

I nodded.

Then Ozzie's hand on my arm stopped me from bumping into Rhett. My jaw dropped at the antique vehicle in front of us.

"Is this real?" It was the dumbest thing I could've said, but I almost didn't care, the thing was so cool.

"Are you asking if it's a car?" Reyna snickered.

Reyna wasn't as bad as Justine, but I swear if she got on my nerves again I was going to punch her. Ignoring her patronizing tone, I gave her one right back.

"It's actually called a truck."

Rhett tried to hide it, but he lifted an amused grin. Reyna hissed and got in the back with Ozzie.

Opening the door for me, Rhett said, "Get in and put on your seatbelt."

"So bossy."

Rhett closed the door without reacting, and went around to the driver's side. He tangled a couple of wires together. The engine roaring to life gave me goosebumps. I wondered where we were headed. I'd thought we'd go out to the street I'd seen earlier, but instead, we went toward the back of the building.

Driving down an empty narrow street where the sun didn't shine made my stomach recoil in dread. Damaged structures loomed all around us, and polluted air hung over us like a heavy blanket. Steel and cement peeked through weedy undergrowth. Not one building stood untouched.

In history class, I'd seen pictures of the natural disaster aftermath. After the meteors, came hurricanes, floods, famine, and destabilized government. It seemed to me, Mother Nature punished us for abusing our resources.

We drove over what debris the truck could handle but often had to swerve around bigger obstacles, like street lamps, flipped over cars, and large blocks of collapsed buildings. My generation and my parents' were the lucky ones. People of my grandparents' era had experienced a horrendous disaster. Their cities crumbled to nothing around them. Everything they'd worked for their entire existence had been wasted and destroyed. The loss of lives had scarred an entire generation.

Ozzie looked out the window. "The Remnant Councils don't care about this side of the world. Which is a good and bad thing. They could make this a workable city. It's far from the main cities, but I don't see why they couldn't."

Reyna kept her eyes on the road. "It would cost too much to supply clean water, electricity, and rebuild homes."

We drove in silence for several miles. My skin crawled when Rhett parked under a half-collapsed building. I had no choice but to trust him. When he got out of the car, I did the same.

"Where are we?"

"This was their main hospital. This is where we get our medical supplies," Rhett said.

"Don't you have enough?" I brought my Taser to the front. Ozzie's description of drifters as zombies didn't inspire comfort, especially when I'd read about zombies not too long before.

Rhett took a couple of steps up the stairs, opened the door, and stopped. "Every time we go hunting, we get what we can. One day, the councils might decide to tear this city down for good. From the information we've gathered, there's a war coming. This time, it won't be from Mother Nature. It will be our own doing. It's the way we are. Anyone with power will take over what they can. A perfect example is ISAN. How many more secret agencies are out there? They might be called something else, but I'm pretty sure they're out there and organized the same way. We're preparing for the worst."

Rhett sprung up the stairs, his footsteps echoing loudly. He slowed when the stairs became uneven, jumping from one to another, avoiding protruding metal rods.

The higher I climbed, the more my muscles wouldn't cooperate. I dared not look down, or it would be the end of my climbing. As I sneezed, I almost slipped on the dusty cement particles. I bent low and grabbed one of the rods to stop my fall.

"This way. Be careful." Rhett leaped to the tilting stairs, then helped his friends and told them to go on ahead.

"Ava, don't look down."

Too late. I already had when I waited for Ozzie to jump to Rhett. The fact that he'd said, "don't look down" meant I would've done it anyway. My curiosity always won. My heart raced a mile a minute when I ascended higher, until it palpitated out of control.

"Ava. Look at me."

Rhett's stern voice grounded me.

"I'm right here. I won't let you fall. You saw Ozzie and Reyna jump with ease. Not a problem, okay?"

My knees buckled and my muscles locked. I couldn't even get my body to move back down.

"That's easy for you to say. You've done this many times."

"I know you're afraid of heights, but you were getting over it because you trusted me. I won't let you fall."

His words, his tone, his eyes, all told me he spoke the truth. The tension eased from my muscles enough to allow movement. Taking tiny scoots to the edge, I focused on my mental mission.

I am stronger than my fear. I don't need Helix. It's all in my head. I can do this.

Rhett leaned as far as he could, anchoring his leg on a broken piece of structure to his left. "That's it, Ava. Keep your eyes on mine. Come to me, Ava. I've got you."

I took a step back, held my breath, and pushed off as hard as I could. One of my feet landed on solid ground, and Rhett grabbed my arm. When Rhett pulled me up, my stomach dropped from my rib cage, but my heart continued to thunder.

"I knew you could do it. That was nothing," he said when I balanced solidly on both feet.

Then his smirk turned to alarm.

"Rhett!"

He'd slipped on a small pile of debris and started to fall backward after he swung me around. Anchoring my leg as he had, I twisted my hands in his shirt, heaved him forward, and slammed his back against the wall with all my weight pressed against him. My fast thinking and the training from ISAN had saved him, but I had no idea where the strength had come from.

"I believe ... I've got you." I panted, my heart racing. Blood drained to my toes, trembling from the near-fall. My fear had almost cost him his life.

"I believe you have." Rhett's amber eyes darkened and heated, inches from mine.

His warm breath met mine halfway, colliding and exchanging. My fists still wrung his shirt, rising and falling on his chest, in rhythm with my heart drumming. I realized my body pressed against his in an intimate way when his hand idly caressed the small of my back. What was he doing to me?

I stood there in silence. Staring. Searching. Connecting with Rhett. Like I'd done that before. The blazing fire of desire inside me—I felt it before in my dreams.

Emotions are the one thing you can't forget. Rhett's voice rang inside my head. For a moment, I forgot I'd been kidnapped.

"What's taking you two so long?" Ozzie's voice echoed from down the hall, breaking the moment.

Rhett closed his eyes, his face contorting as if in pain, and then opened them to focus on the ruined wall behind me.

As he slowly released his hold on me, seemingly not wanting to let go, he murmured, "You first. Go straight and curve right at the dead end. I'm right behind you. I just need a minute."

CHAPTER TWENTY-SIX
THE JOURNAL

Farther in, the middle of the building was not as heavily weathered but had caved in. The air became cooler and thicker, making it harder to breathe. I entered what I guessed to be a supply room.

From the opened cabinets, Ozzie and Reyna had searched the room while waiting for Rhett and me. Syringes, IV bags, Band-Aids of all sizes, clamps, and other tools for surgery rested on a broken dusty table. Rhett packed supplies into his backpack and so did Ozzie and Reyna. Then, we wound back through the eerie halls.

"How about that one?" I pointed and mentally slapped myself for acting like I was part of their group.

"We already raided that room." Ozzie slowed his steps to hike beside me.

"We need to hurry. This way." Rhett's long strides took us down a slope. "Watch your step. It's slippery here." He bored his eyes to mine, making sure I'd heard.

I nodded and followed behind him as usual. Rhett's eyes were always on me. I felt the weight of his stare, and I didn't know if he thought I would try to escape or he just wanted to protect me. Resting my hand on whatever I could grip, I let my leg muscles do all the work as I skidded down.

"Where're we going?" Reyna sounded annoyed, swinging her backpack over her shoulder. "We went down this way last time. We need to try another route."

"I need Ava to see the files," Rhett said.

Reyna's nostrils flared as she placed a hand on her hip. "It's not going to bring her memories back, Rhett. We need to hurry. The sun's going down."

"We have flashlights." Ozzie reminded her.

Reyna's cold stare silenced Ozzie.

Rhett took a step back. "This has nothing to do with that. She might be able to tell us something. I think reading the files will help her understand."

"Fine." She positioned herself and leaped.

Another jump? I relaxed when I peered over the small gap and jumped.

"What is this place?" I asked.

Weak sunlight streamed in from the cracks, but it wasn't bright enough until three flashlights beamed, lighting up the surrounding dark areas.

Rhett placed his flashlight down and handed me a black folder. "You need to see this, Ava."

It had the ISAN logo on it.

"I believe this was the last hiding place of the doctor who created the Helix serum. I also believe ISAN is holding him captive. They obviously didn't know he had been here, or this place would've been destroyed. I also found some recordings. Go ahead." He gestured with a tilt of his chin.

"Reyna and I will be back." Ozzie tugged Reyna out.

My hands shook and my heart thundered as I dove into the folder.

PROJECT HELIXB77—DAY 1: I injected HB77 into a woman pregnant with twins today without her consent. The mother is my special test subject. The ultrasound shows the special subject's twenty-week fetuses are more active, with no sleep during the hour I observed them with Helix in their systems. Though this study is top secret, conducted by a network known as ISAN, it is taking place in my office at a local hospital in the East. ISAN is not aware of the special subject.

PROJECT HELIXB77—DAY 30: I injected 10 milligrams into the thirteenth subject, and the same amount to twenty new pregnant moms. All are from low income families, except the special subject. The serum binds with testosterone and stays in the male babies longer. Injecting them earlier in their pregnancies changed the DNA to adapt to Helix easier and faster I assumed. For this reason, I named the first part of the serum Helix, the shape of a DNA strand, and the second part, Batch 77. It took me 77 batches to finally get it right. Testing of the special subject, the fetuses appeared alert on ultrasound; furthermore, their sense of hearing was heightened. When played a recording of their mother's voice from the next room, something that would've been impossible for normal human ears to hear, the fetuses reacted. Great success.

PROJECT HELIXB77—DAY 60: I injected 20 milligrams into the special subject. Babies' reflexes were impressively faster and stronger. Mother was in great pain from the kicks. I had to inject another serum to counteract Helix. Fifty new moms were injected with Helix today. ISAN will send me more.

PROJECT HELIXB77—DAY 90: The special subject gave birth to twins early, as expected. Though I'm a proud father today, I'm also devastated. ISAN: International Sensory Assassin Network. I'm not sure what they are planning, but training the young to kill is wrong. How many lab-created killers will they create around the world? In order to keep my children safe, I had to separate us. The first child will be going to trusted foster parents. My wife will think her first child is dead. The second child will stay with us, for now. I will inject my children with the last dose of the enhanced serum I have been injecting them with since I began. ISAN is not aware of the enhanced serum. My children will be special. I will not know what their special abilities will be. Their bodies will determine that. I only hope this will work.

Project HelixB77—Month 48: Today will be the day I will lose my wife and my second child. When my wife learns what I've been doing, she will want nothing to do with me. But I have to tell her. They are watching our child too closely. A trusted friend is waiting for their arrival at a safe house with new identities. To my peers and ISAN, I will make it look like my wife and I are separating. And my second child will think her father is dead.

Project HelixB77—Month 60: My family has been gone for so long. I have no choice but to keep enhancing the formula to its full potential. ISAN isn't aware it's as perfect as it can be, for now. I will have to continue to delay and try to find a way to escape from the East territory. The Abandoned City is my only safe haven. There is no one around, except for drifters, but they don't bother me because I bring them food. Maybe someday, someone trustworthy will find my folder. It will be the only evidence I existed. I don't know how long ISAN will allow me to live. Once they think the formula has been perfected, they won't need me anymore.

Project HelixB77—Month 72: It gives me joy to see both of my children, even if from a distance and for a very brief moment. I know I should stay away, but I can't. Those moments give me enough happiness to last for months. My second child is healthy and doing well. My wife sees me from a distance. She knows I'm watching, but she turns away, crying. This is our life now. She despises me. She will hate me even more if she finds out I lied about our first child.

PROJECT HELIXB77—MONTH 96: My second child looks more like my wife every day. When I watch her play in the park, she is full of life. She is brave and thinks fast on her feet, but she is afraid of heights. It didn't cross my mind to alter that gene. The first child is doing well and has moved to the South with the foster parents.

PROJECT HELIXB77—MONTH 144: ISAN has found the first child. I don't know how, but my child will remain in juvie until they are ready to start training the first round of kids. I'm not worried. My child is special. I don't know in what way, but my child will stand out from the others.

PROJECT HELIXB77—MONTH 156: My heart has been ripped to shreds. I have nothing left. My wife died today, supposedly from a new virus. A lie. We have found cures for almost all illnesses. My second child was sent to a foster home. The motions have been set in place. They will bring her in. It's time for me to contact the only person I trust in ISAN. I spoke briefly with my second child today and filmed her without her knowledge. I needed to have this. I can't continue to observe my children secretly anymore.

PROJECT HELIXB77—MONTH 168: My source reported my first child was sent to the West territory. I assume they are planning to organize an ISAN network there. At least I know my child is safe.

PROJECT HELIXB77—MONTH 192: They brought the first batch of kids to ISAN headquarters and started the mental training I designed with another scientist. It makes me proud to see the serum is successful, but I hate what they will be using it for. The serum is flawed. When binding with testosterone, depending on the dosage, it will make the males aggressive, some more so than others. It will turn them into monsters. This will require more testing on male subjects. If I don't find a solution, what will happen to them?

PROJECT HELIXB77—MONTH 204: My second child was brought to ISAN. It had been years since I saw her last. She is as beautiful as her mom. Seeing her brings joy and sadness, mostly sadness, because she doesn't know me. I'm so proud of her. She's doing well in the mental missions, and my trusted contact is looking after her. I hope I live to see her take down ISAN.

As tears streamed down my face, I flipped through the pages as fast as my fingers allowed. My adrenaline pumped rapidly I couldn't keep up with the intensity of the rush. My breath cut short, and it took every ounce of me not to collapse on the floor.

"Where's the rest?" I turned to the beginning and flipped through it again and again. When I saw an envelope on the back, I opened it, but it was empty.

"Ava."

I flinched and shoved Rhett when he placed his hand on me.

"This doctor is not my dad. My dad is dead," I said through clenched teeth.

I didn't want to believe my dad would experiment on his own children, that he'd been the one to create such a powerful serum. The serum that molded killers. The serum that had ruined my life. I had no right to judge him, but how could he?

All my life Mom had told me Dad was an engineer who'd died in a traffic accident. She'd never shown me pictures of him since she claimed to have none. My stomach roiled and I fought nausea. If the doctor was my dad, Mom had to lie to me to keep me safe. Knowing that didn't make it easier to accept.

"I'm not this second child. You didn't come here to get more supplies. You came here to see if I was her, didn't you?"

I didn't realize I was shouting until Ozzie and Reyna returned, looking at me with pity.

Rhett reached for me. "Ava."

I crossed my arms over the folder and staggered back, almost tripping over the stupid cement piece I had stepped on. Rhett tried to catch my fall.

"Don't." I shot out a hand to stop him and glared. "I've got myself."

"Ava, I know this is a lot to handle. Please, let me help you. How do you think I felt when I found this?" Rhett's tender voice did nothing to soothe me.

I shook my head fervently and scoffed. "You don't know me. Everything is a lie. For all I know"—I jabbed a finger at each of them—"you're all ISAN. Or maybe ISAN is the good guy, and you made this folder to make ISAN look bad. Lies."

Rhett extended his arms, reaching ever so slowly for me. "There's no good ISAN, but we can change it. That's what we are trying to do. You're such a skeptic. You'd never believe me without evidence, so I didn't want to reach out to you until I had something solid. You have no idea how much I've missed you. It took me six freakin' torturous months to find something. You're special, Ava, and you know that. Don't deny it. Embrace it and use it for good. Just don't tell anyone. You can't trust anyone but us. We can change what ISAN stands for. Your twin and your father might still be alive."

Hearing they might still be alive should've helped to calm me, but I shook with rage. I didn't want to believe any of it and make a liar out of my mom. Yet something tugged in my gut, and the rational part of me knew Rhett was right.

"Where's the rest of this?" My words cut sharp as I wiped my tears.

"That's it. I swear. But here's more proof the second child he wrote about is you." Rhett reached into his backpack and handed me a phone. "When I found this, it was connected to a charger. Smart move. That type of phone doesn't exist anymore, and you can't find a charger like that since everything is done by solar power. Ozzie rigged up a power source for it."

I didn't waste a second. Touching the screen to activate, I pressed the picture icon. There were baby pictures of a female child and my mom, but there were none of my dad or the first child. I scrolled again and recognized the younger version of me. The more I saw, the harder it became to contain my emotions, especially when it came to the pictures of my mom.

"Mom." My lips quivered, unable to fight the pain crashing through.

I ran my finger down the screen as if I could touch her. Uncontrollable tears streamed down my face. Seeing a photo of her, even after all those years, reopened old wounds.

It didn't matter how much time had passed, and it didn't matter how hard I had shut out the ache, I lost my mother again with every photo. Hating the vulnerability, I wiped my tears and clicked on the video.

Why didn't you tell me the truth, Mom? Why?

CHAPTER TWENTY-SEVEN
THE VIDEO

"*Hello. My name is Dr. Hunt. What's your name?*"

I heard his voice, but he only recorded me. My ragged hair brushed my shoulders. For a thirteen-year-old, I was thin and short. The Ava on the screen shifted nervously, but held her chin high.

"*Hello, Dr. Hunt. My name is Ava. What kind of doctor are you? I need a doctor to fix me.*"

"*Why do you need to be fixed?*"

Young Ava scuffed her shoes on the ground. "Sometimes I see things in my mind, like a map, and sometimes I hear voices and no one's around."

"*Ava, you're too young to understand, but you have to know you're special. Doctors can't fix you.*" *He paused, as if to make sure she understood.*

"You gave me no choice," I cried to the man in the video. "You took my life from me. I'm not special. I'm damned."

I didn't want to listen anymore, but I had to know the truth. There were so many unanswered questions.

"*Can you do me a favor?*" *he asked.*

After Young Ava looked around to see if anyone listened or watched her, she nodded.

"Please don't tell anyone what you can do. They will think you're crazy. You're not crazy, do you understand? When these things happen and you don't want them to, close your eyes and count to ten. Take long, deep breaths and think of something frightening. It will go away. Fear will make it go away. When you're too scared, your special ability shuts down. It's active right now because you're going through changes, but eventually it will become dormant."

Young Ava's eyebrows pulled together. "I don't understand. My mom told me to think of happy thoughts. I don't want to think of something scary."

"It's okay, Ava. Try both ways and see which one works. Will you promise me that?"

Scratching her nose, Young Ava nodded. "My mom is dead." She blinked her teary eyes. "I live with foster parents, but they're not nice to me."

"I'm so sorry, Ava." His voice sank low and his shoulders curved inward. "It's not the life I would have wanted for you." He faltered, choked up. "Your mom loved you very much. She'll always live in your heart. Hold on to her memory and hold on to her love. Days will be brighter. I promise."

"Are you my mom's friend? How do you know her?"

A long sad sigh exhaled from his lips. "Yes, she was my friend."

"Then does that make you my friend, too?"

"Yes." He chuckled lightly. "We are friends."

"Can you take me home with you? I don't like where I am." Young Ava folded her arms and tears spilled onto her cheeks.

"I can't take you with me. You don't know how much I wish I could. Hang in there. You won't be with them much longer."

"How do you know?" Young Ava wiped her tears.

"I just do. Can you hold onto that, knowing you won't be there long? It's a temporary situation. Be strong, Ava. Be brave. It will get you through."

"My mom told me to be brave and be someone important." Young Ava raised her chin, looking proud.

"That's right. Remember those words. I have to go now. Please don't tell anyone we had this conversation. Dr. Hunt doesn't exist to you. Do you understand?"

The screen went dark.

It was the moment of clarity, but not the clarity I wanted. Seeing myself at thirteen made me relive how much I'd missed my mom and how much I'd hated my foster parents.

My dad's sweet, loving voice broke me. Sounds I never knew I could make escaped my mouth. My wails were pain, death, and seeing my whole life taken from me in one second. The room spun with flashing white dots, my knees weakened, and acid filled my stomach.

Why couldn't I recall this interview? *Dr. Hunt doesn't exist to you.* Did my father make me forget? Was it even possible? And if so, how?

While I held onto my father's journal and phone, I kicked the debris and knocked the bottles and remaining items on the dusty table, bellowing.

"It's a lie. Everything's a lie. I hate you. I hate you. I hate you."

"Ava."

Rhett's voice seemed distance away.

I heaved and clasped my arms around my middle to stop the shaking. It had been too much to bear. Everything they told me still seemed like a lie, but denying it had become futile. I wanted to scream again and punch the walls. I wanted to run away fast and far, far away from ISAN, Rhett, and even myself.

I didn't know what my twin's life was like, but if it was anything like mine, they had it rough, too. Though in my dad's journal he said the first child was well taken care of, I didn't believe it. It wasn't fair. I should've lived a happy childhood with a family who loved me and treated me well. But my family was a lie. Instead, it was one messed up nightmare.

Dad's recorded voice buzzed in circles in my head: *Be strong, Ava. Be brave.*

That was all I ever did.

I stumbled back from lack of air as nausea swept through me again.

"I've got you." Rhett caught me before I fell.

I flung my arm out to push him away. I wanted to hurt him for giving me so much grief. But when his eyes pooled with genuine tears, I realized he was not my enemy.

With the folder and phone clutched to my chest, I crushed my body to his as if he was the only solid thing in this world and sobbed until there were no more tears to shed. His warm embrace made it easy for me to feel vulnerable, to need him. The strength and the grip of his strong arms gave me comfort, a solid foundation to my crumbling self.

I hated who I was, hated I had to kill. And worse, I hated I was special.

Memories can be erased, but you can never forget emotions. Rhett's words sprang in my mind.

At that moment, I knew I had felt that raw pain before and had found comfort in someone's arms, but I just couldn't recall whom or why. I remained in his embrace until the sun shifted and the flashlights threw my shadow on the wall.

I finally wiggled out of his arms. Sure, I'd just had the shock of my life, but everyone inside ISAN was a victim. Brooke, Justine, and Tamara all had hard luck stories, and I wondered if their pasts held twists and lies. My father suspected Mom had been murdered. Maybe ISAN had wanted us cut off from people who cared. We were all victims, even the guy who held me.

Rhett and his friends had kidnapped me. My instincts said I should run away or beat the crap out of them. Instead, I felt solace in their presence, a sense of belonging I couldn't explain.

Rhett brushed my hair back as his eyes set tenderly on mine. "I'm sorry, Ava. You can hate me all you want, but I'd rather you know the truth. You don't have to say anything. Let it soak in tonight. We need to get going."

I nodded, sniffling.

"Can you walk?" he asked.

I nodded again, wiping the last tears I planned to allow. Crying meant weakness. Crying meant they had won. I'd fight until my last breath.

"Can I take these?" I held up the folder and the phone.

"Yes, you can. I'll put them in my backpack. You're going to need both hands. We're not going back the way we came."

"Why didn't you just take it with you when you first found them?"

Rhett shoved the folder and the phone inside the backpack and zipped it before meeting my eyes. "In case he came back. Your dad didn't write daily or monthly toward the end of his journal. The last time he wrote was the seventeenth year—not that long ago. You're seventeen. I hoped he'd come back and write more. But maybe it's safer in our hands, in case one of ISAN's people get a hold of it or the Remnant Council bombs this place."

"Okay, thanks. We can go now." My words barely left my mouth as my body drooped from exhaustion.

So tired. I was so tired. Tired from crying. Tired from inconceivable new-found revelations overwhelming me.

"So bossy." He rolled his eyes playfully. "You're lucky I'm not making you jump for that, Ms. Scared of Heights. I'll make you drop instead."

To my surprise, I let out a soft laugh. Laughing through the shock made me feel better. Later, I'd block it out and move on. It was the only way I knew how to be strong, to be brave. If I let all of it get to me, then I had already lost.

I'm an assassin for crying out loud. Get a hold of yourself.

I glanced around, sensing the ghost of my dad's presence. He'd been there, writing in his journal, living with the drifters. But for how long?

I had held the journal he'd touched. Somehow that made me feel close to him. He'd been there the first time I'd done a mental mission. He watched me. He stood a touch away. Knowing what his voice sounded like, he became real to me. I felt his love through the journal and the video, but most of all I felt his pain.

How frightening it must have been for him, always looking over his shoulder, running from his past. It'd be nice to meet him, but I didn't love the man on that video. How could I love someone I didn't know, who I'd thought hadn't existed all those years, and especially the person who had experimented on his own children? I had no memories of what he looked like or any traits we shared, but I wanted to.

The possibility of reuniting with my dad and my twin enticed me. Who had he asked to look after me? Did I have a brother or a sister? I had so many more questions, but no one could tell me the truth except my dad.

I inhaled a deep breath. *Be brave, Ava. Be someone important.* As my mother's last advice echoed, I caught Rhett's attention.

"Let's go."

CHAPTER TWENTY-EIGHT
THE GUARDS

Purple and pink painted thin streaks across the sky, backed by thick clouds. The sun made its last stretch before heading to the other side. I took a moment to enjoy the view and then watched Ozzie looking down. Rhett wasn't kidding when he said, *I'll make you drop instead.*

Reyna swung a rope tied from a steady steel rod. She pointed, letting me know that was my ride down.

Oh, hell no.

"Ready for your first drop?" She snickered. She didn't seem as angry. Perhaps she felt sorry for me.

I frowned at Rhett. "You're not serious, right? You were joking, trying to make me laugh. *Right?*"

I turned to Ozzie for support, but he deflected me with information.

"This is the fastest way down, unless you want to go back the way we came, and that's a long way from here. Plus, it's getting dark, and I don't know if you knew, but our glider works on solar power. We have battery backup, but we don't want to use that unless it's extremely necessary. Unless you want to spend the night here with the possibility of drifters wanting to touch you, I suggest you drop."

I was just about to tell Ozzie to stop talking when several red lights flashed across space, cutting the rope. My heart thudded out of my chest. It happened so fast, it took me a moment to register Rhett had wrapped his arms around me and thrown us behind a broken wall. I felt no pain, only discomfort. Rhett's body had cushioned the impact.

"Drifters have Tasers?" Ozzie roared, crawling to us.

Reyna yanked him down as a light hit the spot where he'd been a second before.

"Thanks, that was close." Ozzie took his Taser out of his backpack and positioned it to aim.

Rhett reached over the boulder and shot. "They're not drifters. Even if they could get a hold of Tasers, they're not this aggressive. They're ISAN guards."

ISAN guards? Confusion filled my mind. How did he know? No ISAN symbol displayed anywhere on their suit. But then again, ISAN wouldn't want to be identified.

What was I supposed to do? Which team was I on? My mind told me to run to the guards, but my heart told me to stay with Rhett. Too late. Again, no time to plan, just do. Clearly when the guards shot at me the decision had been made for me.

Reyna shot a man wearing all black and a mask. "What are we going to do?"

Rhett ducked. "We're going home, that's what we're going to do. There's about twenty of them. Reyna, take the second rope out of your backpack and get it ready. Ozzie and Ava, come with me."

Holding my Taser in front of my chest, I readied to shoot when Rhett stopped me by placing his hand on my shoulder.

"Do you remember what you read? What your father did for you? You're special, Ava. You don't need Helix to be strong or be brave. It's already in you. You just have to believe in yourself. You've been trying to reject this all your life. It's going to take time. If it doesn't work for you today, then fine. We'll find a way. Now … ready?"

I nodded, thanking him silently for his pep talk, but I still trembled. I might freeze up, and then I'd be useless.

"Let's go. On my mark. Three ... two ..."

Rhett never got to say one. I flipped over the boulder and landed with one knee down, and then shot the man in front of me. The lights flashing from behind me came from Ozzie and Rhett, behind the wall on either side.

"You have a bad habit, Ava. You didn't let me say one." Rhett growled, shooting another one. "But that was awesome. Some things never change. You're still the same stubborn, feisty, brave, Ava."

I ducked low behind some debris to escape a shot, and then got back up to stand behind Rhett.

"Miss me already?"

He pressed his body into mine before I could say something back. The chunk of the wall where he'd stood a second before blasted into pieces. Debris and smoke swirled around us.

"Rhett. Ava." Ozzie's voice thundered, filled with concern.

"We're fine." Rhett coughed, switching from Taser to gun. "Ava is trying to make out with me."

I ignored his comment and shot a guard who emerged from the shadows. Too close.

Rhett ducked and gut-punched the guy who came for him and then used the guy's body as a shield. "You want to know why you called me Sniper, Ava?" Rhett pointed his gun away from the targets. "You're about to find out."

"You don't have good aim, Rhett."

"That's what you think." Rhett's body jerked after he pulled the trigger.

The bullet hit the edge of the chipped ceiling, dropped to nick a piece of the thick rod on the ground, and then flew right between the target's eyes. The thumping on the ground confirmed he went down.

"Sniper ... that's what I can do. Perfect aim, all the time."

"Nice shot, Rhett. You're my hero." Ozzie fired his Taser.

"I never miss, right, Ozzie?" Rhett placed the gun back, took out two Tasers, and shot with both at the same time. "Ready, Reyna?"

"Just in time, Rhett. I've re-tied it. It's ready. I'm going first."

"Wait for us down there. Keep safe." He shot like a madman. "Ozzie, you're up. Go. Ava, go after Ozzie."

I did as instructed, but I kept an eye on Rhett. Ozzie and I continued to shoot while heading for the rope. Dust and chips from the cement flew about, making it difficult for me to aim for the target.

"It's easy." Ozzie ducked a bullet, chips of debris blasted like small fireworks. "Pull your sleeve like this and go down. I'll catch you from the bottom. Please don't be afraid of heights. We're running out of time."

Easy for you to say. "Okay, Ozzie. You go first, and then I'll go."

As I watched him descend and land, I pulled my sleeves over my hands and grabbed the rope. Taking deep breaths, I told myself I could do it. My life depended on it, but I couldn't move.

Rhett's words repeated in my mind. *You don't need Helix to be strong or be brave. It's already in you.*

Helix was in me. Just before I let myself go, lights zapped so close I had to veer my body in an awkward position. Still hanging on the rope, I swung like a pendulum on a clock.

"Go, Ava."

The domineering sternness in Rhett's voice had me in a panic mode, and the adrenaline kicked in, thick and heavy.

Anchoring the thick yellow rope with my feet and gripping it with one hand, I shot with the Taser on the way down at the guards. Rhett leaped across to get the rope and slid down while bullets sliced the air around him. Crazy, but amazing, Rhett.

Rhett landed a second after me and aimed the gun to where the rope tied. The rope dropped down with one shot.

I took off and raced around the corner of the building to find the vehicle held hostage by guards armed with Tasers and guns. Pointing their weapons at us, they held up clear, bulletproof shields, and their thick uniforms looked bulletproof, too.

Crap. Now what?

"Put it down, slowly," a guard said. "You didn't think you could escape again, did you, Rhett?"

Rhett sneered.

The guard knew Rhett?

"I'm going to get a huge reward for you. You're lucky I was told to bring Ava and you alive. The rest can drop dead."

Rhett didn't say a word and raised his hands.

We were surrendering?

No. But he gave the impression we were.

I placed my Taser down and knelt like everyone else. Knowing they wouldn't give up easily, I prepared to fight. The guard had made a big mistake by standing in front of Rhett and relaxing his gun arm.

Rhett swiped his leg under the guard, knocking him down. Then he picked up the guard's fallen Taser and shot him in the chest. He spun and yanked the bulletproof shield from the next guard and used that shield to block a bullet flying toward him. Then Rhett went crazy with his Taser, just the way he had above.

Ozzie, Reyna, and I mimicked his moves with the other guards standing in front of us. When I got up, the other ten were down.

I was floored at how sleek, graceful, and swift Rhett, Ozzie, and Reyna moved, and how the four of us battled together as if we were a rehearsed team. We didn't plan, and there was hardly any communication, but we fought together with ease and comfort.

"Get in." Rhett cranked the engine. He shifted into reverse

and the vehicle ran over bodies without a care. After changing to drive, he pushed the gas so fast my body jerked back against the seat.

Two bullets hit the truck. One pierced the back window and continued through the front, between Rhett and me. The truck screeched out into the street. As I watched the road, I had my Tasers ready to shoot, and my elevated pulse descended to find its steady rhythm the farther we drove.

"Anyone hurt?" Ozzie's tone exuded urgently, his eyes fell on all of us. "That was real close." He checked behind his shoulder then turned back to us.

I stole a glance in the side mirror at Reyna since she hadn't answer Ozzie's question. Well, nobody had.

Reyna slapped the door handle, anger seizing her. "How did they know? We've been here plenty of times, and they never came."

"It doesn't matter." Ozzie placed a gentle hand on Reyna's arm. "You know they can't track us. I deactivated Ava's chip. And even if she had another tracker, they can't track us at the compound."

Tracker? As I wondered if they had implanted a tracker inside me, I rubbed the back of my neck. My pinky slipped closer to my ear. Guilt and confusion flooded through me. Without a word, I peeled off the earpiece and tossed it out the window. Could that be a tracker too?

Damn. Why did I care?

"But they can track her here. I guess Ozzie forgot to check." Reyna fisted a handful of her hair and placed her elbow on the door.

"You're wrong. I did it when she slept."

"In her sleep? You're still afraid of her?" Reyna shook her head, a small squeaky noise escaped her throat.

"Kind of." He shrugged.

It wouldn't matter anyhow. If my earpiece was the tracker, a metal detector or any other device they had used wouldn't have found it.

Rhett punched the wheel and swore.

I flinched.

"What happened?" Ozzie asked.

Rhett flashed a glance at me, and then looked back to the road. "ISAN guards will report Ava shot back. I should have killed them all. If they ask you about it, Ava, you lie. Tell them they must have made a mistake. It will be your words against theirs."

Oh, God. Lying wouldn't help me. I needed a miracle.

"Okay," I said.

Rhett remained silent. One of his hands set on the wheel and the other hand rested on his leg. Too busy keeping my eyes on the road, I hadn't noticed he was hurt until then.

"Rhett, you're hurt." I tried to sound calm, but my voice was too loud.

"You're hurt?" Ozzie reached over to get a better view.

Rhett placed his palm on Ozzie's head and shoved him back. "I'm fine."

"He's bleeding?" Reyna gasped.

"I'm fine." Rhett huffed a breath, sounding irate. "It's just a nick. We're almost there. Once we get inside the glider we'll be fine."

Liquid soaked his dark, long-sleeved shirt on his shoulder and I questioned how much blood he'd lost. I had to take his word for it. Secretly, I chastised myself for caring and stared out the window.

CHAPTER TWENTY-NINE
HOME

Rhett stopped Ozzie and Reyna at the entrance of their compound. "Not a word about what happened today, got it?"

They shot a weary glance at me and nodded.

"I'll be in my room. Ava, come with me."

Rhett and I walked quietly and hastily, avoiding others and entered his room. "Have a seat," he said, but it sounded more like a command.

When I sat on the bed, Rhett dropped to his knees. Hands braced on either side of me on the mattress, and he searched my eyes for answers.

Oh God. Move away, Rhett. Don't look at me like that. His closeness made me hot and dizzy, and butterflies swirled, loosening the tightness in my chest. My eyes set on his stubble I'd been wanting to trace with my fingers, and I shook away the thought.

"Are you okay? Do you need to talk about all this? I know you're confused."

No, I'm not okay. I'm never going to be okay. I wanted to say.

"I'm fine. Don't worry about me. Shouldn't you take care of that wound?"

Rhett sighed, dropped his head lower, and met my eyes again. "I'm fine." He paused, seeming to search for words. "Do you know if you have a tracker inside you? Were you injected with anything besides Helix?"

I lowered my eyes to my dry, dirty hands, and then peered

back at Rhett. I hardly knew him. Yet in a couple of days, I'd learned to trust him. He'd keep my secrets safe because he'd do whatever it took to keep *me* safe. Why? What was I to him?

I swallowed nervously. "I think my earpiece was a tracker, too, but I can't be sure. It lost connection long before I got here. I tossed it out the window as soon as I realized I still had it on. I swear I didn't try to contact ISAN."

Rhett nodded. "I know. I believe you."

My eyes shifted to his shoulder. "Are you still bleeding? We need to clean that up. Are you in pain?" I asked the last question when he squinted as he rose.

"Are you trying to show me you care?" His lips curled, wickedly hot.

Rhett dropped his backpack on the floor, opened a drawer to take out a shirt, and then took out what he needed from the medicine cabinet and placed it on the counter. He opened another cabinet, took out a needleless syringe, and shoved it in his back pocket.

Rhett's shirt had apparently soaked up the blood. I didn't see any drops on the floor; I assumed it wasn't too serious. He tugged at his shirt but grunted in pain. I didn't mean to stare, but I knew he needed my help. And maybe I wanted him to need me. Maybe I wanted to return the day's gift.

I twitched when Rhett said my name. "I'm sorry to ask, but do you think you can give me a hand?"

"Sure."

Heat flushed my cheeks at his proximity and seeing Rhett with his shirt half way up, exposing his tanned six packs.

"If I can't take it off, then you're going to have to cut it. But I really don't want to cut my favorite shirt."

"Tell me to stop if I'm hurting you." Slowly, I pulled up from where he'd left off.

He peered down at me. His warm eyes darkened, and something other than pain lurked in them. My heart thumped faster when he placed his hand over mine.

"Stop right there." He groaned, his cheek muscles twitching. "Can you pull it over my head from the back? I'm going to rest my arms on your shoulders, if that's okay?"

I nodded.

When he placed his arms on my shoulders just as he said he would, I gripped the back of his shirt. I stopped when I felt him shudder under my hands.

"I'm sorry. My hands are cold."

"Actually, it feels good."

His words whispered smooth and hot in my ear. Sensual sensations slowly built inside me. A puff of air escaped his mouth at the side of my neck.

Oh, dear God. Ava, control your lustful thoughts.

"I'm going over your head. Let me know if you want me to stop," I said.

"Go for it."

I didn't have to look to see his impish grin.

I trembled when his breath brushed the tip of my ear. His muscles tightened when I slipped the shirt over his head.

"Almost there," I murmured.

As he focused on me with a mischievous grin, my mouth dried.

"Trying to take advantage of me?" He chuckled lightly. Rhett pulled one sleeve off easily. Then he extended his wounded arm to me. "I'm afraid to see blood."

"Now who's taking advantage of whom?" I narrowed my eyes. "You're afraid of blood? Ha."

"Seriously, I need you to peel the shirt off the wound. Don't hurt me, please."

A soft laugh fluttered out of me. Leisurely, I unrolled the rest of the shirt from his arm, trying not to stare at his chest. The wound started at the top of his shoulder and extended to his biceps. Thankfully, it hadn't cut deep.

"We need to clean that," I said.

"Let's go to the sink."

"You have a sink in your room?"

Rhett took several steps before he looked over his shoulder. "This isn't really a bedroom, as you can tell. I didn't want one like the others had. It reminded me of my room in ISAN." He picked up bandages and disappeared behind a wall.

I picked up the pace and almost bumped into him. Rhett moved a large box aside, revealing a small sink with a mirror on top. When Rhett's reflection appeared next to mine, I moved away. He reached underneath the sink and pulled out a small, beige towel.

"Let me help you." I placed the towel under the running water and then wrung it. Timing couldn't have been more perfect. I asked the one question that had been on my mind for a while. "How long have you been here?"

"About six months," he answered without hesitation.

Ozzie had said the same. I had been in ISAN for approximately six months, but if they were here six months ago … Something didn't add up. I asked a different question.

"How long were you in ISAN?"

"I'd already been there for a while before you arrived. But if you're trying to ask me how long we knew each other, it was about six months."

I tried to recall, but as usual, I couldn't and only got frustrated. Rhett bit his lips and winced when I placed the damp towel on his wound. More blood seeped out. I rinsed the towel, but I didn't place it directly on the wound. Squeezing the cloth, I let the water drip down on the cut.

"Do you remember your family?" I asked hesitantly.

"I was brought up by foster parents like you." He tightened his jaw.

"And everyone else?" I knew the answer, but I needed confirmation.

"Yes. We all have different reasons for being sent to juvenile detention. Some are similar, like stealing, but some are more serious, like taking a life. But I'm pretty sure they were framed. Maybe not all, but some of them couldn't kill a fly. Well, they could now. We're all different after coming out of ISAN."

I ran the towel under the water. "Do you have any brothers or sisters?" I thought about my twin. Would my twin recognize me? Did I have a brother or a sister?

"Not that I'm aware of." Rhett gripped the edges of the sink and slumped over. "I try not to think of the past but hope for a brighter future instead. My past molds me to who I am today, and because all I remember is the bad, I know exactly what not to do."

I took another towel from underneath the sink and lightly dabbed the wound.

"Thank you." He grabbed a needleless syringe from his back pocket and pushed the top. It penetrated his skin. "It will help prevent infection and heal it faster."

"Let me help you." I picked up a large square bandage, peeled the first layer, and warily pressed it around his wound.

"You know in some cultures, washing a male is like bonding, committing you'll be with him forever."

I let out a curt snort. "You're full of shit. You're lucky you're hurt. I could seriously take you down."

Rhett slipped his wounded arm through a button-down shirt, wincing. "Yeah, you can. You've done it before."

"And besides, the world has assimilated. There are no cultures.

It's a shame really."

"I agree, but we can create one." He waggled his eyebrows.

I ignored his silly antics and thought about probing more, but I didn't want to just yet. Information about a missing father and twin who never existed was already too much to handle. And hearing more about a past I couldn't remember tormented me.

"Why did you leave ISAN?" I asked just as he finished buttoning his shirt.

Rhett leaned back against the desk, dazed, as if his mind had traveled somewhere else. "I'm going to tell you something, but you have to promise me you won't repeat this under any circumstances. You have to pretend you never heard it. Ozzie and Reyna can't know I told you. Okay?"

"I promise." I plopped on the bed, preparing to listen.

Rhett sat next to me. "The serum was obviously successful. With Helix, we became stronger and our senses were heightened; however, in stronger doses, males became more aggressive, just as you read in your father's journal. The serum binds with testosterone. That's the problem. Sometimes it makes us do crazy things, like bash an instructor's head through the wall for no reason."

I gasped. "Did you?"

"No, but Ozzie did. He was locked up for evaluation. My group went on an assignment, and we killed everyone at the meeting, including the ones we weren't supposed to take out."

"Was I there?" I didn't mean to ask that question. Asking meant I accepted everything he'd told me about my memory being erased.

Rhett studied me a few long seconds, then finally answered. "Yes. We were a team. Thankfully, you and Reyna stopped me, but you couldn't stop the other two. You took them down with your Tasers, but one of our teammates gave you the scar on your back when he grabbed a dagger off the ground."

I brushed the ridge on my back with my finger. The scar was real, but the memory was gone. "What happened next?"

"That was the last time they sent out the males."

"Why didn't they inject smaller dosages instead?"

"At first, everything went well, but ISAN got greedy. They wanted to see what we could do and test our limits. That's when the problems began. The males retained it longer over the course of time, even with a smaller dosage. Doctors could predict females' reactions better. Ten milligrams would last ten minutes and be out of their system completely, something like that, but for the males, it was different for each of us."

I crossed my arms to brace myself to hear more.

"ISAN feared we would revolt one day, so they decided to get rid of the males. If a guy like Ozzie could kill an instructor with one swing, can you imagine what a group of us could do? They didn't announce this. I found out from a source. They were going to say they sent us back to juvenile detention, only they were going to ship us to get cremated."

I ran my fingers through my hair in disbelief. Russ and Lydia didn't seem like the type who would agree to such a murderous act. Would they? I didn't know Lydia well, and come to think of it, I didn't know Russ well, either. But he was my friend. Although, I didn't know if I could trust him anymore. The knowledge gutted me.

"Are you sure?"

Rhett raised his brow, giving me a how-dare-you expression, and continued. "After we found out, we knew we had to escape. Our source found an escape route and made a plan along with Ozzie's help. But things don't always go as planned. We lost a lot of friends that day. It wasn't easy. It was a rough journey to get here."

"How did you know of this place?"

Rhett sauntered to the counter and moved a few items around. "Lots of research before we left and a rumor I happened to hear from my foster father. The knowledge of this secret hideout died with him, hopefully. He was at least good for one thing. His family line was in the military."

"Oh."

"Now you know why there aren't males in ISAN. Someone smart like you must have asked that question in the last six months."

Yeah, I had wondered many times. And the question had been finally answered.

Rhett wiped up the counter and closed the medicine cabinet. "ISAN will get rid of anyone that stands in the way of their power. We are just numbers to them. They don't consider us human beings."

Maybe he was right, but I didn't want to believe I could be a part of such a network.

Rhett picked up his backpack and took out my father's journal and the phone. "I'm going to store these here for safe keeping." He ambled to his wooden desk and unlocked it with the key he had in his back pocket. As he shoved the items inside, he said, "Whenever you feel the need to watch it or read it again, let me know."

"Thanks," I said. Just thinking about the objects drained me.

"We should get going. It's dinnertime. I'm glad I don't have to cook."

"Do you all take turns doing different shifts?"

"Most of us. Some of them are terrible cooks. I make sure they don't have that shift." He laughed lightly. "I do most of the overseeing, checking every department is happy and running smoothly."

"So, are you their leader?"

Rhett rubbed the back of his neck. "Someone has to do the hard work. I don't like to use that word, but I guess you can say that. Reyna and Ozzie are second in command."

Rhett stopped by the door and waited for me. "You're very slow for someone I know is famished."

"I was thinking about these shoes." I looked down at them. "I'm still baffled how you would know my size."

"They're yours. We knew if we made it out alive we would never go back. Why would we? We packed up and stuffed whatever we could in our backpacks."

A knot in my stomach tugged painfully tighter. I wiggled my toes, standing by Rhett. Then I asked a terrifying question. "My backpack made it here, but I didn't. Why?"

Rhett brushed his hand down his face. His expression held sadness and anger. "Something went wrong on the day of our escape. We knew the risks and knew we would have to shoot to kill, but we should have all made it out safely. I'm pretty sure someone ratted us out. In the end, you sacrificed yourself so we could escape. One sacrifice equaled victory is what you used to say to me. My only regret is that I couldn't stop you. I died that day, not from a bullet, but because I lost you."

I shivered. One sacrifice equaled victory was something I believed in. I had sacrificed myself so Tamara could win for us. As much as I wanted to believe he told me lies, I couldn't. I had never shared those words with anyone before.

Rhett tapped the keypad. As the door slid open, I asked another question, even though I wasn't sure he would answer. I needed more. I had to try.

"Who was your source?"

"You," he said without eye contact, and led the way.

CHAPTER THIRTY
OLD TIMES

The enticing aroma burst about the eating room, making my hunger pangs worse. Dinner already sat on the table. Quinn and his friends and a few others I'd met waved at me, and I smiled back. But some looked at me with suspicious eyes, examining me.

"Never mind them." Rhett slid my tray closer to me. "They're afraid. They're worried you'll inform ISAN of our whereabouts."

"I wouldn't." I dropped my voice lower when I realized I had spoken louder than intended. "Not anymore. I don't even know where I am."

I hate to admit it, but I had grown attached to this place.

"I know." Ozzie took a bite of his fresh carrot. "Don't worry—they won't say anything to you. They owe you everything, and they know it." He dropped his head and scrubbed his face. "Crap. I said too much."

Rhett patted Ozzie on the arm like a father to a child. "There, there … It's all good."

Ozzie's expression changed to a somber one. "We used to tell each other everything. The four of us were so close. I don't like to hide things from you."

His words stabbed at me. Though I couldn't remember our friendship before, I felt the sincerity from his tone.

"It's okay, Einstein. I understand."

Ozzie stiffened and stared at me inquisitively. I gasped at the realization I had called him by his nickname without a thought.

"You should eat your spaghetti before it gets cold."

Reyna broke the awkwardness. I was unsure if it had been intentional. It was the first time she had offered me a candid smile.

Spaghetti tasted better at ISAN, but I couldn't complain about noodles and smashed tomatoes. Food was food. It had been the result of someone's hard labor, from planting to picking, and then washing and cooking. I'd never had to cook before, and I didn't have the urge to try. It didn't seem like fun cooking for so many people.

"Thanks." I took a bite, swallowed, and savored the juice from the tomatoes. "It's not too bad."

Reyna snorted, taking a sip of her drink. "Oh hell, Ava. It tastes like crap. You can be honest with us. But food is food, and unfortunately, we have to eat. However, if you put shrimp on my plate in any form, cooked or not, I'll still eat it."

"I guess you like shrimp?" I had asked a stupid question, but I felt the need to say something to her.

"I dream about them." Reyna chuckled.

I smiled and laughed with her. I wanted to know more about her past, but just because she'd gotten a little bit friendlier didn't mean she was ready to share.

"We're going to the city tomorrow." Rhett shoved a bite in his mouth.

"To the city?" My excitement caused me to squeal like a child, who had been told a present waited for her. Then I wondered if "we" included me. I twisted noodles with my finger. "Am I going?"

Rhett's lips slowly spread to a smile, and he tilted his head. Damn, he looked too gorgeous. The way he looked back at me had all my muscles quivering. I couldn't blink, move, or swallow. He had me lost in his eyes, hypnotized.

Then Rhett's mouth moved. Had he said something?

Ozzie's fake cough broke our stare.

"Um ... sure," I answered.

Rhett's amused eyes and grin were too big for his face. "I don't think I asked a question, Ava."

I bit my lip from embarrassment, suppressing a giggle. Then I took sips of water until my face cooled. As I ate the rest of my dinner, I listened to the light conversation at our table and surveyed the people in the room.

Laughter rang in the air, a joyful sound. In ISAN, people rarely smiled. ISAN was all about competing for small rewards and working with your assigned team. Everyone here seemed content, even if an elite team of engineered assassins hunted them.

It didn't seem possible, but in two days I'd developed a sense of belonging with Rhett and his people. Though I couldn't remember them, and some wanted me gone, it felt good to be there. I wasn't afraid. Everyone seemed open and worked together.

I wondered how long Rhett would keep me, and I didn't know if I wanted to ask. He'd shown me what having freedom meant. If I went back to ISAN, I would be a changed person. I wasn't sure how it would affect me. Russ and Brooke were the only people I cared about, if I could still trust Russ. But ISAN was all I knew, all I had.

I was one messed up, confused girl. Knowing I had a twin out there and a father that might still be alive—I had to go back. And I had to go back for Brooke.

Rhett stood up suddenly. "Ozzie, can you take Ava back to my room? I need to take care of something."

"I'm done eating. I can take her." Reyna cut in before Ozzie could answer.

"I can take her." Quinn and his friend appeared, holding their empty trays. "I'm on my way out."

Rhett frowned, his arm muscles flexed, standing guardedly, and a surprising soft growl erupted. "I don't think so. You should go to your station. There's a lot of work to do."

Ozzie snickered. "Jealous much?"

"Shut it, Ozzie, or you'll be working the field."

"Tyrant," he murmured, and tossed a noodle at Rhett.

Rhett furrowed his brow and flicked it off.

"I can go by myself. I don't need anyone to escort me." Blushing because Rhett seemed possessive of me, I looked at Reyna to see her reaction.

"I'm taking precautions," Rhett said. "It's only because—"

"I get it. I wouldn't be happy about someone like me being here either."

"Come on, let's go." Reyna grabbed my arm and escorted me.

* * *

I thought Reyna would take me to Rhett's room and leave, but she came in with me. While she rummaged through the medicine cabinet, I sat on my usual safe spot.

She rearranged the bottles, shuffled some papers on Rhett's desk, and folded some towels, then placed them inside the cabinet. Occasionally she would look at me from the corner of her eyes.

The awkward silence stretched at first while she busied herself, as if she tried to buy time or searched for words.

"I'm sorry if I was rude before. It's just that I thought I'd lost you." Reyna leaned back on the table where Ozzie's equipment was neatly arranged in a line.

"Lost me?"

She bit her bottom lip at the same time she drummed her fingers on the chair. "Dead. I thought they killed you." Her voice wavered. After clearing her throat, she spoke again, "But Rhett wouldn't give up. I know you can't remember, but he really loves you. It isn't just a crush. You two had something special. It breaks my heart you can't remember all of us. When you decide to leave, you'll crush his heart and soul all over again. It's going to take some time for him to adjust, but maybe this time around it'll be easier. At least he'll have had the chance to win you over. I act like I don't care, but I do. I don't know what they did to you. I want to trust you, but I don't know if I can. Just like you're not sure if you can trust us."

Her eyes pooled with tears. She wiped them away and continued, "When Ozzie hacked through ISAN and found out you were alive, Rhett smiled for the first time since we got here. He didn't care if you didn't remember us. He said love would bring you two back together. He believes emotions are stronger than memories. I don't know what your intentions are after today, but please find a way to remember. We need you. We were a family, not by blood, but by loyalty and true friendship. We trusted each other with our lives. We were all we had. I've wanted to open up to you like this since you got here. I wanted to tell you everything to make you remember, but I know I can't. It doesn't work that way, but I wish it did. A war is coming, Ava, and I don't want us to be on opposite sides."

A war? I couldn't believe the words pouring out of her mouth. They crushed me, left me breathless.

"I'm still the same person. I may not remember, but I'm not as bad as you think ISAN is."

"You *don't* think they're evil?" Her tone rose in disagreement, and she tightened her grip on the sliding chair.

"No. I didn't say that." I tried to remain calm. Raising my voice would only tell her I was on their side. "I have friends in there. I need to help them, too. Now that I know my father is possibly still alive, and my twin is out there somewhere, I need to find them. This is a lot to take in in two days."

Reyna relaxed her clutched fingers on the chair and exhaled a short breath. "I know. I can't imagine. I'm sorry. It's a lot for us, too. Ozzie says it would be almost impossible for ISAN to find us, but *almost* is still a percentage I don't feel comfortable with. I'd rather die than go back."

"What did they do to you?" I shifted on the bed to get comfortable. I had given my life to ISAN, but they hadn't mistreated me.

"What did they *not* do to us? For starters, they killed my real parents when I was a toddler and sent me to a foster home. That is all you have to know, because that is what has happened to all of us. I think you need to read your father's journal again." Reyna's nose twitched and rage filled her eyes.

"I'm sorry." I didn't know what else to say.

"It's not your fault." She lowered her head. "But I'm going to find out who started this war and finish it." Anger and determination set in her eyes.

"Me too."

"I think ISAN is run by someone with lots of money, someone who wants to be the sole ruler of the Remnant Councils."

"Are you sure?" Then I remembered Mr. Thorpe's final words: *I believe in keeping the council number count at four. The person who sent you wants to be the only ruler. That person will have everyone killed.*

"No. I know I'm not making sense. I'm just going on instinct. I could be wrong about this. I might have no clue what I'm talking about."

I let out a short laugh.

Reyna's expression changed to something softer. She turned away from me with perked lips, trying to hide a smile.

"I miss talking to you," she said candidly. "We used to talk about so many things, but mostly about guys."

"Do you have a boyfriend?" I thought it was okay to ask.

Reyna plopped on the bed next to me, her face beaming. "I have a crush on this guy named Kaeden. He's about six feet tall, and he has gorgeous brown eyes. I think he likes me, too. He works in the garden. Once in a while, he brings me flowers. They're wildflowers, practically weeds, but it's so sweet."

Talking to Reyna reminded me of Brooke. I hoped she was okay, and I wondered if she missed me as much as I missed her.

Reyna talked nonstop. She chatted about the weather, about a few girls she didn't like, very basic topics about herself. But she was careful not to tell me anything regarding their hideout or personal information about anyone else. She didn't completely trust me yet.

I wouldn't trust me either.

"It was nice talking to you, like old times." She yawned, stretching her arms. "I better get some sleep. We have a long day ahead tomorrow. Rhett should be here soon. Goodnight." Reyna stood with a faint smile and headed to the door.

"Goodnight, Reyna. Before you go, I was wondering if you had the key to Rhett's desk. I left my father's folder in there."

"Rhett has the key with him at all times, but I'll let you in on a secret. If you put your finger under the table near where the lock is located, you'll find a tiny space. Push it up with your pinky. You'll hear a click when you've unlocked it. Don't tell Rhett I told you. He doesn't even know I know." She winked.

After Reyna left, I went straight for the desk and did what she instructed. Success. Instead of pulling the top drawer, I pulled the side one. I shouldn't be snooping, but I was desperate for more answers. Desperate for my missing memories.

I came upon a paper tablet with a long list of names. It appeared to be the names of those who lived in the compound, with some crossed off. Those must be people who hadn't made it. My heart squeezed from seeing so many names, mostly males.

The second name on the list was mine, but it had been circled instead. I put that back and fumbled through lists of duties and chicken-scratch notes I couldn't read. There were also a few colored pens and empty folders.

"Don't you have anything worth my time, Rhett?" I mumbled to myself, listening for his footsteps.

After fumbling through more papers ... *there*. I pulled out a long strip with several photos on it, something you could get at a place called, Fun Zone. An amusement park filled with rides and digitalized carnival booths.

The pictures were of Rhett and me. In the first one, my cheek brushed up against his and we were smiling. In the second one, I made a funny face at him. The third one broke my heart. My lips pressed to his, not in a passionate way, but I could see how much I cared for him in the sparkle in my eyes and my happy expression. But I didn't feel it.

I wanted so badly to remember that day, that moment, but I couldn't. Tears bubbled in my eyes as anger and frustration gripped me. Rounding my fists, I placed the pictures back and shut the drawer.

Then Rhett's footsteps entered the hall. I recognized them. They held their own suave tempo, beating to the sound of my own heartbeat. Music I was getting used to. Music I wasn't sure I wanted to let go. Music I knew I would never forget.

CHAPTER THIRTY-ONE
THE CITY

Rhett's team and I arrived at the hydro-glider to travel across the bay. I entered at the rear, far from the brightly lit first class seats. The lights in our cheaper, more crowded and less legroom section stayed dim and occasionally flickered. The long, fiberglass bullet traveled surprisingly smooth and fast, shooting across the surface of the water.

Some passengers passed the time reading, some slept, while others watched the water slide by the narrow window that spanned the length of the transporter. As for me, I held my breath, wondering whether anyone would recognize me.

Approximately twenty of us went out to the city with our backpacks. We'd split into groups of five. Each group had an electronic map and a specific sector to cover. One went to the west, others went to the north and south, and we went to the east.

Shifting my black hat to hide more of my eyes, I studied Rhett's big, calloused hands in his lap. I closed my eyes and remembered the gentleness of his touch when he'd wiped my tears and the way his hands moved under my shirt. Yet those same hands had killed. Distracted by Rhett shifting in his seat, I let go of my thoughts.

Rhett pressed his shoulder to mine. "You're not nervous, are you?"

I gazed at the people sitting beside us, wondering if they were listening. A woman held her fidgety baby in her lap, her husband by her side. The baby's arm flapped like a bird, and I spotted her bar-code tattoo. Infants were not chipped due to their growing hands. The tattoo would be erased by her physician and she would be chipped at sixteen.

A tinge of jealousy pricked me. The baby laughed in her mother's arms. She would grow up knowing her parents and live a normal life. I turned away.

"I'm fine. I've been through worse," I said curtly, rubbing the sting on my forearm.

Ozzie had activated my chip with fake identification this morning before we'd left. When I'd asked him how he had learned to implant fake IDs, he'd kept his lips sealed and eyes away from mine.

"At least I didn't make you jump. Ms. Afraid of Heights doesn't have motion sickness, does she? You can handle the speed, right?"

I lightly jabbed an elbow into his rib. "If I can't, you'll be the first to find out. I'll leave you a colorful present on your lap."

He gave me a sexy crooked grin that sent wanton tingles down to places it shouldn't have.

"You look good in my hat, by the way. Kind of sexy, if you ask me. I think I should take you on a date."

I scoffed but secretly liked the idea. Briefly, I considered punching him in jest for awakening such inconvenient, but delicious, emotions, but forgot my thought when I saw fire and desire in his eyes. Heat rising in my cheeks, I casually turned my body toward the window.

The hydro-glider came to a halt. The people in first class exited first, and then the next row moved along. Ozzie and Reyna got up and followed the line to exit. When my straps finally unbuckled, I prepared to do the same.

Rhett placed his hand on my lower back and guided me out. It seemed as though he needed to always touch me. I assumed to be protective and, at other times, as if he wanted to confirm I was really there. No one since my mom regarded me with such care.

Ozzie and Reyna were already out, heading in different directions. We pretended not to know each other.

Bright lights shone from the station like the first break of dawn after the dim cabin lights.

"Avoid the cameras and stay with me," Rhett said.

It didn't matter if I avoided the cameras. As soon as I stepped off the hydro-glider and onto a platform, two seven-foot poles on either side of me scanned my chip automatically. My heart raced, thinking an alert sound would blast through the air, but nothing happened. I should trust Rhett's team since they had done this before. Then a hologram of a woman appeared and greeted me.

Holograms of women and men's voices echoed all around, disorienting me. Some were assisting with directions behind a counter. Others helped citizens purchase tickets, appearing next to the ticket machine.

When I stepped onto the walkway, cold wind pushed me forward, and the cool air stung my nose. Ocean water crashed along the road, spraying mist onto my face. Shivering, I zipped up the jacket Rhett had insisted I wear and readjusted my cap.

Salt drops sprinkled my tongue when I opened my mouth to yawn and I cringed at the awful taste. Rhett's lips twitched, no doubt suppressing a laugh when he saw my expression. A soft animalistic growl escaped my throat, catching Rhett's attention. Rhett halted and ever so slowly turned to me.

My stomach lurched when he grabbed my hand for the first time, leading me forward. I was just about to yank my hand back when drones, size of a tennis ball, hoovered too close for comfort, and security guards roamed about. Head down, I sped past them.

My heart collided against my ribcage, and I was afraid I would get caught. But when Rhett's fingers intertwined with mine—the feel of his hands so natural, so familiar—distracted me.

As I continued along, gliders whizzed by, flying in an organized manner. Pedestrians strode through a tinted tunnel walkway mounted above me to get from one building to the next. In the daytime, the city illuminated like a mirage, or a collection of sparkling crystals clumped together.

In the heart of the city, Leviathan Hotel towered to the sky surrounded by skyscrapers, each with unique architecture. A Saturn-like ring encompassed every building—a monstrous solar panel—also used as landing gear for the gliders. Then my eyes were drawn to larger-than-life flat screens displayed throughout the streets—flashing advertisements and commercials for cosmetics, clothes, electronics, and much more.

I wanted to observe everything and enjoy the moment. After that day, I'd never get another chance to pretend to be a normal girl, living in a city like everyone else, strolling down the street, holding my boyfriend's hand. I felt so alive, thrilled to be out and free.

Rhett released me and shoved his hands inside the pockets of his sweatshirt. "We've got ground to cover. Link your arm through mine and keep up."

Rhett's stride was long and swift, and he took off as if the concrete scorched his feet. I sprinted until my legs ached and my throat burned. He stopped somewhere less crowded, and reminded me I had a water container, a pack of crackers, and an apple in my backpack. He'd told me it was going to be a long day and the snacks would be our only meal. After I took a few sips of water, I was back on my feet.

"We're almost there," Rhett said. "When we get there, you can't be seen. I'll point to the truck you need to get in. Don't come out to help. This group of people thinks I'm working for an organization that feeds the hungry, which is kind of true."

"I thought the councils had a program that makes sure everyone is fed?"

"It's true, but it's not enough. And it's complicated."

Rhett withheld information from me. I understood why he would, but that made me more curious.

"And this person, you trust him?"

"I trust *her*. Her name is Cleo." He pointed to my backpack. "I put a Taser in there just in case."

A small neighborhood peppered with quaint shops and paved with gray, beige, and red cobblestones came into view. My mouth dropped when I saw buildings untouched by tsunami, built with wood and plaster, but the cracks and uneven painting of the structure showed their age. I wanted to explore, shop, and pretend I lived there.

I approached the back of a fragrant bakery and the aroma of fresh baked bread made me pause. When five big, black trucks—more like SUVs—drove up, Rhett pointed to the last one.

I climbed in quickly. Though the dark tinted window made the day seem like night, and no one could see me inside, I hunched low to shroud myself.

"Hello, Ava."

Ozzie's greeting startled me. His cute smile reflected from the driver's seat in the rearview mirror. I hadn't recognized him in his shaggy blond wig.

"Did you enjoy your walk?"

"I did." I smiled, studying him. "You look good with blond hair, but I like your dark hair much better."

"Thanks." His cheeks colored pink.

"What's going on?"

"Didn't Rhett explain?"

"Not much. If we're just getting food, why are we worried we'll get caught? Why split up to go to the same place?"

"ISAN alerted the council guards about us. No doubt they did with you. The last time we were here, security almost took Rhett, but his contact Cleo basically bribed the guards. Who knows what will happen this time? They've come around several times. We also need gas. We're lucky we have some at home, and Cleo finds a way to get it for us. We're fortunate to have her help. She's our unexpected angel. Some people are good that way. Stay here. I'm going to help load."

Ozzie adjusted his wig, got out of the car, and slammed the door behind him. Rhett, Ozzie, Reyna, and others exchanged words with a pretty, young, red-haired woman who came out the back door.

Jealousy pricked sharply when she hugged Rhett and kissed his cheek. She must be Cleo. Her flirty smile and the way she caressed his arm made me cringe. I'd assumed he was trying to hide me from ISAN guards, but was he trying to hide me from her?

Ugh! I had to stop having these ridiculous petty thoughts.

Everyone got out of the trucks and loaded crates. Rhett began at the first truck, checking and inspecting, and stopped when he reached the third. He reached inside his bag, took out a pair of glasses and a hat. He put them on, but he flipped his hat backward—nerdy hot, but what was he doing?

Then five men, wearing all black with gold badges on their shoulders, headed straight for Rhett. They had come from the adjacent shop. My heart and stomach collided. Rhett and his friends took out their fake identification cards and showed them to the guards. One of the guards even scanned their chips.

Cleo and another girl brought out some pastries and paper mugs and flirted with the guards. Three guards followed Cleo and her friends inside the shop, but two remained behind to interrogate Rhett. They exchanged conversation, and then ...

One guard swung Rhett around and spread him flat against

the truck. Ozzie and Reyna flinched, but they remained calm. I told myself to do the same, but it didn't last long once the second guard opened the truck doors. Rhett waved his hand, alerting me to get out, I assumed. I had no identification on me and I certainly didn't have a wig handy.

I dug my Taser out of my bag, opened the back door quietly, and slipped out. I sank into the tall grass behind the truck and watched the guard from there. When he'd checked every vehicle, he joined his friends inside. Rhett and his team loaded into the trucks, including me. I thought Ozzie would speed out of there, but he drove like nothing had happened.

"That was close." Reyna took off her short, blonde wig and shifted to face Rhett, who sat in the back next to me. "What happened back there? What did you say to the guard to earn a pat down?"

"I told him he's seen me for the past couple of months, so he didn't need to see my card unless he had dementia or had a thing for me."

"Rhett. What the hell? Don't you ever do that again. You gave me a heart attack. I thought he was going to take you in." Reyna shook her head and narrowed her eyes. "Sometimes I want to sit on your head and crush that ego of yours." She reached over to smack him but missed when Rhett jerked to the side.

Rhett leaned back comfortably and split his lips into a smug grin. "I had it handled. You worry too much." Then he focused on me with an impish grin. "That was smart thinking back there."

I shrugged and gave him the evil eye. "Well, I had no choice. Maybe if you didn't let your fat ego get in the way, the guard wouldn't have checked inside all the trucks, and I wouldn't have had to get out. I had to do what I had to do. Whatever it takes."

I flinched at the last words. Silence filled the truck for a heartbeat until …

Reyna swung around and offered me a high-five hand. "Touché."

From the corner of my eyes, I caught a glimpse of Rhett's smile, and he leaned closer to me. His knee and elbow brushed up against mine. My heart raced from his innocent touch.

I cursed under my breath for liking it way more than I should. Ever so slowly, I broke away from him and pretended to adjust my hat.

CHAPTER THIRTY-TWO
THE CITY LIGHTS

The first truck dropped off crates at a church. Truck two and three unloaded at a facility before heading to their next destination, and truck four hung back to follow us. I pressed my forehead to the window, watching the sun dip lower into the sky.

"Are we going home now?" I yawned.

My body jerked slightly from the bumpy road. I pushed against Rhett's solid chest to stop from smacking into him. The curve of his pecks tightened under my hand.

"Sorry." I excused myself and folded my fingers on the headrest in front of me.

Rhett just smiled. He didn't say anything to annoy me or make me flush with heat.

"One more stop." Ozzie kept his eyes straight ahead.

No gliders, no people traveled the broken street. There was only endless, tall grass beside the upturned cement, poking up through the cracks and swaying against the wind.

"But you can't go far on this route in a ground vehicle," I said. "There are potholes and debris. It's dangerous."

"We're going to the other side of Abandoned City, to an area we call, Hope City." Rhett placed a reassuring hand on my shoulder. "It was the first place we stayed when we got out of ISAN. We met Cleo on our way there, who was nice enough to give us shelter. She knows nothing about ISAN. I'd like to keep it that way to keep her safe. She arranged a meeting for us with a man named Zen. Not all drifters are Ozzie's zombies. Like I said before, they are often good people who were wronged by the councils. That is how they see it, anyway. They want nothing to do with society and avoid technology. As a way to thank them for sheltering us, we take them community food and supplies each month. They don't expect us to, but I need to. If it wasn't for them, we would've been lost."

"Why didn't they go with you? Why didn't you live together?" I asked.

"There are women and children. We didn't want to risk their lives. It doesn't matter. They wouldn't have come anyway."

My gaze drifted out the window again, focusing on the reflection of Rhett, Ozzie, and Reyna. What generous and wonderful people they were. Out of ISAN, they were able to do so much more, be so much more …

Be someone important.

By the time I got to Hope City, clouds decorated the sky with orange and fiery red, like a dragon's angry breath. I couldn't peel my eyes away. I imagined the creature sweeping down to carry me away, and wished I could see the sun set every day.

Men from Hope City helped unload the two trucks. I had imagined them rough and uncivilized, but they dressed casually—pants and shirts—and were surprisingly well groomed.

A few had Tasers or guns tucked under their waistbands. My gut told me there was more than food and supplies in the crates. Weapons perhaps? And the men who rode in the other four trucks—who were they really?

Rhett got out to talk to an older man with gray hair. Zen, I assumed. The man gave Rhett some bottles I recognized from the medicine cabinet and a backpack, probably more medical supplies. Rhett patted the guys who'd helped load crates to our truck, then hopped into the back seat and we took off again.

People from Hope City seemed happy and content, as far as I

could tell. I wondered what they did for entertainment and what their living conditions were like. Did they have electricity or running water?

"You can't see it from here, but they live pretty comfortably. There's even a school," Rhett said, as if he read my mind. "Just beyond those gates is an area with less damage. There are trees, grass, and even small animals. I'll take you one day, if you're curious."

I wanted to say yes, but ISAN could find me any day. Best to not make promises. Instead, I watched the people shrink as we drove away.

Rhett's knee brushed against my leg, then his arm snaked behind my head. I bristled and the weight of his glances unsettled me, so I stared right back at him, only it gave me no reprieve. Our eyes locked for what seemed like an eternity, as time seemed to be nonexistent. I saw love, hope, and life ... until the car jerked.

I wanted to ask where we were headed, but I decided not to bombard them with questions. I'd asked enough for one day.

We took a detour off the street, over dead grass and gravel. Then about a mile later, the truck stopped behind a cluster of tall, abandoned buildings. The outer few had crumbled, but one in the middle looked steady and had an intact solar panel.

"You get one hour and that's it."

I'd never heard Ozzie talk sternly before, especially to Rhett.

"Those jets are in the back of the truck. Have fun, kids. The clock is ticking."

The sound of Ozzie's laughter made me wonder what they were up to.

Jets? I swallowed.

"Try not to fall too hard." Reyna winked at me. "I hope you're not as afraid of the dark as you are of heights."

What were they talking about?

Rhett got out of the truck, took some stuff out of the back, and then opened my door. "You heard the boss, Ava. Leave your backpack and your hat here. We only need mine. Let's go."

When I got out of the truck, he led the way until we reached an elevator shaft.

I took a step back. "Seriously? We're getting on this?"

"You're not afraid to be alone with me inside a dark elevator, are you? Trust me, it's all good." He smirked.

I glared. "Fine." I took a step inside when Rhett opened the door.

The elevator rattled on the way up. Rhett wasn't edgy like the last time I'd seen him inside one. I, on the other hand, held my breath.

Spiders had marked their territory with intricate web designs on each corner. Paint flakes accumulated on the walls, showing the structure's old age. It stunk of something rotting, but other than that, the building proved to be sturdy.

"I forgot to tell you—"

"Forgot to tell me what?" I jumped into Rhett's arms and yelped when the elevator made a loud, screeching noise and rattled to a stop.

"That. It stops one flight short." He lifted a shoulder. "It's an old building. We'll have to climb."

"Thanks for the warning." I pushed away from him. Our bodies had created too much heat and I became lightheaded.

Rhett squeezed his fingers through the narrow gap and pulled the doors open. Then he took out a flashlight from his back pocket to illuminate the stairs in front of us—rickety steps with only a skinny handrail to prevent a fall.

"After you." He gestured.

"Wow. Lucky me."

"You are lucky." He snickered.

ISAN

I held onto the wrought iron banister and made my way up, keeping my eyes on the areas lit by the flashlight.

"Don't look down, Ava." Rhett's words resonated in the shaft.

"Now I want to look down. Thanks for the reminder. Jerk."

"Maybe we should've switched. Instead of me watching your fine ass, you could be concentrating on mine."

My cheeks burned as I let out a short laugh. But ... *He thinks I have a fine ass?*

"Enjoy the view, because that's the most you'll see of it."

Rhett kept quiet the rest of the way. When I reached the top, I found myself on a platform big enough to fit two people. He pushed a square metal door open, went through, then helped me out.

I gasped and covered my mouth. Driving within the Abandoned City, I'd had an idea of the damage, but seeing the whole picture, the gaping ruins and glimpse of former magnificence devastated me. In the center, the aftermath of meteors had left their mark—colossal craters.

As the sun faded, the outline of the destruction disappeared against the darkened sky.

"Wrong side." Rhett shifted me with his hands on my shoulders.

I walked to the edge until panic surged in my throat.

No matter how many times I'd seen a view of the living city from the web and the sub-glider, nothing compared to that moment. The view stole my breath as I gazed upon endless twinkling pinpricks in the distance—colors from the city lights illuminated to life. A vast difference from the other side of the building. Two worlds. One from the past and one in the present.

Rhett set down his bags and steadied the flashlight on the ground. "This is what I wanted to show you. I asked Ozzie and Reyna for this favor. Happy Birthday. You're eighteen today."

"It's my birthday?"

I had forgotten about it. My foster parents had never celebrated my birthday and it had been ignored in juvenile detention all those years. Eventually, it became nonexistent.

Rhett took a step toward me and rubbed the back of his head, seemingly nervous. "I don't have anything expensive to give you. Only a memory. This is my gift to you." He extended his arm and made a complete circle, as if his gift was the world.

The city lights shimmered as I fought back the tears. "I think this is the best birthday present anyone has ever—"

I bit my bottom lip to hold in a sob. It was the only gift since the little doll my mom had given me when I turned thirteen. My last present from her, long since lost.

Without thinking, I reached for his hand and stood next to him under the night sky, under the stars and the moon. The universe joined us in a mesmerizing moment of awe. Nothing mattered. I drifted to another place and time where Rhett and I were a real couple, and I was not an assassin, but a simple girl.

I'd dreamed of moments like that, of being a normal teenager in love. I'd go on dates, and he'd show me how much he cared with thoughtful gestures like this. But like all dreams, I had to wake up.

Rhett wrapped his arms around me when I shuddered. The cold, brisk wind slapped us, breaking our tranquility. He held me tighter when I trembled, and I wanted to hold onto this moment of serenity and stay in his arms forever.

"Thank you," I said. And I meant those simply words to the depth of my core. I closed my eyes as if to still the competing emotions running through me. Then I opened them on his loving smile. "This is very sweet of you. It's breathtaking."

"I knew you'd like it. You used to talk about how you wanted to see the city lights from a tall building."

My smile faltered. The picture I'd seen of the two of us lips to lips, looking so happy, flashed in my mind. Every time he mentioned our past, it felt like an ice pick twisting deep in my heart with each forgotten memory. I still wanted him to be wrong, to catch him making up a lie. But so far, he'd been right about everything.

I didn't want to be reminded about the past. I needed to know about the present. "Is there something going on between you and Cleo?"

Pressing my lips together, I chastised myself. The stupid question had sounded different in my head.

Rhett pulled back and searched my eyes. He curled his lips down at the corners, trying to hide a gloating smile.

Damn.

"Are you jealous?" A happy chuckle rang from his throat.

So jovial. I would never forget the sound of that laugh; music to my ears. But it had to end. I reminded myself I needed to go back to ISAN and find out what happened to my father and my twin. I also needed to tell Brooke about what I knew and had experienced, maybe Tamara, too. I wasn't sure about Justine. Then I had to find a way to get us out.

Rhett would help me if I asked, but I didn't want to get his hopes up. There was no guarantee nothing would happen to me and who knew how long it would take me to find my missing family. At those thoughts, I dropped my hand I'd rested on his arm.

His expression changed, and he laid his big hand over mine. His jaw tightened and his anguish-filled eyes searched mine. "I'm letting you go, Ava. You can leave tomorrow." He stepped back, all playfulness gone. "I can't keep you hostage forever. I only wanted a chance to open your eyes. I know you can't remember any of the things I've told you, but at least I gave us a chance to start over someday. Even if a part of you wants to stay with us, I know you need to go back to ISAN to find answers about your family. I hate that I can't be there for you. It's killing me that I have to let you go after I found you again."

I rubbed my arms and gazed at the stars, not knowing how to respond. Pressure built around my bottled-up emotions; if I opened them, I would explode. Unwanted tears welled in my eyes, pushing at the dam of my lashes.

Girls dreamed of a handsome guy madly in love with them. One stood in front of me and I was tossing him away. For what? A father and a twin who could be dead. A friend who might think I'm crazy. But ISAN was still a part of me. Still coming after me. I couldn't run away without finding answers.

Rhett understood because he was like me. We were fighters. Survivors.

"Rhett?" Calling his name felt more familiar now than it had before. "Did we ever ...?"

I gasped when Rhett set his hands on my hips. He waited for our eyes to connect before he spoke. "Did we ever get this close? Yes. Did I caress your cheeks like this?" Rhett skimmed his hand on my face. "Yes." He paused to run his thumb along the outline of my lips and grabbed my hand to place it on his chest.

Oh, God.

"Did our hearts ever feel like this, like they were going to explode from our chests every time we were near each other? Yes. Million times, yes. You feel that, Ava? My heart thunders for you and no one else. It knows when you're near. You can feel that, can't you?"

I nodded, drowning into him, warmth blazing through my body. My heart beat out of control, just like his. Everywhere he touched burned. Even his words made me dizzy.

"No one can take away my beating heart for you. You're imprinted right there. Memories can be erased, but you can never forget an emotion that's meant to last forever. You are my forever. Find me. Find us in your heart. That is my only request. Whatever it takes."

My head spun. The lights below me whirled in a tunnel around us, and I floated weightless as the breeze. My breaths shortened as I watched his lips inch toward mine.

Rhett stopped and took out a small device from his backpack. Music filled the air. "Dance with me under the stars. I promised you one day I would against the city lights."

I'd never heard the song before, but something told me it had once meant something to us. Another attempt to trigger my memory. Rhett's body pressed against mine, and we swayed to the music.

Put your hand on my beating heart, as we dance under the stars.
I'll sing you a love song, mending all time's scars.
It was clear and simple you see.
We fell in love with just one glance.
We knew it was special when we took a chance.
A gamble worth taking, true love in the making.
We are forever. You and I.

I closed my eyes and listened to him sing. Serenity I'd never known filled me to my core. If it were possible, I would've floated off the roof. How could I have forgotten feeling that way? I wanted to hold on to the moment and make it last forever. Our slow dance broke down something inside me. When the music stopped, he cupped my face into his hands.

"Rhett, did we ever …" I stopped. My face flushed with warmth, and I shyly dipped my chin.

I didn't know how to ask it. Perhaps I didn't want to know, being utterly drunk by his one last attempt to get me to remember him, to remember us.

Rhett ran his fingers through my hair, sending warm shivers through me.

"To answer the question I think you want to ask, yes. We had sex. And it was amazing. It was fireworks, baby. I'm going to kiss you, if you let me. Let me give you something to remember from the present and not from the past."

I shuddered a breath and didn't answer. The happiness suffusing me might have been past or present. It felt so real, so right, and I didn't want to ever let it go. Without waiting for him, I crushed my lips to his.

Rhett pressed my body tighter and kissed me back, all madness and hunger, as if to make up for all the time lost. His stubble grazed my lips, my skin, but I welcomed the gentle pricks.

My lips moved with his in ways I never thought possible, desperate, and wanting more. Our locked lips felt so perfect, so familiar, like we'd kissed thousands of times. Though I couldn't remember us having sex, I knew in my heart he had been incredible. And this kiss … oh, this kiss … this toe curling kiss … utterly mind-blowing. Perfect in every way.

Rhett's lips slowed to tender caresses, taking his time, and then began to nip at my neck. When his hands trailed lower down my spine, I arched my back from the euphoric sensation. Wanting more, my hands greedily explored the curve of his biceps and the defined chest I'd wanted to touch since I first set my eyes on him.

Sliding my fingers through his hair, I twisted his hair in sudden anger. I hated him for making me weak. Falling for him would only break me. If he'd forced me to stay, it would have been a relief in a way. But given a choice, the road I'd been on before was the only way. With this taste of him, Rhett would forever be imprinted on me. I freely gave him a piece of my heart I could never take back … again, apparently.

Lights flashed in the corner of my eye.

"Rhett." I pulled away, out of breath, eyeing his stubble that grazed on my lips. "I think … I think I saw fireworks."

Rhett rewarded me with the sexy smile that left me lusting for him.

"I want to say it was from my kiss, because I'm pretty sure you felt it inside you. But that's Ozzie. Time to go."

Blushing like an idiot, I reached down to find the latch when my body twisted back without my control.

"Not so fast." Rhett rested his forehead against mine and gathered me in his arms. He embraced me as if he wanted to frame that moment forever in his mind. When his lips caressed my cheeks tenderly, I quivered under the warmth of his breath. "Promise me, Ava. Please try to remember us. Whatever it takes."

"I promise," I whispered. I meant it. His words tugged to the depth of my core, and I felt the sincerity and the pain in them.

I stayed in his arms, cheek to cheek, body to body, until another flash lit the sky soon after, and someone honked a horn frantically. A soft growl gushed out of Rhett.

"Second warning." Rhett uttered an annoyed sound. "What's so urgent? We should get going."

CHAPTER THIRTY-THREE
SOARING

"Oh, no." I shook my head. "What's that?" I pointed at a black fabric with a small mechanical thing attached to it.

I had never questioned what Rhett had hidden inside the other bag he'd brought. Perhaps I should've asked him when we were in the truck.

"It's faster this way. We did this before and you loved it."

"That was the old me."

Rhett unzipped the long backpack. It frazzled me at first until I realized it was something else. He slipped his body through it and zipped up. After grabbing the flashlight, he tossed his smaller backpack around his shoulders. The material from his arms expanded outward, connecting to his legs.

"You look like a bat." I giggled, but my amusement died a hard death when he handed me an identical contraption.

"Don't you trust me?" Rhett raised an eyebrow, his eyes daring me. Then he winked.

Oh, hell. It was that wink. Or maybe it was the kiss. I couldn't say no.

"Fine. But you owe me big time."

His brow twitched in a naughty way. "I can suggest ways to pay you."

"Maybe I'll let you." I couldn't believe I flirted back.

Rhett zipped me up and guided me to the edge. My stomach had already dropped to my toes; I didn't know where else it could go. I thought I'd surpassed the point of no return and had become numb. My knees buckled and my muscles tightened, but Rhett's hand in mine gave me the security I needed.

"Ready?" His eyes twinkled brighter than the stars.

As for me, I wanted to spit in his smirking face. "Nope. You're enjoying this, aren't you? You're enjoying the fact I'm doing this for you. You feel like you've won something when I do things you ask, right?"

Rhett's eyebrows pinched at the center. "Well, I never thought of it that way, but yeah, I like that you trust me. One step at a time, that was my goal. When I count down to three, Ava, we jump."

"Okay."

Three …"

"Don't let go, Rhett."

"Never. Two …"

Rhett pressed something on my suit, and then his, and yanked me with him.

"You never said one, Rhett." The wind had tamed my bellowing voice, sounding softer than it should have.

"Just getting you back for the many times you didn't let me say one."

I soared with the breeze toward the city lights. Every thought fled and everyone else ceased to exist. I laughed and smiled, lost to the elation of freedom and lost to Rhett, who held my hand so tightly I felt his love for me.

I trusted him with my life, and that had been his true gift. To show me I could trust him, let myself feel, dream, and hope.

In front of me was the beauty of the city lights, but below, nothing but the gentle darkness. The breeze rocked and cradled me as the flapping of my suit glided like a bird. Fly. Fly. Fly away. So calm. So peaceful. I was free, and bliss filled my heart and my soul.

I continued to stare until the ground rushed toward us. My

happiness disappeared. It might be our last time together. I had to go back, not just for answers regarding my family, but also for my other friends. They needed to know the truth. But truth about what? What could I tell them? Would they even believe me?

Doubt attacked me. What if Rhett and his friends had fed me lies to gain control of my special abilities? How did I know the truth? What if the journal was fiction?

But the video. That was real.

Everything added up.

The guards who had attacked us knew Rhett's name. Rhett and his friends knew about the Helix serum. They'd known about the cyanide capsule. The photo I'd found in Rhett's desk was clearly of the two of us, undeniable proof we had a past.

What the hell do I do?

I wished I could crawl into a cave and hide from reality. Or I could believe my instincts and the evidence.

I landed and took off my suit. In the process of folding the material to fit into a backpack, I spotted someone running toward us in the dark.

"Rhett. Rhett." The panic in Reyna's voice was palpable, and terror filled her eyes. "They have Ozzie." She bawled, pouring anguish into her shout.

Rhett bristled. "Who has Ozzie?"

Reyna bent over, resting her hands on her knees to catch her breath. "ISAN. Mitch was there. He tried to grab me, then ... no, Ozzie. I hid. Ozzie pushed me. I was so scared. Drifters were there." Her eyes danced around in panic.

Rhett placed a hand on her shoulder, in control like a true leader. "Slow down, Reyna. I don't understand. Start from the beginning."

Reyna took a deep breath. Watching her made my lungs hurt.

"Ozzie and I went to Hope City and a bunch of us decided to

visit Abandoned City. We hung out with Zen and his friends. Ozzie and I were on our way back, but before we got to the truck, somebody shot at us. When Ozzie pushed me behind the truck he got tased. Zen helped me escape. Before Mitch left, he said tomorrow at noon we exchange Ozzie for Ava in front of the Leviathan Hotel. If we don't, they're going to kill him." Reyna dropped to the ground, covering her face. "What do we do?"

I was deeply touched she didn't say flat out I needed to leave.

Rhett's shoulders tensed, and he squeezed his fingers into fists, the veins in his muscles bulging.

"You'll get Ozzie back tomorrow, Reyna." I helped her up. Already knowing I was going back made it easier. I just hoped Ozzie was okay.

"Did they take the supplies?" Rhett asked.

"No, but they took our friend." She sobbed, dropping to the ground again.

Rhett got on his knees. With a tilt of his finger, he forced her to meet his gaze. "Listen. We'll get Ozzie back. They're not going to hurt him." Then he looked up at me, his eyes filled with so many emotions, but mostly sadness. "Ava will be leaving tomorrow."

* * *

"I'm sorry," I said.

Rhett paced his room from one wall to the other. My heart seemed to soften around Rhett more and more.

Would ISAN torture Ozzie for information? They said they would release him, but they never promised they wouldn't harm him.

"It's not your fault, Ava. It's mine. I should've predicted this. I wasn't cautious enough. You have nothing to be sorry for." Rhett took a fistful of his hair in his hands. After he exhaled a long breath, he let go. "You should get some sleep."

"I'm going to wash up first, if that's okay?"

I stood from the bed to get clean clothes and saw the book Rhett had let me check out. I'd never even got a chance to read it, but I had skimmed through some parts, especially the ending, which had unsettled my stomach, only because they didn't have a happy ever after. Funny how our situation was kind of similar.

An irrational twinge of hurt flashed through me. If I had wanted to stay, would he have given me a choice? What was I to them if I couldn't remember who they were? Those thoughts weren't fair, especially when I couldn't read Rhett's mind. The little time I'd spent with him told me he was a person who thought things through before he acted them out.

But emotions get in the way, cloud judgment.

Rhett stood by the door with his back toward me. His muscles bulged when his fingers gripped the doorframe. "Just so you know, it's killing me to let you go. It was worse the day we escaped and you didn't make it out with me. I can't seem to get away from losing you." He paused. A breath rushed out of him, as if he needed a moment to collect himself. "If you wanted to stay, I wouldn't have asked you to leave for Ozzie. You mean more to me than that. I would've found another way, even if I had to trade my life. If I have opened your eyes and made you feel even a part of what you can't remember, then the past three days were worth everything.

"Ozzie thinks our memories can be erased by our advanced technology. And with ISAN, anything is possible, I suppose. But I think you did it to yourself. I think the trauma of us being separated, whether it was too painful or whether to protect our final destination, which you knew, is linked to your loss of memories. But that is just my theory."

I blinked and soaked in his words, thinking about that possibility.

Rhett added, "Every second lost without you the past six months drove me insane. I died the day you didn't come with me. And even though you're here with me now, I can't seem to let the pain ease because I have to let you go again. I didn't know if you were alive or ..."

Tears blurred my vision and I quickly dabbed them away.

Rhett took a moment to inhale and carried on. "It won't be easy for you when you go back. You're going to get confused again. You won't know who to trust. Trust your heart. Trust your instincts. And when you're ready to leave ISAN, don't hesitate to ask for my help. I will find a way to get you out. There's a war coming, Ava. I have no evidence to show you, but something is happening, and I don't want us to be on opposite sides."

Reyna had told me the same thing. Hearing it from Rhett as well troubled my heart.

"Will we see each other again?" My voice cracked.

He gave me a sideways glance. "I know we will. I'm not letting you go, Ava. You might not remember me, but I know you feel something for me. Two broken hearts will find a way to each other. Even if it takes a lifetime. And you might have noticed, I'm not the type of guy to wait a lifetime. I make things happen."

The door slid open. He took one step out before I stopped him.

"Wait. I have to see." Catching the edge of his T-shirt, I raised it up to reveal his tattoo.

His brows pinched in confusion, then he lightened his expression to a playful smirk. "Should I undress for you?"

I ignored him, lifted my shirt, and rose on my tiptoes to bump my hip with his. Lining up perfectly, his tattoo and my faded scar became a single snowflake. In the center read the letters, W.I.T. The words slipped from my tongue before I could decipher what they meant.

"Whatever it takes," I mumbled.

My heart stilled. The room became dead silent as seconds passed between us. An image of snowflakes drifting around Rhett and me entered my mind, but just for a split second. I didn't know where we were, but …

His eyes glistened with hope. "You remember?"

Wordlessly, I shook my head.

He took a moment to pause and gently pried my hand off his shirt. With his chin at his chest, he dragged his feet out in silence.

CHAPTER THIRTY-FOUR
GOODBYE

Rhett and his group met briefly in a private room to discuss their plan. When they didn't include me, it stung, though it shouldn't have. Whatever they had planned, I hoped they would outsmart ISAN for the sake of their safety.

The next day, a small team left in the gliders and the rest stayed to protect their home. Luckily for them, the hideout had stored old military equipment—bombs, tanks, rifles, and sleeping gas, to name a few, but would it be enough?

I arrived at Leviathan Hotel. People bustled about their daily lives. I wished I could blend in with the crowd and never look back. Rhett had activated my ISAN chip and instructed me to position myself in front of the hotel. When he gave me one last kiss, my heart shattered in ways I had not expected, especially when his beautiful amber eyes paled. As I stood there waiting for ISAN, I stole a few glances at Rhett, worried for his team, and worried for me.

What did ISAN know of the kidnapping? Had I been captured on camera when I had gone to the city? What if ISAN decided they didn't need me anymore? So many unanswered questions and doubts plagued my mind. Rhett seemed confident ISAN needed me, and they would not terminate their prized possession.

Rhett stood calm and collected. Sporting a black uniform, a black hat, and dark sunglasses, he looked the part of a true leader, or perhaps a legendary assassin. But I still worried for him. An organization like ISAN was a formidable network not to be messed with. As I rubbed my arms in the cold, momentarily distracted by the undulating waves, someone grabbed my arm and pulled me into a brisk walk.

"Ava." Mitch tightened his grip and tugged me like a hunter dragging its squirmy prey.

A hunter. Mitch was one in every sense of that word, a deadly one at that. I'd seen the way he killed, the way his feature showed no emotion, and the way his cruel eyes held its prey with deadly intent.

Hello monster. I know your true face.

"It's nice to see you, too, Mitch." I became repulsed from the lie that left my mouth."

I stole a glance behind me. Rhett and his team had disappeared in the crowd. My heart jolted. The hole had deepened and I became lost, unsure of who I was and where I belonged. My days with him had been a dream, and now I had awoken.

"It's good to see you, Ava. You're looking well."

I wasn't sure if Mitch was being sarcastic. His tone was hard to detect behind his cold expression.

"Where's Ozzie?"

"Keep your eyes straight ahead."

I snarled when he didn't give me an answer, but kept my cool. Being with Rhett, I had softened, especially the last day. Now, it was time to bring Assassin Ava back and find my family.

A group of ISAN girls surrounded us. I spotted Tamara and Brooke. Justine pressed her gun to Ozzie's side, trying not to make it obvious. Neither of them acknowledged me in passing.

"Did you hurt him?" I asked. I didn't want to give any sign I cared about Ozzie, but my tone might have betrayed me.

"What kind of network do you think we are?" He gripped me tighter.

"Why are his lips bloody, then?" I twisted at my waist to see

Ozzie standing alone where I had stood. I assumed Rhett's team would wait to get him when we were out of the way. Most likely, they didn't want to be seen.

Mitch escorted me inside the parked sub-glider without a reply. Once we got in, we took off.

Nobody asked me any questions. Everyone dispersed to their seats without so much as a jovial, "Welcome home. I'm glad you're safe," acknowledgement, not even Brooke. She acted like I wasn't there. Maybe ISAN had told them I had purposely gotten kidnapped, or I had done something wrong. The twenty-minute ride seemed like an hour.

Russ stood by the entrance to the ISAN compound when I got out of the sub-glider. He was the only one who greeted me.

"Are you okay? Are you hurt?"

I stiffened. A part of me felt betrayed, and the other half felt like I had betrayed him.

"I'm fine. Just tired," I said.

Russ gave me a warm smile, satisfied. "Go wash up, get some rest, and we'll meet up after dinner."

I nodded and went down the stark, gray halls to my room. It had only been three days, but an eternity had passed. The room that used to be my safe haven felt wrong when I returned. Rhett had screwed with my mind, my heart, and my life.

Instead of washing up, I powered on my TAB. My heart acted before my mind could tell me what to do. Though I knew it was too soon, I searched for a message from Rhett.

I had a mission of my own. Coming back to the complex made me lonelier than ever before, and I felt like a spy. I cursed under my breath in frustration, changed my clothes, and opened my door.

"Brooke." My heart slammed into the cavity of my chest and I took a moment to breath. I almost ran into her. "You scared me."

She crushed her body into mine in a slightly awkward way. One arm draped around my neck lazily and the other around my waist.

"The one and only," she said. "I wanted to make sure you were okay."

I'd desperately needed that hug and it confirmed Brooke truly cared for me. For her, physical contact was a big deal, and I appreciated the effort.

"I was so worried about you. I want to punch you right now." Brooke lightly socked my arm. "I stayed sick to my stomach for three days, wondering if Mitch activated your cyanide capsule. Did the kidnappers hurt you? Like torture you with electric shocks, cut you with a knife, gag, whip, and chain you?" Brooke crossed her arms, waiting for my answer. "Sorry about when I first saw you. I was acting like—"

I yanked her in.

"I didn't care," she finished. "Whoa ... whiplash."

"Sorry to disappoint, but they didn't do any of those things, thankfully. What happened the day I was kidnapped?"

She leaned in to one side of her hip. "Darn. I would've loved to hear interesting stories. I mean, not that I would want you to be tortured." She twisted her lips, amusement crossing her features. "Russ and I wondered what was taking you so long. Mitch searched for you in the restroom, your dress was on the floor and you were gone. At first, he thought you went down without letting him know, but—"

"How did they know who kidnapped me?"

"I don't know. You know they don't disclose information to us. I was just glad they found you."

"Do you know what they did with Ozzie?"

"I don't know that either. I only saw him twice, when Mitch brought him in and when we exchanged him for you. Too bad he couldn't stay. He's so cute."

From wall to wall, I combed through for something out of place. Though I'd never wondered if a recording device had been implemented in my room, the thought crept in my mind.

"What are you doing? Did you lose something?" Brooke's eyes followed mine.

I stopped, placed my hands on her shoulders, and whispered, "That's the thing. He used to be one of us. Do you remember him?"

Brooke backed away, arching her eyebrows and scratching her chin. "Are you okay, Ava? Did they drug you?"

I pulled her back to me. "Something big happened before you came into the picture. It happened more than six months ago. Whatever happened, I'm going to find out, and you're going to help me."

Brooke lifted her lips to one corner, her eyes radiating mischievously. "Hell yeah I will."

I released a cathartic breath. For a moment there, I thought she was going to tell me I was crazy. After everything I'd learned, I wasn't sure I could trust her, but I was glad I'd come back for her. Emboldened by her support, I didn't feel so alone.

As usual, I sat on my chair and Brooke sat on my bed.

"What have you been up to while I was gone?"

I tried to bring normalcy back into our conversation. If ISAN had ears in my room, I would put on a show.

"Mental and physical training. I have to tell you, though, we're not successful without you, even with double the dosage of Helix."

"You just missed me, that's all."

"Then Tamara missed you the most, because she was hard to handle, but I'm also not patient like you. I had to step in and be the leader. I don't know how you put up with us. I wanted to smack Tamara when she freaked out during mental missions. I don't get it. I know Helix affects us differently, but she can't control her fear unless you're with us."

I laughed, picturing Brooke's frustrated face. But poor Tamara.

"She just needs a little reassurance that she's doing fine."

Brooke leaned back to the wall for support. "I suppose. I don't have your patience. Anyway, you're in luck. You're back just in time. We have another assignment lined up."

"Already?" Dread knocked away what little happiness I had.

"It's Mr. San. He's holding another charity ball in the West. We were informed the Remnant Councils will be there. I don't know why he would want to hold one there with the chance of an earthquake and take a chance on the possibility of being assassinated soon after the other failed attempt. Since we failed the first time, we're going back to get him. I wonder what he did."

I shrugged. "We'll never know."

Brooke placed her hands on her lap, fingers flexing. "Oh, did you hear? A team was sent out on a small assignment, but they weren't successful. Only two came back alive out of eight."

I gasped silently, leaning back in my seat. When my hands trembled, I placed them behind my back. What the hell was wrong with me? I had never shown such fear before.

"What happened to them?"

"I'm not really sure, but the rumor is, some dropped dead on the scene from too much Helix. The others got tased and you know what happens if you get caught."

"That's terrible." I plopped on the bed next to her.

Brooke scratched her head and squinted. "I know. I thought with Helix we would be badass ninjas, invincible. And you'd think more was better. Guess I was wrong."

I hadn't known much before I'd signed the contract. There

were still things I didn't know about the network, but allowing girls to die such gruesome deaths was wrong. I'd expected a short life span with the assassin job but not being experimented on. They were testing our limits. To what extents would they push us? How many of us had to die before they were satisfied?

"Do you like it here, Brooke?" I hadn't meant to ask. I just threw it at her without thinking how I would react if she answered.

Brooke bit her bottom lip. "I'm not sure, and I don't have a choice. This is my life. I'm glad I have you to lean on, Ava. I'm lucky I'm good enough to be on your team. Our friendship is the only thing that keeps me from going crazy."

I embraced Brooke, and she let me as her arms went to my shoulders stiffly. Good enough for me.

"I'm thankful for you, too." With my arms still draped around her, I whispered, "We're going to get out. It might take a while, but I'm going to find a way."

I'm going to take down ISAN and burn it to the ground after I find my family. And everyone standing in my way can go to hell.

"I hope so," she said softly, hardly audible.

"I need to take care of something. I'll meet you at dinner."

CHAPTER THIRTY-FIVE
TRUTH OR LIES

Goosebumps crawled up my arms as I walked past the mental training room. I blamed the unwelcome emotions on Rhett. He'd opened my eyes, and questions I'd never asked filled my head. Could I trust Russ? Who had erased my memories? How long had I been there?

The sliding door to Russ's office was open. He'd known I would come.

"Have a seat, Ava." Russ swung around in his chair to face me. He didn't have his usual friendly face. "You're early, but I figured you would be."

I sat, watching Russ pull out something from his desk. He handed me an envelope.

"What's that?"

"I missed your birthday. Happy belated birthday." He offered a small smile.

"We don't celebrate birthdays here. Why are you doing this?"

"You're eighteen. An eighteenth birthday is a big deal. This isn't from ISAN. It's from me. Open it."

Slowly, I opened the envelope, aware of Russ's eyes on me.

"It's a free night to wherever I want to go with my team?" I read the paper twice to make sure I had read it correctly.

"Let me know when you want to use that. I would have to go with you, along with the bodyguards. You know the drill."

Why? What do you have up your sleeve, Russ?

"Thank you," I said.

I shoved it inside my pocket. For a second, I had forgotten why I'd come in the first place. Handing me a birthday present was a nice distraction.

"I'd like to ask you a question," I said.

Russ didn't respond, so I asked anyway.

"Was it always just girls here? Did you ever have male subjects?"

"You're not a subject." His tone was sharp and cold as if I had offended him.

"If we're being probed and tested, I think that makes us subjects," I said, though I wanted to yell at him.

"You're all special."

His calm neutral tone made me angrier.

I leaned in closer to the desk. "You didn't answer my question."

Russ furrowed his brow. "Does it matter? What did the kidnappers say to you? Don't believe everything you hear. There are always two sides of the story."

"I wouldn't know. Which is your side of the story, Russ?"

"Ava …" He pushed back in his seat, releasing a quick sigh. "Don't ask for stories that aren't meant to be told."

"I'm not going to ask you anymore. I'll make up my own."

"Ava." His tone softened. "You only know the surface of ISAN. You don't want to get involved. Do what you are told and everything will be fine. I'll tell you this much. We had boys in ISAN, but the serum was defective for them. But now it's promising."

Promising? What did that mean?

"What happened to them?"

"Some did not survive the serum and some were sent back to juvenile detention."

I knew he wasn't telling me the truth, but perhaps he was

telling me what he was told. Either he was hiding information from me to keep me safe, or he simply didn't know. I wanted to ask him who had created the serum and where it was manufactured, but I already knew he wouldn't tell me. If he even knew.

"Okay," I said. "Thank you."

"Okay?" His eyelashes fluttered, most likely shocked I agreed so easily. "Now it's my turn to ask you questions." Russ tapped the TAB on his desk and touched the letters. "Can you recall the names of your kidnappers?"

I swallowed and my blood ran cold. *ISAN guards will report Ava shot back. If they ask you about it, you lie. Tell them they must have made a mistake.* I dug my fingers into the armchair and prepared to defend myself.

"No." I bored my eyes into his. "They locked me up in a room. They asked me questions, but I didn't tell them anything."

A screen popped out. Profile pictures scrolled one by one. "Can you recognize anyone?"

"No, I don't so far." When a picture flashed of Rhett, my stomach did a funny tingling flip. "I never saw their faces. They wore masks."

Russ seemed satisfied with my answer. I was getting good at lying. One day I would lie to myself, and I'd believe every word. I might not even be able to distinguish lies from the truth.

The screen came down.

"It doesn't matter if you can't identify them. I have the result of the blood test from the drop of blood he left behind at Shooting Stars. I know who he is."

My heart took a dive, squashed like it hit the cement. "That's great. Who is he?"

"His name is Rhett. He used to be one of our operatives, but he went rogue. I was told he didn't believe in our cause. He formed a group against ISAN. When a group of them escaped, they killed a lot of guards. They will hurt anyone associated with ISAN."

Rocks settled in my stomach. I folded my hands together to keep steady. *Steady Ava. Keep calm.* I would not let Russ see my emotions. I wanted to tell him he was wrong, but I had no evidence. Rhett had told me I was there that day with him. Had Russ been there as well? Nausea coiled in my stomach like a viper ready to attack.

"That's great you found out who he is."

"Did you overhear anything about their plan of attack?"

"No. Like I said, they locked me in a room."

"Do you know where their hiding base is?"

"No."

"You don't have any valuable information to share. I'll let Mr. Novak know you're clean. Enjoy your dinner. See you in the morning."

I didn't bother to be polite. Relieved he hadn't asked me about shooting at the ISAN guards, I sauntered for the door and debated whether I should probe for more answers. Not able to help myself, I halted in the middle of the room.

"How long has ISAN been around?"

"They don't disclose that kind of information. Only the founders would know."

"How long have you been here?"

"I started working for ISAN a little before you came aboard."

"How about Lydia?"

"Same for her."

"How about Mitch?"

Russ rose from his chair, and approached me. "I'm not going to answer for him. You need to ask him yourself. Better yet, don't ask him anything. Why are you asking these questions, Ava?"

I didn't answer. I remembered Mitch had said he'd been out in the field a lot longer than Russ when I'd gone to kill Mr. San.

Reyna had also mentioned Mitch, like she knew who he was, but I hadn't asked. When Mitch and I were next alone, I would drill him with questions. I figured I could ask one question before he decided to stop answering.

"Are there other ISAN facilities besides us?"

Russ placed a hand behind my back and guided me to the side, away from the door. "Yes. There is one in each of the four territories." His voice lowered to a whisper and didn't hesitate. At least he hadn't lied about that.

"We will be meeting the other ISAN groups soon and possibly working together," he added casually, like he was telling me the color of my hair.

The news thrilled and shocked me. According to my father, my twin was in the West. My lips slightly curled at the corner. Would I recognize my twin?

"Where are we located?" Though I knew the answer, I needed a confirmation.

"I can't disclose that information. But you're a smart girl. I think you know."

I had a hunch we were in the East and it had been confirmed when I traveled to the Leviathan Hotel. It wasn't too far. I had recognized the hotel when Rhett had taken me to the city.

Since Russ seemed receptive, I probed more. "Can ISAN erase someone's memories?" As soon as those words left my mouth, I wanted to take them back.

Stupid. Stupid. Stupid. What was I thinking? My desire to find answers made me bold.

Russ chuckled lightly and cocked an eyebrow. "You forgetting things, Ava?"

I scowled. Russ found my question amusing, and obviously he had no idea, or he wasn't going to give me an answer.

"Never mind." I sighed, beyond frustrated. "Was the blood

test the only indicator that pointed to the kidnapper?"

I needed to know if Russ knew about the messages Rhett sent me, or if he had been spotted on cameras when we were out in the city.

Russ glimpsed over his shoulder to his desk and then back to me. "Rhett contacted us. He let Mitch know he was going to release you on the third day. We were to meet them at the Abandoned City. Mitch wanted to go earlier, in case he wasn't telling us the truth. His team wanted to scout out the place, but they ran into trouble."

I wasn't sure what hurt me the most; the possibility Russ had lied to me or Rhett had kicked me out. At the end, just like the book, Rhett walked away after relentlessly pursuing me. Though it wasn't fair of me to think that way. I was the one who had made the decision to go back. He would have let me stay.

"I should be dead." I folded my arms in front.

"What do you mean?" Russ furrowed his brow, his eyes focused in heavy concentration.

"I should've had a heart attack since I never made it back to our sub-glider."

Russ shifted uncomfortably. "It wouldn't have mattered anyway. We wouldn't have let it get that far."

He didn't look away like I thought he would. It meant he told me the truth.

"You said you wouldn't let it get that far for me. Are you trying to tell me Mitch didn't activate my capsule?" I waited for his answer. When he didn't, I pressed more. "But how about Brooke, Tamara, or Justine?"

He bristled and his nostrils flared.

"Why, Russ?"

"This is where I draw the line." Russ wrung his fingers around my wrist and practically dragged me to the door. He let go of me and spoke with an authoritative tone, "Go have a nice meal with your team. Make sure to drink your protein shake. Tomorrow, you'll be sent to the doctor to get detoxed. You've missed three days. You've got a lot to catch up on with your studies and training." Rubbing his chin, he paused to inhale a deep breath. "By the way, if you get another message on your TAB, I forbid you to reply. Don't worry. I don't intend on reporting you, but you need to stop. ISAN monitors your TAB activities."

Blood rushed through me so fast I thought I would faint. I didn't know how Russ knew, but he'd found out. Either he was bluffing to see my reaction, or he had purposely gone out of his way after I had opened my big fat mouth.

Leaning closer to me for my ears only, he added, "Look within yourself. Sometimes trauma can cause memory loss. Don't ever ask me that question again."

Ice coated my spine and my tongue. Russ knew more than he would share. At least he'd told me that much.

Look within yourself. Had I caused my own memory loss? Rhett had mentioned the same.

Without a word, I got the hell out of there.

CHAPTER THIRTY-SIX
RESTRICTED AREA

My tray thumped on the table next to Brooke.

"Who pissed you off?" Brooke asked. She already finished with her meal. "What took you so long?"

"It's a long story. I'll fill you in later." I groaned.

"Hi, Ava." Tamara smiled warmly, her eyes glistening.

I could only muster a half smile.

Nobody else around me seemed to care I existed—even my own teammate Justine didn't acknowledge me. I was beginning to wonder if she was happy to see me.

Tamara grimaced. "You're going to eat rice with your fingers?"

Being used to eating with my fingers for the past few days, I had forgotten to grab a fork. "I'm too lazy to get a fork."

I dropped rice between my fingers when shoving it into my mouth. Heads turned as if I was uncouth. Their heavy stares weighed on me, and their soft whispers rubbed me raw.

Was it about me being gone for three days or the way I was eating? Everyone's words jumbled together. Then I listened past the murmurs. They were definitely talking about me.

"How many days had she been kidnapped?"

"Do you think she tried to run away and they are covering that up?"

"She's eating with her fingers."

I'd had enough. I smacked my hand on the table. "It's fun. You should try it."

Justine narrowed her eyes at me. "What's wrong with you?"

"They were talking about me. Didn't you hear them?" As a burning sensation rose to my face, I voiced louder. "I was kidnapped, held for three days, and now people are looking at me as if I betrayed them."

I couldn't believe I'd said those words. If my emotions had been all over the place when I was with Rhett, they got worse at ISAN. I didn't know how to glue them back together to make me whole again.

I missed Rhett, Ozzie, Reyna, and the other friendly faces. With them, I'd felt a sense of unity and security. At ISAN, I felt disconnected. Their only interest in me was as a weapon.

"Ava." Brooke touched my trembling hand. "I didn't hear anything. No one said anything. I mean, everyone is talking within their groups, so it's not quiet in here. Are you okay?"

Cringing, I dipped my chin in embarrassment at my half-eaten lunch. Was I going crazy?

"Sorry." I scrubbed my face with my hands. "I'm just really tired. I've had a long week."

"Did they torture you?" Tamara swallowed her last bit of asparagus with a crease between her eyes. "Is that what you're upset about? I wanted to ask you questions about it, but I didn't want to bring up bad memories."

"No. They were really nice." I regretted saying it. "I mean ... they didn't ... they treated me fine."

I couldn't find the right words without saying too much. I didn't want to make it sound like they were our enemies, yet I didn't want to make it sound like I'd enjoyed being with them, either.

"Could we talk about something else?" I asked.

That was all I had to say to get Justine chatting away. "You're not going to believe this, but I overheard a conversation between Russ and Mitch when I went to the mental training room earlier to ask Russ if they'd found out any news about you. I only got little bits, here and there, before Lydia spotted me. Anyway, they've recruited more teens and we're going to meet them tomorrow. Mitch sounded really excited. Something is special about this group of newbies."

"I hope they bring in hot guys," Tamara said. "Russ and Mitch are starting to look like one of the girls." She chuckled.

I had to laugh, especially when Brooke spat a mouthful of water on Justine.

That was kind of epic and warranted.

* * *

I asked Brooke to wander to the restricted areas with me after dinner. Instead of going to the hallway to my room, I went the opposite way when the coast seemed clear. Walking with my head down, I listened for the sounds of boots scrapping or voices.

I halted. With a hand I motioned Brooke to stop. "Do you hear that?"

"Hear what? I didn't hear anything." Brooke ogled me like I was her idol.

Brooke's sense of hearing wasn't strong without Helix, but mine was better. I didn't realize it until I heard the footsteps and Brooke didn't.

"Stop staring at me, Brooke." I pointed at the floor. "Stay right here and let me know if you see or hear anyone coming this way. I'm going to see what's behind those doors."

When she nodded confirmation, I went to the first door. I should've known better. The handprint scanner wouldn't let me in.

What are they hiding?

Though my sense of hearing wasn't as acute as when I was in

a mental mission, something was happening to me. While the serum wore off on the others, it lingered in my system. My hearing was heightened to a degree it hadn't been before. It wasn't just that. I saw a faint blueprint of the area—and the red dots that indicated people—but not what was behind the walls. Or maybe there were no bodies in those rooms? It wasn't the first time it had happened without Helix. But it had gotten stronger.

There was one room left to check and the door was unlocked. I went inside to see an empty room and another doorway fixed with a circular-shaped window. Unable to enter, I turned on my heel to go back to Brooke. As I did, a man in a white lab coat stepped out of a room. I got a glimpse of his pale face and gray eyes.

My heart leaped out of my chest. *Dad?* Could he be my father?

A memory flashed like a daydream. I was in a lab room, the same place I had dreamed about when I fell out the window assassinating Mr. Thorpe.

> *"Ava. How long were you standing there?" My father asks.*
>
> *I stiffened from his scolding tone and my four-year-old body goes cold. "I'm sorry, Daddy."*
>
> *My father leans down, his face softening. "Sorry. I didn't mean to scare you." He plants a kiss on my forehead and caresses my cheek. "I love you, Pumpkin."*
>
> *I feel his love expand my heart and everything is fine. "I love you, too, Daddy."*
>
> *"Go to your room. After I finish my work, I'll read you a book."*

ISAN

The memory faded.

I shivered. Shaken by the glimpse of the past, I clutched my chest from the pang, recalling a small treasured memory of my father and realizing how much I loved him.

Look within yourself. How and why had I forgotten this memory of my father?

I tapped on the glass, then the door. He couldn't hear? When I knocked on the glass harder, he entered another room.

What if Brooke and I got caught? I was being reckless. The need to find my family screwed up my judgment.

Get out of there, Ava. Don't get caught. You're not just messing with your life but Brooke's, too.

I stilled and my pulse soared. Mr. Novak came out of the same room the man in the white lab coat entered.

Crap.

Slouching, I stayed clear from the window, and cursed when I heard faint footsteps. Why hadn't Brooke warned me? No, not that she hadn't, but she couldn't.

The sound came near the first door I'd entered. Without Helix, it was undetectable for her, but apparently not for me.

I dashed to Brooke, my heart racing. She had no inkling of what I had done when I grabbed her and hid us down another hallway. When the sound faded, I led her out of the restricted area. I kept the findings to myself, to keep Brooke out of trouble. One day very soon, I would have to tell her everything, but not that day.

CHAPTER THIRTY-SEVEN
REBELS

The next day after breakfast, all of the ISAN girls went to the meeting center. Mr. Novak, Mitch, Russ, and Lydia waited on the raised podium. With my hand behind my back, I stood in line and waited.

"Good morning."

Mr. Novak's cheerfulness didn't settle well with me, and hair rose on my nape.

"I've gathered you here to tell you some good news. First, we had a major breakthrough with our serum. Let me introduce you to the new members of ISAN. Come on out, Miguel, Rex, Payton, Jessie, and Hugo."

Excitement rose in the air with loud cheers and wolf whistles.

Mr. Novak—or whoever picked the subjects—was not biased regarding race. The guys on the stand were from different ethnic backgrounds. They wouldn't be the type of guys I would imagine fighting big men, but then again, no doubt they had the special DNA and would be given Helix.

Had my father finally perfected the serum for male subjects? I guessed I would know soon enough. And why did they need more subjects?

A war is coming, Ava. Both Reyna and Rhett had warned me. Their words invaded my mind, freezing me in place. *I don't want to be on opposite sides.*

Mr. Novak raised his hand to quell the noise. "I know you're excited and so am I. They'll be housed on the opposite end of our facility, in the restricted area. New rules will be implemented regarding the type of physical contact allowed between genders. Don't try to sneak around. More cameras will be installed in places you wouldn't expect. If you're caught breaking the rules, you'll be asked to leave. Leaving would not be to your benefit."

His last sentence made my stomach roil.

"More cameras?" Brooke said through gritted teeth. "Freakin' great."

"Does that mean no physical contact?" Justine sighed.

"As soon as we're done with the meeting, you'll have a short recess. Our new members will be placed on the teams your superiors feel will work best. For the second good news, I can't take all the credit. Ava, please step forward."

I blanched. Though I'd heard his command, I couldn't move.

"Ava." Brooke nudged me out of my stupor. "Mr. Novak called you. Go." She gave me a little push.

The arrogant grin plastering Mr. Novak's face sent a shiver down my spine. My purpose for being there was for his benefit and not mine. Never mine.

My pulse raced, my legs became unsteady, and my jaw clenched. The platform I stood on detached from the ground and ascended, almost to the same level as my superiors.

Mr. Novak cleared his throat, and his gloating eyes warned me I wouldn't like whatever he had planned.

"Ava, you're probably wondering why you were brought up to the front. I want everyone to know what you've done for us. As you all know, Ava was kidnapped by a group of rebels that wants to ensure ISAN falls. This group was created by a known criminal who feeds you lies to make you believe we are the enemy. Your bravery and wisdom has led us to the rebels, and we've taken them down. Lower the screen, Russ."

The screen scrolling down seemed endless. Dread slowly rose

inside me until it stretched into a full panic. Fire and smoke covered the entire screen. I couldn't see through it, but I knew whom he meant by the rebel group.

Let me be wrong. Please.

"There are no survivors," the voice said over the loudspeakers. "I repeat, there are no survivors."

"The rebel group was led by a traitor named Rhett," Mr. Novak continued. "He and his group have now been terminated."

His smug grin made me want to vomit.

"Did you hear that, Ava? This is all because of you."

Shock slammed into me. Heat flooded through my body like a blazing wildfire, and then I went numb, falling … falling to an endless abyss with no end to stop me. As my heart thudded, my mind disconnected from my body. I couldn't focus, couldn't move. Mr. Novak spoke away, but it all jumbled up into foreign sounds, and the clapping of hands muted around me.

Rhett, Ozzie, Reyna, and others who'd been nice to me, were dead. I had just been with them.

Oh God. Please don't let it be true.

The room spun and their faces flashed before me. Rhett's pleasant voice resonated in my mind and his smile haunted me. The comfort and warmth from his arms stayed with me, even the taste of his last kiss.

If I'd had any doubt about how I felt about Rhett and his group, Mr. Novak had forced me to resolve my confusion. I had fought it, didn't want to believe it, but they gave me a sense of belonging I'd yearned for.

You don't forget emotions.

Countless ways to bring ISAN down swarm in my head. I swore I would take my revenge. I might be their greatest weapon, but I would become their biggest mistake.

Mr. Novak is a monster. I wanted him dead.

I pinched myself to stop the tears from wetting my cheeks. I would not let Mr. Novak know I had cared for the so-called rebels. How could they be called *rebels* when they hadn't had a chance? They'd never fought back. They hadn't retaliated. They'd hurt no one in ISAN after their escape.

They'd only kidnapped me because Rhett loved me. He'd needed me to know. Getting a grip, I bit my lip and focused on the pain. I needed to be strong and give him a fake smile. Right then, I needed to get through it.

As the platform lowered to the ground, my peers gawked at me as if I were some kind of a hero. It made me sick to my stomach. My name was attached to a murderous act. I wanted to tell everyone they were being played, but that would do no good for any of us.

When I was dismissed, I peered up to see Russ. His expression gave me no inkling of how he felt. Mitch and Lydia didn't seem to care either. Maybe Russ had been aware of ISAN's plan of attack. It didn't matter. Rhett and his group were gone, and my heart lay in pieces. Finding my dad and my twin didn't seem to matter anymore. I didn't want to know if they were dead. I couldn't handle more pain.

During the times when I was afraid and alone, like the time when my mother passed away, I needed something to believe in, something to keep me going. Russ had given me that. He had given me purpose.

Then Rhett had entered my life with a new hope. But when hope was gone, what did I have left?

CHAPTER THIRTY-EIGHT
FIVE DAYS LATER

I entered the mental mission full of rage. My actions proved impetuousness. For five days, I had shut down. I refused to cry. I refused to feel. I refused to be weak. No one could know how I felt about Rhett's group being murdered—no one.

Brooke, Tamara, and Justine were the only people I smiled at briefly. They needed to believe everything was fine.

I ignored Brooke and shot a glance at Payton to see what he would say. His warm amber eyes and even the style of his chestnut hair reminded me of Rhett. It was hard to be near him.

Payton had scored the fastest during the mental mission testing compared to the other guys, and for that reason he had been placed on my team. Knowing what I knew, I was astounded by how the group of guys tolerated Helix. It only meant one thing; my dad had perfected the serum.

Payton showed no sign of the out-of-control aggression Rhett had described, but I wondered if he would later, or when given a stronger dose.

"She wants to take them down," Payton answered for me.

I turned away from him when his lips curled into a smirk. His expression reminded me of Rhett.

"Are you crazy?" Justine's tone matched the rage in her eyes. "We don't have time. Where's the exit, Ava?"

Tamara gave me a concerned glance. "She's not going to tell us. We can't get out of here on time if we don't know where the exit is. This building is bigger than the ones we've done before."

"We have plenty of time," I said coolly.

"What happened to the cautious Ava?" Tamara rubbed her arms, her nervous habit.

"You're our leader." Justine raised her voice. "You're supposed to get us out of here. What the hell is wrong with you lately? You've changed ever since you became the hero. You having an ego trip or something?" She threw her hands about and tangled her fingers on my shirt. "It's like you don't give a crap. You take unnecessary risks." Her heated breath brushed against my face.

I wanted to tell her I didn't care. Sooner or later, we were all going to die anyway. If not in the upcoming assignment, then possibly the next one. I also wanted to introduce her lips to my fist, but I contained myself. But then again, what the hell?

"Shut the hell up." Out of leadership character, I gave Justine what she deserved and socked her face. Damn that felt so good.

Justine's face whipped sideways, blood spewing from her cut lip. She lunged for me, but Payton blocked her way. She hissed, throwing all kinds of curse words at me.

"It's too late." Brooke tapped her feet anxiously. "They're right around the corner."

I had no fear. My heart didn't pump with the same kind of adrenaline it had before. Anger, sadness, and hate had replaced it. I wanted to hurt those imaginary threats, to release the pain in my heart.

"They're here," Payton announced.

One aimed a gun at me. I kicked it out of his hand and punched his stomach. Then I threw a blow to his face with my other fist.

I dropped to my knee when a sword swooshed, missing my head. Then I swiped my leg across to knock him down. I took the dagger out of my boot and sliced his throat. When I had the chance to evaluate the situation, I realized all ten opponents were down.

"Good job team. Let's go," I said.

More men charged forward and time was running out. I dashed, my team behind me, but I had to stop. A group of men blocked the exit door, and we had no choice but to scatter when bullets came at us.

"How much time do we have left?" Brooke asked. Panic struck in her eyes.

"Eight minutes, Brooke," Payton said. "We have to do something."

"Then let's do something about it." I pulled out my Taser from the back of my waistband. "On the count of three, shoot your way to the door. I'm going first. One ... two ..."

I jumped out with my Taser pointed, shooting like a mad woman, the way Rhett had when we'd been attacked by the ISAN guards. My aim was impeccable. Half of them fell before my group joined me.

Justine reached for the door, but before she could open it, I hauled her away.

"What the hell, Ava. First you punch me and now you're trying to get all the glory?"

"One more stupid comment from you, I'll shoot you myself and leave you behind."

Justine paled, her eyes wide.

"Shut up, Justine." Brooke pushed her away. "Don't you remember what happened last time?"

"I'll open it." Payton twisted the knob.

I should've been a good leader and told him to stop, but I didn't care. I stood with my Tasers pointing at the door, anticipating. Payton swung it open. The room appeared empty. Everybody rushed through except for me.

I paused. A figure appeared and my jaw dropped.

Didn't they see him?

"Rhett?" His name escaped out of me in a quivering breath, and the endless twisting of a dagger in my heart pierced deeper.

Please. Make the pain stop.

Rhett pointing a gun at me brought me back to reality, confirming my mind was screwed up. Rhett was dead. How could he be there? I didn't want to die and fail the team, so I pointed my Taser at him, but I couldn't pull the trigger.

The image faded and flickered. A hologram. When Rhett transformed to Mr. Novak, I didn't hesitate. With a satisfied smile, I shot him. My Taser had transformed into a gun. Mr. Novak collapsed and bled from his chest, and then he changed to Rhett again.

My hands shook. My muscles froze me in place. Mr. Novak's words reverberated in my mind like a broken record. *It is all because of you.*

He'd let me know it was my fault. A warning. Everyone I cared about would die if I didn't cooperate.

Hands gripped my arms, tugging me away. It seemed I'd made it out in the nick of time. I flashed my eyes open and heaved for air. Mr. Novak standing before me produced a wave of icy chills.

Stand your ground, Ava. Don't let him intimidate you. But…

I became instantly paralyzed as I met his gaze. In those cold serpent's eyes and his stark features, there were no evidence of kindness. He wore a perfect mask of a reaper.

Had he been over me during the entire mental mission? Had he seen how easily I could shoot him? My team was wide-eyed, shocked to see him too—except for Payton.

"Great job." Mr. Novak applauded. "I'm glad to see how well Payton is working out with your group. I'll be sending your team out very soon, as soon as I get Ava under control."

There was something hidden behind his visage of cheerfulness. When Mr. Novak leaned into my face, I wished I could sink in my seat to disappear.

"Ava has guilt issues for causing the deaths of all those people. She shouldn't feel bad for being the hero. Perhaps she should be reminded that death is certain."

His words slithered out of him like poisonous venom, so deadly. A warning. I had the strong urge to punch him, or coil his tie around his neck and choke the life out of him. I could probably blame it on Helix. I laughed at that thought, but his words were no laughing matter.

Mr. Novak bent even lower and whispered, "I'm not your enemy, Ava. Be careful who you shoot next time. Let me remind you, shooting an ISAN guard is punishable by death."

You are my enemy and I'm going to kill you if it's the last thing I do.

Wait. What? Punishable by death?

Then his words hit me. Oh, God. He knew. He knew I'd shot ISAN guards in Abandoned City. Why hadn't he said anything about it until now?

The answer—he was going to use it against me one day.

Mr. Novak straightened his spine and moved away from me. His gait was effortless and poised, leaving me immobile and flustered. After exchanging a few words with Russ, he dusted something off his suit, and left.

Russ stepped to the center to give us a clear view of him. "Great job, everyone. I'll see you tomorrow, but Mitch will see you in one hour."

Just before he entered his office, he gave me a sympathetic smile.

I was surprised he'd even acknowledged me. I had been giving him the cold shoulder lately.

Then something burst inside me.

I tore out of there before anyone could stop me. Heartache

won, and I couldn't stop the tears from falling. I also knew my team would want to ask me why I'd just stood there and why I needed Brooke and Payton's help to get me out, and I was not in the mood to answer questions. Why was I the only one who had seen Rhett and Mr. Novak?

Storming into my room, I curled on my bed and let my emotions run free. As tears dampened my face, I wrapped my arms around my legs. For five days I had tried to forget what had happened to Rhett and his friends, tried to keep my tears locked up and remain strong.

Damn Rhett. Why did he open my eyes? I hadn't been happy, but I had been fine. I hated being in ISAN now. I had lost a part of me and my heart was crushed beyond repair.

How do I keep moving on?

I wished the floor would open up and let me sink into an abyss of darkness. I wanted to drown myself in sorrow and let the emptiness take over so I could feel nothing. No matter what I tried to tell myself, I thought of nothing but Rhett.

He'd proved his point. You could forget a memory, but you couldn't forget the emotions. Why was it when you lost someone, you finally realized what you'd had?

I hardly knew anything about Rhett, only what little information he'd shared, and what I'd seen him do. During the time I'd spent with him, he'd shown me he had a good heart. He'd provided me with a sense of security I'd only felt with Russ, but I realized it was an entirely different thing. Rhett had given me so much more.

He'd filled a void I had for so long, and I missed his love. Though I wished I could deny his declaration, I felt it. His actions proved more ways than I could count.

If he'd stood before me, I would thank him for showing me what real love felt like. For so long, maybe since my mom died, I had lived without love or true happiness. I was afraid to open up, but Rhett had broken down my walls. He'd slowly crawled inside my heart and latched on without me knowing.

I didn't know how I knew, but I'd felt that degree of pain before—because grief like that could never be forgotten—so raw, ripping through my heart. Then images flashed in my mind. Rhett jumping inside a trash chute and I stood among the gray hall with guards pointing their guns at me.

One sacrifice equaled victory.

Was I going mad? No. An old forgotten memory. *What happened to my memories?* Then I recalled Rhett's theory and what Russ had whispered in my ear.

Look within yourself.

Indignation blazed in me at those thoughts. It gave me strength, and at the same time, I couldn't think straight. I pounded the wall because there was nothing to hurl across the room. Blood trickled down my knuckles, but I didn't care. I wanted to feel physical pain to release the agony in my heart.

This damn room. My jail. My hell.

I stopped punching the wall when my TAB slid out. I had accidently hit the button and the TAB automatically turned on. When I released a heavy sigh, my heart steadied to a calmer beat.

I had lost all interest in what was happening with celebrities and fashion. There were more important matters at hand. After I wiped my tears, I reached over to shut it down when something appeared in the corner. I dragged a heavy breath, ready to power it off regardless of who it was.

I froze. Icy chills coursed through me hard and fast.

My breath caught in my throat. I couldn't move. I couldn't breathe. I couldn't blink for fear the words would disappear.

Please don't let it be a mistake.

Three words flashed on the screen, but they felt like a page to me, filled with depth and meaning. No matter how many times I read them, I couldn't get enough. I couldn't stop staring. As blissful tears blinded my vision, a glimmer of hope sparked within me.

Ever so slowly, I ran my finger over the words, as if I could actually touch the only person who could have sent them.

Whatever it takes.

MANY THANKS

To my agent with a giant heart, Italia Gandolfo, who never gave up on ISAN. To the superwoman, Liana Gardner, for just about everything. To Holly Atkinson, Jonas Saul, and Jessica Nelson for your guidance.

To my parents, Roy and Maggie, Joshua—my son, Kaitlin—my daughter, Amber Garcia—PA, Mary's angels, and my friends. Thank you for believing in me and for all your support.

To my husband, Richard, my everything. Thank you for encouraging me to reach for the stars and keeping me grounded.

To my bestie, Alexandrea Weis, we've come a long way. We've crawled through mud and though we are still crawling, look how far we've come. Writing world would not be the same without you.

Thank you to my friends *New York Times* and *USA Today* bestselling authors, Addison Moore and Tiffany King, for being awesome and supportive. And to Ednah Walters, who is no longer with us; I know she is rooting for me in Heaven.

To my grandmother, the reason why I started writing. I feel your love, flowing out of my fingertips through every new book and the amazing people I keep meeting through the love of books.

Lastly, to my readers, thank you from the bottom of my heart for taking this incredible journey with me.

ABOUT THE AUTHOR

Mary is an international bestselling, award-winning author. She writes soulful, spellbinding stories that excite the imagination and captivate readers around the world. Her books span a wide range of genres, and her storytelling talents have earned a devoted legion of fans, as well as garnered critical praise.

Becoming an author happened by chance. It was a way to grieve the death of her beloved grandmother, and inspired by a dream she had in high school. After realizing she wanted to become a full-time author, Mary retired from teaching after twenty years. She also had the privileged of touring with the Magic Johnson Foundation to promote literacy and her children's chapter book: *No Bullies Allowed.*

Mary resides in Southern California with her husband, two children, and two little dogs, Mochi and Mocha. She enjoys oil painting and making jewelry. Being a huge Twilight fan, Mary was inspired to make book-themed jewelry and occasionally gives it away as prizes to her fans.

www.isan.agency
www.tangledtalesofting.com